Greyladies

CW00549603

LADY OF LETTERS

'Josephine Elder' was the pseudonym of Dr Olive Potter. She was born in Croydon in 1895 and educated at Croydon High School, where an inspirational Botany mistress helped her to win her scholarship to Girton. She completed her medical training at the London Hospital in Whitechapel, one of the first four women there. After a couple of years in hospital doctor posts, she set up as a GP in Surrey. Patients were slow to come to women doctors in the 1920s, so she turned to writing. Her first book, *Erica Wins Through* (1924) was followed by nine more school stories for girls, and six adult novels (two under the further pen-name 'Margaret Potter'), including *Lady of Letters* (1949) and *The Encircled Heart* (1951). She didn't retire until she was eighty-eight, and died five years later, in 1988.

The characters in this story are
might-have-beens,
not portraits.

LADY OF LETTERS

JOSEPHINE ELDER

Greyladies

Published by
Greyladies
an imprint of The Old Children's Bookshelf
175 Canongate, Edinburgh EH8 8BN

This edition is published by arrangement with
The Lutterworth Press
© Lutterworth Press 1951

This edition first published 2008
Design and layout © Shirley Neilson 2008
Preface © Shirley Neilson 2008

ISBN   978-0-9559413-0-6

Set in Sylfaen / Perpetua
Printed and bound by the MPG Books Group

Preface

By the time *Lady of Letters* was published in 1949, Josephine Elder had already written the books for which she is best known; her ten girls' school stories. These books develop and explore her characteristic themes of friendship, love of learning and being true to oneself. Probably the best concerns the emotional maturing of Evelyn Ingram in *Evelyn Finds Herself,* (1929). Of the books that follow *Evelyn* only the Farm School trilogy has anything really original to say. At this somewhat idealistic school, she deals calmly with mental handicap in *Exile for Annis* and *Cherry Tree Perch*, and the horrors of German anti-Semitism in *Strangers at the Farm School,* but the overall theme is still character development and personal integrity. To this end, the staff are well rounded individuals, "not just school teachers who think of nothing but school". The little biology master with a stammer turns out to be a former scrum-half for England, the maths master is a ballistics expert and the history mistress writes successful plays for the West End.

In fact, the staff are turning out to be a lot more interesting than the pupils. Perhaps this is why Miss Elder now turned to writing for adults.

She had previously experimented with two adult novels; under the pen-name of Margaret Potter, she wrote a hospital novel *Sister Anne Resigns,* (1931) and a thriller *The Mystery of the Purple Bentley,* (1932). They seem to have vanished without trace.

But now, with *Lady of Letters,* she returns to her strength; to a novel set, at least in part, in a girls' school.

Immediately, switching the main focus from girls to staff, she extends the possible scope of the novel enormously. Staff needn't be wise and kind, they can be ineffectual and uninterested in their pupils as their own outside worlds recede ("cardboard figures with nothing inside"). The Headmistress need not be universally loved and respected ("Why's she Head? Oh, because some loud-voiced local draper knew her father, I expect ... she only got a Third at Cambridge..."). She can be blinkered, snobbish and ruthless, and not always right. The pupils too are seen from a different angle and assume a far less important role in the school than in the girls' books. Only one individual stands out - Janet, with her thoughtful intelligence and her determination to make herself do things she is afraid of - but there is no longer emphasis on the minutiae of the girls' lives and little to distinguish most of them.

Writing for adults also offers more scope for friendship to develop in more complex ways than is possible in a book for girls.

Hilary Moore is a fine character ("your integrity simply sticks out"). We see her grow through childhood to the verge of adulthood shaped by "her gentle scholarly father and jealous shrew of a mother" (original publisher's blurb). Because she has been educated at home she has had limited opportunity to mix with her own kind; she appears self-contained and at university stands alone. There are early lukewarm friendships; a brief enthusiasm for the suffrage cause, and the casual companionship of Ruth, another loner (much as in *The Redheads*), but it is not until her first teaching post that she meets her soulmate, Eleanor.

The character of Eleanor Hunt is another tribute to Miss

Elder's own inspirational botany mistress at Croydon High School, Miss Faith Ashford, who greatly helped her win her Girton scholarship. She had already based the character of Miss Yeo, the charismatic science mistress in *Evelyn Finds Herself,* on Miss Ashford; 'Miss Hunt' is the chemistry mistress at the Farm School, and here, in *Lady of Letters,* Eleanor as the slightly older science mistress at Medling High School is given a principal role in the book.

In no girls' school story would you get this level of intensity and joy in a same sex friendship between staff. Here it is quite clear that it is a friendship on an intellectual plane, but none the less overwhelming for that. It causes hilarity among the rest of the staff, and whereas today they would all assume it to be a lesbian affair, here it is shown as a G.P. – a 'grand pash' – of the sort that the staff take care to squash in the girls. In this interpretation they are probably right. It isn't until Hilary's later relationship with the young doctor, Andrew, that there is any hint of anything physical. And though of course Miss Elder is far too well-mannered to use purple prose, she doesn't shirk the problems that Hilary's arousal by Andrew brings.

Well written school and college stories for adults are all too scarce. To find one, like *Lady of Letters,* intelligently and perceptively written by a favourite author of this calibre, is a rare pleasure.

Shirley Neilson, Edinburgh 2008.

With grateful acknowledgement to Hilary Clare, on whose original research this preface is based.

BIBLIOGRAPHY

Girls' school stories
Erica Wins Through. Chambers, 1924
The Scholarship Girl. Chambers, 1925
The Scholarship Girl at Cambridge. Chambers, 1926
Thomasina Toddy. Chambers, 1927
Evelyn Finds Herself. OUP, 1929
Barbara at School. Blackie, 1930
The Redheads. OUP, 1931
Exile for Annis. Collins, 1938
Cherry Tree Perch. Collins, 1939
Strangers at the Farm School. Collins, 1940.

Adult novels
by 'Margaret Potter':
Sister Anne Resigns. Selwyn & Blount, 1931
The Mystery of the Purple Bentley. Selwyn & Blount, 1932

by 'Josephine Elder':
Lady of Letters. Lutterworth, 1949
The Encircled Heart. Lutterworth, 1951
The Doctor's Children. Lutterworth, 1954.
Fantastic Honeymoon. Robert Hale, 1961

PART ONE

Gregory

1

IN the patch of garden on the hillside everything was blue. Bluebells nodded under old apple-trees coated with blue-grey lichen. Blue sky glowed between the masses of blossom whose pink flush tended more to purple than to salmon. Behind the trees the hot air shimmered against the distant blue of hills, and the open side of the garden sloped towards blue sea.

Hilary Moore, asprawl in a pool of sunlight, wriggled with content; glanced at her own faded blue linen dress, then across at the blue shadows on the old grey sheep-dog and on her father's grey flannels, both under the trees. She sat up, roused to a quivering happiness by the harmony of it all.

A tiny impact on one bare knee brought her eyes back to her own person. She drew her breath sharply, for on the knee a bumble-bee sat, brown and gold and dusty, five claws firmly set in her rough skin, and the sixth leg cocked in a business-like, dislocated fashion over the insect's back. Hilary held herself quite still. When the bee began to wave its free leg to and fro, she could contain herself no longer. She called to her father:

"Father, there's a bumble-bee sitting on my knee. D'you think I ought to shoo it off?"

Gregory Moore had been staring at the sea. He brought his chair, with little hops, not getting up from it, nearer the edge of the shade.

"It's combing its back," he said after a second's scrutiny.

"Got too heavy a load of pollen to get home. No, I

11

shouldn't shoo it off. It likes your warm leg to sit on."

The child accepted his explanation silently. "It's scratching its head now," she volunteered after a bit. "Isn't it nice and furry? I've never seen one so close before."

The two bent their heads together over the bee, hardly daring to breathe lest they should startle it.

"He's made a little hill of pollen, d'you see?" Hilary whispered, croaking in her excitement. "Behind him, on my knee! Isn't it *neat*, the way he's put it!"

After a while the bee took a firmer grip with its hooked feet, stretched first one pair of wings and then the other, and kicked itself off into the sunshine. Hilary and her father watched it out of sight, then all of a sudden decided, both at once, to blow away the hillock of pollen from opposite sides of the knee. Hilary rolled over, scuffling like a puppy, and Gregory, laughing, prodded her with his toe.

Presently Hilary stood up and smoothed her rumpled dress; a square-shouldered, straight-limbed child, with delicate hands and feet and crisply curling, gold-flecked hair.

She inquired with studied unconcern, "Would it have stung?" Gregory smiled. "Not unless you'd hurt it. And a bumblebee's sting's nothing much, anyway."

"I wouldn't have hurt it, of course," Hilary said.

She stood for a moment trying to see where the bee had gone, then squatted suddenly at Gregory's side.

"Hadn't we better get on with Sir Thomas, Father?" she suggested, and firmly took the book from his lap and turned over the pages. "I don't think it's any good waiting for Hermione. She was helping Mother, and she's not really very interested. I wouldn't be surprised if she didn't come."

They had settled down in the garden half an hour before for a history lesson, which had not yet begun. Waiting for Hermione was only an excuse, really, for dreaming away part of the summer afternoon. Not that they wanted to shirk the lesson, either of them. Gregory loved Sir Thomas More, from his writings and from the intimate accounts of him in some old chronicles, almost as though he were a man alive, and had so drawn him for Hilary that she loved him too. Only, to Gregory, as well as a great lawyer and a man whose asceticism could not spoil a mellow nature and a ready wit, he was that amazing thing, a really learned man who was ready to die for his religion. Hilary, on the other hand, saw him quite clearly as a gentle, stooping person with keen grey eyes and a happy mouth, exactly like her father. She had other historical heroes, too, all built to this pattern. Sir Thomas was just the one of the moment, because the history lessons had reached his period.

Gregory's daughters, at thirteen and ten, had never been to school, partly because there was no school at hand except the village one, partly because Gregory so much enjoyed teaching them himself. Lessons were spasmodic, taking place with the greatest regularity during school holidays, for in term time Gregory was kept busy at the neighbouring boys' school at which he was a visiting master. The girls had spent the whole of their lives in the Devon village of Redsands, rambling about the country, bathing, rowing the tub-boat about the bay below the house, and, lately, in being haled back by their mother to do those things which daughters, as distinct from children,

13

might be expected to do in a house where there was sometimes a maid and sometimes none. Hermione took kindly to these tasks. Hilary did not, though when she had to do them they were done with a speed and thoroughness which far surpassed her sister's conscientious performances. She had a mania, shared incongruously by her scholarly father, for being out of doors.

She replaced the book on her father's knee. "I know you know it all, but I do like you to read me the bits from the old papers. Like that one where the man said images were idols and Sir Thomas told him not to be silly because even a dog knew a real coney from a carved and painted one. Coney's a much nicer name than rabbit, isn't it? Is there any more about his dear daughter Meg?"

The afternoon slipped away as the pair lost themselves in admiration for More's courage and wit, anxiety as to his fate, and indignation with Thomas Cromwell. When finally More had been condemned and executed, Hilary felt that she had lost a friend and must set out at once to tell King Henry exactly what she thought of him. She was still in this mood of tragic fury when Hermione came out to say that tea had been waiting for them for ten minutes.

Hermione even then was a pale replica of her sister. Where Hilary's hair glinted red-gold, hers was mousey brown. Her cheeks were freckled instead of peach-red, her eyes grey instead of bright hazel. Her shoulders were narrower than Hilary's and already she stooped a little. Her walk lacked Hilary's graceful freedom. Her voice, as she gave the message, had a hint of querulousness about it which made Hilary hump her shoulders and brought anxiety to Gregory's face.

"What have you been doing all the afternoon?" he asked her; more gently than if he had been speaking to Hilary, because Hermione irritated him a little and his immediate reaction, now, to irritation was control.

She ticked off her occupations on her fingers with evident pride. "First I washed up while Mother cut up the rhubarb for jam. Then I stirred it while it boiled, so it shouldn't burn. Then I brought Mother empty jam-pots to pour it into and took away the full ones. They were hot. And then I put the papers on the top and tied them down and wrote on them, 'Rhubarb, 1905'. And then I got tea ready."

Hilary curled her lip. "Rhubarb! Beastly! What's it got in it, ginger or lemon-peel?"

"Lemon-peel," Hermione allowed with some reluctance.

Hilary said, "Beastlier and beastlier!" and stayed behind to sniff delicately at a late primrose.

Hermione ran ahead into the house. And Gregory, as she disappeared, reproached himself a little for so much preferring his Mary to his Martha. His excuse was in recalling that there seemed no doubt which of the children was preferred by their mother.

2

When Hilary came in the others were already seated. Although she was used to the ugly room, she gasped at the difference between it and the garden. Outside was beauty, peace, happiness. Indoors, it was as if the very particles of the atmosphere were jumping up and down in jangling disquiet. It was not that there was noise, for there was none except the occasional tinkle of spoons and cups and saucers and the movement of feet on the floor. Hilary's attention wandered over the dull, harsh colours and heavy furniture, and came finally to her mother's eyes. She slid into her chair, occupied with the impression that all the room's discontent streamed out from them; hard, light brown eyes which darted this way and that and snapped out sparks of hate at all they saw.

The meal was an uneasy one. Gregory, after a glance at his wife, withdrew into himself as though into sanctuary. The children stole quick looks at each other, Hilary's questioning, Hermione's a barrier which seemed to say, "*I* know what's the matter, and so would you if you gave it half a thought!" Hilary supposed she did know, though the fact of two people's having forgotten the time seemed a ridiculously small cause of so much discomfort. She took, defiantly, an enormous bite of bread-and-butter, and, with unconscious mimicry of her father, sat stolidly chewing it, staring at the fields through the open window, her wits far away.

They were brought back by Gregory's movement as he absent-mindedly pushed his cup along the table for more tea. Hermione manoeuvred it into her mother's reach, but Rose Moore did nothing but turn a broad shoulder towards it petulantly and leave it where it was. And so the family sat, the children silent, alert, dominated by their mother's angry mood, Hermione anxious to placate, Hilary waiting in a sort of hopeful terror for the explosion which would end it; Gregory, most irritatingly, outside it all, within the fortress his own mind provided against such situations.

The explosion was brought about by Hilary herself. Gregory, after some minutes, looked round for his tea. Hilary leaned suddenly across the table and emptied the cup's dregs into the basin. She was laying hands on the teapot when her mother restrained her:

"Sit down! How dare you attempt to dictate to me!"

Hilary kept firm hold of the teapot-handle. "He wants his tea!" she objected. "Why shouldn't I give it to him, if you don't want to?"

"Because pouring out tea's my business. Sit down."

Hilary sat, glowering, and Hermione piped out, "She thought you hadn't noticed Father's cup, Mother!"

"I didn't," Hilary contradicted intrepidly. "I saw her notice, and I knew she was just keeping him waiting on purpose, and I don't see why she should. 'Tisn't as if we *tried* to be late!"

Gregory awoke to the discord of three wrangling voices. He said mildly, "Shut up, Hilary! There's no need to be rude over a miserable cup of tea!"

That did it, and his wife's smouldering temper flamed.

"Miserable cup of tea, indeed! That's all it is to you! Miserable food, miserable cleaning and washing and

17

drudging, miserable women who let it take up all their time! It's been taking up my time these days and years, and Hermione's too, while you couple sit outside and pride yourselves *you're* doing the things that really matter! I'd like to see your faces if I downed tools and sat about reading books!"

That, and the instant for which she sat defying them all, were enough to break Hilary's self-restraint. She seized the teapot again - her mother took hold of it, too, and jerked an elbow against Hilary to make her let go - and between them the heavy thing rolled over, shivered Gregory's cup to fragments, and crashed to the floor.

The hot tea stung Hilary's legs. She looked this way and that in terror, saw her father's face, gentle, deprecating, as he pulled himself to his feet. Hermione was craning her thin neck, open-mouthed, like a pullet. Her mother's cheeks were almost purple, her eyes bright, her mouth a thin line. The ruin of the teapot, the brown mound of tea-leaves, the liquid soaking into the carpet, made her feel as though she had pulled the house about their ears. They couldn't have tea, or breakfast even, without that teapot - it had always been there.

She caught sight of the long shadows in the garden, the spring green of the fields beyond; pounced on a slab of bread-and-butter and dived without a word into the cool kitchen and out of doors.

She ran as if there were demons behind her to the place where a drop of a few feet divided field from rocky shore, then leaped down and sat on a big rock, facing outwards, to finish her tea. She could not swallow it. She was still shaking with rage and fright and her mouth was dry.

She could not remember a time when such scenes - only never one quite so bad - had not been part of her life. They were always started by some trivial thing: a chair out of place, a door left ajar, a small unpunctuality like to-day's; always worked up to a climax of menace, thrust-out chin, hands which would have made claws or fists but for some quality in Gregory before which physical violence sank and died; always dragged on for hours during which her mother flounced about, did the work of three women in a third of the usual time, glared with tight lips and darting eyes and would not speak a word to any of them.

Hilary thought of life as spotted, black and gold. The black was her mother's rages, her incalculable changes, the impossibility of pleasing her. Even now she wanted, sometimes, to please her. Then there was her own fear of her mother, making her creep into the house after any absence from it, to find out her mother's mood; and shame at her fear, for wasn't it shameful to be afraid of anything? There was no peace, in the red cottage by the sea.

The golden background to this blackness varied in intensity. There was the quiet, glowing gold of the hours with her father, walking, bathing, talking, doing lessons. There was the blaze of adventures in the boat, alone or with Hermione, to whom, away from the house, she assumed naturally the role of protector and egger-on; on her bicycle, exploring; and of expeditions with the boys from her father's school.

To these expeditions Hilary had been admitted since, at the age of about ten, she had shown that she could do with

19

ease most of the things the boys did. The boys were fond of her father, and accepted her, when he brought her, as one of themselves. The sort of boy who could not was not attracted by Gregory's rambles. She bathed and played with them in the summer, walked and cycled, wrangled and scuffled with them in the winter, as she might have done with brothers and cousins in an age of larger families. Sometimes Hermione came with them, more often she stayed at home with her mother.

The evening was quiet. Sky shaded from golden in the west, through delicate greens to blue in the east. The sun had just gone down. The red after-glow would come presently. Waves splashed softly, hypnotic in their rhythm. A cormorant on the rocks sat so still that Hilary was persuaded he was nothing but a stranded bottle, then stretched his neck and flapped away.

She sat still, not thinking, hardly feeling; and in time the quiet worked its miracle, her trembling stopped, her rage was forgotten. Even the red was fading from the sky as she climbed the bank to go indoors. She was hungry, but she disregarded that. Her one thought was to get to bed unseen.

3

It was during that summer that she was given a glimpse, no more, of what the atmosphere of an ordinary home might be. Funds must have been low that year, or Rose Moore more than usually amenable, for she agreed to take two of Gregory's boys for the holidays, their parents being abroad.

They were pleasant boys. Henry was a little older than Hilary, Kenneth two years younger. Henry was above the average in brains, a quiet boy, always whittling bits of wood into heads or animals, never happier than when he could get a bit of clay into his hands. Kenneth, round-faced, with eyes like saucers, bubbled over with health and spirits.

They treated Hilary's mother with no respect at all: called her "Mrs. Greg" or "Ma" to her face, and "the Tartar" when she was not there to hear; doubled up with unbearable laughter when she scolded and banged things about, answered her back, and with all this did for her, without permission, odd jobs which she would never let her daughters do, and, if she issued an order, obeyed it without question. And Rose Moore put up with it. She could not resist them. When they were outrageously cheeky she smiled, as though it hurt her to, but still, smiled. The "get along now" with which she indicated that she had had enough of them was almost good-humoured. Unusual delicacies appeared at table, and before many days had passed young Kenneth was made a pet and could get out of her anything he pleased.

Hilary looked on open-mouthed at the change. At first she was definitely uneasy. To be alert for the first sign of storm was natural to her, so that she might have time to make her mind up whether to run or fight. To watch for clouds in broad sunlight was unnatural. She began to wonder, dimly, if her mother's ill temper could be the

21

family's fault, which, before, had never occurred to her. When at last she realised that the barometer was set fair, she stopped wondering about anything and just enjoyed herself. The change in her, from a defiant girl into a happy, high-spirited child, was as great as that in her mother.

One grilling day the four youngsters went out in the tub-boat - the first time they had been in it together, for the weather had been rough. Hilary, without thinking, began to shove the boat down the shingle herself and shouted to the others what to do to help. It was what she always did with Hermione.

The effect on the boys was funny. They glanced at each other, and Henry, without a word, joined her to such effect that the boat was at the water's edge in no time. Kenneth, ridiculous, squeaked out, "Aye, aye, sir!", tilted his cap over one eye, rolled up his sleeves, hitched his shorts up, strutted, and finally applied his weight to the boat at the exact second which was the best to get her afloat. Hilary realized that they knew as much about boats as she did.

She said, "Shall we sail her?" and they helped expertly in getting up the sail. Then Henry took charge of the sail and Hilary of the tiller and they skimmed across the bay as though they had worked together all their lives. Hilary, who had suggested sailing with the idea at the back of her head that if they did she would be able to show without question that she knew more than they did, was first surprised and then delighted. This smooth progress was better than anything she could achieve with Hermione, who always took a command the wrong way if she could and forgot at some critical moment what she was supposed to be doing, so that they went by jumps and jerks, with Hilary's heart in her mouth half the time. She watched Henry's movements critically at first, then with a content which she had never felt before. There was hardly need for a word between them. Each kept an eye on the other's actions and followed with his own, and the boat leaped ahead. When they had rounded the point which shut the bay off from the open sea, Henry settled down to the following breeze and grinned across at her appreciatively.

"Smart sailing," he said. "We could win a race, you and I." Hilary, thinking it over, agreed. "I believe we could." She had never worked with anyone on equal terms before, only either done as she was told or harried her sister into doing it. This was fun.

Kenneth and Hermione sat in the bows out of the way. Hilary hardly noticed them.

They sailed eastwards along the coast and put in presently to another bay, almost landlocked, facing west. They beached the boat and waded ashore with the same fine efficiency which had sailed her. They bathed at some length and found that Hilary was a faster and stronger swimmer than Henry but that Kenneth beat Hermione every time. They had lunch, leisurely and very cheerfully, and after it lay about and talked in little spurts and drowsed. Hilary, dreaming day-dreams rather than dozing, caught sight of Henry going up the cliff path to explore and heard Kenneth wheedling Hermione to come with him to look for sea-anemones in the pools.

She stayed where she was, flat on her back, watching gulls and, higher, swallows, wheeling in the blue. She felt

23

an affection, always, for the gulls, but the clean rise and swoop of the swallows filled her with a happiness which she was almost afraid of - it was as if she rose and swooped with them. This peace was too precious to be frittered.

Presently Henry came into her vision, squatting beside her rather seriously, his face towards the bay's narrow opening. He said, "There's a great wind getting up. Look out there at the white horses."

She sat up and looked where he pointed. He went on, "It's thunder, I think. See that bank of cloud? I could see it better from the top. Like ink."

The thunder grumbled as he spoke, and a gust whipped up even the smooth water of the little bay.

Kenneth and Hermione came running back. "There's a cave along there," Kenneth volunteered, "if it rains."
Hermione, looking fearfully at the sky, said, "I'm frightened of thunderstorms!"

Kenneth, his hands deep in his pockets, reassured her. "Hoo! You can't get struck in a cave!"

Hilary was unreasonably annoyed that her sister should own to fear in front of the boys. Hermione never did mind acknowledging fear, or weakness. It made her very difficult to coerce.

Henry said, "It looks to me as if it's going to be a good storm. What about putting some of the stores in the cave, in case it pours and we have to stay here? Show us where it is, Ken!"

They took the remains of the food, between them, and no sooner were they in the shelter of the cave than the storm broke. Hail-stones jewelled the water and made little sullen fountains of the wet sand. Jagged streaks of lightning rent the inky cloud and lit the grey dusk which had shut out the day. There seemed no respite from the thunder which echoed and re-echoed across the bay, even across the cave from one side to the other and back again. Hilary wanted to shout and dance for joy. She did not, because she was afraid the boys would call it showing off; but the feeling stayed inside her, as though she were really doing it in spite of them.

Hermione was sitting huddled, with her eyes tight shut and both hands over her ears. She *was* showing off - sitting like that didn't do any good. Hilary called across to her, scornfully, "Cowardy! I'd rather be struck with my eyes open, if I were you!"

Hermione, surprisingly, opened her eyes malevolently and answered back. She said shrilly, "Cowardy yourself! What about the day you broke the teapot and ran away so that Mother shouldn't blow you up! *I* saw Father looking at you!" She screwed her eyes up again, and shivered at a specially loud clap of thunder. Kenneth, with a grin, made a bound for her and squatted beside her, an arm about her shoulders. Hilary could not hear what he said, but Hermione managed a smile. Hilary wanted to hit her. She stalked to the mouth of the cave to watch the storm with Henry.

He turned for an instant to look at her. "D'you mind it?"

"No, I like it, rather," she told him; then was impelled by some deep sense of honesty to add, "I'm not afraid of things like storms. But I am a bit of people. I never know what to say to them."

To her surprise Henry agreed with her. "'M! They spoil things, most of them. Want to know too much." He was scraping at a chip of rock. Hilary was prevented by his words from asking what it was going to be. He looked up to say comfortably, "Crumbs, that was a crack!"

Yes, in spite of the cracks and the lightning and the turmoil, Hilary knew that she had never felt so safe or so contented in her life. It was as though, cut off, with no possibility of doing anything, she had got out of prison. She hoped the grey wall of rain would not lift for a long time.

It lifted in no more than half an hour, and the thunder went grumbling away into the distance. But the wind had split the black cloud into untidy pieces and strewn them over the sky, and now was whining as it swirled in and out of the funnel of cliff which made the little bay. The four stepped out to have a look at the boat.

"We'll have to bale - or tip her over," Hilary said.

Henry was looking doubtfully at the sea. "D'you think we can get round the point, in this? *I'm* not certain that we can even get out of the cove, till the wind drops."

Hilary snorted. "I've never been put off by a spot of bad weather yet," she said, "if I've really wanted to get anywhere."

She expected Henry to be furious, but he was not. He only said mildly, "I don't know that I have either. But I don't think I ever have wanted to get anywhere in a gale like this. Let's go up on top and have a look round."

They went up the cliff path side by side, in step. When they came to the top the wind took them and would have hurled them down again if they had not clung together, gasping and laughing, and ducked from its violence down to the short turf.

"You're quite right," Hilary said, when they could speak, "I never have been out in a wind like this." She knew she was giving in handsomely, but somehow one had to be honest with this boy. "D'you think it will drop?"

"Oh, I expect so. It's only a storm wind," Henry said, and they went down again. Kenneth and Hermione had gone back to the cave and were playing naughts and crosses in the sand. The other two joined them.

They waited another half-hour and a bit over, and every time they looked out the wind seemed to howl the louder. Hermione said, "We shall be late for tea."

Hilary made a face and Henry, seeing it, said, "Why, does it matter?"

She explained, shamefacedly: "Only, Mother gets into such a fury if we're late for things."

Kenneth opened wide eyes to say, "Well, we couldn't help a storm, could we?"

"She'll say we ought to have seen it coming and turned back."

Henry chuckled. "Well, we didn't and that's that. Nobody could have, it was behind the hills. Will she keep tea for us?"

Hilary didn't know. They had never, any of them, dared to be as late as all that. "She always seems to think we've done it on purpose to annoy her. Never believes we've simply forgotten the time, or gone farther than we meant to, or whatever it is."

"She can't help believing us about this," Henry objected.

"Look at the sea!"

Hilary said gloomily, "She'll ask millions of questions to try to catch us out, and get someone into a muddle so that they contradict themselves, and then she'll pounce and say we're not telling her the truth the whole truth and nothing but the truth. You see."

But Henry was shouting with laughter, refusing to take things seriously. "If she asks us millions of questions we'll give her millions of answers. Tell her we were kidnapped by buccaneers and haled off to the West Indies, working before the mast, and escaped and stole an aeroplane and here we are. And give her this as a proof." He picked up a boulder in both hands and stood astraddle, balancing it. "It's a ruby of fabulous worth. If you don't believe me, look for the red streaks. You only find the streaky sort in the West Indies." He laid the stone down carefully and tiptoed round it, dazed with admiration.

Hilary giggled. He talked such priceless bosh!

Hermione had been looking more and more shocked. She said solemnly, "But we shouldn't be telling the truth. And she'd *know* we weren't."

Kenneth doubled up with laughter. "Of course she'd know. That's why it doesn't matter."

Henry left his ruby and expounded. "We call those Timbuctoo sort of lies. People know they're lies, so they're not mean. They're just a not quite so rude way of saying, 'Mind your own business!'"

"If you try that on Mother," Hilary said positively, "I think she'll burst. Or p'raps she wouldn't - to you."

Kenneth came close to her, mysteriously. "Methylated

spirit's awfully good if she whacks you," he confided. "Whether it's hands - or backsides. Rub it in every night - not after the whacking, it smarts - and it hardens the skin." Hermione, scandalized, said, "No one *ever* whacks us! How dare you, Ken, say things about Mother like that?"

Kenneth sighed. "Well, I expect you deserve it. All children do!" he said, like a little old man. A snort from Henry made Hilary chase him and smack his head.

There was still the question of getting back. Hilary said, "We can't leave the boat here. The tidemark's right up to the cave, and she won't go inside. We could anchor her, I s'pose - but it would be a risk."

Henry said, "I believe it is dropping a bit. What about sending these two home overland, Hilary, to tell them we're all right, and you and I waiting a bit longer? It'll die down before sunset, almost for certain, and we can bring her along."

Violent objections from Kenneth were firmly squashed. "There's no earthly point in all of us getting wet through, and we really ought to let them know we're not drowned - we easily might be - and Hermione won't go all that way alone. Get along with you," Henry ordered, and after some grumbling the couple climbed the cliff path and disappeared. Alone with Henry, Hilary felt a moment's fright. She didn't know what to say to him, now, although she had chattered away easily enough with the others there as buffers. Mercifully, Henry was not so afflicted. He brought out his bit of sandstone and exhibited it. It had turned into a duck, such a lively, beady-eyed duck that Hilary cried out with pleasure.

"You can have it, if you like it," he said carelessly. "I can make another for myself any day."

Hilary turned it this way and that, stroked it, stowed it away in the pocket of her knickers. That led to a discussion on pockets in general, and when that was done Henry pointed out that the wind had veered a little and was no longer sending great waves jostling and crowding into the bay's narrow mouth.

"I think we could just about do it," he said. "Game to try?"

As they baled out the rain-water and stowed their tins away, Henry talked about sailing on the east coast, which he and Kenneth did with an uncle almost every holidays. He looked with knowledgeable eyes at the flurry of grey sea and gave his opinion that it was not too bad at all. "If she was a little bit bigger it'd be simply nothing."

Hilary's heart was racing again, but pleasurably. She had never been out in a small boat in anything like so rough a sea, and she wasn't going to say so for the world.

She hadn't a chance to think about it, once they got out of the bay. The wind made it impossible, it seemed, to breathe, the spray stung her cheeks and got into her eyes so that she could barely see, and every minute there was something to be done in the way of steering, trimming, baling, while Henry managed the fierce little sail. She was wet through in the first two minutes. She wondered whether Henry's rather gentle swimming would keep him afloat in a sea like this if they did turn over. She wanted to tell him to hang on to the boat if it did happen, but the wind would not let her. Soon she forgot her own discomforts altogether in the exhilaration of feeling the little boat's going where they wanted it to, in spite of everything. She never pretended for a minute, after that, that she knew as much about sailing as the Swains did.

Getting into their own little bay was a job. Henry managed that entirely. Hilary just did as she was told. When they were in, Hilary shook the damp, salty, sandy mass of hair out of her face and turned to Henry with laughing, shining eyes. "I've never enjoyed myself so much in all my life!" she said.

Henry's own pleasure was more tempered. It wasn't the first time he had sailed in a rough sea. He said, "She's not a bad little tub . . . I've split my finger-nail on that beastly rope." He added grudgingly, "You're a better crew than young Ken, although he's done it since he was two."

Hilary was absurdly proud. She said rather crossly, "Well, I've done it since I was two as well, and I'm older than Ken."

"Girls don't do rough things like that, much. That was what I meant," he said, unperturbed.

"I do. I do anything I like," she insisted.

He had the last word. "Most of them haven't the guts."
Hermione met them glumly in the garden. "Mother's furious!" But Rose Moore's annoyance, which after all was partly anxiety, dissolved when she saw their state of dampness. She hustled them off to hot baths and took endless trouble over a dressing for Henry's split finger-nail. Hilary nearly wept in her bath because she hadn't a brother. It would have made life so absolutely different.

After they had filled themselves as full as was humanly possible with tea, Hilary managed to slip into the garden

31

with her father alone. He thought she wanted to talk about the afternoon, and asked her kindly questions and was glad she had enjoyed herself. She answered him absently, only biding her time until she could get a question in herself. "Father, d'you think I'm a coward?"

She saw him look her up and down, as though considering, and braced herself to meet a blow if one should come. "Honest, please," she added.

He said seriously, "No. I shouldn't say so. Why?"

"Because," she said, and braced herself again, "I ran away the day I broke the teapot." The memory of that day still gave her cold shivers. She could not get used to the two small green teapots which replaced the big brown one, big ones being impossible to get in the village.

Gregory's kind, serious gaze relaxed into a smile. He said serenely, "That was a dreadful moment, wasn't it? Enough to knock anybody sideways!"

Hilary could have hugged him. She did not, because they did not hug each other in her family. Besides, she had not quite finished confessing her baseness. "I was quite a lot afraid when we started back in the boat to-day. And I'm awfully afraid of Mother, very often."

Gregory did not speak for a while, and Hilary did not know what he was thinking or what to do. She played with a grass stalk and began to nibble it, then remembered that there was a disease you could get from eating grass and stopped in a panic. Your jaw swelled, or your tongue, or something.

Gregory said, "There's nothing to be afraid of in your mother, you know. She's got" - he grinned - "a most alarming bark, but she never bites."

Hilary felt suddenly grown up. First, Henry and Kenneth plotting to tell her mother a ribald tale if she intruded on their private concerns. Then, Father saying quite calmly that her bark was worse than her bite! Had she been funking a shadow after all?

"It only annoys her if you're frightened," Gregory went on. "She's ashamed of you for being a donkey and not seeing she doesn't mean it. Just don't be afraid and you'll find things are much better." He paused, then said, as if he had forgotten Hilary was there, "Being married's a rotten life for a woman."

Hilary felt a need to explain herself. "I'm not quite sure what being a coward is. If I've got time to think it over, I can generally make myself do the thing I'm afraid of. But if something takes me all of a sudden - like the teapot - I'm just terrified and run. I suppose if I'd been brave, I should've come back, instead of staying down on the shore, as soon as I *had* had time to think."

"You might have, if you'd thought of it," he allowed.

She protested eagerly, "I didn't! It simply never came into my head! I'm not kidding myself!"

He surveyed her, amused. "Then that's all right. Kidding yourself is the very worst sort of cowardice - running away from something and then pretending you didn't really mean to go that way at all! If you *do* funk something, acknowledge to yourself that you've done so - there's no need to go acknowledging it to other people; 'tisn't their business - and you'll probably never funk that particular thing again. Don't make excuses for yourself, ever. Your

33

failure's your failure, and if you'd been a better person you'd never have made it."

She followed that stark doctrine with attention. It appealed to her, made her brace her shoulders even while she shivered. Then she warmed suddenly, for her father was saying, "Don't worry about yourself. You've got courage all right. Everyone has these moments of terror, except the few who are so insensitive that nothing can get through their hides. It's courage that counts, all the time. Pull yourself up, when you've started running, and go back. Make yourself do the things you hate doing. You'll find you soon do them as a matter of course. It isn't the things that happen to you that matter, it's how you take them - that's the only important thing."

4

After that holiday together, the Swain boys became as much part of Hilary's life as though they had been her brothers. They spent most of their school holidays for several years at the red cottage, and a great deal of their free time. While they were at hand, the gold dazzled the black right out of existence, and even when they were away Hilary could deal with the shadows high-handedly by herself if they did not last too long. The very hint that her mother was not terrifying to everyone took away much of the bewildered fear which had given Rose Moore such power.

"If you can understand a thing, it can't frighten you any more," she said one day to the boys.

Kenneth, flat on his back in the sun, and bored by these abstract vapours, said pompously, "Some old bird in Greece said that. 'Knowledge is power'. And of course it is. If you know how to do a thing you can do it, and if you don't you can't. Q.E.D. and anything else is absurd."

Henry launched a punch at him, from force of habit.

"You're all wrong, both of you. It was Socrates, but he said it was virtue, not power. And some things frighten you however much you understand them - more than if you didn't, I should say. If you fell under a steam roller you'd understand quite well that it was going to flatten you out - but don't tell me you wouldn't be frightened."

Hilary could not be bothered to explain that she hadn't meant that sort of understanding. She said, "Mother *is* rather like a steam roller. The only thing to do about her when she comes at you is to dodge."

Kenneth said, "Pah! Let's go and play cricket on the sands. Bags I to bat."

"It's Hilary's turn," Henry remarked, and Kenneth made a face, protesting, "She hasn't got to practise for any eleven. I don't see *why* she should have turns."

Henry said, "Well, she's going to, that's all!" And Hilary did, though she did not really mind much whether she batted or not. She was quite a good bat, but there didn't seem any point in it.

She missed the boys terribly when they went off to stay with a relative. A tension arose in the cottage almost as soon as they had gone, for neither the girls nor their

35

mother had quite enough to do. Rose Moore furiously cleaned the house and poured imprecations on anyone who brought mud into it. Hermione shared her labours and echoed her mood, and Hilary, in unbearable irritation, took herself out of doors.

In the afternoon she was joined by Gregory and Hermione for a bathe. Their mother would never bother to learn to swim, but Gregory had taught both the children when they were young and they were happy in the water. They could not have been more than six years old when, in turn, they discovered the opposite side of their rectangular bay, where the rocks went down sheer into blue water, with golden banks of seaweed showing far below which turned the blue into swirls of vivid green. There were bits of lapis lazuli in the rocks, and the far shore, too, had the attraction of being almost inaccessible except by water. Once there, you must swim back, or take a long and prickly scramble inland in nothing but your bathing dress.

On this afternoon, the three of them had started, together as usual, by swimming across. Gregory and Hermione climbed out and sat on a rocky shelf in the sun. Hilary swam back to the middle of the bay, where the water was so smooth that it looked like jelly which you could cut with a knife and make it gape. She floated, flapping gently with her hands, and stared at the sky till she was dazzled, then turned over suddenly and darted along with her head under water, then made her legs into a paddle-wheel and enveloped herself in spray; then floated again, for so long that she lost all sense of time. When at last she doubled up and turned herself over to swim back, her father and

Hermione had left their shelf. Hermione was lying on the sand of the home shore, Gregory was nowhere to be seen.

A faint uneasiness took hold of Hilary. Her father was not swimming in the bay. He was not dressing, for his towel still lay in a bundle near her own. She could not see him anywhere on the shore.

Far away at the mouth of the bay something dark and round caught Hilary's eye. It floated for a second, then sank out of sight; then floated; then sank again . . . and did not reappear. Terror ran through her like a lightning flash, forced its way and was gone, leaving her numb. He was out there, drowning, and she was helpless. She began to swim, head down, hand over hand, as hard as she could go, towards the place where he had disappeared.

Problems crowded into her mind. What had he been doing, so far out? Had he got cramp, or banged his head, or what? How would she know when she came to the place, if he didn't come up? Would there be bubbles to tell her where he was? Could she dive to the very bottom? Would she be strong enough to get him up, if she did find him? Hadn't she better yell for Hermione to come and help? She turned her head to do so, but her voice would not come, it stuck in her throat and she could not make a sound. . . She must be nearly there, she had swum so fast. . . There was not a single bubble, nothing but a bunch of seaweed floating in the smooth sea.

She hesitated, treading water, peering every way for anything to guide her - and her ears caught a thin hail from the far shore.

"Oi! Hilary! Not—too—far—out!"

Looking up, she saw her father, high on the rocky point, sitting with his knees under his chin.

She could not believe it - thought he must be his own ghost resting on the way to Heaven. It was only when he made a peremptory gesture shoreward with hand and head, that she was convinced that whatever the floating thing was it was not he. She began to swim towards him, and found that her arms and legs had gone weak from sheer fright.

She thought, "I was sure he was drowned - now I'm going to be drowned myself . . . ! Well, I just won't!" With reaction, the strength came back into her muscles and she swam on carefully, not even now quite sure of herself.

She scrambled out of the water and up towards him. Part of the time he was out of sight, hidden by projecting rocks, and she wondered, "Is he really there? Shall I really see him again in a minute?" There was a feeling in her stomach as though she had swallowed a gallon of water.

Then she was beside him and he was looking her over, whimsically, with a sort of unwilling admiration, as he often did. She threw herself on the short turf and let the sun dry her. The sound of his voice made her jump. It sounded different, like a voice she had never heard before.
"Were you going after that floating thing?" he asked, just casually, as a matter of interest.

She said, "'M! I didn't know what it was," and he went on, "I started off after it myself, and then I lost it, so I came up here to have a look. There it is - see? It's got right into the current."

The black object was bobbing up and down now on the

waves, out beyond the bay. From her height, Hilary could see that it was nothing as heavy as a man. Her father's voice went on, "But I still can't see what it is. Someone's hat, perhaps - or a child's big ball."

Hilary shivered and he fixed a mildly accusing eye on her. "You're cold. Stayed in too long."

"No. Goose over my grave," she protested. "How could I be cold, in this sun?"

He insisted on her running about, all the same, on the little patch of turf. She turned cart-wheels and jumped, and presently they swam back, side by side, across the bay.

Hermione greeted them peevishly. "I thought you were never coming. I'm getting most horribly cold!"

Whereat Hilary, in an access of high spirits now that things were normal again, threw sand at her and chased her, shouting, in and out of the rocks, till she cried pax and they both rushed panting into their shallow cave to dress.

Days later, they found the floating thing, washed up by the returning tide. It was a woman's handbag, with nothing in it but a mirror; discarded by some petty pilferer, perhaps. Hermione wanted to take it home, but Hilary gave it a great kick which landed it in a tangle of blackberry where no one could get it. She never wanted to see it again.

The terror of the one moment, the flooding relief of the other, never left Hilary for good. Early next morning she half woke, trembling and clutching at the bedclothes, oppressed by the most terrible sense of desolation. The whitewashed attic was grey, cell-like and very cold. Hermione's bed was empty, she was all alone. No, there was a movement in the room below. She wasn't even alone, her mother was there. She almost screamed. She was alone with her mother for ever. She could bear anything but that. She must get away.

She sat up, with the idea of dressing at once. The movement woke her properly, and with awakening came memory. She was not alone. Her father was not drowned, but downstairs asleep. Even Hermione had not really left her. She was just lying flat and breathing very quietly.

Relief was like a drug. She lay down and slept again immediately, and woke later hazily conscious that she had had a nightmare. It didn't matter. The morning was full of blue haze and pale gold sunbeams.

5

Another, later, summer was marked by Hermione's having pneumonia. The usual party of four went picnicking one day, were cajoled by Hilary into taking a longer round than they need have done, and were caught by a shower on the way home. Hilary was as happy wet as dry, but Hermione must have been overtired. Even before she got home she had dark rings round her eyes. In the night, she woke Hilary by her restless tossing, and by the morning, when the doctor came, the diagnosis was easy for him.

Rose Moore stormed at Hilary, and Hilary, as usual, stood up to her and threw back, defiantly, word for word. But no sooner had her mother flounced out than Hilary rushed to the shore and wept, her face to the sea. Hermione's illness was her fault, there wasn't any doubt. She never could remember that some people weren't as strong as she was. She never thought about being tired, herself. It was awful to think of Hermione dying because her elder sister, who ought to have been looking after her, wanted to see if a particular plant in a particular wood was in flower.

By way of penance she flung herself into the performance of household jobs, leaving her mother free to look after the invalid. She found that cleaning, cooking, and even washing and ironing, were not so dull, done on her own without her mother's eye on her. Dusting she had no patience with unless there was enough dust to make a pattern in. Then she would remove it with a fine sweep and squint along the shiny surface it had been hiding. She would deliberately leave some bits of furniture undusted, in places where she was sure her mother would not look, till they were sufficiently covered to give her that particular thrill. But the essential things she did heartily, and got through them in about half the time her mother usually took. She began to wonder why her mother made such a fuss about running the house. It seemed to her a business one could take in one's stride.

Another thing which puzzled her was the complete contrast between Rose Moore as she usually was and Rose Moore as a nurse. In Hermione's room she was quiet and deft, firm and astonishingly gentle. When the child was delirious she cried out continuously for her mother and was immediately quiet at the touch of her hand, while nothing else would calm her. Nothing was too much trouble for Rose Moore in the sick room, nothing so little trouble in her ordinary life but she must grumble about it.

Hilary watched her in utter amazement coaxing Hermione into taking her food, moving her without hurting when it was agony for her to be handled by anyone else, arranging her pillows in just the right position, washing her, carrying bed-pans about, sitting up all night with her at her worst - all without the faintest complaint and with a look about her which Hilary had never seen before, almost of serenity.

Hermione did not die, and she lost for ever her fear of her mother. For always, after that, the smallest hint of illness brought Rose Moore to her solicitously, waiting on her hand and foot. The weakness left by this attack stayed with her all her life; whether as an outcome of the pneumonia or as a defence against her mother, no one, except perhaps Dr. Tomkins, ever knew.

Hilary spoke to Henry one day about the change in her mother. He and Kenneth were at a neighbouring cottage now - Rose Moore could not manage both them and Hermione. But Hilary continued in spite of her housekeeping to spend hours in their company, and although this summer was not as good as those before, it had a golden-ness all its own.

She and Henry, Gregory and Kenneth, had set out after midday dinner for a walk. It was the first week of September, but the damp, sheltered south country kept the green of early summer. Such breeze as there was came from the east, stinging hot cheeks. Kenneth shouted that the air felt like sherbet. A haze hung over the sea, joining it imperceptibly to the sky and turning its indigo to turquoise and amethyst.

The party soon turned away from the sea and started along a lane which ran inland between high banks. Little streams trickled, chuckling, at the roadsides, the big stones in the banks glittered wetly and grew rosettes of liverwort, some like green velvet, some leathery brown or black. Foxgloves still flowered, and blue veronica, and navelwort's spikes of green sprang from among padded, coppery leaves.

The four of them crunched along the stony road abreast, the sheep-dog lumbering ahead. Hens scuttled from him as they passed a farm, a square house set back from the road with a pump in the farmyard and turkeys with angry faces gobble-gobbling round it.

Hilary said she would like to keep turkeys, Kenneth said he would hate to, and Henry supplied learnedly the information that they were delicate and difficult to rear.

"And their eggs are too big for one person to eat at a meal," Gregory said.

Henry and Hilary shouted both together, "Are they? Let's try!" and Kenneth called them greedy blighters.

The road began to climb, and took them past a church with a sloping churchyard and a tower with four tapering spires. They argued a lot about those. Why were there spikes on churches?

"To bump off evil spirits who try to sit on them!" Henry said.

"For lightning conductors!" Kenneth decided.

"For angels to balance on," Hilary suggested, with a vague memory of something that happened in a wilderness.

Gregory said, "To guide you up to Heaven," and they fell

silent, wondering.

The lane was banked on only one side now. To the left, it fell away to fields which rose gradually to rounded hummocks and merged in the distance into black moor. Nearer, the fields gave place to forest, which looked as though a jump from only a little farther along the road would land one in the tree-tops. Really, it was ten miles or so away.

They wrangled as to what trees they were. Hilary and her father both said, "Oaks," at once, with no thought at all. Henry said, "Couldn't they be beeches?" Kenneth was sure it was impossible, at that distance, to tell.

Hilary said, "They look like oaks. Colour and shape."

"You can't see the shape, from here, and the colour's just tree-colour."

"It's oak-colour. Beech colour's quite different, however far away you are."

Kenneth jeered, "You're just talking! You can't see either their colour *or* their shape!"

Hilary, perfectly sure she was right, became heated. "I can see! I can see they're oaks! You silly gowks, I don't believe you've ever looked at an oak to *see* it! If you had, you'd know them a hundred miles away, winter or summer or out of an aeroplane!" She could not bear to be argued with by ignoramuses when she knew she was right.

Gregory intervened: "They are oaks - I've been there," and Kenneth subsided.

Henry enlarged on Hilary's theme. "You know them because you live in the country. Country people take in things without knowing they do. That's why they can

44

always find their way about - isn't it, sir? They see the landmarks and pouch them, without thinking about it, and there they are when they're wanted. Town people just learn names of roads by heart or ask a policeman."

Gregory said, "That's true, I think. But townsfolk are more all there about *people* - know what they mean and when they're telling the truth and what they're likely to do next. The same process: subconscious observation and deduction. They see more people than we do."

"People!" Hilary said dejectedly. "Then I wish I lived in a town! I never know what they mean or what they want. I don't see how anybody possibly can!"

Gregory looked at her a little sadly. Her patterns, for people, were so limited, and one at least so incalculable. He said dryly, "You seem to follow the meanings of a rather abstruse old schoolmaster with some agility!"

"Oh - you!" She hung on his arm for a moment. "You're not a person. I mean ordinary people. Nasty people. Boys." She screwed up her nose at Kenneth, who became a gargoyle. "Grubby little reptile!" she said, but could not help laughing at him.

They turned aside presently from the lane across a farmyard, where dogs barked and geese hissed at them, then through a gate and so on to the mossy, pale green turf which covers the lower slopes of Dartmoor.

The sheep-dog bounded away and rolled, and Kenneth, with a yell, hurled himself on top of him. Henry and Hilary, intent on reaching the sky-line, climbed on. Gregory stayed behind, laughing at the scuffle, and by the time it was over and dog and boy had shaken off some of the clinging moss, the other two were a hundred yards ahead.

They were quite unselfconscious together now, they had seen so much of each other over many years. Sometimes they trudged silently, whistled, or twitted each other, argued, or fell into serious talk. Lately they often found themselves together, with the others either in front or behind, without having made any conscious effort that it should be so.

It was Henry who introduced the subject of Rose Moore. "How's Hermione?"

"Heaps better. Her temperature's been down five days."

He commented, "It's wonderful, isn't it? I heard Dr. Tomkins telling your father - it must have been a fortnight ago - that she hadn't an earthly chance. And yesterday he said your mother was the best nurse he'd ever come across and that it was all due to her the kid was still here. He generally comes and talks when we're having our history coaching, that's how we hear."

Hilary turned on him. "Why didn't you tell me he said she wasn't going to get better?"

Henry kicked a pebble accurately into a hole in the path. "Didn't seem any point in telling you a nasty thing that might not come true. And it hasn't, so there wasn't."

"I ought to have known. I might have been nicer to her," Hilary objected.

Henry said matter-of-factly, "If she was as ill as all that she wouldn't have noticed however nice you'd been. I didn't notice anything when I had measles. Anyway, it wasn't my business to tell you; it was old Greg's if he wanted you to know."

Hilary accepted that masculine reason without comment. It fitted in exactly with the standard she approved of. Her father and the boys never asked personal questions, never went probing into people's private minds, and nor did she. It seemed indecent to her that anyone should. Yet Rose Moore and Hermione, and the vicar's wife, and women in general, could not leave anything alone. The more it wasn't their business, the less you wanted them to know about it, the more interested and insistent they became.

"It's simply *mad*, the difference in Mother," she said. "Almost as though she likes doing all the horrible things she has to do for Hermione. I've had to do them once or twice, and I simply hated it, and then of course I felt a pig for hating it. The ordinary things in the house, Mother seems to hate, and they're nothing to make a fuss about compared with the others."

Henry said, "I expect she gets bored, doing the same old things over and over again. I should myself, I'm sure. I think your mother looks like a saint."

Hilary opened her mouth and shut it again. "*Mother?* A saint? I should've said that suited Father better!"

Henry objected. "No. Old Greg's awfully - sort of - good. And awfully wise, of course, which isn't the same thing as being brainy. But when your mother *is* good - I know she isn't always - she's superlatively good. D'you see what I mean? She can go very high or very low. Most people paddle along on the level, some on higher levels than others, and Old Greg's is a high one. But he never gets as high as she does at her best. D'you see?"

Hilary said at once, "Yes, I see. But I don't agree. I don't agree that a person who can be as perfectly horrible as Mother can is a saint when someone as good as Father isn't."

"The Head's been preaching sermons about saints," Henry said. "That's what started me off thinking about them. He said something like this. Some people - most people - don't find it difficult to be fairly decent. They don't want to do bad things - don't get a chance to, perhaps - don't get tempted. They have some sort of a standard and they don't fall far below it. If someone like that has a terrifically high standard, he's a saint, without any particular effort. That little Saint Theresa was like that - the Little Flower, they called her. She couldn't help being one, she was born like it. Then there are the people who are always getting into rows - who do find it terribly difficult to be even ordinarily decent. A lot of them don't try. But if they do manage to get on top of their beastly bits - bad tempers, or greediness or whatever it is - they're saints too, because it's been so difficult to conquer the beastly bits that if they've done that they've sort of automatically conquered the ordinarily nasty bits as well. That's the sort your mother would be - *is*, sometimes, I think . . . And I think it's ever so much more wonderful than the other sort."

Hilary nodded. "Father's the other sort," she insisted. "I like them best. You can depend on them. I don't think it's any good being a saint in spots and a perfect devil the rest of the time . . . D'you think it's awful of me to feel like that about Mother?"

"Not to feel like it. I don't see how you can help it, if she's always at you. I think it's fairly awful to say it."

"I shouldn't to anyone except you. I just say what comes into my head, to you," Hilary informed him lightly. She liked to be serious - but not for as long at a time as Henry did. In a minute she said, "I've got a hollow in my tum as big as a house. D'you think if we began now we could eat *all* the sandwiches before Father and Ken came along?"

Henry came down from his heights and giggled. "Let's try!" But the other two, ambling behind, saw them bending over the rucksack and broke into a trot.

6

It was some days later that Henry came rushing into the garden, to Hilary lying on her favourite moss-patch under the apple tree.

"I say! There's a Fair on the green at Buckleigh! Ken and I are going! Will you come?"

"Rather! When?" She sat up, her eyes alight.

Henry threw himself down beside her and Kenneth joined them.

"This afternoon. Start directly after lunch, same as usual?" It was the "same as usual" which made up Hilary's mind. There was a Fair at Buckleigh every second year, and whenever it came Rose Moore held forth against the iniquities of fairs, the waste of money, the noisiness and rudeness and bad behaviour, the hideous side-shows, the poisonous ices and sweets. She always finished up with the same prophecy - that there would be an epidemic of diphtheria and scarlet fever in the village before the week was out. When it came to Dolbey, fifteen miles away, in the intervening years, she rejoiced that it was not nearer and lamented that it was not still farther away. It had always been such an accepted fact that the Fair was a Bad Place that the children had never felt any desire to go. But here were the Swain boys taking it for granted that to go was the thing to do, chattering of other fairs they had been to. It could not be such a bad place after all.

She nodded. "Right-oh. You'd better wait for me out here. Mother's cleaned the hall; she won't want you indoors."

Long before dinner she had tied up buns and apples in a parcel for tea. After the meal, she washed up in a tremendous hurry and made for her room. Hermione had been moved downstairs at the beginning of her illness and Gregory was sleeping in a tiny cupboard called, by courtesy, the dressing-room. So Hilary could gloat over the luxury of a place to herself.

She considered what she should put on; looked at the cream silk she wore on Sundays and decided that it would not do for a Fair. It was the only nice dress she had. The alternative was a clean cotton one, new, certainly, only this spring, because she had been growing so fast, but quite plain. She put it on. The colour brought out the glow of her cheeks and the gold in her hair and, because it was longer than her older frocks, made her look more grown-up, less leggy than usual. She stood in front of the dressing-table mirror, tilting it to try to see the whole of herself at once.

A step on the stair made her turn sharply, and she saw her mother, on the way to the linen-cupboard, looking at her from the door.

"I'm going out with the boys," Hilary gabbled in a hurry. "I've set the tea and I'll be back in time to get supper ready."

Rose Moore was watching her sardonically. "Prinking for the beloved Henry, are you? You're starting early, young woman!"

Hilary, her conscience pricking, looked up, startled. She protested, "It's not so very early - it's after two!"

Her mother only cackled on a high note and turned away. "Dear Henry!" she taunted.

She was gone, but the look in her eyes and some quality in her voice left the girl quivering with rage. She made a movement to tear off the clean dress, but checked herself and scolded, "Don't be silly!" She brushed her hair and tied it back with deliberate care. "I always do tidy myself up to go out - I don't see why she should be sarky about it!" But her lips pressed themselves tightly together. She wasn't going to *try* to think what her mother had meant.

She put on a shady hat of golden-brown straw - old, but she was fond of it - and ran out into the sunshine.

Henry and Kenneth were waiting for her astride the fence. They jumped down when they saw her. She scrutinized Henry as though she had never seen him before. Indeed she had not: she had only taken him for granted as a person who was there, with whom she could comfortably do things; just as she did Hermione and Kenneth and the village girls she sometimes chatted to. She

51

had never received any shock or snub from him to awaken dislike or fear, though she was jealous, a bit, when her mother was nice to him, or showed any special favour to inspire gratitude. She approved of him and depended on him, that was all. There was no trouble about it.

She saw him now, a tall boy with an untidy, unfinished look; sunburned, rather beaked, with solemn grey eyes, wide, friendly mouth and pointed chin; fair hair which stood up, always, in a wispy crown at the top of his head. There was nothing unusual about him except the long, strong fingers which could make ducks or anything you liked out of bits of stone and wood. If she liked him better than the other boys at his school, it was because of those things he made and the way he always had something to talk about, and, most of all, just because she knew him better. She had never called him "Dear Henry" in her life, and if she did he would only mimic her with "*Dar*-ling Hilary!"

He called to her, "We've got your bike out - you needn't go into the shed!"

Kenneth jigged up and down and squeaked out, "Hurry up, hurry up, Hilary!" He was only fourteen and full of enthusiasm. Hilary became infected with it. She scuttled across the grass and flung herself on her bicycle and rode away down the hill with the boys pedalling furiously to catch her up.

The Fair ground was surrounded by a high barrier of sacking to prevent unpaid-for prying. The three, having arrived hot and somewhat tumbled, left their bicycles with a red-faced receiver of sixpences whom Henry tipped, shyly, yet with a lordly air, as they went in. Once in, he paused, Kenneth beside him like a little eager dog, and looked round him with an air of sophistication which impressed Hilary enormously. She had never been in such a crowd before and would have been terrified alone.

There was already a good sprinkling of country folk in the field, but it was possible to walk about with ease. Hilary caught sight of a face she knew and was seized with panic. Suppose someone told her mother she had been there!

She took hold of Henry's elbow. "I say, I've no earthly business to have come, you know! Mother thinks Fairs are simply awful - I knew she'd never let me come, so I didn't tell her!" She swung round to face him, too proud to say, "Don't tell her we've been!", too much attracted by everything round her to go home at once. "And I didn't tell you, because I thought you wouldn't bring me if you knew!"

A slow smile spread over Henry's face as he took in what she was saying. Hilary was glad he did not think she had been too terribly mean. "Well, now you're here you may as well be hanged for a sheep as a lamb and enjoy yourself a bit! And if we all keep our mouths shut, there's no reason why you should be hanged at all - is there?"

Hilary grinned. "I suppose not. There's not anything very awful about it, is there, honestly?"

Henry said comfortably, "*I've* never seen anything! D'you hear, young Ken? If you breathe a word that Hilary's been here, I'll wring your neck!"

Hilary wriggled with enjoyment. There was something rather nice about Henry, after all. Most people would have laughed at her and not minded whether her mother found out or not.

Henry turned seriously to the business of deciding what they should do. All around there were booths with queer-looking games inside them: "Ring the bell and you get your penny back!" "First to bust the balloon wins a handsome prize!" - before this one three perspiring youths worked away at hand-pumps which blew up big coloured balloons. *Pop!* One of them had burst. The others threw away their pumps with shouts of panting laughter. Henry said, "We'll have a look at those presently. What about swings, first? They'll be crowded later on."

They moved across the ground and Hilary heard him wrangling amiably with the fat lady, broad-bosomed, aproned, with black greasy curls and a big hat on one side, who looked after the swing-boats; protesting that Hilary and Kenneth were light enough to occupy one end of a boat while he took the other. He had his way, and they climbed up wooden steps and wedged themselves into the red-cushioned, gilded canoe. Someone gave them a shove - and in a few seconds Hilary was ecstatically aware of nothing but the red plush cord in her hands and Kenneth's, the swish of air past her, and the vigorous, rhythmic movement of her body as they timed the pull to the exact instant which would increase their speed to the uttermost. The tightening of all her muscles for the pull-up - the breathtaking pause so high in the air that the field below seemed peopled with pygmies - the dizzy downward swoop, clutching at the rope - the steadying bend of the knees before the ascent began again . . . There had never been anything like it!

The fat woman had to give in three times to her demand for "another go". She could not tear herself away.

When at last it was over, she wobbled uncertainly down the steps and stumbled in the business-like wake of the boys as though in a dream.

They stopped at a stall and bought brandy-snaps and crunched them. Hilary had never tasted anything half so good. They hurriedly skirted a great cauldron out of which saucers of some concoction were filled with a dipper and sipped by the buyers, giving off a peculiar aromatic smell; paused, fascinated, by a rifle-range whose targets were many-coloured balls dancing on a fountain spray, and had a more modest shot themselves, with darts, at the spots on a black-and-white dog - "If you hit the patch on his tail you get *two* prizes!" Hilary hit one in the middle of his fat stomach and went off triumphantly with a packet of milk chocolate; and later, Kenneth knocked down a coconut and carried it away by its hair.

Hilary wanted to have her fortune told, but Henry dissuaded her. "It's all bosh, the stuff they tell you. You cross the water - it may be the sea, or a puddle in the path. You marry someone with golden hair - or black - and have umpteen children.

Who wants to know things like that? If you want to spend some more, let's go into the circus. It's only a little one, but I heard a man say there's some good riding."

The atmosphere inside the circus tent seemed to Hilary almost solid. They came out limp and dripping, but while they were inside they forgot everything in the antics of a lithe girl and boy on a couple of graceful ponies and of a racketty painted clown who held hoops for them and egged them on and rolled about himself. As they paused outside, uncertain what to do next, Hilary found herself more in accord with young Kenneth's plans for going at once to train as a circus-rider than with Henry's grown-up conviction that such careers were not for such as they.

Their minds full of what they had seen, they sauntered towards the Merry-go-round. Here they could at least pretend that they were controlling one of those grey wizards of the circus. The thing was in motion when they reached it. Fat horses, dappled and brown, bobbed up and down in rhythmic gallop. Or, if you preferred it, you could ride a pig or a camel, or even a dragon, whose movements were just the same. The three of them watched, choosing which steed they would have.

"That little brown one - no, the dapple with the long white tail . . . *Henry - look!*"

Hilary clutched Henry with such force that he would have shouted if he had not been as dumbfounded as she was herself. For the dapple with the long tail bore, proudly, a tall, thin figure sitting stiffly upright but giving to the horse's action as he would have done to a real horse; his face grave, his vision far away; a schoolboy lost in knight-errantry, a grown-up lost in his own childhood. The horse bore him round, out of sight.

"Did you see? It's Father!"

Henry was chuckling. "The funny old dear! Whoever would have thought of him doing a thing like that!"

Kenneth was laughing delightedly. "Won't the chaps

fairly hoot next term when we tell them! I say, Hilary, what a good thing you didn't go home! Mrs. Moore can't possibly mind your being here now he's here too!"

Hilary's mind pounced backwards to a scene years ago, at tea, in the red cottage dining-room. Her father, recounting, eagerly, what he had seen and done at the Fair. His wife, expressing grim surprise, then pouring biting, stinging scorn on him for going to such a place, for his incredibly low tastes; the boyish happiness fading out, leaving his face grey. Hilary could not have been more than five then, for Hermione was a baby tucked up on the sofa. The picture flashed before her as though in a mirror. Ever since, the Fair had been spoken of as though unclean.

She turned on Kenneth. "No! She mustn't ever know he's been!" She took hold of his arm in her excitement and worked it up and down. "You don't know what Mother's like when she disapproves of something! She disapproves most terribly of fairs, thinks they're wicked; they're like red rags to her and we never mention them! I don't really mind much if she knows about me, because I don't care really what she does to me. But he does care if she's beastly to him" - she could not have told how she knew this, but she did - "and if she gets to know about me he'd have to tell her he'd been too, and we shouldn't hear the last of it for weeks and weeks! So she mustn't know about either of us! She'll spoil it so, and he's enjoying it! You do see, don't you? Henry, make him see, please!"

Henry said, "I think you make too much fuss about Mrs. Greg. But if you don't want her to know, we won't tell her, of course. Mind, now, Ken, you keep your big mouth shut!"

Kenneth grinned villainously and said, "Right-oh. I'll be mum!" and Hilary grinned back in the violence of her relief.

"What d'you want to do now?" Henry asked her. "D'you want him to see you, or not?"

Hilary jumped. In contemplating the remote danger she had forgotten the nearer one. "No, he mustn't see us! Of course he mustn't - didn't I say that if he knew I'd been here he'd have to tell her he'd been? He'll be getting off in a minute, won't he? It's slowing up!"

She dived away into the crowd, the boys behind her. Henry, turning round for a last look, saw that the Merry-go-round had started again, with the tall figure still upright on the dapple horse, having "another go" just as his daughter had done on the swings.

They went home soon after that. Hilary was so jumpy that it seemed the only thing to do. They ate their apples and buns, forgotten in the excitement of the afternoon, on a bank in a little wood by the way. Kenneth, who always lived contentedly in the present, relieved the tension by chattering all the time. But Hilary's thoughts kept going back to her father, solemnly, all by himself, riding his little fat horse.

As they approached the village she pulled herself together. Since Hermione had begun to get well, their mother's temper had become less angelic again; and because Hermione, in her weak state, so hated anything approaching a scene, Hilary had grown more subtle in preventing displays of wrath. Rose Moore's attention was, she had found, easily diverted from a late arrival or from curiosity as to where one had been, by some interesting bit of information imparted immediately on entering the house. Accordingly, she looked about for something - anything - out of which a good story could be made.

She found it to-day in the sight of the doctor's dog-cart, with which she had only lately become familiar, stopping outside a house in the village street. That would do; illness among one's neighbours was always news. The doctor, a cheerful little red-faced man, waved a hand to her as he climbed down.

At the gate, she thrust her packet of chocolate into Henry's hands. To take it in was only to court inquiries as to where it came from. She admonished the boys again - "Don't for any sake let out about it, will you?" At their grins, she was impelled to defend herself. "It isn't that I mind being punished. I don't. It's the fuss and rumpus before and after the punishment that upsets the whole house. And then there's Father. You will be careful, won't you?"

Before her earnestness the amusement faded. They promised the greatest caution. She flung her bicycle into the shed and bounced into the house. The boys, cycling away, heard her calling, "Mother! Mother!" as though her one wish was to tell Mrs. Moore all about the afternoon.

She imparted her news as soon as she was inside the sitting-room door. Hermione was downstairs to-day, sitting wrapped up by the window.

"Dr. Tomkins is at Mrs. Bennett's! He looked in a most awful hurry! He waved to me, though, as he went in."

The ruse succeeded. Rose Moore appeared to be looking

back into her own head, and her lips moved as though she was counting. "Is he, though? Had he got his black bag?"

Hilary considered. "Yes, I think it was black. A much bigger one than he brings here. I noticed him hauling it down."

"That'll be sooner than she thought, poor thing," Rose Moore commented. "That's the bag he brings the babies in," Hermione supplied.

Hilary had gone back to the hall and hitched her hat on a peg. She was not the least bit interested either in Mrs. Bennett's illness or in babies. She neither questioned nor believed the theory of the black bag; it simply passed her by. She had been too young to wonder about Hermione's arrival, and she knew no families intimately enough in the village to inquire about their increase. Village women were so often a queer shape, with great chests and large aproned stomachs, that a little more here or there seemed to her no cause for comment.

Just now she was filled, to the exclusion of all else, with unholy joy at having focused her mother's attention on something other than herself. She began to think about the business of getting supper.

When Gregory came in, she felt a great rush of affection for him. She was glad he liked fairs, indignant that he could not just say he did and take her with him so that they could have enjoyed it together. It must, she thought, have been almost dull for him alone. She longed to ask him if he had been on the swings or to the circus, but could not. It would have meant a conspiracy to deceive her mother, and that, somehow, was unthinkable, however much she might do it by herself.

Supper progressed calmly. They chatted about picking the apple crop in the garden, about Hermione's recovery and whether she ought to go away for a change. No one asked anyone where they had spent the afternoon.

As she went to bed, Hilary discovered that she was disappointed, and wondered why; then realized that she had been conjuring up a scene in which her father said boldly that he had been to the Fair and was going again, as often as he liked; challenged his wife to prevent him if she could, and gave her, Hilary, a chance to stand up with him and shout, "We don't care what you say, we're going to do as we like!"

But that wouldn't happen, of course. That was why she was disappointed.

Then, a few days later, she and her father, walking together, came out of the lane into the village street just in time to see a great unwieldy procession going by. A fiery little traction engine with a brass breast-plate, puffing brown smoke; yellow vans lumbering, the little circus horses stepping delicately; and, on a lorry, the roundabout, with the animals packed into piles and the dapple pony on top of them all, grinning down at the village with open mouth and dilated nostrils.

Hilary looked up at her father; to find him looking down at her. She knew at once, for certain, that when he had been sitting on that dappled horse, he had seen her and the boys standing in the crowd.

Neither of them spoke a word, just watched the procession go by. Hilary thought, all in a whirl, "I shall

61

trust him as long as I live, and he'll trust me, and *she* doesn't matter."

Then Gregory shattered all that by inquiring dryly, "Does it occur to you, Hilary, that we're being cowardly in not owning up to our misdeeds?"

Hilary jumped. Then, clinging to the exact truth, as was her way with her father - it made up, she felt, for the frequent lapses from it which her mother occasioned - she said, "No. Not cowardly. I should've told her, for myself. I didn't, because I was afraid it would get you into a row." She looked up to see what he thought, and to her surprise, found him laughing. She said indignantly, "I don't think that's funny!"

"It struck me as funny," he explained, "because it was just what I was doing myself. It never occurred to me that *you* were - for one thing, I didn't know you'd seen me."

She said absently, "Oh yes, we saw you . . . What did you think, then? That I was just funking?"

He considered that. "No. Dodging, perhaps. I mean, I knew you'd tell, if you were asked. I don't see any reason, now, why you should tell either your mother or me exactly what you do with every minute of the day. You're old enough to do what you please, within limits."

That was new. "D'you mean - I needn't - only do things that Mother thinks are all right?"

"I do. Or that I think are all right either, as long as you think they're all right yourself."

"If you didn't, I shouldn't," she said instantly.

He could not help showing his pleasure. Soon he was serious again.

"I think, perhaps, though, we ought to tell your mother about this," he said.

'Why, if we can do as we like? I don't think going to the Fair was wrong."

"Just because not telling her makes us feel mean. So there must be something the matter with it."

"But it's not to stop us doing what we like in future?"

He smiled. "By no means. You must be your own judge."

She felt so grown-up after that conversation that she really was not afraid when they marched into the sitting-room together and Gregory said gaily, "We think you ought to know, Rose, that Hilary and I went to the Fair the other day."

Rose Moore looked from one to the other of them and snapped out, "Like father, like daughter! I bring her up carefully and you lead her into your own flighty ways!" The scorn in her glance was so biting that Hilary could not hold on to her rage. She stammered, "You needn't l-look like that! We shall g-go again whatever you look like! I shall, anyway! I'm going to do anything I like! He didn't lead me, I went alone!"

Her mother did nothing, surprisingly, but sniff and smile maliciously over her shoulder as she swept into the kitchen. Hilary heard nothing more of the matter at all. Whether Gregory did or not she never knew.

7

Hilary was just eighteen when Gregory asked her seriously what she wanted to do with her life. They were sitting in the garden in the late afternoon, and it seemed to her, drinking in the near peace and the distant beauty, that no other existence was possible for her but this. Her hands were occupied with odd jobs in the house and garden, her mind with the work she did with her father. It was only when she was very tired, now, that she could not dodge her mother's rages, and though they were bad at the time, they did not trouble her in between as they had done when she was younger.

She said, "Go on the same, I suppose. There's really plenty for both Mother and me, now Hermione doesn't do anything. And you know I love working with you."

"All that won't earn you a living, though," he told her.

She sat still for a minute, startled. The idea of earning a living had never entered her head.

"Do I want it to?" she asked at length.

"I can imagine situations in which you might," he said, and went on in a hurry, seeing by her eyes that she was imagining them too, and loath to hurt her. "Besides, I feel very strongly that everyone ought to have a trade he - or she - can ply at a pinch. It's a horrid feeling, to be dependent on other people."

She said unwillingly, "I suppose it must be," and added, "The only thing I want to do is to know as much history as you do. And if you go on teaching me, I suppose I shall, one day."

Gregory said, "Henry's going to the University next term. I wondered whether you wouldn't like to do something of the sort, too. You'd learn a lot more there than I can teach you."

"To Cambridge?" But that would mean being away from him.

He smiled. "No. I couldn't run to that, unless you carried off a big scholarship. You might do it, if you tried - you've a good clear brain - but that wasn't my idea. I was thinking of Ardlemouth. You could go over every day by train, and take a London Honours degree at the end of your three years. That would fit you for teaching, or research, or some sort of secretarial work if you preferred it."

She meditated for such a long time, fear of the unknown battling with her love of learning, that he asked, "Well - does it appeal, to you at all?"

"It appeals to me ever so much," she said at length. "It was just - I'd simply never thought of such a thing. And then - I was wondering whether it was fair to let you spend a lot of money on me, when I'm perfectly certain I shall never want to go away to teach or anything else, and there aren't any schools to teach in or people to secretary round about here."

He insisted, "You ought to be fit for it, anyway. You can't possibly tell now what you may want to do in three years' time. I don't want you to be one of those women who aren't fit for anything but marriage."

She had no impulse to ask him why his opinion of marriage as a career was so low. There was no need. With her mother's continual dissatisfaction before her, she had grown up in the belief that the lot of a wife and mother was one of drudgery and discontent. No other aspect of it had ever come before her.

He went on, "Think it over for a day or two, and then, if you like, we'll fix it all up."

She smiled at him. He was so eager and yet so shy - so much more like an older Henry than a parent: showing her a way, yet not pushing her along it. "Only if I like?"

He looked at her with some wistfulness. "I do want you to be happy as well as useful."

Her heart bounded suddenly. It was so nice of him to want her to be happy - so surprising to her that he should think of it. She had never considered happiness as an end. Sometimes you were happy and sometimes you weren't. To take steps to make yourself happy was somehow mean. Besides, she had a suspicion that it would not work if you did. Perhaps it was all right to do it for other people.

"If you frightfully want to go to Cambridge," her father was saying, "you might try for a scholarship. It would mean waiting a year, but you wouldn't be any the worse for that, and we could keep Ardlemouth as a second string if you didn't get it."

Hilary said promptly, "I don't want to go to Cambridge a bit. I wouldn't if I could. But I think the other idea is simply marvellous. Can we do something about it now at once, instead of waiting for me to think?"

8

She and Hermione went to bed rather early that night, for no particular reason. As a rule Rose Moore came up soon after they did. Gregory often stayed downstairs late to work.

To-night, a murmur of voices began below as soon as the girls had left. Hermione had gone to have a bath, and Hilary, moving across the room to brush her hair by the open window, caught a word here and there and could not bear to go out of earshot. A quiet monologue from Gregory was followed by a series of staccatos from Rose. Then, Gregory - "She must have a chance to make a life of her own" - and Rose, a burst of words which ended scornfully, "As though every woman hadn't the chance to make her own life if she's got the sense to take it!" Gregory answered that in a hurry with something Hilary could not hear, and then came another impassioned spate from her mother, then silence.

Hilary's breath came painfully. Supposing Mother refused to let her go! Suppose. Father let himself be over-ruled and it all fizzled out! It would be too cruel, to dangle such a wonderful prospect in front of her nose and then let it be dashed away! As a rule she scorned praying for definite things - had done so since a day when she had prayed for one thing and heard Hermione praying for the opposite and her sense of fair play had been offended. But this time she yielded. "Oh God, please, *please* let him get his own way, *please* let me go to Ardlemouth!"

Then Gregory's voice came, gentle no longer, but thin

and clipped, as Hilary had never heard it. "I've made up my mind about this, Rose. I spoke to you about it, because, of course, it affects you - you'll have to get help in the house, if Hermione can't do more. Besides, you've a right to an opinion about the children's future. But when your opinion's nothing but a hotch-potch of silly prejudices and you've no better suggestion to offer - why, then I must take my own way in spite of you. I'm sorry: I'd hoped you'd be proud of Hilary. She's a clever youngster. She'll make the best of it."

The last sentences had about them the wistful note of the afternoon. Hilary bit her lip. It was much worse to over-hear praise of oneself, all of a sudden like that, than just argument. It made one ashamed.

To her surprise there was no outburst from her mother, only a low rumble of words, but so charged with resentment that Hilary shivered. Gregory said, "Hermione can go when she's older, if her health's good enough and she wants to . . . And isn't that an additional reason to make sure that Hilary's qualified for something? She may have to keep her sister as well as herself, when we're gone."

Hilary thought, "How awful!" It felt as though an earthquake were taking place - change, and the hint of more change still to come. She wished herself back in the day before, when everything was as she had always known it.

Hermione came back from the bathroom then, and Hilary left the window hurriedly. Eavesdropping wasn't so bad if you kept it to yourself - but she was bothered if she was going to have her sister joining in.

By the end of the summer holidays the whole thing was arranged, entrance examinations passed, new clothes - a few of them - bought, and the future an exciting plunge instead of an effortless amble along a set path.

The last day of the holidays was more a festival than a farewell. The boys and Gregory and Hilary set out early for a day's tramp. They had tried to arrange something which would include Rose and Hermione, but Rose was surly that day and Hermione unwilling for physical exertion. So the four went off light-heartedly, really glad, their consciences having been placated, to have the day to themselves.

They walked for miles along the indented shore, gorse towering above them on the one hand, blazing gold and smelling of apple pie, and on the other, sand and blue sea, or rocky chasms and white foam. They had lunch - crusty sandwiches and fruit - on a ledge of sweet-smelling turf with a cluster of marvellous blue rampion beside them, and drank ginger-beer on a hot, worm-eaten bench outside an old inn. They went on again for some miles, and then Kenneth developed a blister on his heel and the question was, what should be done about getting back? Gregory made a pad in the shoe, and Kenneth pluckily announced that he could go on indefinitely. But it was not long before he began to limp again, and, although he made no complaint, the pace of the whole party dropped to keep in line with him.

Gregory said, "We'll strike inland to St. Brelan's station. It's only about two miles from here."

The others said nothing; felt nothing, for it was obvious that Kenneth could not go on like that. But Gregory, looking at them and at the lovely day, said, "I don't see really why we should all cut short our trip. Or why we should pay four train fares when two would do. I'll take Kenneth home, and you two carry on."

"Wouldn't you mind?" Hilary said, surprised.

Henry made feeble obeisance to his conscience and suggested, "Let me take the kid, sir, and you go on with Hilary."

Gregory swept their objections away. "No, I'd just as soon get home. Don't be too late - be sure you're back by dark. Got any money in case you need it? Yes? Well, come on, Kenneth, if we're to catch the four o'clock train - it'll take us an hour, at this pace."

They turned away, up a side-lane. Henry hitched the rucksack higher, and he and Hilary went on; and it was not long before the heat of the sun induced them to sit down on a grassy ledge and drowse.

They were too young to sleep long. First Hilary roused, then Henry, and they began to talk. It did not matter what they talked about; themselves and their futures more than anything. Henry had given serious thought to his; he was going to study to be an architect after leaving Cambridge. Hilary had only just, with Ardlemouth before her, realized that she had a future to think about. She talked about that - "Fancy having a library to burrow in just as I like! D'you think they'll let me take sandwiches in there in the middle of the day and read while I eat - meals are such waste of time!"

Henry chuckled that he had never noticed that she was in any hurry to stop eating, and was sure the library authorities would not risk getting crumbs squashed between their important pages. "Besides," he added, "you'll soon stop wanting to spend all your spare time reading. What about games, and the river? I'm going to put in all the time I can at those, you bet. Or don't girls do those things?"

"Games - I don't know. I've never played any, and they won't want beginners. The river I should like, of course - I've seen girl students on it at Ardlemouth. We'll see. I don't understand how they have any spare time - you should see the stuff they have to get through!"

"They're not all as studious as you are!" Henry teased, and they wrangled as to whether she were abnormally studious or not.

They touched on religion, which had its lure for both of them.

"Of course there's a God," Hilary snorted. "It's perfectly obvious that *somebody* made all this - " she waved a comprehensive arm - "and somebody with a jolly fine mind too, an enormous mind, that could see round everything; and a most scrupulously accurate one, to make butterflies' wings and give all the animals proper joints and things that really do work . . . "

Henry said, "There are a whole lot of people who think it could all have evolved on its own, without any mind behind it. I don't, but lots of brainy bugs do - "

"They can't be brainy if they think that," Hilary objected. "Or if they are, they've got those brains that only, see along a narrow passage and shut out anything they don't like the look of. Besides, if there isn't a God, what's the good of praying to Him?"

"Is it any good?" he teased.

"Of course it is. My being able to stand up to Mother, for instance. I was nearly just a door mat, and I prayed I might be braver; and then you came along that summer and laughed at Mother - *laughed* at her, when I'd thought she was terrifying - and made everything all different. And then my going to college: Father was within tuppence of giving in and saying, 'Have it your own way, my dear, I didn't realize you really *needed* her in the house!' but I prayed and he suddenly went quite different and snapped her head off and said he'd made up his mind - I've never heard him talk like it in my life, before *or* since!"

Henry said, "Good old Greg! *I* know he can be fierce enough, of course - he isn't often, but when he is, it's devastating! I don't think that was a miracle!"

Hilary said obstinately, "I do. His voice just changed all of a sudden as soon as I'd said, 'Please!' . . . He's got a prayer, he told me, about believing in God - something about seeing Thy hand in everything. St. Patrick said it - I can't remember it."

Henry had lost interest, suddenly, in prayers. He had seen a collection of iridescent butterfly's eggs, neatly arranged in a pattern on the end of a leaf, and one after another was cracking in the sun and letting out a tiny, active caterpillar no thicker than a hair. Hilary joined him in watching them. Each one looped purposefully away until it found something tender to eat - a harebell, or a white convolvulus flower - and then it ate, and grew, and turned from grey to green under their eyes. There must have been a hundred or more of the little things.

When they grew tired of caterpillars, they walked on again, and talked again as they walked. Henry was keen, naturally, on buildings, Hilary more on natural history or, when there were buildings, on surmises about the people who had built them. They were both very earnest, and both paid more attention to their own utterances than to each other's. And whatever they talked about, Henry came back to hard facts and Hilary to themselves and their own reactions.

By the time they turned inland to come home by another way, they had talked themselves out. There was a companionable silence between them; a magic silence of which both were conscious and which both were loath to break. They did not analyze their state of mind. They only knew that they had, both of them, enjoyed that day more than any before.

As they climbed the last hill before the village, dusk was gathering; September dusk, with clear blue sky from which a fiery red was fading, a tang in the air, and with the tang, a melancholy. Hilary, throwing back her hair and opening her nostrils like a horse to the breeze, tried vainly to call back the glittering joy of the day. "Wasn't it a *heavenly* afternoon?" she said. "Why can't it be like that always?"

Henry, frowning a little, answered her. "It's the best day I've ever had. But happiness like that's too near unhappiness to last. It's - fragile, somehow."

They walked on, their mood now according with the autumnal smells, the hint of cold winds coming; with the flaming beech-trees which would soon be bare, the flaming

73

sky which would soon be cool, aloof, impersonal.

They stopped, suddenly, without a word, at a place where a pine grove was cleft by a green ride. The dark, slim trees were rusted on one side by the sunset, and framed sombre fields, clear sea, and clearer, rippled sky.

Hilary gasped, transported beyond herself and her petty sadness by the beauty, as though something streamed out of her to blend with it. She felt immeasurably small, yet part of an immense whole and, so, not insignificant.

Moved by an impulse to share with him, she turned to Henry; to find him regarding not the sunset, but herself, with owls' eyes. Her own were shining with the wonder of the sky and sea.

Henry blinked and moved closer to her.

"It'll be ages before I see you again, Hilary," he was saying. "May I kiss you?"

She laughed, brought suddenly down to human ground from her god-like height.

"Of course, you old idiot," she said, "if you want to," and she flung an affectionate arm round his neck. He kissed her cheek, clumsily, and she smudged his chin with her lips.

"It'll be *perfectly beastly* without you," she told him, tragic because she really did know she would miss him, cheerful because the day had been so lovely and she was going to College soon.

Henry flushed slowly to the tips of his ears and seized her hand, and so they wandered back towards the road.

On the edge of it, Hilary realized suddenly that it really was the last time they would walk together just like this. Next time they would be grown up, or nearly so. She did not mind about herself - one had to grow - but she didn't want Henry altered. There was something so nice about him as he was, his seriousness, his sun-flushed face, his hair standing on end. He was looking straight ahead, his eyes on nothing, his mouth, generally so good-humoured, almost grim. She stopped and said, "You can't think how beastly it'll be! I wouldn't go to Ardlemouth - though I do want to - if you were still going to be here!" Turning, she faced him and put her free arm round him, gently this time, and kissed him of her own accord. His lips sought hers and found them, shyly, and clung to them, and his arm at her waist pressed her to him and let her go. She stood away and looked at him, wondering what access of feeling had so queerly come to them both, and saw that his flush had gone and left him pale. She felt pale herself - pale and bright-eyed and tremulously happy.

She said aloud, "It's just because we're going away from each other, I suppose."

He agreed, "I suppose it is. But we shan't forget it, shall we, Hilary? And we'll see each other every single holidays."

"Vac, we've got to call it now," she bubbled.

"Vac, then. I'll simply make them let me come down here. Ken'll be here for a year or two, that'll be an excuse."

"I shall be here - no fear of my going away!"

They were laughing at everything now, everything was fun. They could not keep their eyes off each other; and when they caught each other looking, that was fun too.

On the road, Hilary took charge; squeezed Henry's hand and flung it from her and tramped along, well away from him, chattering all the time. If she didn't, they might find themselves caught up in that magic again and doing the queerest things. She wondered why she, who never kissed anyone, even her family, should have been moved to kiss him and why she wanted to again, unless it was to show him, better than any words could, how much she liked to be with him. That must be the reason, she decided, because there obviously wasn't any other.

They parted at the cottage gate; most circumspectly, it seemed to them, stiffly, almost, with no more than a jibe and a shy, quick look into each other's eyes, and Hilary went in whistling. She saw her mother in the front room and thanked her stars she had not walked hand in hand with Henry down the road. She knew so well her mother's knack of planting a square thumb on the frail wings of some lovely fancy, destroying it utterly or so spoiling it that it died a maimed and scarcely regretted death.

At supper, Gregory asked her which way they had come home, and she talked happily about the sunset and the colour of the pine trees. She finished up, "It was the loveliest evening sky I've ever seen!"

Rose Moore looked at her daughter with hard, sparkling eyes. "Everything's luv-ly when you're with the be-luv-ed!" she mocked. "*Dear* Henry - have you let him kiss you yet?" She smacked her lips.

The colour flamed in Hilary's face and died again. Rose Moore cackled. "Aha!" she said, "aha, young woman, I know the signs! I've been through it myself - haven't I, Gregory?"

Gregory was looking out of the window, his face a grey mask devoid of all expression. He said nothing at all. His wife rose, still laughing, and began to carry dishes into the kitchen.

Hilary, after a glance at her father, helped silently with the washing-up. In the garden afterwards, she stood for a moment looking towards the house. "You beast!" she said under her breath. "You beast, you beast!" And, for some reason which she could not fathom, she ran sobbing towards her refuge, the shore.

9

She had two long, shy letters from Henry during his first week at Cambridge, which she replied to, eagerly, at once. The following week another came, shorter, referring many times to people she had never heard of. She put off answering that, and finally did not answer it at all. She had forgotten all about it under the battery of new impressions. Going to the University was like going to a new world. Ardlemouth is a small University, but it has its own pride. Its standards, both in work and in conduct, are high. It has several halls of residence for men students and one for women, and separate common rooms for each.

Hilary had mèt no educated girls at all. The cottage was not at a holiday resort, and none of Gregory's colleagues happened to have daughters past the infant stage. Women to her were typified by her mother and Hermione, the shabby, good, but quite brainless wife of the vicar, and the people of the village. The girl students, and still more the women lecturers at the College, were something quite new. The women who taught her aroused an almost terrified admiration. They were all of a type - unmarried, round about forty, with plainly dressed hair, tweed coats and skirts and sensible shoes, and faces which had the serenity of those who have found life's battles enough for their strength and no more, and wrinkles of humour about the eyes and mouth; a good type, and they were good specimens of it. She was far too shy to approach them. Instead, she observed them minutely, adopted their rather pedantic mode of speech; and insisted on a tailor-made coat and skirt and brogues for the winter.

One of them, Miss Buckley, was an ardent suffragist, and Hilary drank in her tirades on women's rights with no criticism at all. The difference between these women and those she was used to, in brain-power, in independence, in happiness, was so enormous that she could not but conclude that if all women were educated and given the chance to stand on their own legs, all would be as sturdy as these. She went to suffrage meetings, and, in an access of enthusiasm after one, had her lovely hair cut off and by so doing shook Gregory's trust in her good sense. The hair defeated her aim of stern sexlessness by curling entrancingly at the nape of her neck and making her head look like that of a lovely boy.

She was a little above middle height now. Her square, upright carriage, her big brow and determined chin combined with her beautiful colouring and her small hands and feet to produce a fascinating mixture of strength and delicacy in her appearance. This union of masculine with undefeated feminine in her made everyone who saw her exclaim and look again.

Nowadays her type is everywhere - or imitations of it. Then it was new.

During her first term, she was something of a nine-days' wonder. Miss Buckley took her up at once, realizing how much more powerful youth and beauty would be than elderly plainness, however earnest, in furthering the Suffrage cause. But when she suggested that Hilary should go with her to speak at meetings, and talked about the nobility of going to prison, the girl took fright. To face crowds, be heckled perhaps and pelted with tomatoes and dead herrings, to be shut up alone, to have to promise not to eat and perhaps be forced to; these were more than she could bear. She could not sleep for bothering about it, and finally talked it over with Gregory.

"D'you think I ought to? I'll do it - any of it - if you think I ought," she said. But her eyes were wide and her breath panting even as she protested, and Gregory found such hardships for her unthinkable.

"I don't think you're old enough to have an opinion that's worth anything, yet," he told her. "Wait a bit. Find out all you can about both sides - whether the majority of women really are ill-treated - and then, if you're convinced, go for it bald-headed." He tweaked her shorn hair with a grin. "But just now your job is to get through your exams. You can't take them twice."

So she withdrew, thankfully, from active service in the suffrage movement, and Miss Buckley, disgusted, dropped her like a hot coal. She was sorry about that - but not for

79

long, there were so many others for her to be interested in. The men students and lecturers, objects of tremendous interest to the other girls, were to her only older or cleverer editions of the schoolmasters and schoolboys she had known all her life, all of them inferior to Gregory or Henry, and so not worth attention. There was not much mixing, in any case, between men and women at the University - a few flirtations, which were discouraged; rarely an engagement, which had to be surreptitious and which generally fizzled out as soon as the participants went down. The atmosphere was not right for any relations except the most casual between the sexes.

The girl students made advances to her at first, attracted by her healthy good looks, and at first she liked them. They went about in gangs and talked a lot, and Hilary, thirsting for discussions such as she had had with Gregory and the boys, listened eagerly. But she found that the talk was chiefly about games which she did not play, and gossip about the Dons, especially the men, and the teams, and that work was simply a laborious road towards the necessity of making a living, to be taken in strictly measured laps. She was disappointed in them, and they soon found her dull and left her alone.

There were others - less pleasant to look at but possessed, it seemed, of more brains - who mooched about in ones or twos, and with whom, at meal-times and in the garden, she had talks which really interested her. But she found that to talk with one aroused passionate resentment in another, and that the highbrow conversations degenerated very soon into personalities and led to kissing and embracing, pet names, confidences, quarrels and makings up; and, somehow, she could not enter into these. The minds of these people attracted her, but their wallowing affections she found revolting. Such cataclysmic loves and hatreds, so unstable that in spite of their violence they changed from week to week, were outside her experience altogether. School might have given her some warning; home life had left her totally unprepared.

She did make one friend; or rather, the friend made herself: a small, mousey member of her own year, Ruth Barnicott, who simply attached herself and made no demands. The two sat next to each other at meals and lectures, walked in the garden together, and in the summer took lunch and books together on the river in a canoe.

These afternoons on the river were the only happy memories which Hilary carried away with her clear-cut from her University life; still water slap-slapping against the nose of the canoe and dripping from the paddle poised for a stealthy stroke; buttercup fields, a blazing mosaic of gold and green, on a level with one's head; Ruth, small and firm, at the other end of the canoe, gravely listening to Hilary's monologues on historical persons and now and then inserting some shrewdly devastating comment of her own. The only differences they had were that Ruth objected to direct sunlight and to midge bites, and Hilary loved the sun and was always much too taken up with conversation or with the scenery to notice whether she was being midge-bitten or not; and these were settled easily enough by arranging Ruth's end of the canoe in the shade and Hilary's in the sun, and by always going home before dusk. Hilary did not remember feeling any affection at all for Ruth, despised her a little perhaps for being so inoffensive and minding so much about her bodily comfort. But without Ruth at her elbow, admiring her, protecting her from the stigma of solitariness, she would probably have been unhappy instead of only disappointed during that first year. It never occurred to her to invite Ruth to the cottage or to talk of home things to her, and Ruth might have had no family for all she ever heard of it.

At home, she sought Gregory's company more and more; naturally, for he was the only one of them who could understand her other world at all.

The only protest Rose Moore made against her elder daughter's new life was not a verbal one. There were a certain number of lectures in the evenings, from which Hilary did not get home till round about ten. Gregory would meet her most evenings at the station, and they would walk up slowly to the cottage, two miles or so, talking all the way.

On one such evening, Hilary sat down to a light supper as usual when she came in, and Hermione came and chatted for a minute or two and then went up to bed. No sooner had she arrived upstairs than there came a yell - "Hilary! I say, there's been a burglar! Do come, he may be still here!"

Hilary raced upstairs, half frightened, half amused; and indeed, the room did look like the scene of a robbery, for the drawers were all open and their contents higgledy-piggledly everywhere.

Hilary said, "What on earth! 'Tisn't as if we'd got a pearl necklace between us for anyone to steal!" Then, looking more closely, she saw that most of the garments scattered about were her own. Those of Hermione's which had been taken out were only a top-dressing to the general mess. She stood back from it and grinned. "That's not a burglar, that's Mother! If she wanted to protest that I hadn't tidied for about a year, why the dickens couldn't she do it in the daytime? And not just when we want to get into bed!"

Hermione was chammering that it must be a burglar, it must. Hilary cut her short scornfully. "All right, I'll *look* under the bed - there's nothing there, of course! *And* in the cupboard - it might be Mother Hubbard's by the look of it! There, are you satisfied now? Of course it's Mother! Bother the woman! - if she thinks I'm going to tidy this lot up at this time of night she's jolly well mistaken!"

Hermione gasped, "Hilary! You talk so *wildly* since you've been to college!" But she did not dispute Hilary's conclusion. It was obvious enough, once thought of. She said doubtfully, "I didn't think mine were untidy! I did them only a week or two ago - "

Hilary was gathering up armfuls of garments and stuffing them into drawers. "They weren't. Mine were, horribly - and now they're worse, and that's all she'll get out of it!"

Over the clothes from the cupboard she took more care.

Her best dress and coat she smoothed tenderly, and hung upon hangers - she liked them, they were pleasant in themselves and she looked nice in them. Hermione was still methodically folding petticoats and rolling up stockings when Hilary leaped into bed. Sitting with her arms round her knees, she watched her sister's precise movements, and the grotesque ones of the diving, grabbing shadow which the candle threw on the wall and the sloping ceiling behind her. The shadow's actions were more like her own, she thought, than Hermione's. And her own shadow, sitting quietly there, was more like Hermione than herself. Yet she was never Hermione's shadow, and Hermione, for all her timidity, had an obstinacy which prevented her being her sister's. Yawning, Hilary regretfully gave up the attempt to trace the relations between shadows and selves, resemblances and differences.

"I'm not going to say a single word about this to Mother," she announced, lying down flat and staring upwards, "and you're not to either!"

Hermione, still preoccupied with the present, asked, "Why not?"

"Because it'll be such a swizzle for her, silly! She'd love us to go down straight away and rail at her, or weep and say she'd rrrr-uined our clothes, and make a grand old scene! And if we don't do that, she'd like us to crawl to her in the morning and say we're sorry we were so untidy, so that she could sniff at us. If we don't say anything, she'll think we don't care even enough to remember about it! See? And sucks for her!"

Hermione said nothing, and Hilary knew that she would not keep this pact. Hermione was no good as an ally, less than ever since her illness. Their mother could worm anything out of her she liked.

She was saying her prayers now. Hilary recollected that she had not said hers. Well, how could she, in such a rage as she was? That was her mother's fault. She dug her nose into the pillow and went to sleep unrepentant.

In the morning, she heard Rose Moore banging about the house in one of her furies. She lay and shivered. She might defy her mother when she was not there, but she simply could not, in the cold morning, go down and face that vicious hatred.

She did not get up until there was only just time to snatch an apple to eat on the way and catch her train.

The incident of the drawers nagged so insistently at her brain that she departed from her habit of not talking of home things and told Ruth Barnicott about it. Ruth listened solemnly, as she always did, and her comment was, "Jealousy's the only vice which has absolutely no pleasure attached to it . . . You deprived her even of the pleasure of knowing she'd annoyed you, by keeping quiet about it."

"That's what I meant to do - though Hermione'll have told her by this time," Hilary said absently. She was thinking about Ruth's first remark, really. "What d'you mean, 'jealousy', anyway? There's nothing in my clothes for anyone to be jealous of, and Mother's got heaps of pretty ones of her own, stuffed away . . . "

But Ruth, feeling perhaps that she did not really know enough of Hilary's people to dogmatize about them, began to talk about something else.

10

Hilary's life went on much the same throughout her first college year and into her second. Then one day she found the doctor's dog-cart outside the cottage when she came home. He still looked in sometimes to see Hermione, and Hilary took it for granted that this was the object of his visit to-day. But when she went into the sitting-room, she found Hermione there alone.

"Hullo," she said, "where's Dr. Tomkins? Discussing your future with Mother in the other room?"

Hermione looked solemn. "No. Seeing Father. He's in bed."

Hilary blinked. "Father - in bed?"

"Yes. He went to bed as soon as he came in, and Dr. Tomkins came a few minutes after. I think they must have arranged it. I don't think Father was ill when he came in - not *taken* ill, I mean."

Hilary breathed again. She had been medically examined before going to college. Perhaps this was the same sort of thing. She said so to Hermione, but Hermione shook her head. She was quite ignorant about the matter and not much interested. She did not see how her father could be working and yet be ill. It did not fit her own experience.

Rose Moore and the doctor came downstairs together. Hilary heard fragments of conversation and was glad she had left the door ajar: " . . . absolute rest for a few weeks," she heard the doctor say. What struck her most was his serious tone. She was used to him as a cheerful, jokey little man. He was speaking again and she had missed some of it:

" . . . the heart of a man of seventy." Her father wasn't seventy, or anything like it. Then the voice took on again the cheerful quality, she knew in it: "However, it's amazing what rest will do for a heart, even in that condition. Absolute rest of body and mind, that's what he's got to have. I'll see him again this day week, Mrs. Moore. Good night."

The street door closed behind him. Hilary would have made a dash for the bedroom, but her mother came in and blocked her way. Rose Moore's mouth was grim. "Just what I've always told him. Tired himself out. All this dashing about with the boys and - " she turned on Hilary - "trapesing round after you late at night! Now he's got to have three weeks' rest, and it's me that'll bear the brunt, with one of you out all day and the other not much better than an invalid! Oh, well - I'm used to hard work!"

She sniffed and bustled out. Hilary sensed a spice of enjoyment in her martyrdom, just as there had been in her nursing of Hermione.

When Hilary did manage to get to the room where her father was in bed, she found him sitting up, his greying hair on end, a twinkle in his eye and a smile on his lips, looking years younger than usual. She was relieved. She had expected him to be drawn and panting, or languid, as Hermione had been. She dragged the whole story out of him.

At first he would do nothing but tease, gloat over the leisure he would have, detail the reading he had longed for years to do and would now have time for. Then he allowed that, yes, there had been a pain in his chest, and lately rather worse; that he had had an attack of it at school under the eye of the Head - a silly, tactless thing to do, but he had not known that the Head was there - and the old man, who fussed a good deal about his own health, had bullied him into seeing a doctor. And that was all.

"And you've got to stay there for three weeks."

Gregory looked at her between glasses and raised brows, and grinned. "Yes. Great fun!" Hilary thought again that she had never seen him look so youthful. He seemed to have shed all responsibility with his working clothes. "I shall stay at home and help take care of you," she said positively.

Gregory looked distressed. "Oh, no! There's not the slightest need for that. I should simply hate to spoil your work. It might put you back a whole year. Please don't think of doing that for a single minute."

His whole outlook was youthful. It might have been Henry chatting with her. Reluctantly she gave up the idea of long days spent reading to him and talking.

He read her thought. "You see, I really have got to rest. Mind as well as body, Tommy said. Sleep and sleep. And if you were here we should talk all the time."

"'M! All right. Only I shall rush home as early as ever I can. You must do your sleeping while I'm away. Will that be enough? Can you perk up in the evenings if you sleep all day?"

He chuckled. "I should think I might. Listen, here, comes your mother with some food. That's another way I shall score. You know what heavenly food she gave Hermione when she was ill - ?"

It was the schoolboy who had gone to the Fair who twinkled in his eyes. Hilary nearly told him so. She helped her mother with the tray and went down to tea, cheered enormously by the interview.

"After all," she said to Hermione, "it's only a holiday he wants. He's simply never had one, as long as I can remember. Teaching boys, all the term; teaching us and coaching the Swains and writing, all the vacs . . . P'raps he'll get fat!"

They had a number of cheerful days. Rose Moore would not let anyone help her look after her husband. She was tireless and deft, gentle and firm, forestalling his wishes before he was conscious of them, even teasing him without a spice of malice. It was as if they had been transported back to their honeymoon. The girls watched them with amazement.

"I wish to goodness it would last!" Hermione said.

Hilary said, "I suppose it's how they were before we came. What on earth made them ever lose it?"

There were visitors whom the girls had never seen, who came from long distances because they had heard of Gregory's illness, and had to be content with half an hour's chat with him. Several young schoolmasters who had been boys at his school; fishermen, whom Rose Moore hated to let in but had to because Gregory must not be annoyed; an elderly Professor of History, now in the northern university of Fenchester, under whom he had studied; and various "old boys" of different professions, a number of them clergymen. They talked to the girls when they came down from the bedroom. Hilary was astonished at the love

89

and admiration they had for him, so many different types of them. She had looked upon the feeling as her own prerogative.

His sister came, too; an angular woman fifteen years his senior, whom Rose had hitherto refused to have in the house because she was a Roman Catholic. She, too, lived away in the north. Her three children were married. Hilary took to her at once, for she was a stronger edition of Gregory, not unlike Hilary herself; his goodness in her was allied to a robust common sense which delighted Hilary and terrified Hermione. She returned Hilary's liking and said so to Gregory.

"But take care of her," she said. "She's the type who'll always live by her affections. The sort of girl the boys go mad after. My eldest's like that. Took her two years to make up her mind which she'd have of half a dozen. She's happy enough now."

Gregory laughed and said, "Maybe. Hilary doesn't go mad after them, thank goodness. She simply isn't aware of them, yet. She's got a splendid brain and I'm hoping she'll find happiness in the intellectual side of life. The best women I know are old maids."

Aunt Nell snorted. "Stuff! The sort of thing a man like you would say! Not aware of them, at nineteen? - she ought to be aware of them! What's her mother thinking about? Though, mind you, I think you're chiefly to blame, filling her head with the idea that learning's the only thing that matters!"

Gregory said serenely, "It does matter quite a lot. She'll have to earn her living. And there's no comparison between the happiness one gets from the intellect and the - I won't call it happiness, the pleasure - that comes from the emotions. The one lasts a lifetime; the other burns out and leaves nothing but an irritating smoke."

Aunt Nell spread out her hands in despair. "I'm sorry for the girl, if that's what you've been drumming into her! It wouldn't have mattered, if she'd been a boy!"

She invited Hilary warmly to come and stay with her next holidays, and Hilary thought she would like to. Gregory watched her minutely the next time she came up to talk to him. When she rocketed off straight away into a discussion of the deeper causes of the Reformation, he subsided comfortably into his pillows to answer her questions and give some direction to her enthusiasms. Aunt Nell was all wrong. She had the inevitable married woman's bee in the bonnet and, for all her sense, could not be credited with a particle of the real stuff of intellect; so how could she possibly understand his and Hilary's point of view?

With Hilary, the memory of these evenings with her father always lived; the faded blue-green curtains stirring with the breeze from the open windows behind them; the salt tang, mixed with the smell of flowers, which the breeze brought in; the lamp, throwing queer flickering shadows on the sprigged wall-paper, showing up irregularities in the old walls, dancing on the few coloured prints of saints and madonnas, brought from Italy years ago, which were the room's only adornment; the gentle, clever face of the man propped against the mound of pillows, alight with laughter sometimes, sometimes serious and indrawn as he followed an argument, wistful again as now and then he inserted, shyly, some piece of wisdom into the helter-skelter of his daughter's deductions. They talked of college, of literature and life; a little, of death, and Gregory said that he had always held that one's only immortality was in one's children, but now he wondered how he had ever presumed to question the clear teaching of the Gospels which said we shall rise again. To Hilary, death seemed a far-away thing then. She could not imagine how she could ever stop living, if not on earth then somewhere else, and being very much herself the whole time. Another part of the joy of these short evenings was the feeling of herself, curled up in the old arm-chair, alert in brain for their talking, in heart for the first sign that her father was tired.

He did get tired, very easily. Dr. Tomkins hinted that the visitors were too many and they ceased to come so often. Two of the Sixth Form boys came one day when Hilary was in charge - her mother was resting - and she let them in without a thought. They laughed and chatted for ten minutes and then went away. As she shut the street door after them, Hilary heard a noise in her mother's room, and Rose Moore flounced out, her temper, as so often when she had just awoken, quite out of control. "You didn't let those boys go up to your father?"

Hilary felt a start of surprise that her mother should hate her so much. It showed, unmistakably, at moments like this. It did not exactly hurt her, just gave her a cold, stiff feeling. She said, "They went up for a few minutes. They didn't worry him at all."

"Worry him! As though the very sight of them didn't

always make him stew about the exams they'll probably fail in without his coachings! As though I didn't spend half the day turning the little wretches away! I was a fool to think you'd a ha'porth of sense, anyway, as you've never shown the slightest sign of it!"

Hilary brushed past her into her father's room. No good taking any notice of her in that mood. She knew quite well the boys hadn't done her father the smallest harm. He liked them to come. She pretended not to see his questioning glance. They exchanged a word or two about the boys, then returned to the book she had been reading to him. When Rose brought his supper she was calm and friendly, and no reference was made to the incident.

When Hilary came back from college the next day, the doctor was in the house again. He was coming downstairs, alone, as she let herself in. His face had a tired, defeated look. He said to her, "He's just gone."

Hilary stood still. She repeated stupidly, "Gone? D'you mean you've had to send him to the hospital?"

Dr. Tomkins turned sad eyes on her. "No. I don't mean that," he said.

It was his expression more than his words which made her understand.

"D'you mean - he's dead?"

He nodded. "All in a minute." Then, struck by the girl's utter bewilderment, he added, "Didn't your mother tell you there was this probability?"

Hilary dumbly shook her head, and he murmured, "She should have, she should have - poor child . . . " Then, more briskly, "You'd better go and see what you can do with her.

I'll attend to all the arrangements for you."

She let him out, then looked into the sitting-room. Hermione was shivering by the fire and did not move. Hilary ran upstairs - not to find her mother, but to see for herself whether the doctor's dreadful words were true. They couldn't be - they couldn't . . .

A glance at the waxen face on the pillows showed her that they were. It was peaceful, but there was a sort of high scorn about it which Gregory had never shown in life; as if he knew now that life was a little thing and death too. Hilary found herself saying, "They don't matter - it's how you take them that matters " He had said that again only the other day.

Rose Moore spoke harshly from the window, where she stood upright, gripping the sill. "I don't want you in here. I can do all that's necessary myself."

Hilary, recoiling from her, stumbled downstairs and out into the November night.

11

When she did at last get to bed and to sleep, it was to be dragged at once into her old, dreadful dream that she was alone with her mother. This time, when she woke, she could not free herself from the terror of it. How was freedom possible, when the thing was true? She lay and trembled, and presently made a solemn resolution not to stay with her mother a day longer than she had to. Why should she? Hermione would be there. She had neither duty nor affection to bind her. She fell asleep after that.

There followed gloomy days with drawn blinds, which she resented, both for herself and for her father, who had so loved the sun. Aunts and uncles in black came and went. From them, Hilary gathered that there was next to no money now that Gregory's salary had stopped. Aunt Nell, surveying the cottage critically, suggested paying-guests. "It's warm enough here to attract people even at this time of year."

Rose Moore tossed her handsome head at that. "I've got two daughters! Haven't I slaved for them all their lives? It's their turn to keep me now," she said, "after all he's spent educating them!"

Her eyes met Hilary's, challenging, but Hilary did not pick up her glove. It seemed quite a reasonable claim for her mother to make. Gregory had kept her. Now Hilary would - as soon as she was able. The only thing she must do was to get her degree as quickly as she could and begin to earn. It made no difference to her what she did.

Her numbness was pierced only once; that was while she stood at the grave-side in the churchyard, which was beautiful with quiet trees and close-cut grass banks, even in the greyness of November. "The Lord gave, and the Lord hath taken away. Blessed be the name of the Lord." It was not resignation, it was defiance to despair. An end - and a beginning. For an instant the peace of the place enveloped her.

Then, looking round as people began to stir, she saw the

phalanx of sixth-form boys drawn up solemnly, expressionless; the red-nosed aunts and uncles all close together, protectively; Rose Moore standing upright and grim, Hermione holding her hand and weeping. The pain of loneliness came down on her again, an encircling mist which shut out sorrow and joy alike.

As they moved away, Henry came to her and linked his arm in hers and talked. But she did not remember what he said, or how it was that he left her.

During the evening she noticed, dully, that her mother was watching her. The watching culminated in a briskly spoken command. "You'll be getting back to work as usual to-morrow, Hilary." Then, as Hilary said nothing, "*I'd* have sent you out to look for a job right away. But the Head says you'll make more in the long run if you finish your time at college, and I dare say he's right. He's offered to pay for the rest of it, anyway, and I don't see why he shouldn't. Your father's good teaching brought a lot of pupils to him, I do know."

Hilary said listlessly, "Decent of him. I'll pay it back, one day . . . Of course it would be idiotic not to stay on." It was unthinkable, to be at college and not have her father to talk to. But no more unthinkable than any other nightmare, now.

So she went back, and by so doing set her mind, though not her emotions, in action again. She observed things, though she did not feel them.

There, for instance, something new about her mother, something which was not sorrow at her loss. She was always grumbling, never pleased, however much one tried to please her - nothing new about that - but she did not fly into rages any more. There was a sort of sly triumph about her, a sneering triumph which gloated out of narrowed eyes; some connection with it and the transformation in her relationship with Gregory during the last weeks of his life. She said nothing. But her expression conveyed to Hilary better than words could have done, a sense of the girl's presumption in supposing, ever, that she could have been of more importance to Gregory than Gregory's wife.

"He's mine. He has always been mine. What did it matter if we quarrelled with our surface selves? What have you shared with him that is comparable with our years together?" she seemed to say.

And Hilary knew that it was true. She was humiliated even in this which had given her so much happiness. She had taken it for granted that her father had loved her more than anyone in the world, had depended on her as much as she did on him. But in trouble he had turned back to his wife, on whom he had always depended. It was of no use to tell herself that it was only her mother's thought, not the truth at all, or to protest that, he had loved her as much as any man can love a daughter. It wasn't enough. The one relationship which she had thought impregnable seemed now a false one.

She got it into her head, too, that he might not have died if she had not let the two boys in that evening. Her mother had said it was too much for him, and perhaps it had been. She couldn't forgive herself for that.

The days were flat, dead. Or perhaps it was she herself

who was dead. She went to college, got through her work quite well; threw herself into it, for abstract thinking brought relief. It was feeling that she shrank from. Any advance of friendliness or praise sent her running, for she knew that if she let herself feel one thing she must feel all, and if she started feeling about her father heaven knew what would happen. She avoided contact with everyone but Ruth, quiet, mousey Ruth, who was always there when one wanted her, but about whom emotion was plainly impossible, who seemed to want it as little as she did herself.

Her one devouring thought was to get away from the red cottage as soon as she could. She knew she could not put off feeling for ever, if she stayed there. In the ordinary course of events she would have had a year-and-a-half more at college. She arranged, instead, to take a pass instead of an honours degree, which would shorten the time by a year. She did literally nothing, during the following spring and summer, but work day after day at her books, and walk, alone or with Ruth, in the country; arriving home late and leaving early and paying no more attention to her mother's objections than she would have done to the wind wailing in the chimneys at night.

PART TWO

Eleanor

1

AT the end of her last term at Ardlemouth, Hilary was appointed History mistress to a big girls' secondary school in Kent. The interviews which preceded the appointment were swallowed up in the apathy from which she made no attempt, then, to escape. She remembered nothing about them. The Principal of the college must have taken some trouble over the matter, for the school was a good one which did not as a rule take people with Pass degrees on its staff. Hilary's appearance, too, had a distinction about it which must have told in her favour. She herself had no feelings at all, neither gratitude nor apprehension. She had to get away from home, and this was the first step which must be taken - that was all.

She did not feel anything until she got out of the train at Medling station. Then she was conscious that, far from standing squarely on her legs as a member of a big school's staff might be expected to do, she had no legs at all, but two useless columns of jelly which wobbled and would not move one in front of the other. It was definitely unpleasant, but it was a feeling. The apathy was lifting. Once free of the surroundings which she had grown up in and never left, she had begun to notice things round her: the little hills and vales of Dorset, Hampshire woods, the downs of Berkshire, like the back of some great animal asleep, with villages tucked in between its paws; the Thames, peaceful, silvery, slow, here deserted except for waterfowl, there alive with houseboats, motor-boats and people in bright colours, a much more sophisticated river than the one she was used to. The warrens of the suburbs were like nothing she could have imagined - little clean houses, but so many of them, with gardens which were cheerful at first but grew sadder as London was neared, degenerating by stages into untidy backyards flanked by windows from which hung rags of all shapes, all the colour washed out of them. Then there was London - a porter who put her into a taxi whether she liked it or not, a roar and a rattle, tall, secret buildings, a green park, another station - and then the little fields of Kent, orchards where red apples still hung on the trees, hop-gardens being demolished by hordes of hop-pickers, who looked picturesque, like Italian peasants, from the train; tall red cones with Dutchwomen's caps on, which she learned only later were oast-houses; and at last the old, wide station where nobody seemed in a hurry, where horse-drawn cabs waited, and carts piled with round baskets topped gaily with blue paper, and wagons behind sleek Shire horses, from whose load of fat sacks came the queer, sweet, pungent smell of hops.

Hilary found her way to the school building, and was at once beset by doubts as to the proper way to go in. There was a big front door which looked deserted and terribly grand, a little door labelled "Tradesmen", a gate which seemed to lead into the garden, and a flight of steps, very well worn, leading downwards, called "Pupils' Entrance". She had almost decided on that when a heavy body threw itself off a bicycle at her elbow and a voice said heartily, "New staff? Come along, I'll show you where to go!"

They went by the garden gate. Hilary, standing back, saw a big woman, stout as well as broad, who rolled along with toes turned out. As she walked she chatted; wanted to know Hilary's name and what her subject was. There were three new mistresses, she said. She herself was Miss Hornibrook, taught Art, and had been there since the year one. "Twenty-five years as a teacher, and ten before that as a pupil." Showed she got on well with people, didn't it? Leave? Never, till she was carried out feet foremost. She hadn't any life apart from the school, she said, and was proud of it. Hilary's heart warmed to anyone who could be so friendly and so contented.

"Wouldn't think I taught Art, would you?" she asked.

Hilary, cautiously, smiled and said, "Why not?"

"Oh, I don't know. Djibbahs and all that, and hair all over the place, and sandals. I rather believe in being tidy and ordinary, myself. But I might be doing something better than teaching if I didn't. I mind too much about trifles, I expect. Tidiness and manners. The unessentials. This your first job? Yes, of course. It's not a bad job, as they go, from what I hear of others. Here's the staff cloakroom."

Half a dozen women of varying ages were tidying themselves. The Art mistress greeted them severally. "Hullo, Banks! Cheerio, G.K.! Good holidays? Morning, Miss Tindal Smith!"

Hilary made herself inconspicuous in a corner. Conversation buzzed round her, more women came in.

"Been to Brittany, have you? Looking at architecture's too much like work, *I* think! I've been to Cornwall, all by my lones except for my dog. He's the perfect companion, does whatever I want to do, never argues, listens intelligently to everything I say. Nothing to do except lie on my back and look at the sky!"

Somebody giggled. "Don't weep for me now, don't weep for me never, I'm going to do nothing for ever and ever!' That your idea of heaven, Horners?"

Miss Hornibrook replied serenely, "Something like it. You wait till you've been teaching as long as I have. No harps and child angels for me, anyway! Child angels! Who's got Lower Fifth B this year?"

They all slewed round and looked at Hilary. "You have, Miss Moore, haven't you?"

Lower Fifth B? - Hilary believed she had.

"Good luck to you! Why are the Lower Fifths always *the* most unpleasant of all the forms? They're not bad in the Fourths, and they're perfectly polite in the Upper Fifth - but once over the doorstep of the Lower Fifth rooms and they turn into little demons . . . You don't see why they should? Awkward age, I suppose - fourteen or so, with a few clever thirteens all cock-a-hoop with themselves for being so young. First job? Oh, you'll see!"

Hilary felt a sinking at her stomach. There was a menace in that "First job?" whoever spoke it. As though they were all going to be rather amused to watch her floundering.

The big Art mistress turned to her. "Ready? Here's another new person: Miss - what? - Farrisey? Goodness, what an unfortunate name to have - the brats'll fall on it like vultures! But I suppose you've had that to put up with all your life!"

Miss Farrisey was little and plump, like a partridge. She laughed. "Scribe or Pharisee, all my life," she admitted. "But never, so far, hypocrite, I think. So I've something to be thankful for. No, I've done a job before - three years at Addiscombe High. Not bad, but I wanted a move. Don't believe in staying in one place all my days, turn into a stick in the mud

There was a ripple of laughter all round. She turned unconcernedly. "Have I dropped a brick? Well, we're all entitled to our own opinions, aren't we? Some do and some don't. I don't."

Hilary envied her the easy way she dealt with these people whom she had never, presumably, seen before. She herself felt as if she had one of those lumps of jelly instead of a tongue, this time. They were straggling out of the cloakroom now and up the stairs. Someone whispered, "I bet you Lilian Jane's been sitting bolt upright in her little chair waiting for us this ten minutes - "

There was only one person sitting when they arrived at the library, and that was Miss Barrington, the Head. Lilian Jane! It suited her - slim and straight, pale, with a crown of white hair; dressed in something dark and silky, with flowing lines; cold, beautiful, almost, yet austere. The words she said as each one shook hands with her were commonplace - welcome, questions about the holidays - yet did not sound so. The mistresses treated her with respect, almost, it seemed to Hilary, with caution.

When the meeting was over, she was waylaid by Miss Tindal Smith, a thin woman with wispy hair and pince-nez; and a suspicious, snappy look about her. "I'll show you your form-room. It's the form above mine - I have the Fourth Remove. So I can tell you something about them. Little wretches! *I've* never had such a naughty form!

2

She took up a position early the next morning on the platform where she was expected to perch, and watched the girls as they came in by ones and twos. They scuttled in, gave her polite good mornings, and studied her covertly as they stowed away their books. After the first dozen or so she felt definitely easier. They were just like Gregory's small boys in different clothes, after all. Of course they didn't get on with Miss Tindal Smith! Who would?

She smiled to herself at the bare idea, and immediately a rustle among the girls announced that the smile had been noticed. Goodness, what a life! One's smallest gesture, from now on, would be a subject for their conversation.

Her first lesson was with her own form. She had to begin in the middle of history, because school exams demanded a knowledge of the Tudor period from this particular set of girls. She wondered how much they knew of what had gone before, and tried to find out by questioning. But their answers were so vague that she wondered, then, if they had learnt any history at all.

She began quietly, in Gregory's conversational style. She had never heard him take a class, but that was how he had always taught her. Some of the girls looked at each other and grimaced, as though surprised. Miss Tindal Smith was right - they had no manners. None of them showed any signs of taking notes. She realized that they were too young to do anything but what they were told. What a mass of things like that one had to learn! She wished she could have gone to a teachers' training college, but so few intending teachers did in those days, that she had not even thought of it. She went on talking to them, and was pleased when a mildly funny anecdote was greeted with giggles from all corners of the room. They were attending, anyway.

She glanced at the clock, and immediately half a dozen hands shot up.

"We go on till ten, please, Miss Moore!"

"Then it's maths!"

"Miss Moore, please, you haven't given us any homework!"

"We only have twenty minutes for it this time!"

She looked them over, amused. So much for their interest in her lesson. They grinned expectantly. She said, "You know, I knew all those things already. They're on the time-table here in front of my nose!" They shouted with laughter. Hilary never ceased to be surprised at the things which tickled them: they would chuckle delightedly at a turn of phrase, and sit glum at what was meant to be a joke. The laughter exhausted itself in little pops and gurgles and they settled down again to listen.

In a minute a fat girl, whose face had grown more and more painfully puzzled as time went on, put up a hand to ask, "Please, you haven't told us what date it was or who the king was."

Hilary gravely supplied these wants.

"Miss Firth always told us those right at the beginning," the girl informed her; "then we knew where we were." The class tittered. Evidently the fat girl was an acknowledged clown, but whether rude or stupid she was not sure.

The class was watching with the look of a mischievous child who wonders what it can do next. Two of them, at the back, began a whispered conversation. Hilary noticed it immediately and stopped speaking, wondering for a second what to do about it. As she wondered, the whole form slewed round to look at the speakers and they, struck by the sudden silence, glanced up, startled. Their abashed expression tickled Hilary and she laughed, and the form laughed too, as though relieved that she had taken it so easily. She wondered what Miss Tindal Smith would have done. She said to the offenders, "Thank you. Now we'll go on." They flushed and giggled, but there was no more talking. The girls liked people who laughed at them instead of lecturing, and respected people who did not let things pass.

When the lesson was over, most of them simply buried their heads in their desks, pushing books in and pulling them out. But two of them came up to the platform and said, "Please, Miss Moore, could we make a little model of that village? And little cardboard people, dressed as they really were dressed? And p'raps one big house with a kitchen and a great hall like you said?"

The other followed, tumbling over the words in her eagerness. "I've got an old dolls' house. Couldn't we furnish it like it would have been? We should remember it all heaps better if we could see it!"

Hilary could have hugged them for being infected with her own interest. It didn't matter that the rest had already forgotten the whole lesson. She said, "I've got some pictures. If you went by them you could do it perfectly -

you *must* do it perfectly if you do it at all, or you'll give yourselves and everyone else a false impression and that wouldn't do, would it . . . ?" Looking up, she saw the Maths mistress hovering in the doorway. "I'll bring them for you to-morrow," she promised, and caught up her books and hurried out. There was no expression on the Maths mistress's face as Hilary murmured apologies for keeping her waiting . . . Hilary wondered if she was annoyed because one couldn't expect Lower Fifth formers to get up much interest in maths. Someone was proclaiming shrilly, "Miss Moore says we can make models! Hurrah!" Then, "Sssh!" as the Maths mistress walked to her place.

The Staff Common Room she found not unlike college; but, disappointingly, on a lower level, lacking the sense of striving, whether for learning, for excellence at games, for social success or for spiritual experience which pervades any collection of late adolescents. A few of these mistresses were still pressing on, in one way or another. Most were resting on their oars, apparently content - actually, inside themselves, deeply disappointed that they could get no farther towards whatever type of fame they had dreamed of; buttressing their self-respect with the easy comparison between their trained minds and the immature ones of the children, giving in to the pleasant fallacy of being all-knowing, avoiding contact with those whose standards were higher than their own, always ready to give advice and never to take it. There were no apparent friendships among them; they seemed to be a collection of more or less neutral acquaintances, having come to the conclusion that neutrality was the only state in which they could live and work comfortably together. To anyone who probed, strains of attraction and repulsion would have appeared. Hilary did not probe. She had seen so little of people that she took a completely surface valuation of them.

Only a few days after the beginning of term, she was surprised to find that she was fitting in. It was such a relief to be free of her mother's harrying, to be able to do what she wanted, within limits, without a fight. For she did not have to fight the girls. She made them laugh without knowing how, did not nag them, was really interested in their gawky, inexplicable ways, and they liked her.

The purely personal element soon came in. An aggresive-looking girl called Rhoda, against whom Miss Tindal Smith had specially warned her, brought it first. She came up to Hilary's desk one morning and said, "I've got to report myself for being rude to Miss Tindal Smith - " and waited, expectantly.

Hilary was thinking, "This kid's awfully like young Kenneth." She said, as she would have said to a Kenneth recounting his misdeeds with a spice of bravado, "How were you rude to her?"

The girl grinned. "It isn't a bit difficult to be rude to Miss Tindal Smith! I always say it's because she's rude to me first, but I suppose that isn't really any excuse!"

Hilary agreed: "None at all. There aren't really excuses for things, are there? Or are you one of the people who think there are?"

Rhoda stared. "I don't know about that. There's awful provocation sometimes! What happened this morning was that T.S. (sorry, Miss Tindal Smith) made a laughing-stock

of my Latin prose to the whole form, in a *nasty* sort of way
- not the way *you* laugh at us and I lost my temper and said
Latin doesn't interest me in the least. That was all. I was in
a rage, but I didn't mean to be rude. I *do* hate Latin; it's so
niminy-piminy and unnecessary. She took it as if I'd
insulted her."

"Well, so you had, if you insulted something she was fond
of. Love me, love my dog. That's sense, isn't it?"

"Fond of *Latin*? Oh, my *goodness*!" Rhoda exploded.

"Some people are . . . What am I expected to do about it?"

Rhoda looked horrified. "Don't you really know?"

Hilary laughed. "Of course I don't know. How could I,
when I've only been here ten days? I can go and ask Miss
Tindal Smith, if you like - but I should think you're quite
well qualified to tell me."

Rhoda's grin and a droop of the eyelids acknowledged the
thrust. She said, "You know, I could pull your leg - like
anything."

"You could. But I should very soon find out that you had,
and then I suppose there would have to be - retaliation."

The girl crowed with laughter at that. "Wouldn't there
just! I won't pull it, anyway. You produce the report book -
big red one - that's it - inscribe my name in it - give me a
jaw - and urge me to go and apologize to whoever it is. And
if I get more than six reports in the term I have to go to the
Head . . . I was always being rude last year."

Hilary said dryly, "You certainly know the procedure
very well."

Rhoda sighed gustily. "I do. P'raps - "she looked up
sideways - "p'raps I shan't this year so much."

"I hope not. Isn't there some little matter of competitions in conduct between forms? I'd rather mine wasn't at the bottom . . . What I meant about excuses was, that really they don't exist. Your failure's your failure whatever the circumstances. If you'd been a better person you wouldn't have made it. Your particular failure, this time, was in losing your temper - one's always in a stronger position if one doesn't - and in judging the person you were talking to, perhaps. You were surprised because your remark was taken personally - but most people do take things personally, and the sooner you find that out the better, then you'll be more careful what you say. But while you lose your temper and say the wrong thing, you can't grouse if you're made to suffer for it. See?"

Rhoda was regarding her with delight. "I like that. It's sort of clean and tight and exhilarating," she said. "Having no excuses, I mean. D'you think I ought to go and apologize to her?"

"Only if you think you ought."

The girl considered, her head on one side. "I think perhaps I do. *Because* I lost my temper and said the wrong thing. I never have apologized to her before. I've been rude heaps of times."

Hilary, her pen poised, said, "I've forgotten your name."

Rhoda told her it, and added, "Most people call me Bill. My friends, anyway."

Hilary made the entry. "Well, that's all, isn't it? You'd better go or you won't have any time for dinner." She refrained from calling her anything. It seemed presumptuous to label herself a friend so soon, yet she certainly did not want to declare war.

The girl smiled at her squarely, eye to eye, and took herself off. Hilary wondered what on earth she would say to Miss Tindal Smith.

3

It was not long before the mistresses became definite persons, too, although there was not much contact between them beyond hurried meetings on the way from one lesson to another, free hours spent elbow to elbow in the Staff-room doing corrections, lunch hour conversations - "*Is* Maureen O'Reilly half-witted, or does she only pretend to be?" "Banks, when *are* you going to do decimals with Lower Four A? My physics calculations are completely held up until you do!" "I'll do them when the little monsters have got vulgar fractions into their heads and not before!" "What a way to teach arithmetic - where did you learn methods of education, Banks?" "Methods of education are all blather - give me a good knowledge of my subject and a spot of common sense and I'll teach them all they can assimilate, I promise you!" "My dears, L.J.'s unloaded *all* the junior Scripture on to me, just because I'm supposed to be able to teach Geography! I've never read the Acts of the Apostles in my life, and I've got to ram it into the Thirds and Fourths!" "Dog's body, that's what I am!" "Never read the Acts? Time you did - do you all the good in the world!"

There were a few who were near enough to their college days to talk of plays they had seen, of this or that modern philosophy which interested them. But they were scowled upon by the elders. "There simply isn't time for that and work too - I don't suppose you have the slightest idea who's on duty for Break this week! No, I thought not - well, don't forget to go out, and leave them all in the garden five minutes too long like someone I know did the other day!"

There was, too, the matter of chairs. Miss Tindal Smith, too old for a Headship now and knowing it, professing a scorn for Heads as persons who chatted with parents - "*Parents!* Nitwits! The mere business of producing a child robs even the most intelligent of all the sense they ever had!" - yet asserted her seniority by appropriating the couch for her sole use and glaring at anyone else who presumed to sit on a corner of it. Miss Hornibrook was allotted the big arm-chair, because the others liked her, not because she insisted on it. The rest of them, particularly the newest, had to be content with seats of varying age and hardness whose merits they very soon learned to distinguish one from another.

There were Music mistresses who sidled in and out apolo-getically, knowing that they did not really belong, and Miss Hunt, the spare, weather-beaten guardian of the laboratories, who rarely appeared in the Staff room because she had a den of her own in the Science wing.

They were amiable enough; an ordinary crowd, it seemed to Hilary, well fitted to the room's drab walls, ink-spotted tablecloth, and the arty-crafty vases which were filled from time to time by floral tributes from this admirer or that of

114

some one of them; filled crossly, with a snort and a push, all the flowers in at once, because adorations were not encouraged and the recipients were rather ashamed of the gifts, which could not be hidden.

After the novelty had worn off, Hilary became conscious that she was lonely. Her father had been friend and hero both at once to her. Hero he still was, but she could not look to him for daily inspiration. She was a person who must have a hero. Even to her memories of him she did not voluntarily turn, because nearly every recollection of Gregory was bound up with the pain of the realization that her mother meant more to him than she did. Silly, unreasonable, presumptuous, but she could not get over it.

She could not imagine the High School producing either hero or friend, until one day when, leaving the building, she heard at her elbow a voice which she had never, to her knowledge, heard before.

"Fond of walking, Miss Moore?"

Turning, she saw the Science mistress, thin, wiry, with a face like a Red Indian's, all high cheekbones and brown, stretched skin. It struck Hilary as an amusing face, and she definitely liked the voice, which was crisp and cultivated.

"Very," she said. "Though I haven't done much here so far."

The other fell into step beside her. "There's some good country round about, if you know where to look for it. I've got to take a party of the Lower Sixth fungus-hunting to-morrow afternoon. Would you care to come?"

Hilary assented, chiefly because she found Miss Hunt attractive. She enjoyed the walk, being entertained, at first with difficulty and then uproariously, by two of the girls. When it was over and the party had been shepherded into the school dining-room for tea, she would have turned aside to the Staff-room, but the Science mistress prevented her.

"Tea in there'll be cold and black. Will you come and have it with me?"

Hilary looked inquiring. Mistresses did not, in her experience, order tea for themselves and friends in their own rooms.

The other smiled; a curious, crooked smile which made her bony face oddly attractive. "I've a little house along the lane. I expect you've seen it - all covered with honeysuckle."

Hilary cried out, "Why, of course! It's a darling little house! I'd love to come!"

The crooked smile widened, and disclosed, unexpectedly, a dimple. "Good. Come along, then."

Once inside the garden gate, Hilary drew a deep breath. She felt at home for the first time since she had sat with Gregory by lamplight in the shadowy bedroom.

The garden was peopled, now, with prim clumps of sunflower and Michaelmas daisy, set about with lavender and low box hedges. The house was small, and not an old one. Its floors were polished, and covered only with rugs which glowed ruby and russet-brown. Bookcases ran round three sides of the sitting-room, open shelves full of books which looked well used. A low desk was littered with papers, a stool by the fireplace with more books. The chairs were small round wicker ones, with hand-woven cushion-

116

covers. The curtains were hand-woven too, of a delicate yellow. The pictures were sketches, wood-cuts, water-colours, some of them unframed, just fastened up with drawing-pins. It was not a room to loll in. It had the air of inspiring to work, and only to the best work. Although there was no physical resemblance between them, the room's atmosphere took Hilary back with a bound to her father's study at school.

A round-faced country girl brought tea on a tray and set it on a little table; a simple tea, new loaf and a lump of butter, honey and home-made cake. A huge sandy cat came in with her and jumped into Miss Hunt's lap.

As she poured out tea, Miss Hunt threw out little quiet questions and comments. "Your first experience of Secondary schools, is it? You're not quite like most of the young staff we get - all built to the same pattern."

Hilary explained herself, shortly. Miss Hunt, evidently interested, led her on. She would not say much about her home - she could not, yet, to a stranger - and the Science mistress, respecting a reticence which she only sensed, turned the talk to more impersonal things. Hilary let herself go, then. Perhaps it was the room that did it, taking her back to similar talks with her father. They ranged over prose and poetry, old books and new books, philosophy and education; fascinating talk, in which each skimmed the surface of the other's mind and sent down, now and then, a plumb-line to see how deep the knowledge went. The results were entirely satisfactory. Neither was interested in the snippets of information which most people love to pick up and pouch, like monkeys, to produce boastfully and pouch again. They talked of what they knew.

They talked till seven. Then Miss Hunt said, "Heavens, I'm having supper with someone at half-past. I must go and change, this minute!"

Hilary sprang up, half ashamed but wholly alive again. She had been coming alive ever since she had left Redsands and this was the climax. "Have I been jabbering too much? I'm awfully sorry!"

The Science mistress frankly laughed at her. "Not a bit too much. I've liked it. You jabber very well. Will you come again?"

Hilary said, with a fervency which surprised them both, "Rather!"

She noticed with pleasure the kindness in Miss Hunt's blue eyes as she went out. On the way home she hummed to herself. It was almost as if the two half-dead years had never been.

4

So far, Hilary had found week-ends a problem. She had no friends to spend them with and nothing special to do. Then she discovered the Medway, lapping through hop-gardens and water-meadows, and a friendly boatman with a good supply of boats. The first day she went out, she took a canoe. Then, prowling round the big shed which glistened with brown paint and smelt of varnish, she saw, slung up to the rafters, the slim lines of a whiff. She turned to the man impulsively. "Can I have that to-morrow?"

Then, seeing him dubious at the notion of a woman alone in such a craft, she laughed and added, "I'm used to one," and talked of the West Country river on which she had rowed before. He knew that river, and she got her whiff.

On Sunday morning she came down to the boathouse early, with a long coat over her gym-dress. Nothing else was safe in that sort of boat; a skirt might get caught up in the sliding seat and pitch one out. She left the coat in the boathouse, knelt at the water's edge to arrange the stretcher, took the long, light sculls from the boatman and let him push her off. She saw him nod his head in approval as she skimmed upstream. She smiled back at him, knowing that she sculled well, liking the approval, glorying in the smooth motion of her muscles; thankful that she was able to glory in it after all these months of not enjoying anything.

Glancing over her shoulder from time to time to make sure she was going straight, she saw presently that she was coming to a weir, with the black structure of a lock gate beside it. She went in to the near bank, turning a scull sideways and lodging the rowlock on a low tussock of grass, and looked about. On the opposite side, green meadow rose to a rounded hill. Above her was a towpath, rich with purple loosestrife and tansy and backed by slim trees and a tangle of blackberry. She slewed round to watch the weir; green translucent streaks rushing down to tumbling froth, then swirls and bubbles and then the still, clear pool.

As she sat there, three cyclists came along the towpath. They glanced at her, then stared, then one of them smiled and she recognized Rhoda Grey and two more of her form. The three of them tumbled off in a hurry and came and looked at her over the edge.

One of them said, "I say, how topping! What a perfectly heavenly little boat!"

"It's quite a nice one," Hilary allowed.

Rhoda inquired if she were going through the lock, and, having heard their verdict on the reach above it, Hilary thought she would. "At least, I'll go over. It's a bit risky taking a little thing like this through - they upset so easily."

"Over? Carry it?" the three girls exclaimed. "Do let us help!"

So Hilary climbed out and stood with her sculls upright beside her while they shouldered the boat. She saw them look her up and down and was glad that she had straight legs. She walked beside them as they carried the boat, and as they walked they chattered.

Had she been rowing long?

"Since I was six," she said, and did not tell them how short a time ago that was. After all, they were fourteen, and well grown, themselves.

Would she teach them to row in a thing like this?

She countered by asking them if they had ever wielded an oar, and they laughed and said no, they didn't really know an oar accurately from a winnowing-fan, and cocked an eye to see if she recognized the allusion. She did. "No excuse - *you* don't live in a waterless city in the mountains!"

"Will you teach us?" they implored.

"Why, yes. I'll teach you to scull. It'll be a long time

before you'll be safe in a whiff, though. Can you swim?"

They could. Watching her embark, they supposed regretfully that she was right about the long time. She thanked them for their help, and they sat down and watched her out of sight round the bend. Nice of them, she thought. They might so easily have raced along beside her on their bicycles.

When she came to the next lock she turned regretfully back. She could not afford to have the little boat out too long. The day, after an early morning of blue mist, was marvellously hot and sunny. Swarms of hop-pickers' children, at the edge of a partly dismantled hop-garden, came to the bank and pointed at her and were yelled at raucously by their parents, who were cooking the Sunday dinner at open fires. Hilary did not like their harsh voices. She rowed on as fast as she could.

A lock-keeper carried her boat over, this time, for sixpence. She rested below the weir again, because it was so lovely to watch. When, after some time, she passed under the town bridge near which she had started, several of the churchgoers, on the way home to lunch, paused to look at her over the parapet.

As she told the boatman she had had a heavenly morning, her eyes were dancing and her cheeks glowing, and he smiled with pleasure at the sight of her and promised that she should have the whiff whenever she liked. It was hardly ever used, he said, except by a Cambridge undergraduate who came there for his vacations sometimes. The man had at one time gone out in it himself, but now he was too stiff and too heavy.

121

That made her think of Henry. She wished he were here. He was in his third year at Cambridge now, very proper, she supposed, and stuffed with culture. She had never seen him since the dreadful day of the funeral, never written, hardly thought of him. Queer, how one lost touch . . . She must write.

She retrieved her hat and coat and, in them, cycled home as decorously as though she had been to church herself. The Headmistress, meeting her by chance, positively jumped at the radiant friendliness of her smile. She was not used to smiles like that from members of her staff.

On Monday morning, the three, Rhoda, Virginia, and Gillian, greeted her when they came in as an old friend. Indeed, there was an air of amiability about the whole room. Nearly everyone there gave her some sort of a grin, shy, self-conscious, frank or deprecating according to the state of the giver's conscience. Hilary beamed back at them. She felt as though the sun had come out after a long grey winter, and if anyone had asked her why she could not have told them.

At the end of the afternoon she was striding, in high spirits, along the corridor to the Staff-room, when she was stopped by the Headmistress's secretary, with a face as long as a fiddle. She gabbled, "Miss Moore, please! Miss Barrington would like to see you in her room!"

Hilary smiled down at her. She looked dowdy and faded, frightened, as though she needed pumping from some reservoir of courage. She jumped, and said, "Now, at once, Miss Moore, please!"

So Hilary went, at once, wondering faintly but not

overmuch what it was all about, knocked at the solid, green-painted door, and saw Miss Barrington behind her desk, scribbling on a pad of blotting-paper. Her eyes, as she looked up, had the same expression of snappy enmity as Rose Moore's eyes. Hilary, catching sight of it, went all weak at the knees.

It was veiled in an instant and the eyes had no expression at all. Hilary was motioned to a chair. The Headmistress's voice, when she spoke, was as expressionless as her eyes.

"Just a little matter I have to speak to you about, Miss Moore. You were on the river yesterday?"

Hilary blinked. She did not know whether to say "Yes", or "Well?" or nothing at all. She shot out at length, "D'you mean - I'm not to go on the river?"

Miss Barrington's eyebrows were raised for an instant. She scribbled, then, still holding her pencil, sat back and looked up.

"You're very young, Miss Moore."

"I suppose I am. But I'm very experienced with boats." She could not see what being young - if she was young - had to do with going on the river.

Miss Barrington continued firmly, "A great deal younger than most of my staff. I appointed you on my friend Miss Haslitt's recommendation. She is an excellent judge of people. I'm content to abide by her judgement. But your being here does mean, I'm afraid, that you must learn to behave as though you were older than you really are. We're very anxious that our girls shall go out into the world *womenly* women, Miss Moore, not hoydens. And so - our staff must be womenly women, not hoydens."

She paused. Hilary could not believe that she was being given notice after three weeks' trial.

The thin, musical but determined voice went on. (Lilian Jane - how it suited her!) "I'm sure, Miss Moore, that you are a womanly woman at heart. We all are, if we're not spoilt. You may say that what my mistresses do in their spare time is no concern of mine. That's not quite true, as you'll see if you think it over. Anything a mistress does which might injure the reputation of the school is very much my concern."

She scribbled a complicated pattern on her blotting pad, as though waiting for Hilary to give her views. But Hilary was much too frightened to argue. She must know whether she was losing her job or not.

"There's no question, of course," Miss Barrington went on, "of your being allowed to do this or that. For the staff there are no rules. I trust to their good sense. I see no objection to your using the river - tidily, shall we say, in a punt or an ordinary rowing-boat. Although most of the better local people prefer to keep away from the hop gardens just now. But to appear on the river - " the sagging cheeks became suddenly taut with the firm closure of Miss Barrington's mouth - "*in* a gymnasium tunic, *on* a Sunday morning, for all the Board of Management to see on their way home from church - well, you must be thankful that if they did see you, it was not by them that you were recognized but by one of your colleagues."

So she had not been given the sack - yet. But she might be, any minute, as the result of knocking up against some convention which was in force in a country town though not at the seaside, and which therefore had never occurred to her. She was so panic-stricken that she could only say, very low and ashamed of herself, "I'm sorry. I didn't think about people seeing me. Of course I won't do it again."

Miss Barrington appeared to be placated by this submission. She smiled. "I quite understand that it was nothing but lack of thought, and we must be glad that there was no harm done. If you will bear in mind" - she leaned forward confidentially - "that you have to be an example to the girls on every single occasion that one of them might catch sight of you, out of school as well as in - then I'm sure we shall get on together very well."

She rose, majestically, and Hilary thanked her - she wasn't quite sure for what - and escaped.

She was still in a panic. What would happen if she did, through that ridiculous inability of hers to foretell what people would think, lose her job? What would happen to her mother and Hermione, if she couldn't find work to support them?

She gulped some tea in the Staff-room and rushed out of the building without speaking to anyone. Once started along the road, she felt better. She must talk to someone now - someone who could warn her of the pitfalls she was too silly to see for herself. What about that promise to go and see Miss Hunt again? She wheeled about, swiftly and competently, on her bicycle. A group of girls, unknown but wearing school hats, turned and gaped at her. Heavens, couldn't she even change her mind in the middle of the road without someone taking note of it? The girls giggled. She turned thankfully off the main road and down the lane which led to Miss Hunt's house.

There was an air of self-sufficiency about the little place which soothed her jangled nerves. The round-faced maid smiled at her and showed her straight out to the back garden. The Science mistress, in an incredibly old and dirty Burberry, with a tweed hat crammed on her head, was trimming a hedge. Watching her as she snipped, her whole body expressing grim determination, Hilary was seized with a desire to laugh. At the sound of her steps Miss Hunt turned about and screwed up her eyes. The hat was ludicrously crooked and there was a smudge on her cheek. She threw down the shears and came forward with outstretched hands. Relief at the welcome and amusement at the comic figure brought Hilary's laughter and the question which had sprung to her lips bubbling out together.

"I say - are you a womanly woman?"

Miss Hunt checked and stared. She had been a senior mistress for some years now, kept strict discipline, and was, by this time, quite unused to impudence. Hilary thought for a sickening instant that she had bumped up against another rock. Then the blue eyes twinkled and a pop of laughter came, explosively, as though against resistance.

"I'm afraid not - here, anyway. In school's another matter. What have you been doing that wasn't womanly?"

Insensibly the terrifying interview was reduced to the level of a joke. Hilary sat on the grass and watched the continuation of the hedge cutting, and as she snipped, Miss Hunt talked.

"She's right, of course. In school and in the town - any

where where the local people go - we must be circumspect if we want to keep our jobs. The Board's rather timid. It likes mistresses to be cardboard figures, guaranteed to impart much knowledge and to do no harm. They mustn't have political opinions or religious views other than strictly orthodox and moderate ones - or eccentricities unless they don't show. And if we take the Board's money, obviously we must conform to their fads. That's sense, isn't it?"

She went on, furiously attacking the hedge. "One must have a refuge, unless one is a cardboard figure. Lots of them are - worked by the Head's strings. This is mine - good high hedges and a charming dragon to keep undesirables away from the door - girls and others - when I'm being wild."

Hilary chuckled. "She didn't breathe any fire at me."

The blue eyes met hers, appraising. "She's a very discriminating dragon . . . Are you comfortable down there?"

"'M! Lovely to be on the ground. I've sat in chairs and been proper ever since I came."

"As for the Head - " Miss Hunt stopped snipping and seemed to choose her words - "I think her malicious look was not at you, as a person, but at you as a possible menace to the school. It's her one devouring passion. Become an asset to it, and she'll fawn on you . . . You'll find her - difficult. She's built exactly to the Board's pattern. Victorian. Expensive ornamentation of the very best material. The uglier the better as long as it's in the fashion, and good. What's underneath doesn't matter. Flannel petticoat and feather-stitched drawers, all different shades of pink. And combinations."

She laughed at Hilary's gasp. "Metaphorically speaking, of

127

course. I've never studied her wardrobe closely. Certainly never the innermost. I mean, as long as you behave as she wishes you to she doesn't worry what you're like inside. The less inside you've got, the better, really. I've got more than she approves of - but my examination results and my discipline are both excellent, so she puts up with me. You've got too much, too, I think - "

The agony of apprehension took hold of Hilary again. She remembered Miss Barrington's angry eyes. She would not need much excuse for getting rid of someone with too much inside. Couldn't one tear it out, or smother it?

Miss Hunt divined her mood. "I shouldn't worry. Your looks are tremendously in your favour. We haven't had anyone as distinguished-looking ever, I do believe. She'll love pointing you out to parents. And didn't you have a recommendation from an old friend - someone she'd hate to offend? That's a good start. You make your brats interested and get a few distinctions in the public exams, and think before you do anything out of the usual, and you'll be all right. You won't have any difficulty with discipline."

"How do you know that?" Hilary asked. The fright had buried its head again.

"Brats like you. Can see that. Besides, they would . . . One good thing about the Head, she's not jealous. Some of the others are, you'll find. And she doesn't interfere with one's work. I don't think she knows much really. She only got a third at Cambridge, and she's not the sort to have real scholarship outside her own shop."

"Why did they make her Head, then?" Hilary asked idly,

biting at a grass stem.

"Oh, she's not a bad Head. She's an amazing organizer - the numbers have trebled themselves since she came - and there's very seldom any sort of a dust-up. Why's she Head? Oh, because some loud-voiced local draper knew her father, I expect. That's how Heads are made in this sort of school, not because they're great scholars, or even great people, which would be a better reason."

Hilary was horrified. She had been brought up to believe that jobs, high and low, were acquired by merit and merit alone. She said so, forcibly.

Miss Hunt said, "My poor child! It's the truth I'm telling you - in every walk of life, I should think. And it's not so unjust either, when you come to think of it. You, for instance, got your job because the Head of your college thought well of you. She got hers because a member of the committee thought well of her father, perhaps. Thought well enough of her father to be pretty sure he'd be pleased with her. Ability to get on with those in authority is a most useful asset, more useful than good looks, whole heaps more than good brains or high exam results. If you've got it, and the sense to cultivate the right people, you get the plums. If you haven't, you don't. I don't quarrel with it."

Hilary, dimpling, said, "Have you got it?"

The other looked amused. "Not to any marked extent. But then, I don't want the plums. I've no ambition at all to be a Head. So it works out all right . . . Would you like to do a job of work and sweep up these bits? I may not have many wires to pull - but I can make people work!"

Laughing, Hilary worked; and as a reward was asked to

supper. Throughout the meal, and after it, the talk went on; not on quite such a high level as last time; more about themselves, their views of life, their relations with other people.

When she left, Hilary felt quite sure of herself. Her panic had vanished. She could deal with Miss Barrington, the Board, and anyone who might come along. She said so, shyly and very gratefully.

Miss Hunt went shy, too - gruffly, stiffly shy. She said, "I've so enjoyed having you. I don't get many visitors - because I'm not a cardboard figure, perhaps. Most of them are afraid of me . . . I've stopped minding now, almost. I haven't been cheeked - or talked so much - for I don't know how many years."

Hilary, studying her, said, "No, I'm not afraid of you. You're real. I'm afraid of Miss Barrington."

"Because you can't see through her shell. 'M! I used to be, till I found out how little there was on the other side of it. Most people think the shell charming and don't look beyond. Best just to do that and remember how keen she is on the school, I think. Well, come and be cheeky another day, won't you?"

5

The following morning, Hilary was set upon by her three friends of the tow-path and many others, all clamouring to be taught river-craft. On Miss Hunt's advice, she went to the Head about it. After a lot of discussion and hesitation, she was given permission to teach those girls to row, paddle and punt whose parents wished them to learn and who could pass a swimming-test. One influential parent, it seemed, had stormed, a term ago, because there was no one on the Staff who could instruct his daughters in these things.

Miss Hunt chuckled and said, "One - no, several - up to you. Increases the school's popularity. Other schools don't do it because they haven't an expert to teach - we have. Improves your standing no end with L.J., and with the girls because it's a new thing and they like it. Oh, you don't need to worry about losing your job."

And so, gradually, Hilary lost her fear; both of losing her job and of people. The other mistresses invited her to coffee with them, and, from being shy at first, she grew able to enjoy going. School gossip became intelligible, although even now she listened to it chiefly for the pleasure of retailing it to Miss Hunt and hearing her caustic comments. Everything, somehow, had come to centre round Miss Hunt in the few weeks that Hilary had known her. She could not tell how this had come about, for she had not expected or engineered it. It had simply happened.

It was after a coffee-party at Miss Hornibrook's that, passing the little house and seeing a light in the sitting-room, Hilary turned in at the gate and, being admitted, found the Science mistress grumpily sitting over some corrections.

"I came in just because I saw a light; I've been listening to the chatter of Farrisey and Co. and learning to play Bridge -

I'm getting quite keen about it: jolly good exercise for the brain!"

Miss Hunt grunted. "My brain's had about all the exercise it can stand by the evening. Counting up trumps and doing post-mortems on what I might have done doesn't appeal to me in the least. I'm very bad at it. I hate the people who play it, and I frequently lose my temper."

She jabbed so fiercely with her pen at somebody's chemistry book that Hilary wished she had not come to cause such irritation.

"I hate Bridge. I hate all games that grown-up people waste their time over. Golf and bowls and all of them. Games are for children. Adults ought to have something better to think about."

"And if they haven't?" Hilary said, amused. "Anyway, games are a good way of getting to know people, aren't they?"

"If you want to know people like that. Can you imagine that you and I would have got to know each other across a pack of cards?"

"I think - I like to think" - she had to speak, but did so with difficulty - "that you and I would have got to know each other however we'd met."

Miss Hunt said, "Humph!" and seemed to be winding herself up inside. "If I'd met you at a Bridge table I should've said, `Here's another of them!' and that would've been that. And you'd have said, 'What's that old scarecrow think she's playing, Bridge or Demon Patience? And why can't she learn to keep her hair on?' And that would have been that, too."

She scratched a red line across the whole page of an exercise book, and made a blot. Hilary laughed because she could not help it, then wished she hadn't. At the sound, perversely, the Science mistress came out of her bad temper and laughed too.

"Sorry. I've got a headache and l stayed out in the garden and put off doing these till I simply had to, and they're the worst lot of rubbish I've ever come across, which means I must've given a pretty poor lesson for them to be done from. I've nearly finished. Sit down, do, Hilary, and we'll have some cocoa in a minute."

Hilary started at the sound of her Christian name. She had been "Miss Moore" to everyone for so many weeks now that she almost thought of herself as it. The Science mistress was smiling across at her.

"It slipped out," she said. "D'you mind? It's a nice name. Mine's Eleanor. Now be quiet till I've done this last wretched book."

Hilary did not stay long. It was too late and they were both too tired. But while she stayed, they talked as though they could never stop, about themselves entirely this time, and when she left, Eleanor Hunt walked to the gate with an arm about her shoulders. "Good night, bless you," she said, and Hilary impulsively returned the light pressure with a hug and, "Good night, Eleanor - dear."

The moon was full and yellow, the dark trees against a sky of misty green had the sharpness of a drop-scene, all unreal. Hilary, cycling home, was surprised at the strength of her own emotion. She had thought she could never feel acutely again - and now this had come. She did not so much think about Eleanor as feel over again the mental stimulation, the amusement, the bubbling, unreasonable happiness, which their encounters evolved in her.

School was fun, for Eleanor was there and might crop up at any minute. It needed restraint (which Hilary rigidly applied, knowing instinctively that this friendship was too precious to be cheapened) not to make occasions to go up the back stairs, past the labs, instead of up the front which led directly to her own form room. When legitimate business did take her near the labs, she was plunged in disappointment if Eleanor were not visible. When, occasionally, Eleanor appeared at her end of the building and chatted with her at her form room door, she gasped with pleasure. It was a long time before she let herself understand that Eleanor did make occasions for meeting and got as much pleasure out of them as she did herself.

Indeed, it was Eleanor, relying inadequately on her seniority and her reputation for being stand-offish, who gave the other mistresses the chance of enjoying the spectacle of a "G.P.", despised and discouraged among the girls, between two of their own members. Some of them shrugged and smiled and said, "Don't worry; these things never last - they'll be scratching each other's eyes out in a week and then not speaking!" They all - except Miss Hornibrook, who had some kindly idea of plucking a brand from the burning - ceased abruptly to invite Hilary to coffee or Bridge, saying in excuse that they knew quite well she would simply forget to come. Hilary did not mind, did not even notice. She accepted Miss Hornibrook's invitations and did not forget to go. After all, she could not spend every single evening at Eleanor's house. But when she was with Eleanor she was happy, and when she was not with her she was planning to be. Everything else skimmed off the surface of her mind, hardly perceived.

The only other person who made an individual impression on her at this time was Janet Brock, a sixth-former who was working for a History scholarship. She was a hard worker with a strong artistic streak, and an appearance which belied her good brain. She had the eyes of a startled fawn, and the slim grace of a daffodil bending to the wind. She had coachings alone with Hilary in the afternoons, and would arrive punctually, take down all she was told, ask quiet, intelligent questions, and go off without a word when the hour was over. Between the coachings, which took place twice a week, Hilary hardly saw her.

Then one day she appeared in the Lower Fifth room with the request that she might miss her coaching on the following afternoon to go to an extra hockey practice. The association of rough games with the lovely, timid face seemed to Hilary so incongruous that she asked why she was so anxious to play.

"It's not so long before your exam that you can afford to scamp your work just for a game!" she said accusingly.

The girl flushed and as quickly paled. "It isn't just an ordinary game," she said. "It's a special practice for the teams. We've lost so many games because of the rain, and the first Cup Match is on Friday, so Miss Reeve thought we ought to have a practice on the junior school's day as well as on our own."

Never having played school games herself, Hilary was unmoved. She was on the point of saying no. Then, struck by the agonized eagerness of Janet's expression, she temporized. "I didn't know you were in a team."

The girl smiled "I've been in the First for a year."

"Then you've had plenty of practice."

Janet looked away out of the window, then brought her eyes to Hilary's and spoke as one who has, with an effort, made up her mind. "There's a new person come this term. Joan Scudamore - the Captain, you know - is awfully keen on her. I'm so afraid, if I cut this practice, they'll push me out and put her in instead."

"And you'd mind if they did? It would leave you more time for work!"

The girl's great eyes opened wider than ever. "Well, it's pretty much of a disgrace to get pushed out of a team, isn't it? And - and I didn't know my work was so frightfully bad!"

She was bewildered, not defiant. Hilary, realizing that she simply had not apprehended a point of view which all her pupils, probably, shared, relented at once. "It isn't. It's quite good. Right - only we must make up the coaching another day."

Janet beamed her relief and ran away.

Two days later Hilary met her in a corridor. "Well - playing to-morrow?"

She laughed and shuffled her feet. "Yes. I've just been to look at the team list. P'raps I was just making a fuss."

Hilary said, "I'm glad it's all right," and would have passed on. Janet said in a hurry, "Miss Moore! I wish you'd come and watch! It's going to be a good match, and I'd love to

136

show you the way to the ground!"

"I might," Hilary conceded, "if it's a fine day!" and left it at that. She never had taken any interest in school games; but that was no reason why she shouldn't.

She rode to the field at Janet's side and had to do all the talking because Janet was so shy. From the touch-line, with Rhoda and company in attendance, she was smiled upon by the Head, who took Cup matches nearly as seriously as examination results and liked her staff to do the same. She watched Janet dashing up and down the left wing, infusing into the game such speed and grace and neatness that its normal scuffle and fight seemed entirely absent.

She turned to the three, who were in the Second Eleven. "Is Janet Brock a specially good player?"

Virginia said, "She's playing toppingly to-day. Sometimes she's marvellously good and sometimes she's feeble. What did you say, Miss Moore, please? Graceful? Yes, I s 'pose she is. But it's beef you want in hockey more than gracefulness. Still, she *is* playing well to-day."

Queer, how physical beauty made no appeal to these youngsters, yet.

"Joan's *really* far the best person in the First," Virginia went on, reverence in her tones. Hilary watched Joan, at centre-half, charging here and there, untiring, stocky, hitting great swipes which always went in the right direction and showed that she used her brain as well as her sturdy body. It was a close match, and before it was over Hilary was as excited as the girls beside her, more at the spectacle of a well-fought battle than with any appreciation of the points of the game.

Once, as Janet tussled with an enemy half, Hilary caught sight of her face, nostrils dilated, teeth bared in grim determination. Hilary drew breath sharply. She knew that look, she had felt it on her own face, though not at games. You simply couldn't - and yet you must, or you were a coward.

Then Janet had jerked the ball away and shot a goal - her third, the winning one - just as the whistle blew for time, and was standing before her, laughing, triumphant.

"Your match!" Hilary said.

"No, yours! But for you, I shouldn't have played!"

"Ours, then - though I don't think that's true!"

Janet ran off to the pavilion. Joan, the captain, called, "Played, Janet!" as she passed; but did not link arms with her or show any special sign of pleasure. Was that effort Janet had to make, the effort not to funk, the reason she was brilliant one day and poor another? Was it why she was not more popular with the hefty, insensitive people like Joan, who never thought of funking? Was it, in Hilary's own case - only it wasn't funk of physical things, with her - the reason she was not quite most peoples' sort of person?

The three Lower Fifth formers surrounded her again. They had melted away discreetly at the Sixth form girl's approach.

She was not surprised when, a few days later, Janet invited her to tea. She felt nearer to Janet, at this time, than to anyone else, even Eleanor, who was on a far higher plane. Intuitive understanding of this one girl went far to help her understand others, less like herself, and helped in the cure of her fear of other people.

138

Eleanor said, "Don't get too friendly with the girls. L.J. doesn't like it." So, against her inclination, she saw less of Janet and even of the other three than she might have done without the warning. She was glad to find that they accepted her attitude as natural. A mistress was a mistress, and the fact that she could not be bothered with girls out of school made no difference at all to their preference for her. She threw herself into the business of getting Janet's scholarship, realizing the judicious mixture of encouragement and bracing which the girl required. "You didn't seem to think much of my work, so I had to show you that I could play games," Janet might have said if she had been more articulate. There was no need for her to say it; Hilary understood it quite well.

6

In spite of the forecasts of the other mistresses, the friendship between Hilary and Eleanor Hunt neither exploded nor declined. It grew, steadily, with no effort from either. Perhaps the original attraction lay in Eleanor's resemblance to those lecturers who had so excited Hilary's admiration at college - that, and Hilary's need for someone to lean on and Eleanor's for a friend of her own calibre. Eleanor was a good friend, not so far from her own early twenties as to have forgotten their violent ups and downs and the tenderness and teasing, the emotional brake and the intellectual stimulus to which they react. In Hilary she recognized a kindred spirit who might, she felt, have been her daughter with only a few more years' difference between them. She seemed to demand nothing; just to accept gladly all that Hilary freely gave. Nor did she herself give ostentatiously and so make the younger woman her debtor. Hilary's affection was much like that which she had given her father; an upward affection, compounded mainly of reverence for the genuine goodness, the intellectual honesty, round which the rest of both Eleanor's and Gregory's personalities were built; and of enjoyment of Eleanor's dry humour, her common sense, the downrightness which smote, sometimes, with the bracing shock of a cold shower, the sensitiveness of other peoples' moods which softened these harder qualities. Their effect on each other was of acid upon alkali. Each, in other company, was quiet almost to dullness - except with the girls, who loved Hilary and respected Eleanor. Together, they fizzed and sparkled, in feeling, action, and speech. Much of this, Hilary consciously knew and revelled in. Subconsciously, she sank gratefully into the safety of Eleanor's presence, into the mothering, crisp yet tender, which she had never longed for because she had never known.

With the spring, the river called again. A boating-club was formed. Hilary found her spare time completely filled with teaching girls and even staff to manage the various craft they chose. She did not grudge the time. She could not have too much of the river, and, having no fear of the water herself, was unmoved when her pupils caught crabs, swung their punts round in midstream again and again till everyone, punter and all, was hysterical with laughter, or bumped the noses of their canoes full tilt into the rushy banks. She only had one casualty, and that was a clumsy girl who let herself get stuck with one foot in a punt and one on shore and sank down at last between the two into deep water. She fished her out and reported the matter at once to Miss Barrington, on Eleanor's advice, instead of hushing it up, and gained, for that and her constant calm, a very great deal of admiration. Both the club and she grew immensely popular.

A discussion arose as to the form which should be taken by the annual entertainment in aid of the local hospital. The usual concert or play seemed somehow stale, and the very idea of a bazaar set everyone groaning. Hilary's suggestion of a Regatta was received with a tempered enthusiasm which grew more intense as it was thought about. Miss Barrington deliberated; then went to the Board; weighed pros and cons for a week, and then allowed it.

Then Hilary hit on the plan of asking Henry, now a member of the Cambridge crew, to come and judge the various events.

"Henry? That's one of the boys who used to spend their holidays with you?" Eleanor queried, having, as usual, been the first recipient of the idea.

"'M . . . I haven't seen him for ages, but we've written once or twice lately, and I believe he would."

"You'll have," Eleanor said positively, "to say he's your brother."

"Goodness, why? Besides," Hilary protested, "heaps of people know I haven't any brothers!"

"You go and ask L.J. and see what she says about it," Eleanor advised. "You *may* get away with it, being so much in favour as you are; but don't go off the deep end if she refuses point blank."

Hilary went, and was tickled almost beyond restraint by the sight of Miss Barrington struggling with, on the one hand, a lively appreciation of the lure Henry would be to the visitors and therefore to her Box Office, and on the other a quaking doubt as to the wisdom of introducing anything male under sixty among her flock. In the end, the Box Office won.

"But you must understand, Miss Moore, that I depend on your good sense to do nothing - *nothing* - which would be a bad example to the girls. There must be no question of your being seen alone with this young man."

"Alone with him? But," Hilary said, "I've known him since I was so high! He's just like a brother, even though he isn't one!"

Miss Barrington's chin went down on her chest and her lips tightened. I'm not questioning your - er - moral character. The matter is simply one of example, nothing else. With girls on the verge of womanhood, one cannot be too careful. It must not be said that anything - anyone - connected with the school puts ideas into their heads."

Hilary said, "I'll be terribly careful. I do think it would draw people to have him, don't you, Miss Barrington, if he'll come? We could get Mr. Fry - or someone else on the Board - to take charge of him, and, you know, I shall be far too busy to see anything of him at all!"

She was so eager for the success of the project that she

forgot even to be afraid of Miss Barrington's eyes; which indeed were inwards, calculating the impression the school could make, and not on Hilary except as on a cog in the machinery of success. Miss Barrington said at length, "As long as that's understood, we shall be very glad to see your friend. I'll leave the actual arrangement to you, Miss Moore."

Henry, in an amused little letter, agreed to come. He would be in London then, so it would not be too difficult.

As a lure, he surpassed all expectation. The school bought autograph albums by the dozen. The staff talked of little else and twitted Hilary until she longed to knock their heads together.

She grumbled to Eleanor, "Anyone would think they hadn't a brother between them, the way they behave!"

Eleanor said, "I don't suppose they have. People with brothers - decent brothers, not the superior sort - don't become assistant mistresses at secondary schools. They either get married or do something less henny."

Hilary wondered if that was true. She found, on inquiry, that, in this case at any rate, it was. But she had no time either to wonder or to be irritated very much.

She watched the weather forecasts anxiously for a week; and the morning of the regatta dawned, gloriously fine, grillingly hot, a perfect river day.

The school, its parents and its friends, turned out in force to watch the novelty. Hilary's friendly boatman, as well as the hospital, must have made a handsome haul from the letting of seats for them, on the banks, and on old river barges brought up from heaven knew where. They sat in

143

their flowery dresses, under gay sunshades, eating ices and listening to music by the school orchestra, for all the world as at a miniature May Week.

"All because you dared to be seen in a whiff in your gym dress on a Sunday morning!" Eleanor laughed.

Hilary had not dared to go to the station to meet Henry, after Miss Barrington's warning. Instead, she watched him descend solemnly from Mr. Fry's car, and be conducted, resplendent in white flannels and azure blazer, into the enclosure reserved for the Board and the other big-wigs. Only when he had been introduced all round and stood waiting to begin his official duties did she catch the Head's eye and go in to greet him.

He was different from the Henry she remembered: taller, stronger, even more sunburnt; but still quiet and scholarly, with a look of Gregory about him which made her catch her breath. After all, he had had a lively admiration for his old schoolmaster at a very impressionable age.

They shook hands, under a fire of observation, exchanged a word or two, then went together along the bank. He looked this way and that to make sure they were out of earshot, then shed his company manners and lapsed into schoolboy indignation. "I was looking for you at the station - what on earth did you send that pompous old geyser along for?"

"Send him along? He went!" Hilary gasped. "I'm very small beer here except in a boat, you know, and he's the Chairman of the Board! You're frightfully honoured to get him!"

"He's honoured to get me!" Henry corrected, and Hilary

laughed. She might have remembered his lack of reverence. "I suppose he's the local candlestick-maker when he's at home!"

"Brewer. At least, he owns the brewery. And as the town exists for the making of beer, he's an important person."

"Why didn't you come, too?"

"Nobody asked me. Besides - " she waved a comprehensive arm - "I had to see to all this! Nobody here knows the first thing about rivers, except as places where, very occasionally, you sit in a boat and let a man row you up to the old mill for tea. Look, here's your punt. The 'old geyser' is coming with you, I'm afraid. Two geysers in fact. That's why you had an awning, for their, bald pates, not for your own elegant locks!" Henry smoothed them absently, with no effect at all; they were on end on the top of his head as they had always been.

She punted him, and the two elders who had elected to help him, to the position from which she thought they would get the best view, and tied them to a stump. Henry left the others under the green awning and came and stood with her on the platform while she told him, shortly, what she wanted him to do.

They made a pleasant couple for the crowd to see; both fair and sunburnt, both beautifully made, he with a gentleness about his manhood, she, feminine enough but with a hint of gallant boyishness. They might well have passed for brother and sister, did so, indeed, with the less inquiring of the onlookers. Their easy familiarity added to this impression. Even Miss Barrington, watching them at first with the eye of a lynx, was satisfied that the idea in her girls' heads would not be polluted. The gossip-mongers turned elsewhere for inspiration. There was plainly nothing to interest them there.

Small girls, then rather bigger girls, raced in rob-roys, their faces tense, their paddles going round like windmills. Hilary shepherded competitors to the start and set them going. The three men in the punt bent seriously over their notebooks, the spectators craned their necks and cheered their offspring on. Miss Barrington realized thankfully that the afternoon was going to run itself with no help from her, and settled down to chat with the more influential of the parents.

Teams of Red Indians, in feathers and ochre, raced grimly in Canadian canoes, and the three who came in first paraded in front of the judges for comments on their style. Hilary could not help being pleased when the team from her own form, the trio and three others, were pronounced easy winners and as nearly perfect as a Red Indian team could be. They had been her first river pupils, and were so keen that they deserved recognition.

The double and single scullers were not allowed to race. It was said to be too strenuous for growing girls. They processed up and down for judgement of strength and style, and processed again in order of merit. Most of them really sculled beautifully. The last pair created some amusement by catching crabs which sent first one and then the other over backwards and would have upset the boat but for the steadiness of their cox, who leaned out at the appropriate time and place, as nonchalantly as Hilary herself might have done, and righted it again. "We thought as we couldn't be perfectly good we'd give a demonstration of how bad we could be without falling out," they told Hilary blandly when she reproached them, and watched to see her laugh. They could always make her laugh and they knew it. If ever they failed they knew there were storms ahead.

A picked team of good swimmers showed exactly what would happen in the case of an accident. First a rowing boat came along, with three girls dressed up as ladies of uncertain age (one of them terribly like Miss Tindal Smith, Hilary noticed with dismay). Two of them rowed, their elbows sticking out, their blades chopping first the air and then the water, banging against each other because neither of them kept any sort of time. Stroke turned round and harangued bow, her hat cocked over one eye, her spectacles sliding off her nose. "*One - two* . . . *One -* two . . . Bend - stretch - *can't* you follow me?" Those were Hilary's own accents, and half the school recognized them and went into fits of laughter. Hilary herself, standing by in the boatman's dinghy, shook an admonitory fist. Bow, more agitated than ever, worked her oars at a tremendous pace. Cox gave a great heave to the wrong line and slewed them round into the bank, where they stopped and engaged in shrill altercation. Bow refused to row any more. Cox said: "All right, if you don't like the way I steer you can change places with me!" And they proceeded to do so, while the spectators held their breath.

They both stood up at the same minute, both decided to pass stroke on the same side, glared at each other, and toppled into the river shrieking. Stroke, grabbing vainly at them, capsized the boat neatly on the other side.

A punt, apparently empty, tied up under the bank, sprang into life. Heads bobbed up. Three divers went in swiftly over the edge with hardly a splash. Two of them grasped one each of the spluttering ladies and towed her to shore. The third lady, after a frenzied waving of the arms, jerked herself safely into a lifebuoy which Hilary threw from the dinghy. The third rescuer, baulked of her prey, collected the boat and the oars and pushed them before her to the landing stage. The rescued were hauled up the bank, submitted to a course of artificial respiration, given hot drinks and carried away on stretchers, all with the greatest dispatch.

"We insist that they shall all be able to swim really well before they're allowed to go in a boat at all," Miss Barrington was telling her neighbour. "And the seniors must be able to life-save as well. No, they never go without at least one mistress in the party. There's really no possibility of accidents . . . We're extraordinarily lucky in that new History mistress of ours - doesn't mind how much time she gives up to them charming - most talented - splendid influence on the girls . . . "

All Hilary saw was that the Head and several other ladies had their heads together confidentially and were looking at her as the Head spoke. Neither of her ears was burning - but their expressions were envying more than venomous, so she hoped it was all right. The Fifth forms had started on their historical pageant - Mary Queen of Scots escaping to her island and being hauled away again by her captors. They did it well, infusing an air of stealth and terror into it which the onlookers readily caught.

Then there were speeches and prizes, thanks and congratulations, and then it was over and the people swarming away. It had all gone swimmingly with never a hitch.

Hilary had decided that she could not invite Henry to her bed-sitting room. So she had asked Eleanor if they might come, both of them, to the little house for part of the evening. It had seemed the obvious thing to do, now that she spent so much of her own time there, and Eleanor, after one small, surprised glance, had agreed. The surprise was so momentary that it escaped Hilary's notice altogether.

Henry had to sign scores of autograph albums and talk to dozens of interested parents. But at last they got away, and found Eleanor in the garden waiting for them, with the most inviting cold meal ready, ending up with raspberries and cream. They tucked into it like a couple of schoolboys, talking over the afternoon whenever their mouths were not too full to prevent them. Henry was enthusiastic. For girls to be really competent in boats was unusual, then, and he saw no reason for this.

"Ordinary games are all right - they give you the team spirit and all that - but there's something brutal about them. *I* don't think they're awfully suitable for girls. I suppose you'll flay me for that, but look at the frightful females they produce when they're carried too far - the ones who go in for county hockey till they're fifty, loud voices, giggles, and jab you in the ribs with an elbow and lurch about if you say anything they think's a bit funny. A friend of mine's got a sister like that: I simply cut and run when I see her coming - her and her friends - and so does

149

her brother . . ." He looked at Hilary's sunny good looks with approval and took no notice of Eleanor at all.

Hilary murmured that it was not fair to take extreme types as examples.

"It's the type these sport-mad girls' schools tend to produce. The kids like it, of course. There'll be more and more of such places unless they take warning! Anyway, on the river you can get the team spirit by having definite boats for definite forms or something like that; and over it all there's that calm that the water gives one (I don't know anything else that does): one comes away feeling gracious and peaceful, even though one may have been sculling like blazes or getting the punt pole stuck in the mud!"

Hilary said, "Isn't it just something to do with getting close to nature?"

He caught her up: "Getting the better of nature's a whole lot healthier than getting the better of a crowd of other fighting sweaty people with a ball!"

Eleanor laughed. "And here's the whole staff gnashing because you've been clever enough to hit on a successful novelty which makes you indispensable to the Head! None of them has the remotest conception that the river's not a novelty to you, but a religion! I hadn't myself!"

She rose as she spoke and moved into the house.

Henry said, "I say, is she shocked?"

"What on earth would she be shocked at?" Hilary asked.

"Oh, I don't know - some people don't like the word sweaty! Or she might object to my views on girls and games."

"I don't think so. I think she's just gone because she's got things to do," Hilary said. But she knew that she had no idea, really, whether Eleanor was likely to be shocked or not. She had seen so little of her in the company of other people.

It seemed to Hilary that she had neither heard nor told one half of what was absolutely necessary by the time Henry had to go. She made Eleanor come with them to the station, because of Miss Barrington's warning. The older woman spoke little all the way, answered Henry in monosyllables when he tried to draw her in, until at last the unease of her mood filtered through the gaiety of the other two and dried up their flow of talk, so that it came in spurts, stiltedly, and finally died out altogether. Hilary was actually glad when the train came in and Henry's long form disappeared into it.

He leaned out and looked down at them. "I believe I've stayed too long and tired you out!"

Hilary seized on the excuse thankfully. "I am tired - but you haven't stayed too long! You've no idea, the work the thing took - and then there was a certain anxiety as to whether it was going to march or not! I knew it would be visited on me if it didn't, you see! But I'm sorry it's made me bad company!"

He smiled, "It's only just begun to! Home and bed for you, right away! I shall see you in the Vac if I go - down there?" She nodded. "I'll be there!"

Before they could go into detail the train drew out. Hilary and Eleanor walked home almost in silence. For Hilary it was a crowded, happy silence, full of bits of childhood which she could remember now, all of a sudden, without pain, of glittering ripples on water, flashing drips from the tips of sculls, the eager faces of the girls. She hardly noticed Eleanor until they came to the little honeysuckled house and switched on the light in the sitting-room. Then she turned to her - "Hasn't it been a heavenly day?"

But Eleanor did not respond. She stood plucking at the papers on the table, her expression so hurt and indrawn that Hilary cried out in dismay, "Why, my dear, whatever's the matter? Are you simply dead to the world?"

She shook her head. "No, I'm not tired," and wandered over to the window.

Hilary persisted. "What is it, then? Have I done something horrible?" She searched frenziedly round her mind. She could not remember anything; but then, she couldn't remember half the things which had happened during the afternoon. Had Eleanor been shocked? "Didn't you like having Henry here? I thought I was showing off something so nice to you in having him!"

Eleanor appeared to be wrestling with herself. "P'raps I was bored," she said.

Hilary was distressed. "But how awful of us, to bore you. We did talk a lot of stuff about home. I'm most terribly sorry."

Eleanor said dully, "You couldn't help it." There was a long pause, Hilary instinctively waiting for more. It came, when Eleanor had flung herself into the little round chair. She sat looking up to the ceiling, her head on the cushion.

"I'm never at ease with young men. Any men, for that matter. I don't know how to treat them or what to say."

Hilary said cheerfully, "Just the same things that you'd

152

say to young women," and Eleanor smiled and shook her head.

"I was brought up in a silly way, I think," she said. "There was nothing which frightened my parents quite as much as sex. It disgusted them. They wouldn't talk about it - wouldn't tell us about it - wouldn't give us a chance to learn about it - and so, when we began to go about alone, they were simply terrified we should 'get into trouble'. Their safeguard was to drum into us, as early as I can remember - and earlier, I expect, if the psychologists are right - that no nice girl was ever seen speaking to a boy. Also that one never did behind one's mother's back what one would not do in front of her face. So that way of escape was cut off. I didn't question either the one rule or the other, I just imbibed them both and acted on them. So did my sisters. So did several other people at my school who'd been brought up in the same way. We just despised anyone who thought differently; obviously, if they did, they weren't nice girls. We could afford to despise them; we were leaders, hard workers, good at games. At Cambridge it was the same. And we'd got authority on our side, of course; the University didn't want to be turned into a marriage market. People who flirted were letting the women's colleges down. People who had brothers up and saw a lot of them were sailing near the wind. I hardly ever saw a young man to speak to. Now, as I say, I don't know what to say to them. Feel as if I was doing something wrong all the time - at forty! It's villainous, to bring up a girl like that! I'm sorry I was uncouth with your friend, Hilary. But that's the explanation. You've never seen me

153

badly at a loss before, have you?"

Hilary touched her hand gently with one finger. "It's rotten luck. We simply had to talk to boys, all the time, of course, with Father teaching at a boys' school. But we never thought of them specially as boys, or ourselves specially as girls - we did all the same things, pretty well. It didn't seem to matter which we were."

Eleanor was looking at her curiously. She went on hurriedly, she did not quite know why. "I wish I could dig out the reasons for the things I do, as you can!"

The dimple came in Eleanor's cheek. It was blessed to be reverenced so much that one wasn't despised even for one's little confessions. She said bitterly, "People make jokes about school-marms being school-marmy. It isn't our faults, it's our parents'. If they hadn't brought us up like that we shouldn't be school-marms!"

"You put an awful lot of blame on parents, don't you?" Hilary said.

Eleanor snapped out, "All of it. We're as they make us. Warped, most of us."

Hilary said, "No. If a child's got guts, it'll pull straight again. And be all the better person that it's had something to go through. Tempered, like steel. Isn't that true?"

Eleanor sighed. "Steel's not human flesh."

Hilary saw what she meant. She was like steel - unadaptable; like steel she must spring back to her original form even after she had been bent. She felt suddenly that she had a great deal to make up to Eleanor. "I believe if you saw lots of Henries you'd soon not think twice about them. What did you say to me about courage being experience?"

154

Eleanor grunted, "It's too late, now," but Hilary went on: "It's all rubbish, saying they're different. The children here are just like Father's little boys. And you're - " the note of reverence gladdened Eleanor again - "awfully like my father in lots of ways."

"And your mother? And L.J. and all the other measly lot of them?" Eleanor teased. Hilary was glad, because she could tease again, had lost some of her grimness.

She said, "I expect there are men to correspond with them. There was a Games master awfully like Hornibrook - and a Maths master quite like T.S. As for Mother, we always thought she'd have made a better man than woman - more scope! Let's make Henry come and see us often, then you'll get used to him!"

7

After the regatta, things settled down into the ordinary routine again. Janet and her scholarship work were Hilary's chief interest apart from Eleanor. Janet had pluck and a good brain, but she was diffident. It was easy to understand her fears when one came to know her family. Her environment was almost the antithesis of Hilary's own. All her life she had been sheltered from every unpleasantness, given everything she wanted, praised always and never blamed. It was natural for her to shrink from rough games, snubs and uncongenial work, be discontented if she was not admired. Natural, too, when one saw the fine stuff of which her parents were made, that she should overcome her timidity to such an extent as to excel at the very things she feared, attack the very things which repelled her. It was like seeing a dragon-fly on the marshes struggling out of its ugly, confining shell, to watch the girl develop. Hilary watched her with fascination, derived some inspiration herself from watching, and felt it a privilege to be able, now and then, to offer a helping hand.

At the end of term, Miss Barrington formally congratulated her on her first year at the school. There had been marked progress, she said, in History; there was little doubt, from what she had heard from the examiners, that Janet would get her scholarship, and the school had not carried off a big one for many years; the boating club had been a great success. In short, Miss Moore was just the type of mistress she required and she hoped to keep her for a very long time.

Hilary could not think of anything to say but a bare, "Thank you." She was considering the queerness of a person who could be so bound up with an undertaking such as the school as to base her likes and dislikes simply on one's value to it. Or rather, to have no likes and dislikes, but simply tools and junk. The junk was quickly thrown out. Miss Farrisey had turned out to be junk. She was going. She talked too much and looked too frivolous. Hilary remembered envying Miss Farrisey. She still envied her, a bit, for the calm with which she had taken the intimation that she would do well to resign.

The next day, Eleanor came home with Hilary to the Red

Cottage. Hilary had frankly hated being away from her during the Easter holiday, and this time she said so.

To her surprise, for she always thought of herself as the leaner and Eleanor the oak, Eleanor said, "Well, let's do something about it. I never knew I could miss anyone as I missed you then - it was like toothache, I couldn't get away from it. Makes one understand what sloppy novelists mean when they talk about tugging at somebody's heart-strings - it really did feel like that." She grinned sheepishly, and Hilary, who had been taken in so completely by her gruffness and her cynical talk as not to credit her with feelings, cried out, "Why, Eleanor! I never thought of your missing me! I simply don't believe it!"

Eleanor said simply, "Why not? You've dug yourself in pretty thoroughly, haven't you? Anyway, I'm not a bit anxious to face eight weeks without you, so it's just as well you spoke. I didn't want to tag on, or I'd have mentioned it myself."

Hilary gasped, "Eleanor! *You*, tagging on! You perfect idiot, you know you couldn't possibly!" Such humility only made her reverence Eleanor more; think of her more, too; she fitted Eleanor's name to the tune made by the whirr of her bicycle wheels, the drop of the bath tap, the lilt of any air she happened to hear. The birds sang it when they woke her in the morning.

So, for the first weeks of the summer holiday, she showed Eleanor South Devon. Rose Moore grumbled a bit, but Hilary, not afraid of her any more, pointed out loftily that she was already sending her mother half her salary and was willing to contribute a little more, temporarily, for the pleasure of having her friend with her. When they did arrive, she caught her mother pointing her out to a new resident in the village with such an air that she realized that Rose was actually proud of her. She laughed quite a lot about that.

Hermione took to Eleanor at once, shook off her languid ill health and went for long days out with them and was all the better for it. She had stayed at home ever since Gregory's death, a pale, nervous ghost of a girl with no interests outside the narrow ones of the Red Cottage, and an education which had stopped abruptly at the age of fourteen.

Hilary did not worry about her; accepted her, as she did everyone, as she was, and thought her frailness a sufficient excuse for her lack of enterprise. What could she possibly do but stay at home and be glad there was a home to stay in?

Eleanor, after a few days' observation, differed sharply from her. "You ought to get her away from your mother," she insisted, "while she's still young enough to develop. I don't believe there's anything physically wrong with her at all. Take her to a doctor and see, if you don't believe me. Your mother simply drains her vitality - keeps her an invalid because, inside, she likes to have her so. As Mr. Barrett did Elizabeth Browning. Your mother's the sort of woman who ought to have had a baby once a year for as long as she could and then gone on to looking after her grandchildren. She'd have been happy, then. D'you mind my talking about her like this?"

Hilary said absently, "No, of course not. I've talked about

her pretty frankly to you, haven't I?" She was searching back in her mind for verification of Eleanor's theories and finding it abundantly. "It's perfectly true."

"And poor little Hermione's just the victim of her rampageous maternal instinct." Eleanor was so much in earnest that she got up and strode about the shore. Hilary had never seen her so wound-up about anything. "Girls ought not to be mothered after they're about twelve. They ought to be turned out to stand on their own legs. Your mother's the type to go on mothering till she's eighty and Hermione's over fifty and then die and leave the poor thing stranded, incapable even of looking after herself, much less of doing a job for anyone else. Haven't you seen them? Poor boneless spinsters, living in cheap boarding-houses, trailing about with no interest in the world but their own ill health. Simply the victims of their mothers' lust for power. I've seen them go into mental asylums, even . . . And that's what Hermione'll turn into!"

Hilary objected, "I don't know what you mean by mothering. We've never, either of us, had any real affection from Mother. Except when we were babies, p'raps: I have got a memory of her kissing Hermione, over and over again, when she was a very little thing. I was jealous. But apart from that, she's been - well, 'harsh' expresses it best, I think. Unless we were ill. I never was ill."

Eleanor sat down and stretched her thin arms above her head. "All that only bears out what I've said. They're almost entirely animal, women like that. Their real instinct is for babies. If they can't get babies, they'll spend themselves on weak things. And if they can't get weak things, they make

159

them. That's why they're dangerous."

Hilary was gravely digesting this new point of view, fitting the jigsaw pieces of her family's life with uncanny accuracy into Eleanor's picture.

"She ought to have married some rumbumptious country squire instead of my father," she remarked.

Eleanor nodded. "She married a child instead of a mate." Hilary said presently, "And what do you want to do about Hermione?"

Eleanor spread out her hands. "It's difficult, isn't it? The only practicable plan I can think of is to send her abroad, to some family where she can help in the house and learn the language. France'd be best. Then she could get a job as a French mistress in a small school. Another possibility's a Domestic Science diploma, which I don't suppose she could afford. Or nursing - but she'd never stand the strain of that unless she simply had to . . ."

Hilary said, "And what about Mother? You're proposing to deprive her even of her Peter Pan - "

Eleanor shrugged. "All my sympathy's with the child. Your mother would find some activity, even if it was only a cat. They always do."

Hilary, struggling with a feeling that her mother and Hermione were safer, as far as she herself was concerned, together than apart, said, "You'd better talk to her. To Hermione, I mean."

But Hermione, when the idea was put to her, listened in silence, and in the afternoon excused herself from going out with them, saying she was too tired. In the evening Rose Moore descended on them like a fury. What did they mean by upsetting the poor child? Just because they were strong and healthy themselves, they couldn't understand that there were people who needed care. Didn't they realize that Hermione would be dead but for the way her mother looked after her? Did they grudge the poor little thing such comfort as she had, that they must try to push her out into the world to kill herself? If Hilary did not see her way to continuing to help her own sister, she herself would go out charing, to-morrow, and work her fingers to the bone.

She would not listen to Eleanor. She shouted them down and flounced into the kitchen.

Hilary, half laughing, said, "You see what it's like. You might as well try to argue with a thunderstorm. I ought to have remembered that Hermione always blabs to her."

Then, in the second week of the holidays, came the unbelieveable rumour, swiftly confirmed - war.

It hit them lightly in the Devonshire village. A few sons of the larger houses on the outskirts appeared in khaki; one or two older men remembered that they were reservists and went off; there was a lot of heated talk - and that was all. Why worry? It would be over in a few weeks. Meanwhile, there was fruit to be picked, ripening corn to be got in. Henry wrote to Hilary, joyously, to say that he was going into a training-camp at once, and Hilary was sorry, because it meant that she would not see him.

When Eleanor had gone to her own home, life was incredibly empty. Incredible, too, that this, tinkering with household jobs, walking on the moor, bickering in the cottage, had once been all Hilary's life and had satisfied her.

She wondered if all households narrowed so when they had no man about them.

A letter from Janet was a breath from the world. She had got her scholarship and was touchingly grateful for Hilary's help. Hilary wrote warmly - so warmly that she had another letter by return and wondered if she had said too much, then reflected that Janet was not a pupil any more and could grow into a friend if both of them felt inclined for it. She was glad about that.

Joining Eleanor seemed like going back to life, although the country Vicarage was not really any more lively than the country cottage. The mere fact that it was Eleanor's home made it appear in a rosy light.

School, in that first year of the war, was much as it had been before, Girls carried knitting about with them and took an interest in maps, the news in the papers lent a spice to life, nothing more.

But as the year wore on, changes came. Elder girls' brothers, younger girls' fathers even, were joining up. Kitchener's Army was coming into being. Others than regular soldiers and territorials began to go to France - and not to come back. Food was dull and difficult to get.

In spite of these things the outstanding event of the year for Hilary was centred not on the war but on Eleanor. Coming into the little house one day at tea-time, she found Eleanor pale and unwilling to move, on the wicker settee which was the sitting-room's nearest approach to comfort. She admitted to a tummy-ache, would have nothing to eat, and after a sip at her tea was suddenly sick. She looked so alarmingly ill that Hilary took matters into her own hands and went out, her heart pounding, for a doctor.

Eleanor took this with surprising calm. "I knew I should have to have her. If you never are ill, you know jolly well when something's got you. When's she coming?"

Hilary paused in the act of slipping a hot-water bottle into its case. "She? I went to Dr. Ryan. You know, the man who lives a few doors away from the school. We saw him come out one day and you said you liked his face."

Eleanor said, "That's no reason for letting him come and paw me. You've seen Dr. Hill - Isobel Hill - at school; why on earth didn't you get her? Her face is all right, if you must be ruled by faces!"

Hilary looked blank. "I never even thought of her. I know she inspects the brats, but they're not ill. I can't imagine a woman tackling a real illness - giving orders and calming people down as Dr. Tomkins used to at home. Just because I've always had a man, I suppose."

Eleanor said, "Well, you'd better go and ring up Doctor what's his name - Ryan - and tell him we don't want him after all. And then get on to Dr. Hill. I won't have a man messing me about, and that's flat. Tell Dr. Hill to come soon; I've about had enough of this pain."

Hilary lingered to say, "You're sure you haven't picked up a green gooseberry or something and swallowed it, in the garden?"

Eleanor looked unutterable snorts. "Would I? How old d'you think I am? Get along, there's a good kid, or that man'll be on us and I shall have the unpleasantness of refusing to see him."

Hilary relinquished the hope that he would come before

he could be put off. She hated the idea of trusting anything as precious as Eleanor to a woman. To her, illness meant pneumonia - or her father. She said, "I think you're silly. I'm sure Dr. Tomkins never thought whether a person who was ill was a man or a woman or a canary. They were just sick, and it was his job to make them better and he did. So why should you mind, if the doctor doesn't?"

Eleanor said vigorously, "Well, I do." Hilary gave up the skirmish and went out. She wished she could have telephoned, but she was frightened of the instrument, being unused to it. She gave both her messages, hurriedly, and rushed back. She hated leaving Eleanor alone in pain.

Dr. Hill, when she did come, proved so kind and confident that Hilary's bump of admiration was stirred again. Silly of her, she told herself, to think that merely being a woman made anyone less efficient than being a man. It was education that counted, not sex. Even when the doctor said, in a perfectly matter-of-fact tone, that Eleanor had appendicitis and must be operated on as soon as might be, she believed her, instead of demanding a second opinion.

This was partly, no doubt, because Eleanor simply grunted and said, "I thought it was. My sister had it, a few years ago. Appendices run in families, like noses, don't they?"

She was whisked off to the cottage hospital and operated on that same evening. Hilary lived through a more dreadful three days than she had ever experienced. There was no merciful deadening of her pain by shock, as there had been after Gregory's death. This time imagination could, and did, run rife - how could anyone possibly get better, looking as awful as Eleanor did? Why couldn't they give her something to buck her up, instead of letting her lie there half asleep? Why hadn't she insisted - insisted, whatever Eleanor had said - on a proper doctor instead of that woman, who had even gone so far as to call in another woman to operate and had given the anaesthetic herself? How could she herself live if Eleanor died? One did, of course. But she could not face the misery of it again.

The girls were charming to her. Their various devotions among themselves, and their fondness for Hilary, made their sympathy very understanding. There was something romantic, to them, in the friendship between the two mistresses who were, perhaps, respected more than any others.

Then, after three days, Eleanor had her tube out and slid into convalescence, and Hilary's fears went into the background. Her days were shaped, now, round her visits to the hospital. Everything else was mechanical. When Eleanor showed gratitude for her attentions, she was amazed, for the visits were paid entirely for her own pleasure.

When the necessary three weeks in hospital were over, Eleanor went back to the little house and Hilary went with her, to be there in case she needed help. She did not; she got well very quickly. But Hilary stayed on. Neither of them could bear the idea of living alone again, having once grown used to being together.

It was during Eleanor's first week at home that Henry came; in uniform, looking ridiculously smart, and very brown and spare and strong. He was in high spirits, kept exploding into jokes, more mannish jokes than had been habitual to him. He was going to France very soon. Thrilled? Of course. Young Kenneth had joined up too, and was on Salisbury Plain. He talked as though the whole thing was an exciting game.

Only, when Hilary went in from the garden to get tea ready, he came with her, leaving Eleanor lying in her deck-chair alone.

"Aren't I ever going to see you away from that old crone?" he demanded.

"Henry! She isn't!" Hilary stood back from him, her colour high, her small breasts heaving with indignation under her bright green linen dress. She was beautiful - vivid, young and very strong.

Henry grumbled, "All right - she isn't. I only meant, can't we get away by ourselves for a bit?"

Hilary, who was not placated, said quite sincerely, "What for? She doesn't mind our burbling." She turned to her cutting of bread-and-butter, and he watched her.

He tried again presently. "It's just - it's not - all jam out there, Hilary. One's talked to people who have come back."

Hilary, who had not, raised shining eyes. "Not jam, exactly - but wonderful . . . Eleanor and I have been cursing in concert that we aren't men . . . She always does - I don't except for this. But no - you can't think how I envy you!"

He came towards her; but she misunderstood his purpose, not coquettishly but just because she was thinking of other things; said, "Thanks, very much", and handed him a tray to carry. 'Old crone!' - was that how people thought of

Eleanor?

Henry gave it up, then. Perhaps he was not quite sure exactly what he did want of her - some sort of encouragement and comfort. After all, when they had been alone together before, they had been little more than children, and done little more than talk. He carried the tray into the garden and set it on the table.

He did not stay long after tea. Hilary did say regretfully,

"I wish I could come to the station with you. But it's the maid's day out, and I don't like to leave Eleanor alone."

The following week he went to France.

Some days after he had gone, Hilary found the girl she had always liked least in her form in tears in the cloakroom, and asked her, impulsively, what was the matter, expecting to hear of a squabble with a friend or a snub from a prefect.

Instead, the girl said dully, "It's my brother. He's - killed," and relapsed again into shuddering sobs. She looked up again presently to say, "I know I oughtn't to be doing this. I know it's really 'business as usual'. But I simply couldn't help it. I'll - go back to my form-room in a minute."

Hilary found things to say to her, somehow, and presently the girl had control of herself again. She said, "I'm glad it was you, Miss Moore. I couldn't have *borne* any other mistress to speak to me."

Even then, the first thought that came into Hilary's head was gladness that even this girl, to whom she had never been attracted, thought of her as a friend. She was proud of her success with the girls; partly because it seemed to echo her father's relations with his boys, but more, lately, because it satisfied Eleanor's standards. Eleanor could not bear inefficiency of any kind.

It was her first intimate contact with the losses of war. She told herself, "That may happen to Henry. Henry may be killed, any day - may have been already", and then, that people like Henry did not get killed: he was too cautious, too steady, not one of those who ran foolishly into danger without a thought. But tell herself what she might, the possibility did not go beyond her reason. There was no stark fear for Henry, no physical pain which she could not get away from, as there had been during that three days of Eleanor's illness.

8

It was about this time, too, that she heard from Janet; doubtfully, at first - was it fair, to stay comfortably working at Cambridge when there were Waac's and Wren's, V.A.D.'s and the Land Army, crying out for recruits? Hilary could only repeat to her Gregory's advice to herself over the matter of Women's Suffrage, knowing that the situation this time was different. Janet knew it, too. Her next letter was more definite. She had asked the University authorities if they would hold over her scholarship till the war was over, and they had replied that they would not. She had asked her father what he thought about it - and he said she must do as she thought best. And, after a lot of thought, she had decided to throw up the scholarship and become a

V.A.D. She was coming down in a day or two. Might she come and talk to Hilary about it as soon as ever she could?

She was bubbling with excitement when she did come. "I expect I'm silly. I expect there are heaps of people who could do it better then me. But I felt such a *worm* stuck away up there when there were things to do. I couldn't bear it, somehow . . . It didn't seem to affect most of them so much - perhaps they liked college life better than I did."

"Didn't you like it?" Hilary asked, interested.

"I was disappointed. They're so schoolgirlish. Much more thrilled about calling people a year ahead of them by Christian names than in making their minds work . . . Silly and gossipy and keen on this person one week and that one another . . . Busy being funny and bright . . . It didn't seem proper, with all this going on. There were some decent ones, of course. Two, who are joining up with me, I really do like . . . Even the work wasn't as exciting as I'd thought it would be. None of the lecturers is a patch on you as a teacher, Hilary."

"And you think you're going to enjoy - messing about in hospital wards?" Hilary asked. They were alone now; Eleanor had gone to lie down after lunch.

Janet looked solemn, at that. "No, I don't think I shall enjoy it a bit. In fact, now I've made up my mind, I'm funking it most horribly. But I'd rather do it than - feel a worm."

That was just like Janet.

"You don't think I'm an ass, do you?" she asked.

Hilary said forcibly, "I do not. You're following a star - no one can do better than that. Most people haven't the courage for it."

Janet flushed with pleasure and began, in a hurry, to chatter about uniform. It was not until she rose to go that she said, "Hilary, I do wish most frightfully that you could come too."

Hilary jumped. She had been wishing the same thing. But Janet's putting it into words seemed to convert the dream into a possibility. If Janet went - why shouldn't she? They stood looking at each other, Hilary reviewing pros and cons, Janet watching her.

Hilary said at last. "The trouble would be the money. You don't get paid, do you?"

"Not at first. They're hoping to attach us to something later so that we shall get our expenses at least . . . Hilary, do."

Hilary said, "I must think about it. There *are* things that get paid. You've made me feel a worm, too."

Janet grinned. "I'm not a bit sorry, if it makes you come."

Hilary did not broach the question to Eleanor until she had made some inquiries. Munition-workers, of course, were paid well. But she hankered for something less confined than that. Waacs and Wrens were paid, and some of the lorry drivers - Hilary rather fancied herself driving a lorry. She heard that the Gym mistress, who had a car already, was going to drive one. She had a post card from Miss Farissey, who was helping to run a canteen "Somewhere in France". Frivolous Farrisey - and lovely, timid Janet!

She said to Eleanor, "I'll have to go, I think. It seems awful not to, when I'm so strong and fit."

Eleanor said, "D'you know anything about the work you'd have to do?"

"Not a thing. But everyone'll be in the same boat. It's not skilled work, any of it. Only common sense."

Eleanor clasped her bony hands round her knees. "I've been thinking about this a lot," she said. "For me as well as for you. I doubt if they'd have me, so soon after my operation. They'd have you all right, any of the women's things. Jump at you."

"Then you think I ought to go?" Hilary put in joyously. She had rather expected opposition from Eleanor. "Which one of them do you think 'ud be best?"

"No," Eleanor said. "Honestly, I don't."

Hilary felt like a punctured balloon. "Oh, Eleanor - why?"

"'Tisn't as if school teachers weren't wanted. Or as if you were only an ordinary medium sort of one like most of them. Like Farrisey. You're far above the average as a teacher, and you're good for the girls as a person. If you went out there, you'd just be one of a crowd, scrubbing floors very likely, anyway doing things someone with no brains and no personality could do as well or better. Someone's got to stay and educate the generation who'll have to clear up the mess. Oughtn't it to be the very best of us, not the poor ones who can't do anything else?"

She paused. "I'm not trying to flatter you. I'm just telling you what I think. There's another thing, too. You've got a good job here, and a certain one, as long as you choose to stay. You've got a distinguished future, if you play your cards properly. You could get the plums, and you ought to take them, not shirk. Goodness knows the teaching profession's in need of good people . . . While if you go off looking for excitement - isn't that all it is, honestly? - they won't keep your job open for you. I found out about that, when the Head was here the other day; and they're not encouraging people to go. You're good at your work, but not good enough to throw it up for a year - two years - and come back to it. The younger ones'll have stepped into your place by then. If you stay and work for an honours degree, your future's assured. If you don't - you'll be mediocre all your life. And you're not the sort of person to be satisfied with mediocrity."

Hilary was looking out of the window, her back squarely to the room.

Eleanor's voice took on a tone of entreaty. "Hilary, do think about it sanely. It's different for Janet. She isn't doing work that matters. You are . . . And what about your mother and Hermione, if you play ducks and drakes?"

Hilary's shoulders moved irritably. Was she to be hampered all her life by her mother and Hermione? What *would* happen, if she didn't go on helping them? Her mother was active - she *could* take lodgers in the cottage, if she had to. Any decent mother would, rather than sponge on a daughter who had to work for every penny she sent her. As for Hermione, she would be better if she did have to work, according to Eleanor . . . Still, it was true, she did have to think of them . . . Perhaps it *was* just excitement, change, that drew her after Janet - rivalry, even, perhaps, pique that Janet could do something that she couldn't. Stay and educate the generation that's got to clear up the mess? - perhaps that was one's drab duty, after all.

172

She turned from the wide fields where the wind was blowing to the quiet, book-lined room. I expect you're right," she said. "I expect I am - just beglamoured. I haven't done much thinking. I will, before I make up my mind."

Janet went off to London for a hurried training, the Gym mistress left at the half-term and another one came. Everyone, somehow, was twice as busy as usual, for girls came to the day-school from boarding-schools which were on the coast or which their parents could no longer afford, and there were bandage-making afternoons, knitting hours, talks on this and that connected with the war.

Eleanor came back to work, but she was not yet quite the same Eleanor as before her illness. She was glad to have small things done for her, routine things like writing letters and entering up marks, and odd jobs in the house and garden.

Hilary's war-service ambitions merged into the background of her thoughts. She really was wanted where she was, there was no doubt about it. The next term, they vanished altogether, for she was promoted to the Upper Fifth, whose form-mistress had left to look after a wounded brother; with a rise in salary and corresponding seniority among the other members of staff. In such spare time as she had she worked for her honours degree and obtained it. She had to acknowledge that she was filling a place which no one, perhaps, could have filled better. She forgot her ambitions, or smiled at them, and was content.

She loved her cell of a bedroom in Eleanor's house. The very simplicity of the house itself filled a need in her. It echoed, in its clear colours, clean lines and its austerity, the whipping stimulus of the cold sea winds which she had welcomed in her childhood. In the evenings, when work was done, she would sit on the step of the french window which led from the sitting-room to the garden. It faced westward, and in autumn showed them some lovely sunsets. She would sit with her knees drawn up, watching the changing colours of the sky, and the trees beyond the garden; listening to the quiet, broken by the joyous rush of a thrush's song, alternately scolding and enticing; by voices, muted by distance, of people playing tennis, by the muffled beat of a car's engine on the main road behind the hill. Comparing this life, so peaceful and yet so full, with the strain of her childhood, when even the golden days had held presage of disaster, she would look round into the darkening room to see Eleanor reading, tilting her book to catch the last light, and would wonder at the rush of pleasure, the sense of utter safety, which the presence of this spare, stern woman gave her. Or, the light having failed and her reading being unimportant, Eleanor would pull her chair to the window and Hilary would lean against her knee, not speaking, in deep content. She liked to picture their growing old together, quietly, so.

They had few visitors. Eleanor was not sociable, and Hilary was so happy with Eleanor that she felt no need for anyone else. Janet came, in her rare leaves, and told them tales which made even Eleanor laugh. It would have taken more than Eleanor's grimness to keep Janet away from Hilary, and Hilary loved to hear her talk. Another old girl came, once, but Eleanor's silence froze her. Eleanor spoke of her afterwards as a dull fish, and she never came again.

Neither mistresses nor girls from the High School came at all.

So the war years, with their possibility of emotional development, passed over Hilary in her backwater and left her unchanged, making hardly an impression. There were warnings of air-raids, but nothing near at hand. There were letters from Henry, full of life in the trenches, impossible to picture, perhaps because so much was left out. She heard with regret, no more, that Kenneth had been killed, and presently, that Henry had been wounded; and then, with no regret at all, only curiosity, that he had married the sister of a brother officer, a nurse at his hospital.

She heard from the girls of fathers or brothers who were prisoners, wounded, or missing; heard, but did not apprehend, because, as it happened, none of the people concerned was intimate with her. These and Janet's stories - which were so much more like fiction than hard fact - were the only contacts she had with the events which were making and shattering lives all round her. She was immersed in the small matters of school life, and Eleanor held her affections. At twenty-five she was as she had been at twenty-two, a contented, highly efficient schoolmistress.

PART THREE

Andrew

1

THE war had been over a year before Janet came back to Medling; a quieter Janet, more mature, less timid and more serenely lovely. When she spoke of her work, she became grim. The stories she told were not funny any more. She did not tell them often, and they were dreadful, or tender with a tenderness which hurt. She was trying to get a post at Geneva. The only thing to do, now, was to give oneself up to making sure that there was never a horror like this again.

The Gym mistress came back, too, her successor having conveniently left. Her stories were still funny, and rather coarse, not at all tender. She had broadened, both in body and mind. She was not capable of tenderness, for she had no imagination. But she was different. She looked out at the world now, not in at herself; not even only at the school, or at the school's impression of herself. Those points of view interested her no longer. She took them in her stride and looked beyond them, read the papers, went to London at week-ends, to meetings, to an ex-service club which included men as well as women.

Hilary, listening, realized quite for certain that by staying at home she had missed an experience which nothing could make up to her. Perhaps it *had* been her duty to stay - one couldn't tell, now. But wouldn't the earnest, anaemic ones among her colleagues, who hadn't even wanted to go, have done just as well, really? Wasn't this the inevitable punishment for thinking oneself indispensable, which nobody was, at any time, anywhere? Seen against the stark facts which Janet told, against Miss Reeve's racy anecdotes with their kernel of real horror and real heroism, the quiet, contented years had the interest and consistency of pea-soup.

In 1920, Miss Barrington electrified them all by retiring. She was growing old, she said, must make way for younger women with younger ideas.

The new Head was not much over thirty, a brilliant Oxford graduate who had been teaching at a big boys' school during the war, and then at one of the famous girls' boarding-schools. A go-ahead person, everyone said. Hilary was pleasantly excited at the prospect of working under her. After all, Miss Barrington was rather a stick.

She chatted to Eleanor about it. "Things are going to hum. Reeve's going to insist on lacrosse as a regular game - all the best schools are playing it. I shall try to make her let my kids wear gym-dresses on the river. And they say she's very keen on catering for other professions beside teaching - letting people do First M.B. from school, and doing something about the masses who want to be secretaries and saleswomen and go into offices. It's going to be fun . . . L.J. *was* growing old, there's no doubt about it."

Eleanor, sitting back in her chair, said, "I'm growing old, too. I can't stand this new, smart type of schoolmistress who thinks, because she's been about a bit, that she can be a Society lady as well. Worldly, sensual, devilish, my father would have called them. Old L.J. was devoted to the school, whatever her faults; lived her whole life for it; resigned for it, even, because she thought she was letting it get behind the times. This one lives her life for herself. Look at her ear-rings! I suppose her generation *has* had its ideals shattered, can't believe there *is* anything but oneself to live for . . . But why impose that point of view on children? They'd be far better off with a nun out of a convent . . . I shall leave."

Hilary stopped exploring an interesting future and came to rest with a bump. "Are you pulling my leg?" But Eleanor's face left no doubt about that.

"I am not. I've been contemplating this for some time. I've done my share of teaching. Besides, if she's going to put them in for First Medical she'll want someone who can teach Zoology, and it's more dignified, at my age, to get out than to be kicked out . . . I can afford to do something less paying and less infuriating, now, and I'm going to try to."

Hilary said, "I've wondered, of course, if you'd go on with it, ever since your people died. Only, you're so good at it. It's impossible to think of school without you."

Eleanor smiled dryly. "If it can get on without L.J., it can get on without me. I've no illusions about that. I'm too set in my habits to change them without changing my surroundings. D'you realize I've been here sixteen years? No, I'm going. And if you take my advice, you'll go too. You're younger than I am, but you're pre-war. You haven't been through it, or grown up in it, or seen anything of it at all. You can't talk its language any more than I can. She can - this new one - because of her boys'-school job, I expect, but she can. If you try to work with her, you'll be at cross purposes all the time."

Hilary was half inclined to be angry. After all, she was a good many years younger than Eleanor, and surely far more adaptable? It was rubbish to talk as if she were too old to work with someone several years her senior. She said so.

Eleanor said, "You must do as you think best, of course. But I think you'll find it pretty ghastly, after being L.J.'s pet lamb, to be treated as an outsider totally without understanding. It's the people like Reeve who'll be the pet lambs in this regime . . . You can rent this place from me, if you like, and get someone to share it with you."

That was grim. Eleanor's house without Eleanor! Someone hearty, like Miss Hornibrook, or ineffectual, like little Banks, sitting in Eleanor's chair! Bridge parties, gossip over coffee, instead of their quiet, companionable evenings!

"And we'll spend our holiday together, of course," Eleanor went on chattily.

Hilary said absently, "Yes. Yes, we must do that." She was so taken aback that her mind would not work. She had pictured their growing old together in this house - and now Eleanor, Eleanor, whose terror was that she would have to grow old alone, sprang this upon her. What on earth was the matter with Eleanor? She added as an afterthought, "What are you going to do?" Then wished she hadn't, for they had always delicately prided themselves on not asking each other personal questions.

Eleanor did not resent this one. She might have been courting it. She said, "I've always hankered after doing botanical research. I've done a certain amount as I went along - published bits here and there, corresponded with the people who are doing it properly, though I couldn't afford to give up my whole time to it. Now I can. So I've written to the man at the head of the Plant Diseases station at Fenchester to ask if he's got a job for me."

Hilary said, "Fenchester? That's where that old professor friend of Father's is. He came to see us. A dear old person. You'll like him. Why, Eleanor - Eleanor, what on earth's the matter?"

They were sitting each in a chair, on the two sides of the fireplace. Hilary had given up, for some time now, sitting on the floor at Eleanor's feet. If she had been asked why, she would have said, "But I do - sometimes, when I'm not working . . . generally I've got writing to do." She simply had not noticed that the change had come about.

Eleanor's face had crumpled suddenly. She dropped it on one hand, and held out the other, groping. She said in a little choked voice, "I thought you'd be sure to come too."

Hilary was dumbfounded. "But - *I* can't do botanical research! I - and anyway, you've only just sprung it on me! I haven't had a second to think! And it was you who began to talk about my having the house - assuming I was going to stay!" Eleanor said, "That was after you'd p-practically said you were!"

Hilary came and knelt beside her, "I just never thought of changing, that's all," she said. "I didn't know you had. Now I have thought of it, I don't know that it's a bad idea. We haven't any special friends here. There's no particular reason why we should stay. I don't want to break away from you - I should hate it. I thought - while you were talking - that you'd grown tired of me, and I was trying to take it without a fuss. *Now* - have you made a plan?"

Eleanor looked up from her sheltering hand. Hilary was shocked by the way, in an instant, she had aged; as though

183

she had been brought suddenly face to face with something she had dreaded, as though something she depended on had fallen away and left her helpless. She was bewildered at her own pain, angry at her bewilderment. A breathless pity for her surged through Hilary. She flung her strong arm round Eleanor's shoulders, felt Eleanor's head; round, knobbly, with hairpins in it, beneath her chin. Her momentary sense of independence, her light-hearted interest in a changed future, fell away. She said, "Of course I'll come with you, if we can work it in any way at all . . . Is there a High School at Fenchester?"

Eleanor jerked out, "I don't want to *make* you do anything. It wouldn't be fair. But - you don't know how lonely I was before you came! I simply can't imagine my life without you, now."

Hilary, immensely touched, hugged her the tighter. "Tell me the plan," she coaxed. "I'm sure you've got one. Let's have it!"

Eleanor sat up. "I'm silly. I've never been so silly about anyone in all my life . . . Well, here's the plan. You mentioned Professor Hewer once before. That's why I chose Fenchester. I thought he might give you a job."

Hilary sat back on her heels. "At the University? Me? Eleanor, you've gone mad!"

Eleanor achieved a smile. "I don't think so. You're as good as anyone else, now you've got your honours degree. He thought a lot of your father. He knows your father taught you. And there's your looks, again. It's worth trying, Hilary! Write to him and see!"

After that, it was all plain sailing. Professor Hewer wrote

184

warmly. He had thought of appointing a junior lecturer in History the following term. The University had doubled its numbers in the post-war years. He was growing old. The post would have to be advertised - but would Hilary apply, and come down and talk things over?

She went, and was approved and presently appointed.

Hilary said, "It's a miracle, I think!" She really did, it was all so opportune, the post so enormously more to her liking than any she would have tried for in the open market.

Eleanor said, "Nonsense! Unless you call careful planning miraculous."

"Not when you do it!" Hilary laughed. "But I do think this is, all the same: you didn't know he wanted an assistant just now!"

"I knew he was getting old and the place was growing. Common sense. That's the sort of miracle it was. A modern one."

They house-hunted during the holidays, and found a cottage in a village beyond the big town, towards the moors. It would mean a train journey every day, but only a short one, and that, they thought, was infinitely preferable to living among the smuts which poured from the chimneys of Fenchester's mills and factories.

It was the first northern town Hilary had seen, and at first it appalled her. It lived in a permanent dusky haze, which a country dweller takes at first for "the pride o' the morning" only to find it worse still at eleven, pierced reluctantly by an anaemic sun at midday, and brooding more sullenly than ever over the town at three. Trams screamed down narrow hills, lorries thundered over cobbles, into dips where oily rivers, stained here and there with repulsive mixtures of colours, crawled, and corrugated iron fences took the place of banks. The people were like foreigners to her - hurrying women with grey shawls over their heads, lounging men with caps over one eye, clogs, and a whippet to heel. It was impossible to imagine such a town supporting a university. Eleanor, Hilary thought with alarm, had made a bad bargain for them.

When she had explored a bit, she was comforted by two things: the nearness and beauty of the country - for the town did not, like southern towns, throw out unsightly arms all round, but stayed where it was; and the direct, go-ahead outlook of the people. By the time the new term was due to begin, she was looking forward to it with pleasant excitement.

2

Hilary stood in the doorway of the Staff Common Room. She stood there not because she was shy or uncertain what to do, but because, for the moment, she had lost all consciousness of herself in amazement at the difference between the scene before her and any in which she had been before.

The very physical atmosphere was different. In contrast to the hygienic airiness of Medling, the windows here were shut and the air misty with tobacco smoke. Two men stood by the fire-place, an elderly, stout one with his back to it, and another tall and craggy, who leaned on an elbow and waved his pipe as he talked, his stretched neck and the movement of his Adam's-apple giving the impression of a large, ill-clothed bird. A leather arm-chair was blotted almost entirely from view by an open newspaper, from which on one side a pair of grey-flannelled legs lolled over the chair's arm and ended in neat woollen socks and brown brogues. From behind another newspaper, in another chair, stretched a slim feminine hand with a long cigarette-holder between finger and thumb, and below it a woollen skirt and silken ankles. In the middle of the room, on the table, sat a young woman with sleek, waved hair and a string of beads round her neck, matching her brightly coloured jumper. She, too, was smoking, as was the young man who stood beside her. Both wore heavy horn-rimmed spectacles. They might have been brother and sister. There was an older woman reading a magazine in a corner, and a broad, fat back whose owner was seated at a desk, writing, with swift, vicious jabs of pen on paper.

The pipe-waving man saw Hilary, all of a sudden, and stopped talking. The stout man's eyes followed his, and the boy and girl at the table swivelled round. The broad back proved to belong to a short-haired, masculine-looking woman of something over fifty, who bounced up from her chair as soon as she saw what was going on. She reached Hilary in two strides, holding out a hand and booming, "You must be Miss Moore. I saw Miss Barrington in town the other day - "

Hilary, far too much interested to give a thought to any impression she might be creating, smiled and took the hand. "Then you're Miss Cronshaw I'm lucky to find a friend of Miss Barrington's here - "

"We're waiting for the V.C. He's always late. Come over here and sit down."

The rest of the company turned back, with grunts of relief, to their former occupations.

Most of the meaning of the staff-meeting which followed was lost upon Hilary, who did not yet know the place. The arguments, sometimes sharp, about rooms and times, left her unmoved. She was surprised, when it was over, to find that she had a room of her own, a small square comfortable den with her name already printed on the door, in which to interview students, carry on coachings, and do her own private work. Fresh from the scramble of the High School, it made her feel very important.

She joined the rest of the staff for lunch, sitting next to Miss Cronshaw, who beckoned to her as she entered the room. She was served immediately, by a trim maid who brought her what she ordered from a quite extensive menu. It was all extremely civilized. She felt suddenly a little frightened. She had not lived a very civilized life. There would be rules she did not know, she would drop bricks and disgrace herself and Professor Hewer who had given her the post. She threw covert glances round to see what everyone else was doing.

Miss Cronshaw was engaged in conversation with her neighbour on the other side, into which she drew Hilary when she remembered to. She talked all the time, whether her mouth was full or empty, and gesticulated sometimes with her knife and fork. Hilary took heart. Not quite so civilized after all.

For the most part, she was left free to listen to the talk round her. Opposite, Grey Flannels and Silken Ankles were chatting about variety shows. "I'd go miles to see Gracie Fields! She's so full of vim, enjoys herself so enormously! And so nice to look at. And such a tip-top actress, in spite of all the funny bits!"

Grey Bags did not altogether agree. "I liked her the first time, and the second. The third, I felt I'd seen all there was to see."

"I've seen her about twenty times," Silken Ankles confessed, "and still want to. I've got all her records, of course, but they're not a patch on the real thing! I wish she'd been a straight actress - I like her best of all in the tragic sketches she wedges into the other things . . . I wonder what she's like as a person."

Grey Bags didn't know. Wasn't interested, very much, and didn't pretend to be. Lately, if he'd wanted a laugh, he went to one of Ian Hay's things, "They're shoutingly funny, and they're never low."

Silken Ankles chuckled. "Good, clean fun!"

Grey Bags grumbled, "Well, one gets a bit fed up with some of the muck they're always putting across nowadays!"

He saw Hilary's eyes on them and stared, unsmiling, and she felt she had intruded. Yet one could not help listening, at such a distance. Silken Ankles caught her eye and laughed and leaned across, friendly. "Do you like Ian Hay?"

Hilary had read one of his books, seen none of his plays at all. But gratitude for the woman's smile stimulated in her the sense to give such opinion as she had. She said, "Funny

- but a bit thin!"

Silken Ankles thumped the table and said, "That's just what I think! And I don't like my plays thin!"

Grey Bags grinned now, and said, "But you don't mind them low," and she laughed again. "Shakespeare's low enough!" They went on to argue about cinemas, which Hilary hardly ever went to because they gave Eleanor headaches. She decided to go more often, by herself if need be, if the people here liked to talk about such things.

On her right, the woman who had been sitting alone in the Common Room was talking about a summer school to another very much like her - a pair of quietly dressed, grey-haired spinsters, with nothing remarkable about them except, perhaps, the high level of intelligence in their rather mincing conversation.

Miss Cronshaw turned suddenly and addressed Hilary; not afresh, merely as an expansion of her audience. "Just what I always say about these Americans. Not worthy of the name of scientist. Rush into print on the result of one experiment, the Press gets hold of it and hails some epoch-making discovery - and the next experimenter finds that there was an impurity in the material and the whole thing fizzles out. And that happens not once, but again and again. As for this man Henderson, I've just made out a rough draft of a letter refuting *all* his conclusions in the light of ten years' work in this laboratory. I'm sending it straight to the *Journal* as soon as ever I can get it typed!"

To Hilary's relief she did not seem to expect comment. She just went on eating, inelegantly, as though she were stoking up for the next outburst.

The horn-rimmed boy and girl came stalking down the room on the other side of the table. The boy looked at Hilary with curiosity, the girl stared over her head. When she had nearly finished her meal, the Professor of History stopped behind her chair. She rose, with an instinctive respect for an older person who was her chief.

He motioned her down again. "Don't hurry. But come along to my room when you've done, will you? There are just one or two things to talk over - "

She found the room - the place was a maze of passages - and spent an hour falling in with the Professor's arrangements for the term. She found him reasonable, a little querulous, but genuinely convinced that history was the most important subject in the curriculum and that the way it was taught mattered most enormously. Hilary found him stimulating. He talked about the students, whom he sized up quickly, and, as Hilary found by later observation, with great accuracy. "We've got a good lot this year. That lad Bellingham, and Miss Falkner, are both real scholars. They should both get Firsts and do really good work afterwards. Then there's the little Jap - wants to know all about European history, and is already a perfect mine of information on his own country's. They always are, if they know anything at all. Very interesting. Pump him, if you don't know much of it; he loves to talk . . . I shall be coaching those three myself, but they'll come to you for papers. There's the usual crowd who'll go in for teaching, mostly second class, with one or two - " he named them - "who'll get firsts from sheer grind; and some who'll scrape a third with luck because they're lazy or too gay. But they're a good, intelligent lot on the whole . . . Then you'll be lecturing to the Inter Arts people - that's no more than you've been doing already at school. It's your own province and you can arrange it as you like. I don't want to have anything to do with it. And there's your own work - you ought to get your M.A. this year or next; the authorities'll expect it. Think of something for a thesis and I'll tell you if it's any good. You'll be kept busy!"

He looked up at her critically, to see if she minded being worked hard. She smiled and said she preferred to have plenty to do. Indeed, she was feeling that she had been suddenly promoted to adult society from the nursery. She would be kept busy - sharpening her brain to keep up to adult level after the society of children only. Her mind had been asleep, except on the surface, ever since her own college days. School work had just been a more or less happy way of earning one's living. Here, it was the work itself that mattered. Wage-earning and happiness were mere adjuncts, not to be taken into serious consideration.

In the Common Room again, Silken Ankles made further advances; offered a cigarette, which Hilary took and smoked gingerly, and remarked, for want, it seemed, of a better opening, upon the foulness of college tea.

Hilary said, "I wish you'd tell me who all these people are." And Silken Ankles laughed and lost her shyness in a moment.

"Me, for instance. Helen Martin, Classics, Croydon High School and Cambridge. This is my second year here - I'm junior enough to be fairly irreverent. Had a minor coaching job at Newnham, but apart from that came straight from college. The man I was talking to was Mitchell. He's Maths: a sociable, entertaining creature - at least, I think so. Some people don't. It's not fair to bias you, is it? Anyway, that's who he is. Cronshaw you know. Everyone seems to, she's one of those amoebic sort of people - puts out pseudopodia in every direction. A.B.C. we call her - Adelaide Beatrice - always punctual to her time-table. Kind old soul. There I go again. The two on your other side at lunch were Miss Hawes and Miss Jago - Education and English. You probably won't know them apart for a very long time. The fat man's Professor Taylor - runs the Fine Arts Department - you wouldn't think so, would you? And the long, badly dressed one's the Curator of the Museum. Blake, his name is. The very young thing in horners is lecturer in Philosophy - yes, he does look a bit callow for a philosopher, doesn't he, but I think they often are, don't you? Professor Byles, his chief, is hoary enough for them to make a decent average of years between them. And the girl who was with him does weaving and all that sort of thing. This man who's just come in is a medical bloke - they wander in and out, but they have their own place, really, over at the Hospital . . . Now, all about you, please."

Hilary set forth a modest account of her own past, and Miss Martin nodded. "That's the sort of thing we rather want, here. Something different. First-class brain and not quite the usual look-down-your-nose outlook of the people who come straight from Oxford or Cambridge."

Hilary, startled, said, "I think I got it simply because Professor Hewer taught my father and knew that my father taught me. There's nothing special about my brain, I'm

193

afraid."

The other gave a little musical gurgle. "I don't know anything as to why you were appointed, though that's a good enough reason - there were several candidates who were very hot on paper. Since you've arrived, everyone's taken for granted that it was the shape of your cranium and the look in your eye. You *look* as if you could grow into the perfect Don, which the V.C. says is dying out. So it is. A.B.C. is the only approach we have to it on the female side, and Hewer and the V.C. himself on the male. I don't really know anything about your brain, of course - but one feels it must be all right behind a forehead like that!"

Hilary was laughing helplessly before these crisp personalities. Silken Ankles heaved herself to her feet, laughing too. "I do run on, don't I? If I tread on your corns, you must just lash out. I shan't mind. Well, I'm buzzing off - good-bye."

The impression of promotion to adulthood was heightened next day when Hilary interviewed students, one by one, in her room. There were a curious, mixed crowd, most of them North-country, many of them rough, so that through the differences in manner she caught glimpses of the primitive country types, uncultured and uncowed, whom she had known in the villages in the south; people in the same stage of civilization as those at the University at Ardlemouth. They were all very young in appearance, like colts; some frankly countrified, some with a veneer of gentility, some spoilt by town life into an unpleasing vulgarity; all self-possessed, as though they had passed, at any rate in their own opinions, through all the experiences possible to life and found them disappointing. She liked them, saw, without even knowing that she did so, through the uncouth or mincing manners to the person beneath. They, on their side, threw her one sharp, appraising glance as they entered, and accepted her without question as their superior. She reacted to the attitude and to her own interest in them, and became gracious and confident, giving all her thought to their problems and losing all consciousness of herself as she talked with them.

She found that Helen Martin was one of the most popular people in the Common Room, always chatting with someone, generally the centre of a group. Hilary, listening to her and to the discussions she provoked, realized that something as well as her intellect had been asleep all these years. There had been no need for ambition, at Medling; success had come without her giving it a thought. Conversation in the Staff Room there had been the merest chit-chat, and she and Eleanor had exhausted all the deeper topics of discussion years ago and lapsed into a series of contented grunts and comments. Here, with these people, a social sense awoke. She wanted to talk to them, to do the things they did, to be one of them. And, because they were, most of them, fiercely individual though united by common interests, she felt that she could do so without losing her own individuality, without becoming one of a mediocre crowd, as would have been the result of sociability with the High School staff.

In the meantime, she listened to them with delight as they sharpened their wits one against the other, and tentatively tried a little sharpening of her own with her students. She was horrified to find how slow and blunted they had become.

She talked more to Eleanor, too; and found, to her surprised pleasure, that Eleanor, like herself, was waking up. The change of surroundings had given them both a shaking. It was nearly - quite, perhaps, it was so impossible to remember - as much fun talking to Eleanor now as it had been six years ago. Even in spite of the years, she still loved the small things about Eleanor. The way her eyes wrinkled up at the corners when she smiled, her straight glance under thick tawny lashes, the sensitive lips opening over even white teeth, the deft movement of her long thin hands - all these, even now, could strike in Hilary a note of pure pleasure which made her heart lift.

Chatting about her new colleagues on the second evening of term, she finished up, "You must come over to tea and meet them."

Eleanor laughed. "I'd thought of that, too," she said. "I mentioned to one of the people in the lab that you and I lived together, and she looked at me in a queer sort of way and said it was a good thing we did live together if we wanted to see much of each other. When I asked what she meant, she said that research students rank as students, not staff, and aren't allowed to poke a nose into the staff common rooms. There's been some fuss about it, some time or other, I gathered, about some research worker who got a bit above himself. So I'm afraid I shan't be able to come to tea with you. And it seems that it isn't usual, either, for the teaching staff to come into the students' common room, at any rate for more than a minute at a time. It cramps the students' style."

"It looks like an impasse," Hilary agreed. "How frightfully funny, though! You a student and me a Donlet! Well, anyway, there's always my room. Nobody can keep you out of that!"

"Except you," Eleanor said, with a side-glance which Hilary simply did not see.

"Me? Oh, well," she said seriously, "I shan't keep you out unless you arrive in the middle of a coaching. And if I give you a copy of my time-table you won't do that."

Eleanor looked across at her, humped in a chair; blue handwoven jumper, cheeks like a half-ripe peach; corn-gold, crisply curling hair, grey eyes which looked out eager, friendly, but ready to dream; and her smile had in it wonder, and a question. Hilary was not looking at her.

3

With the students, Hilary's relations soon grew from formal to friendly. Both men and women would come into her room to ask a question and stay to talk. They liked her easy way with them as much as the schoolgirls had done. The one or two girls who whipped themselves into the inevitable sentimentality about her were steadied by her inability to perceive anything in their advances but friendliness.

With only one of them did she become involved in any relationship which extended outside the college. This one was Margaret Falkner, the girl whose scholarship Professor Hewer had praised. She was a downright northerner, who had been to a good school and was one of a large family. There was no nonsense about her except the affection which her tutor excited in her, and a passion for music which all her family shared. In face, she was plain, but she had fine eyes and a slim, pretty figure. There was a shy wildness about her which reminded Hilary of Janet and contrasted with the sturdy courage of her character.

It was towards the end of the first term that she invited Hilary to spend Sunday afternoon and evening at her home. Her father was a cotton-waste merchant, moderately wealthy, with a house on the north side of the city, which meant a long tram ride from Hilary's suburb. Eleanor, fortunately, had invited to tea the wife of one of the Dons whom she knew slightly, so Hilary left her with no qualms of conscience at possible loneliness.

She found a grey stone house in a shabby garden; an ancient maid and a dog, who ambled to the door together and together inspected her; and a well-used drawing-room in which Margaret Falkner rose from the depths of one of innumerable armchairs. There was a log fire to temper the autumn shortening of the days, a piano pulled out into the room, music-stands about; books everywhere, a big gramophone, an oil-painting of trees in autumn, full of glorious colour, and another of a lake in moonlight, both new-looking, as if a member of the household had done them; french windows, leading out to a smooth lawn.

Margaret said, "The others have gone for a walk, and Daddy's playing billiards Here's Mother - "

Mother was thin and grey; worn, but with a shrewd humour gleaming in her eyes and a very sweet smile. She put Hilary into a chair and began to talk to her, easily, about books, about college and things in the town, and Margaret joined in.

Presently Mr. Falkner came in, a bearded, energetic man who monopolized the conversation, but so excellently that no one wanted him to stop. Then another daughter, a pretty, dark girl, older than Margaret, already teaching, and her fiancé, a little shy man with a lively, darting glance and a younger brother who was studying medicine, a good-looking boy not yet past the stage of trying to be funny.

For a while they all talked. Then Mrs. Falkner said, "Shall we have some music? Do you play, Miss Moore? Well, then, do you mind being the audience? We're so seldom all together that when we are there's no holding us - "

She was very young, Hilary thought, to be the mother of all these almost grown-up children - less in years, perhaps, than in mind. She caught them up, in the quick give and take of conversation, as patly as they did each other. She wondered whether Eleanor would have stigmatized the family as "hearty". They were very lively, very good-humoured and friendly, more then commonly intellectual; but there was a simplicity about them, a wisdom and humour about their talk, whether it was culture, uplift or pure nonsense, which saved them from being highbrow.

Their music was beautiful. They all seemed to play one instrument as easily as another - piano, violin, viola and 'cello - and took turns with them. They played Beethoven and Brahms, César Franck - the last movement made Hilary sit bolt upright with pleasure - and an arrangement of Kreisler's which frankly made her laugh with delight. Margaret, who was playing the piano for that, looked round and saw her and laughed too.

"Enjoying it?" she asked when it was over, and Hilary nodded, "Enormously. I haven't heard any decent music - oh, since I used to go to college 'musicals' myself. And I do so love it."

They all surveyed her benevolently, thinking transparently that college musicals couldn't have been, for her, very long ago; for she looked hardly older than Margaret.

Other people had come in while the music was going on. Two young men and another girl stepped in through the french window, softly, and settled themselves about the room, giving Hilary a glance as they came, and blowing kisses to Mrs. Falkner, who smiled around her 'cello. Hilary had a good view of them. The girl was a small person, plump and merry, as old, perhaps, as Hilary was herself. One of the young men was puck-like, thin and frail-looking; the other, in contrast, dapper, stoutish and ruddy, wearing the orthodox Sunday get-up of morning-coat and striped trousers. The others were all in flannels or plus-fours.

Hilary, her conscious thoughts on the music, stared at him. He must have felt her eyes on him, for he raised his sleek head and looked straight at her. She saw that his eyes were vivid blue. He watched her for a second, as though he knew her and yet could not recall her; then dropped his head again.

Margaret introduced them, when the music was over. The girl was a neighbour, Mary Richardson, who was always in and out of the house; the thin man, Billy Thomas, the fat one, Andrew Fraser, friends of Margaret's elder brother who was now abroad.

"They generally drop in on Sundays. Where did you put your cars, people?"

Andrew, in a voice surprisingly deep and rumbling for his civilized appearance, said, "Out in the road. Philip's hearse is in the middle of the garden, and I didn't dare go into that junk-house you call a garage, in case something might fall over on me."

Margaret explained: "It's full of Daddy's painting things. There really isn't room in it for a car. We don't use ours much, and when we do we have to unpack stacks of canvases that are leaning against it, and if we're not careful we sit down on a tube of cobalt blue or something, that's been left on the seat . . . Will it be all right, Andrew? Philip can move his - "

"If anyone touches it except me, it'll most likely explode," Andrew said. "I've got an aeroplane engine in it and it goes like the wind. I did eighty-two with it on the north road last night . . . But it takes a bit of starting."

Hilary thought what a lot of unexpected qualities one surprised in people - Margaret, stolid and commonsensical until you knew her, and then with this gift for music and dreams; Janet, with her mixture of timidity and courage; Eleanor, apparently as self-sufficient as anyone could be, yet in tears because she thought she had to leave Medling alone; and now this dapper little man who was perfectly at home in a racing-car with an aeroplane engine!

They went in to tea soon - nursery tea round a big table - and he showed another side by eating steadily on like a schoolboy ("One might have expected that, he's so tubby," she thought), and another by engaging Margaret's father in a critical discussion of a modern painter whose work, it seemed, one either loved or hated. He was growing more and more lyrical and Mr. Falkner more and more grumpy with every sentence until Margaret, opposite, broke into the conversation.

"Oh, Andrew, come off it! You know you don't really like his rotten pictures! You're behaving as if you'd painted them yourself!"

Andrew was imperturbable. "How d'you know I don't? It's just the sort of *nom de* - what would you say? *Pinceau?* - thanks - that I should choose if I wanted one. Paul Verntbloem - luv-ly! Whitechapel?"

"Idiot! *Do* you?"

Andrew simpered. "Oh well - it's a stage we all go through, isn't it? Don't be too hard on me!"

Margaret shrugged. "Time you grew out of it . . . You'd never think he was a budding surgeon - "

" 'Blooming'," the younger brother put in.

" 'Full-blown' surgeon, would you, Miss Moore? Spends his life chopping out people's brains and livers - "

"She would hit on the only two - practically - parts of human anatomy that one can't chop out!" Andrew inserted sorrowfully.

"Oh well - lights and stomachs then - and inventing horrid little hooks and pokers with lamps on them: 'One of the Royal's most brilliant younger men', they called him in the local paper the other day - "

Andrew leaned across the table and asked earnestly, "What *would* you think I was?"

Hilary, with equal solemnity, replied, "I'd been wondering, and the only thing I could think of was an undertaker!"

There were shouts of laughter all round the table. The young medical student thumped on it and cried out, "Oh, that's a jolly good one, that really is a good one!" Andrew himself looked sheepish and said, "Well, it's not such a far cry, I suppose!"

Billy remarked, "You'd better change into plus-fours next week, Andrew, then there won't be any mistake!"

The talk became general again. Andrew and Mr. Falkner, both released from public attention, returned to their food. It was the jolliest meal Hilary had ever known - never a pause in the bubbling talk, one spurt of laughter following another, plates of this and that travelling round almost automatically; all the rivalry of the friendliest, all the personalities devoid of malice. One felt that the Falkners really did love and respect each other without fuss and with a healthy amount of friendly criticism; and they expected and found the same attitude in their friends.

When tea was over, Margaret attempted to shoo Hilary into the other room; but Hilary resisted her and joined the rest of them, men and women alike, in clearing the table and washing up. Everyone chaffed and jostled everyone else; Margaret, with turned-up sleeves, and rubber apron, splashed at the sink, Mary languidly polished spoons, Billy shook tea-leaves carefully into a sink-basket and bore them away outside; Andrew, looking like a waiter now, rushed about with piles of plates, the medical student brother puffed upstairs with a bucket of coal; all behaving as though they performed these duties every day, instead of only as a weekly relaxation.

In the drawing-room, they found Mr. and Mrs. Falkner sitting by the fire, dropped into chairs themselves, one after another, where they found themselves; played a word-game with pencil and paper, at which Hilary, to her own surprise, shone. Andrew, who was opposite her again, congratulated her seriously whenever she scored a point. She did not know quite what to make of him.

They listened to some gramophone records - beautiful things, which again surprised her, for she had literally never heard a good gramophone. Then cards were brought out, and her heart sank, wishing that she had kept up her learning of Bridge in spite of Eleanor's scorn. But it was not Bridge, only lighthearted games, Newmarket, Rummy; which she had indeed to learn but got the knack of without much trouble. Margaret constituted herself teacher; and Andrew, this time, jeered at her mistakes and baulked her villainously whenever he could.

Margaret said, "Andrew, you're being a pig! You've played this since you were thirteen and Miss Moore's only just begun!"

Andrew, grinning, said, "All's fair - isn't it?" and banged down the seven of diamonds just in time to prevent her being "Out".

She met his twinkling, bright blue eyes gaily. There was,

it seemed, a silent battle between them - well-fed, civilized, rather pampered man against the austere, hardworking womanhood which had been Hilary's life.

They sat round the fire after that and talked of all the things which were going on in the world. It was when, after a long time, someone suggested more music that Hilary glanced at her watch and sprang up in a hurry at what she saw.

"Goodness, it's nearly twelve, and I've got to get right across the city and out the other side!"

"I'll take you!" Andrew said at once. "Do it in twenty minutes at this time of night, with no traffic. Where, exactly?"

She told him, amid a chorus of protest and warning.

"You take care, Miss Moore: he'll tip you into the river and go off singing!"

"He'll take you a toot to show off the engine, and you'll find yourself in Scotland in the morning instead of at college!"

Andrew said, "Don't you believe them! I'm a very careful driver and I've got a whole lot of work to do in the morning myself."

She tucked herself into the long, insect-like car. The whole party had surged into the road to see them off, and presently off they jerked, to an accompaniment of bangs from the engine and good wishes from the onlookers which must have annoyed the neighbourhood more than a little.

The jerking settled down in a minute into a steady glide.

"Got enough rugs?" Andrew asked. "It's cold, after the fug we raised in there."

Hilary said, "I like it - lovely and fresh. Yes, I'm as cosy as anything."

He negotiated a cross-road. "Smart bit of work, your word-making," he hazarded, looking round at her with a smile.

Hilary smiled too. "It's too easy." Then, "But aren't they ripping people? Are they always like that - the Falkners?" She was still excited - too excited to mind, in the dark, who she was talking to or what she said.

He said, "Always, more or less. We generally do something balmy on Sundays. And music and proper talk, always, as well. I was at school with Norman, the eldest brother - he's married now, and in Persia doing something about oil - and they've had that sort of open house at week-ends ever since I've known them. Sometimes it's crowded out, for everyone who's ever been comes again. They're such happy people - no grousing, no even wanting to grouse and keeping it inside: that's the attraction, I think."

Hilary nodded. "Happy and kind - that sounds awful, but it isn't, because they're brainy too. They can talk about anything, and yet fool like children."

Andrew said, "'M! It's just the sort of relaxation one wants, in my job, where one's always in a state of anxiety, more or less. The responsibility's so great, in surgery - you decide that something's got to be done, and you do it, and if you're wrong, or if you make a mistake in technique, it's not you that suffers, it's someone else. They say one grows callous as one grows older - I don't believe one does. I should go batty, I sometimes think, if I hadn't these Sundays to wipe it all away. A physician has quite a different time - he just brings his great mind to bear, at leisure, on a difficult case, writes a prescription or two, speaks some big words and leaves it to nature. We butt in and try to help nature - do help her, nine times out of ten - and the tenth, she goes back on us and the patient dies and one wonders whether it wouldn't have been better to be less bold and leave things alone - "

Hilary, her hands eagerly round her knees, said, "Isn't that losing courage?"

He smiled, his fingers moving on the wheel. "I suppose it is . . . I've just lost an appendix case - a child of nine - that's why I talk like that . . . What are *you* going to do when you've done with college?"

Hilary, her interest fixed on this picture of yet another, unexpectedly sensitive, Andrew, said vaguely, "Done with college? Well, I hope I shan't have done with it for quite a time. When I have, I'll retire and keep hens."

Andrew stared for a moment. Then he inquired, "Have I made a bloomer? I thought you were a pal of Margaret's."

She laughed. "So I am. Only, worse luck, not a student any more. History staff. This is my first term here."

He appeared to be relieved. "Not such a bloomer. There's not much difference between a last-year student and a first-year don."

"A tremendous difference between teacher and taught," she teased him.

He assented, gloomily. "'M! Perhaps there is. I do a good bit of teaching myself, now. You weren't a student here, were you? No, of course you weren't, I should have seen you . . . I grouse at it for a mouldy provincial place, but honestly I believe one gets more real experience at a small university than a big one."

They wrangled amiably about universities until they came to Hilary's front gate. She told him the little there was to tell about her own student days, and it was only because the talk flowed on so effortlessly that she did not tell him how long ago they were.

She stood for a minute with her hand on the car door, thanking him for the ride. He called, "Sleep well," and she laughed, and said, "I shall most likely have a nightmare - I got thoroughly worked up over those games! Ridiculous, at my age!"

He shook his head with an air of great wisdom. "One's never too old to feel! If people tell you so, they're fools. The older one gets, the more feelings can grind one . . . That's why one develops a sort of armour - "

This was intriguing. She wanted it to go on. But Andrew, who had looked as though he might sit there talking till dawn, changed his mind suddenly and let in his clutch, waving to her as he roared away.

She went in with a great feeling of exhilaration. The Falkners were the sort of people she had hankered after all her life. It was natural to her, to play silly games with them and to be liked, and admired a little, and mistaken for a student years younger than her age. Armour, had Andrew said? She thought she had none, thought she would rather have none. It kept one young, to be made to feel.

She had forgotten all about time. It did not surprise her to see a light in the sitting-room. It did surprise her, very much, to hear a scuffle and a rush as she put her key into the lock, and to see Eleanor standing in the hall, a hand at her breast, her face pale under its tan, her eyes wide. Hilary pulled the key out and came in, and Eleanor sagged back against the wall.

"Thank goodness you're safe! I've been nearly frantic!"

Hilary blinked. "Safe? Of course I'm safe! Why not?"

"You've never been so late, in all these years!"

Hilary realized a situation which called for management. She tucked an arm into Eleanor's and bustled her into the sitting-room. "I've never been so entertained in all these years - " She plumped Eleanor down on the couch and sat beside her. "They're darlings, the Falkners - we had the loveliest, silliest evening - " and she began to tell Eleanor all about it.

It was quite a time before, engrossed in her anecdotes, she understood that her management was not succeeding, that she was talking to deaf ears. Eleanor was sitting upright, staring straight in front of her, her eyes hard bright balls, her mouth a thin line. Hilary stopped abruptly and considered what to do next. This was an Eleanor she had not met before. She flung an arm about her and said, "Old silly, were you *really* worried about me?"

Eleanor said coldly, "Perhaps I am silly. But I think it was reasonable to expect you home before midnight when you'd gone out to tea at a house you'd never been to before."

Hilary laughed, a bubble of pure exuberance which had nothing, really, to do with Eleanor. "I suppose it was . . . We just forgot about time, somehow."

Eleanor got up. "Exactly. And - perhaps this is silly, too -

209

I'm not used to *your* forgetting all about me and what I may be suffering. Now you are in, I shall go to bed. I can't, at my age, do decent work without a proper amount of sleep. Good night."

She went stiffly across the room and upstairs, without looking back.

Hilary sat still, her enjoyment all gone. One hadn't one's freedom, joined up with someone else as she was with Eleanor. Lack of it was the price one had to pay. She had never thought about it before, because she had not wanted to do things by herself. One had to choose, it seemed. Which was best - freedom, or safety from that bogy of growing old alone? Freedom, to go out when one pleased for as long as one liked - or affection and peace? All rubbish, to talk like this, of course, and no one would do it except in the middle of the night - all that was necessary was a little thought and consideration. She *had* forgotten all about Eleanor. If she hadn't, if she had even said to Eleanor, "I simply don't know anything about these people, it may be a formal tea-party or I may come back with the milk," she could have had her cake and eaten it, both, without any trouble. Selfish, horrible of her, to have forgotten how Eleanor might have been feeling . . . How would Eleanor have fitted into the party, she wondered? It was amazing, how people did change, in changed surroundings. She could never have imagined that she could have fitted into it herself, if she had thought about it beforehand.

Impulsively, she went two steps at a time to Eleanor's room; and found Eleanor in bed, in floods of tears. Hilary nearly wept too, she felt so sorry for her.

"I really won't be so silly next time," Eleanor sobbed. "Only tell me when you're going to be late again!"

Hilary, thoroughly repentant, protested that she would. "Only there won't be a next time," she said, "because next time you'll come too. Margaret said she'd like you to come, to-night. You'll like them - "

In her own room, her mind went back joyously to the shabby, crowded house. She dreamed about it, and about a racing car which carried her heaven knew where. Eleanor did not come into her dreams at all. She woke in that mood of exaltation which comes after a night of happiness of which only the feeling remains.

4

At the University, life moved with relative smoothness. Helen Martin was definitely friendly, Miss Cronshaw condescending and sometimes expansive. Miss Cronshaw did not quite approve of Helen, who was on good terms with men and women alike. Still less did she tolerate the young woman in horners, whom she suspected of a secret engagement to the young man. She had been a militant suffragette and was still aggressively feminist. She did not see that the younger generation of women, with no first-hand knowledge of the battle which had won them their present fighting position, pitied and laughed at her for being behind the times.

On Friday, Margaret Falkner came to her and said, "Could

you bear to come to us again on Sunday? We've got a special friend coming who plays the violin most beautifully. He doesn't often come, or I wouldn't have dared to ask you again so soon . . . Or were we too rowdy for you?"

Hilary said, "I haven't enjoyed myself so much for years - in fact, it took ten or so of them off my age."

"Then you'll come? And Miss Hunt too, if she'd like to."

"We'd both like to, very much indeed," Hilary said.

Margaret, standing on one leg and rubbing it with the other, said, "Most people come quite often, once they've been. We'd love you to, any Sunday you feel inclined."

The girl's shy reverence was warming. "My dear, it's nice of you to want a couple of middle-aged spinster ladies." At which Margaret opened her mouth and hooted and said, "What rubbish!" as though to an equal, and then darted a look which justified her rudeness and asked forgiveness for it all at once, dismissing Hilary's description of herself as the merest affectation. In her heart, she so dismissed it herself. She felt more one with these energetic young things than she did with Eleanor's rigid elderly regime of rest and work and nothing else.

On Sunday, there were several other University students at the Falkners but no other members of staff. Andrew, still in his correct Sunday dress - "I don't play golf, so why should I pretend I do?" he answered Hilary's taunt - came quickly and sat beside her.

The music began soon. In deference, perhaps, to the violinist friend, it was taken very seriously. The talk in the intervals was nearly all of music. Hilary, who always liked to hear people talk their own shop, listened with enjoyment and now and then asked a question. Eleanor sat silent; but she generally was silent in company, and Hilary was so happy herself that she could not doubt that Eleanor felt the atmosphere of the house and was interested and at ease.

At tea, Eleanor sat next to Mrs. Falkner and talked with her. Hilary was too far away to hear what they talked about, but saw no awkward pauses. One couldn't imagine awkward pauses and Mrs. Falkner in the same room. There was much less fooling than on the Sunday before. It would begin spurting up from one of the young men, only to fizzle out before the solemn looks of another. There was some factor which damped them; the presence of more strangers than usual, perhaps. The talk was good, and Hilary enjoyed it, but not with the magic, exuberant enjoyment of the week before.

The only game they played was Rummy. Hilary looked a little anxiously at Eleanor when it was suggested. Suppose she refused to play, let off some of her fireworks against card games - what would happen? But Eleanor's manners were too good for that. She sat bolt upright, serious, collecting sequences and grabbing jokers as fast and as efficiently as anyone else. Seeing her laugh suddenly at some remark made by Philip, next to her, Hilary wondered if, perhaps, this was the way to dispel the awkwardness with young men which had haunted her all her life. A great person, Eleanor, to be able to do things she didn't like doing with such an air. Or had this happy atmosphere dispelled her dislike for play as it had dispelled Hilary's own shyness?

Andrew, at her side, abstracted a card of hers and twitted her for being absentminded. She turned to him, laughing, and gave back as good as he had given, and made a ripple of laughter all round them. "Don't expect a schoolmarm - oh yes you are, even if your pupils are a bit older than some - to be so quick at the uptake," someone said. Hilary said, "My father was a schoolmaster; I'm used to little boys," and Andrew chuckled. She saw Eleanor looking across at her and thought that Eleanor was seeing a new side of her. The only company they had been together in before had been ladylike tea-parties in the Medling parents' houses, with talk of nothing but maids and children, which they had been agreed in their desire to leave as soon as possible. Queer, she thought, how two people could live together for ten years and only half know each other.

Andrew banged down his last two cards and yelled, "Out!" triumphantly.

Hilary said, "Pig! - I've got twenty pips!"

"Fifty years ago, I should've peeked over your shoulder and held on till you were out," Andrew said. "And twiddled my moustachios and thought I was no end of a fellow!"

Hilary said, "Chivalry's dead!" and Andrew retorted, "Don't you believe it! Gone underground, and not far down. That's all. Been stamped on. It'll sprout."

The party broke up before eleven. The younger people grouped themselves together, as though they would stay and talk round the fire. Hilary, for Eleanor's sake, did not join them.

On the way upstairs, Margaret drew her aside. "Squash

me if I'm trying to get too much of your company, won't you. But we're making up a party on Wednesday evening to go to the Rep - we know some of the people there, so we go when we can, and they really are jolly good. Will you come? We shall have a cheap dinner somewhere first."

Hilary agreed with hardly a thought. It was all part of this exciting new life which she was waking up to, which she felt she ought to have belonged to for years and years.

When she came down, with her coat on, Andrew was waiting for her in the hall.

"I'll drive you home again," he announced, and only added, "If I may," when he saw a shade of doubt across her face.

"I was only trying to remember whether there was room for Miss Hunt," she explained. "We're going together."

He became gallant at once, less natural. "Of course. We can take three in front if you don't mind a bit of a squash. It's more comfortable squashed than in the dickey, I think."

So they bunched together, Eleanor stiffly on the outside, Hilary wedged in the middle. Watching Andrew's hands on the wheel and feeling the hard bulk of him beside her, she realized that in spite of his quaint tubbiness he was very strong. His hands were broad and well kept, with dark hairs on them, like no other hands she had seen so near.

When they arrived, Eleanor thanked him, shortly, but with the dignity which Hilary had always found charming, and went straight in. Hilary hesitated, then said, "Come in and have a cigarette. The only drink I can offer you's cider."

He smiled and declined. "No. I don't like being too late

too often, and I've a heavy week ahead, and another behind me. You're coming on Wednesday, aren't you?"

She said with some surprise, "Yes." She was so used to hen-parties that she had hardly thought of Andrew's being there.

"I'll call for you about seven," he remarked, and waved as he turned the car. There was no opportunity to tell him to do no such thing. And anyway, she liked Andrew, and his car was a good deal more comfortable than a crowded bus.

Indoors again, she asked Eleanor what she thought of them all, and Eleanor yawned. "Just nice ordinary people. Reasonably intelligent, but no more - that's why they go in for silly games. Really brainy people talk instead. I liked them . . . But I don't see quite why you're so filled with enthusiasm."

Hilary was unreasonably piqued. Why must Eleanor be so highbrow and different? She said crossly, "I suppose I haven't met many ordinary people in their own homes. I think they're darlings."

She could not have said - perhaps it was just that pique - why she did not tell Eleanor until the following day about the theatre party. When she did tell her, Eleanor just said, "Nice for you," and added that she would not wait up for her. Hilary was relieved. She had expected some sort of objection. She was going to have her cake and eat it after all. She hugged Eleanor.

5

The party was not exactly rowdy but very cheerful. The play was a good one, well acted. The cast were all women, the scene a West-end shop for hats and dresses. Mary, whose suggestion the expedition had been, apologized for bringing them to "such a henny show".

Young Don was frankly bored, and said the whole thing was a fuss about nothing.

"The he-man's point of view," Margaret commented. "Any woman's business is nothing except looking after a man."

In the interval she looked at the faces round her and was struck by the differences between men and women. She had never noticed it before. Rarely, on an old man's face, there was a baffled, bewildered look, as though he could not believe that life had no more to offer him than he had already had of it. But the younger men - and there were many of them, for the Repertory Players were popular in the city - were for the most part either contented or pugnacious: either they had got what they wanted or were confident of getting it. The younger women here had a hungry look - life was a scramble, and the devil took the hindmost; or something less exciting than the devil, the workhouse, or some dreary drudgery in someone else's home. The older ones were tired; disappointed, but too tired to bother about wanting any more; or embittered, or cross, or hard, scheming, predatory, with beaked noses and eyes as metallic as their jangling ear-rings. One woman with a ruddy, contented face was remarkable among them.

There were no more like her, though Hilary craned her neck to see.

Andrew asked her what she was looking at and, impulsively, she told him. He shattered her new conviction of an unbridgeable chasm by nodding gravely and saying, "Yes, women - on the whole - do have a thin time. Lots of soul-destroying little worries. We have worries all right, but they're more clean-cut. One can deal with them, or one can't. They don't nag. I've wondered, sometimes, if it's all right for a woman who's made a success of a career - old A.B.C., for instance. She's got a hard-boiled look about her."

Hilary considered Miss Cronshaw. "I should think she's been through something and come out the other side," she said presently. "She's content enough now, in a thoroughly discontented sort of way; always making a fight if there's not one there for her."

"Thwarted, but sublimated," Andrew murmured, and squinted sideways at her. "Even a surgeon knows a spot of the jargon of psychology."

She laughed. "More than I do, I expect."

He went on, "That's what I liked about you, at the very beginning. You don't fit into any type. I can't place you. You're not a discontented spinster, or a successful, hardened one, or one of those who know all about men inside as well as out, or a spiritualized prude. There's something child-like about you, and yet not childish - you're strong and weak both together - "

Hilary said, "Andrew, stop it! I'm not used to being dissected, and I'd no idea you were so observant!"

He looked round at her cautiously, to see if she were annoyed. He was so like one of the smaller children at Medling who had dug up a seed-bed in mistake for weeds one day that she laughed. He was watching her gravely, as though he would unearth more contrasts in her. She was glad when the lights went out and they settled themselves for the third Act.

On the way home she harked back to the conversation about women, teased Andrew for classifying them. "As though it's possible, with any lot of human beings! They simply won't fit!"

But he persisted that they did fit - all except her.

She did not accept his bait. Instead, she asked curiously, "What about Eleanor?"

He answered at once. "Undeveloped. Psychologically, still adolescent. A good brain, and emotions shelled in till they've gone queer. Sorry, but you asked. I should think she was brought up in a country vicarage."

She was startled by his perspicacity. "Did you know?"

"Was she?" he asked, amused. "No, of course I didn't know. It was just a good shot."

Hilary was wondering with a fascinated horror if everyone knew as much as this about everyone else - everyone except her. She asked him.

"No. Most people are too busy thinking about themselves. A doctor grows pretty shrewd about people. He's got to, if he's to get on. And I'm interested in the human race. I like to know about them."

Hilary said, a little defiantly, "I don't suppose you're always right. Eleanor's a wonderful person. Perfectly splendid."

Andrew said, "I should think you're quite right. In the old days she'd have been an Abbess - almost a saint. She'd have let off her emotions on her religion, and they'd have expanded and developed her, instead of drying up."

Hilary wondered what the piercing blue eyes had really found out about her. Nothing, she hoped. She liked to puzzle him. She did not inquire, lest she should give something away.

At the gate he said, "When am I going to see you again? Friday?"

She echoed stupidly, "Friday? I didn't know there was anything - "

He laughed, the blue eyes twinkling in the light of the street lamp. "There isn't. But we always seem to break off in the middle of a conversation, while there's still heaps more to say, and then I chew it all over till I can go on with it."

Surprised, she said, "I've been doing that, too."

"So much the better. Friday, then. Can I pick you up at the University?"

"For Goodness' sake, no. Think of Miss Cronshaw - and all of them! Can't I meet you somewhere?"

He chuckled. "I wondered if you'd discovered what a gossip-shop the place is. Right - let's meet at Mackie's then: a meal and a drive, so that we can talk. Say a quarter past one?"

She could find no reason to refuse, and before she could manufacture one, he was gone. Why should she refuse, anyway? Making a new friend was the most exciting thing

220

in the world, and she had not made an intimate one since Janet, years ago - had never thought to make another. One didn't, people said, as one grew older.

As she undressed, she wondered again what Andrew - how abominably cocksure he was! - thought he had found out about her. What was there to find out? What was she like? What were her principles, her ambitions, her interests, even? Surprised because she could not at once reply to any of these questions, she sat down on the bed to think about them.

You had to be efficient - that, quite certainly, came first. If you weren't, there was something about you to be despised.

You had to be brave. You couldn't, in fact, be efficient for long if you were not.

You had to be kind to people who were not as strong as you were - though there were not, it seemed, many of these. And not conceited, to think you were better than even the charlady who cleaned the corridors and wiped her face on her apron and said, "Moi!"

So much for principles. Those were all she had, and to them she held as far as she was able, though it was difficult always to be brave.

Ambitions? She did not think she had any. She never thought about the future much. She had got out of the way of it after her father's death. As long as she had Eleanor and a job, she was content.

Interests? She considered. History ought to have come first - had come first, once upon a time. She had wanted nothing better than to know more and more, to spend hours poring over old books and documents. But now, somehow, history had gone dry. People, she thought, were her chief interest now. What had Andrew said? The human race. He liked to know about them - so did she, now she had the chance. She had always liked it, really, she thought. The girls at Medling had never bored her, or even the other mistresses, when she had had time to give them her attention, though Eleanor had always put them down as dull. Her friends had interested her enormously. Her friends - and herself. That was new. She had never thought much about herself before. She had no idea at all what impression she made on people.

Heavens, it was late! How silly she was being. She bundled into her nightdress, suddenly sleepy, thinking confusedly that she was glad she had a decent, strong body as well as a good brain. That was her childhood in the country, most likely - and her mother, perhaps, for Gregory had not been physically strong. Funny, to think she owed something so pleasant to her mother.

6

Andrew gave her a careful lunch - which amused her, for she was used only to good plain food - and then tucked her into the car.

"You like going fast, don't you?" he asked, when they were out of the town, and accelerated to sixty miles an hour without waiting for her reply.

She did like going fast, when she realized that it was possible to breathe in spite of the rush of air past her nostrils. She thought with some amusement, "What a spinster I am!" because she was not used to having it taken for granted that her likes would fall in with someone else's. She was surprised that she did not resent it. Then, slewing round to look at Andrew, she thought, "One couldn't, of course," because he did look so absurdly like a chubby schoolboy in spite of the speed he was driving at and the skill of his hands on the wheel.

They left the straggling bungalows and came into woodland, up a hill which curved through miniature cliffs of red sandstone, with caves in them and bosses like gargoyles over church doors, and above, beech trunks crowned with copper and gold. The sun lit fires in the trees, the sharp smell of wood-smoke came from some cottager's garden. Hilary could have sung with pleasure. She snuggled into the rug, her eyes shining. Andrew, who could not go so fast now because of the winding road, looked round and smiled. "All right, there?"

She nodded, "Rather. Lovely."

She was glad that he did not seem to want to talk. They passed through the beechwoods, to fields of soft, tawny grass where sheep grazed. Pointed slabs of rock, scattered at random, lent the fields a wildness, foretelling the brown moorland, to which the road climbed, here flat and stark, there falling sheer away below parapets of stone to a valley where one surmised a rushing river. Its chief beauty was its colour - the purple brown of faded heather, pink near at hand, and in the distance a misty, rosy grey.

It was bleaker moor than Hilary was used to, higher, colder, less friendly, though she had a feeling that its friendship, once gained through effort and pain, would be more binding, perhaps more sweet, than that of the South Country moors.

Andrew drove on over the high land, scaring grouse whose queer, angry cry made Hilary laugh - "Go back! Go back!" Perhaps she was ready to laugh at anything.

"They're like angry old gentlemen," she said, and Andrew rejoined, "They *are* angry old gentlemen! Right up in the air about nothing at all!"

They saw a village, far down on their left - a clump of trees, a square tower of old-gold stone with four pinnacles, some grey roofs. Andrew said, "Stockton Monarchorum - jolly names these old places have!"

"Why was there more than one monarch," Hilary asked, "in such a little place?" Then wondered why she should have said anything so inane, and why, all in a day or two, she had discovered what it meant to be self-conscious, to hear one's own words and see one's own actions.

Andrew said, "The king and his queen, of course," and stole a look at her.

She had taken off her hat, and her crisp hair was blowing, showing its gold and russet lights and the bleached curls over her brow, which the sun had dotted with little golden freckles. The fine, fair down on her cheeks was more effective than any powder. She felt Andrew's eyes on her and smiled at him - frankly at first, then, unexpectedly, with a catch of the breath. She turned in a hurry towards the village in its dip in the hills. Andrew, following her gaze, said, "Let's go there for tea."

They had tea in the garden of the village inn - a plain, country tea, home-made bread, butter and jam, and tea so strong that they could almost cut it. They talked all the time; or rather, Andrew talked, stories of hospital life which made Hilary alternately shiver and laugh. The mental honesty which his calling had forced upon Andrew found its echo in Hilary's nature, his outspokenness about natural things tallied with the absence of veneer which Hilary's country upbringing had given her; the pity for human suffering, the determination to alleviate it, which shone, now and then, through the gaps in his rather earthy humour, excited her to poignant admiration.

He said very little about the war, which seemed to make him less far away from her than others of her generation. He had spent nearly all of it at a base hospital, and the rest in England. His service had been solid and useful, but not exciting. He was perhaps, at heart, ashamed because it had not been more exciting, just as Hilary was ashamed of having done nothing but teach. They spoke little of it.

Then Andrew drove uphill again. Even to the shadowed valley, the sky had given a smouldering hint of sunset. Over the hill's brow it faced them in all its glory of flaming bars of gold. The turn of the road took them eastward, and Hilary cried out, "Oh, Andrew, do let's wait and watch it a bit! I've never seen anything so lovely!"

Andrew stopped. He said, "There's a ledge down there. I've watched sunsets from it before. I hoped it would be a good one for you."

He swung out of the car and led the way, and Hilary

225

followed, liking him more than ever because he made time, sometimes, to watch sunsets, and because of his absurd showman assumption that the sun was performing its fireworks on purpose for them. She, too, had the light-heartedness which comes from good weather, good food, and everything falling out according to plan. It didn't matter what they did - the gods were on their side.

Andrew's ledge was a rocky shelf, carpeted with thyme and with some late bells of pink, cross-leaved heath. It faced due west across a lower stretch of moor, rusty with bracken, with little twisted trees which stood out black against the sky. Hilary flung herself down to enjoy it, and Andrew adroitly slipped the rug between her and the ground.

She laughed. "Andrew, it hasn't rained for weeks!"

He said solemnly, "There's a dew. Besides, you're a rheumatic type. People who freckle always are."

She looked to see if he meant it, and laughed again because it seemed that he did. "Nonsense! I've never had a single twinge!"

He sat down carefully beside her. "The time is not yet ripe. Don't boast."

It was amusing, she felt, to be taken care of. At home, she had taken pride in being the strongest of the family and in never considering bodily comfort at all. At Medling, it had never been considered until Eleanor's illness, and then only for Eleanor, who had accepted care grudgingly, as though the need of it were something to be ashamed of. They had both of them tacitly despised it a little. It was soft, to bother about your body. Now, here was someone who looked on comfort as a necessity, who was a hard worker and not at all soft, who forestalled her wishes, thought out plans to please her, and ran about after her with rugs. And instead of snorting at it, she liked it.

She sat sideways, with most of her weight on one hand, watching the wisps of gold turn to red, from red to sullen purple, and then to grey which gathered the whole scene into its restful arms; and sighed, because the vivid loveliness had passed. She felt a touch on the hand which rested on the ground, and Andrew's fingers closed on it. She shifted her weight, but it did not occur to her to take the hand away. Andrew picked it up and turned it over so that it lay on his palm.

"Tiny, for your size, aren't they? And soft. But lovely, supple fingers. They'd be good hands for surgery. The best surgeon I've ever watched is a woman."

"I'd have liked your job, I think," Hilary said.

He pulled her fingers and bent them, very gently, then laid one of his own across her palm, so that she curled hers over it instinctively and held it. "Why?" he asked.

"P'raps just because of the things you've told me about it. But I like doing things, rather than talking. If I had been a doctor, I'd have been a surgeon."

He nodded. "Surgery and faith healing - psycho-therapy, now perhaps - they're the only logical branches of the craft. Either cut out the ill, or make the soil which grew it healthy again. Both, sometimes. But anything else is a makeshift. Medicines do no good."

Hilary was interested. She hardly noticed her own grip on Andrew's finger. "D'you mean - that one's mental state's at the bottom of it all?"

He said vigorously, "I'm sure of it. The actual diseases, of course, are due to germs - or irritation, or what-not - but if you're not worried, or in a state at least of mental unrest, they don't get you. We're all in such a state at some time or other - so they get all of us at some time or other. But I'm perfectly certain that the two factors are necessary, always, before we're ill. The Christian Scientists score by trying to get the mental condition right; the doctor, by killing the germ or removing the irritation or just husbanding the patient's strength so that he can do those things for himself. What's really wanted is a profession which can do both."

That absorbed Hilary so much that she did not even notice that Andrew was talking only with his surface mind, marking time, as though he had something underneath to say but lacked courage to say it. She remarked, "That would account for - my father. And my sister Hermione. My mother, though, lived in a state of mental unrest, but she was never ill. And I don't see why Eleanor got appendicitis just when she did, or why I've never been ill myself, for I had my share of worry when I was a child."

Andrew said, "You were lucky to have such a good healthy body to start with. It would take a lifetime of worry or a lethal dose of germs to wear its resistance down. I expect your mother's the same . . . Don't you ever realize how lovely you are, Hilary?"

She had looked up, her attention still on his theory of illness, and, her mind refusing to switch so suddenly from one thing to another, echoed, "Lovely - what?"

Then she met his eyes, laughing, tender, eager. He said,

"Silly - *you*!"

She stayed, wide-eyed, for a second, then flushed up all at once, and turned in confusion to the gathering darkness. She said - and her voice, to herself, sounded composed - "I suppose that's it. I had a better start than Hermione. Thank goodness for it, that's all." Her heart was thumping. She wanted, Andrew to go on talking shop. And yet - wouldn't she be disappointed if he did?

He said, "It was the mixture of loveliness and intelligence that bowled me over, right at the beginning. All the intelligent women I've met before - and I've met a good few, of course - they're mostly plain, and even if they've got a certain amount of looks, they ram their cleverness down one's throat. Talk shop, or ride some hobby to death - show off their knowledge as though there's something unnatural about it. Yours is so much part of you that one hardly notices it. Wisdom, it is, more than cleverness, I think."

Hilary, laughing, said, "Poor intelligent ones. What about the lovely ones, then?"

He swept them aside with a movement of his arm. "There haven't been any. Little soft, pretty ones I've seen - and heard. They giggle and wriggle and roll an eye. But no lovely ones - like you."

She was helpless before him. She had liked him so much because he talked to her mind to mind - and now there was this, and she liked this too.

"I don't think most people think I'm lovely," she said.

"Most of them don't dare to tell you so. You're rather fierce, you know. And a Don. But they can't help thinking so. Margaret does, of course, and the rest of the crowd. You *are* lovely. And clever and brave, and - kind? I don't know whether you're kind or not."

She laughed, getting control of herself again. "Of course I'm kind. Soft-hearted, ridiculous. You should have heard me getting the children out of rows at Medling!"

He watched her, broodingly, for so long that she took matters firmly into her own hands, and scrambled up, saying, "I'm getting cold. Fancy being able to sit about like this, in October!"

He was upright before her, and stretching out a hand. She took it, and he pulled her up and found his face on a level with her own, his eyes, with a light in them, shining into hers. She laughed again, and murmured "Dear Andrew!" happily, as though she were enchanted. He pulled her to him, and she felt the hardness of his chest and smelt the unaccustomed smell of cloth and smoke and some male soapy fragrance. A great sense of comfort enveloped her. Henry's gentleness, Eleanor's restrained affection, flashed into memory and were blotted out.

When she raised her head from under his rain of kisses, he was stroking her hair and murmuring her name. "Hilary - Hilary. It's a dear, funny name. Boyish. You're like a boy, on first sight - but not afterwards."

"They wanted me to be a boy," she said, and he derided, "Stupid! They didn't know what you were going to grow into!"

She stood back, her hands on his arms, surveying him, wondering what Gregory would have said of him. Through his strength and his ardour she saw again the chubby,

230

grubby schoolboy. Gregory had liked schoolboys. She let his arms go round her again and felt, this time, his lips on hers. He laughed delightedly and did it again, and this time she kissed him too.

She said, inconsequently, it seemed to her, "I've always distrusted - bodies. I've only had to do with minds."

"Both useful instruments," he said. "We couldn't do without either, and if one's warped the other goes a bit wrong too. But the other one of the trinity - spirit rules them both."

"Andrew," she said, "you really are the most surprising person. One doesn't expect you to think things like that - much less say them!"

He was standing back from her now, holding her hand, but looking beyond her. "Why? Because I'm tubby and spruce and - sometimes rather coarse?"

She caught her breath, then laughed. "I suppose so. I hadn't put it so crudely, even to myself. Well-fed, well-dressed, and a bit Rabelaisian, I should have said."

He grinned, swinging her hand. "Oh, I can recognize spirit when I see it. It's you, of course, who've made me do obeisance to it just now. They're all three of them strong in you - but spirit's strongest."

She marvelled again at his clear sight, when they had hardly touched, in conversation, on any matter the least bit spiritual. Was it true, that spirit was strongest in her? Thinking of her father, she concluded that it might be. She could not have admired Gregory so whole-heartedly if her values had differed much from his. It was strongest in Eleanor too. She said so.

Andrew treated Eleanor tenderly. "Poor lady, yes. It's a pity the religious life's gone out of fashion. Spirit would have won in her, then."

"And now?" Hilary asked, startled.

"Mind, I should hope. That would be happiest."

Hilary, twinkling, asked, "Which wins in you, Andrew?"

He spread out his hands, "Don't ask! They're all at war! I'm terribly fond of my food!"

They were silent as he tucked the rugs round her, and during the first part of the drive home. Before they came into the town, he stopped by the roadside.

"What's the matter?" Hilary asked. "Run out of petrol?"

He snorted. "I don't run out of petrol! Didn't we agree that we hated inefficiency more than anything? No, I just wanted - please - to kiss you again."

She was charmed. "Andrew, how funny and nice of you!"

He did not only kiss her. He took her in his arms, gently, as though she were something breakable She lay there, inexpressibly comfortable, conscious of the comfort, of her own quick-beating heart and, with surprise, of his tapping just as quickly under her cheek.

He said deeply, "I do love you, Hilary. All the best bits of me love you."

She rubbed her head against his chin. "I think I love you too. It's absurd - only the fourth time we've ever seen each other. Can one love as quickly as all that?"

"I knew I could, the first minute I set eyes on you," he avowed. "I've always told myself that love's a thing one allows oneself - or doesn't . . . That one can take it or refuse it at will, once the initial attraction's recognized. Now, that

232

conviction's shaken. I didn't specially want to love anyone, just now. I'm too busy. But - I could no more keep myself from coming where there was a chance of seeing you than I could go without sleep for a week."

She said, "I've never thought about loving. About friendship, a lot. How one must trust a friend, absolutely, and never expect things as a right."

"One must trust a lover, too," he said, sternly, almost, and she corrected him dreamily.

"One couldn't help trusting a person one loved."

He took her home, and, a little doubtfully, she invited him to supper. She was glad, though, when he shook his head. "No. Anticlimax. Don't you agree?"

She did. "Only, I don't want you to go. Where *do* you go, Andrew?"

"When I'm here, to my people. Not very far from the Falkners' house. My father's still alive - my mother died some years ago - and one of my sisters keeps house for him. It's a dullish household - the gov'nor's getting old and crotchety, and Ena's a bit of a Martha: bustles about the kitchen and hasn't time for much else. She's a good old sort though - one day you must meet her. And when I'm not here - when I'm in London - I live in the students' hostel next door to St. Patrick's Hospital. It gives me good food and a good bed and chaps to talk to . . ."

They both wanted to stay, talking, indefinitely; but they were literally talked out, and they could not stay by the kerb and simply gaze. So Hilary left him, and went round the garden and indoors by the back way.

Eleanor was working at the table. About her, sitting stiff

233

as a ramrod, Hilary threw an arm. (Poor Eleanor, who had never lived and was withering already!) Eleanor grunted, "I shan't be long with this." She really meant, "Don't bother, I'm busy," and Hilary smiled and turned away. On the mantelpiece was a letter from Hermione. (Poor Hermione, who was less than half alive!)

Eleanor's work lasted her for the evening. Hilary, glancing up at her, recalled Andrew's words - "Mind, I hope - that would be happiest." Dear Andrew, it was nice of him to hope for Eleanor!

She could not, somehow, talk of him. It was a good thing Eleanor was busy. After all, what was there to tell? Nothing, but magic, and a flaming sunset, and a lot of talk which had been wonderful at the time but which, she knew, would fall flat, retailed by herself, before Eleanor's critical acuity. "Woolly," Eleanor would call it, and ask how Andrew's theories could be proved.

But in spite of this, and because of Hilary's inefficiency at any but "Timbuctoo sort of lies", Andrew's name kept cropping up in conversation, and Hilary's eyes shone and she walked with a spring and sang as she walked.

This extreme of happiness brought a new alertness to her mind, as though, with the awakening of a dormant part of her, she was altogether more alive. She took her work in her stride, chaffed and chivied her students until they made greater efforts than they had thought possible and enjoyed making them. Professor Hewer was delighted with her. She was an experiment and she had succeeded. He chatted with his wife about his power of rightly estimating human character.

The senior common room regarded her with some caution. They were not used to such abounding vitality. They had learnt long ago to control exuberant spirits; Hilary, only to hide exuberant pain.

Sooner or later, of course, Andrew had to come into the little house. The first time she saw him there, Hilary shouted with laughter. He was standing in the sitting-room, enormously broad in his muffler and leather coat. There were flowers on the mantelpiece - beech-leaves and Michaelmas daisies - the new check curtains, yellow and white, were daintily clean, there were books, but not too many books, lying about, the floor was polished, the hand-woven cushion covers all tidily shaken up. And the room looked anaemic. There wasn't a single chair which would hold Andrew comfortably, and one felt that the smell of a pipe would be a desecration. Andrew could not see what she was laughing at. But then, he could not see himself in that room.

Supper, too, was an awkward meal. The little maid was thrown into a panic by the unusual presence of a man in the house. She undercooked the potatoes and spilled the gravy on the cloth, and listened so anxiously for the bell that she heard it before it rang and burst in before the meat course was half over and whisked away Andrew's plate. And although they laughed to pass it off, there was something exasperated about Hilary's laughter and almost faintly malicious about Eleanor's. It was the sort of thing Andrew could make a funny story of, and Hilary couldn't bear to think of his making funny stories about her household.

Eleanor behaved, in her own style, perfectly - she was dignified, ready to talk intelligently on any subject which was brought up and to introduce promising new themes when a pause came. Hilary had admired the attitude hundreds of times when she had seen it used on parents at school functions. Now, somehow, it did not fit. Andrew's joyous self-confidence was subdued before it, and Hilary fiercely resented the subduing. He told a story and Eleanor did not laugh - did not understand, most likely, though it was not a dirty story. He encouraged her to talk, but she was so academic that Hilary could have screamed. When they had drunk their coffee, by the gas fire in the sitting-room, with Andrew wedged firmly into one of the basket-chairs, he suggested taking them both to a popular film which was being shown in Fenchester. Even about that he was charming - "I wouldn't try to hook you out, only this is its last night and it really is worth seeing," he said.

Eleanor declined, because films always gave her a headache. "But you go, please," she said. "I've heaps of things to do here." And they went, thankfully.

In the car, Andrew sighed with gusty relief. "Must we do that again?" he said, with the guilelessness of a child of six.

Hilary could not help laughing. She ought to have been cross, but she felt exactly the same herself. "Poor Andrew! Did you simply hate it?"

"I felt very Agag," he allowed; "as though I might put my foot in something, heavily, at any minute. Uncharted country, to me. I didn't belong. Extraordinary, that you should live like that!"

It seemed extraordinary to Hilary herself, then; a queer,

arid, limited existence whose only merit was its stability. She said, "I suppose, one way or another, I've always been hemmed in, so I don't notice it. It's almost more extraordinary to me to be unhampered."

Every few days she saw Andrew. He had demanded a copy of her time-table and carried it in his pocket, and would ring her up, with unfailing accuracy, at moments when she was free to reply to him. They would arrange an appointment and go off together - sometimes just to lunch, when Hilary had a heavy day, sometimes for a whole afternoon and evening, sometimes to a cinema or theatre with some of the Falkner party. To these Eleanor now and then came, too, and seemed to enjoy them. Of the other excursions, Hilary spoke to her when long absences had to be explained and not otherwise. She had an idea that Eleanor's feelings would be hurt if she knew how many they were.

She was taken to Andrew's father's house. The old man was in bed, as it happened, and not on view, and Ena Fraser was as cold to her as Eleanor had been to Andrew. Hilary was disappointed. She liked to be liked, and specially by Andrew's people. He made light of it. "She's always like that with strangers. Inferiority feeling, I suppose. She'll soon grow out of it, with you - anyone would: you're so sweetly unsuperior."

They learnt more about each other than Hilary had ever learnt of Eleanor: about each other's childhood, each other's moods, each other's temper, as well as everyday tastes and manners.

On the days when they did not meet, she dreamed of

him, treasured up thoughts and incidents to tell him, heard his name in every harmony of art or nature, and had no shadowy remembrance of ever having been in a similar state before. Because she was so intensely alive, her work did not suffer. But her real life was outside college, she could not even pretend an interest in its small talk and the internal relationships of the people there. She seemed literally to glow with happiness, and a new gentleness crept into her ways, perhaps from having no longer, in the part of her life which mattered, to fight for herself. She was more popular than ever with her students, and even the common room thawed at last and treated her as one of its inner circle.

While Hilary grew softer and more sensitive, Eleanor seemed to harden in her new life. She had never been very much interested in clothes; now she became so careless as to appear eccentric. Her garments, once good, were shabby and years behind the fashion. Her greying hair was untidy, so she had it off and it hung in wisps round her face, straining back from her high forehead to a school-girl's slide. Her manner had always been downright, now it became abrupt. She spoke of little but her work and the people connected with it, all of whom she seemed to dislike. When Hilary talked of her own doings, Eleanor as likely as not would open a book or ostentatiously take out a wad of papers to look through. She did not even keep up an appearance of interest.

Hilary noticed this last, though, up in the clouds as she was, the other changes escaped her. She was hurt. Half the enjoyment of doing things apart from Eleanor had always lain in recounting them to her afterwards. She wondered anxiously if Eleanor was working too hard, yet hesitated, because they had never fussed each other, to ask.

The vacation came, and they saw, by necessity, more of each other; and the more they had of each other's company, the more snappy did Eleanor become. She had not a kind word for Hilary or for anyone else. Hilary realized at last that the thing must be dealt with. Even through her haze of happiness she felt the discomfort of it. Yet to criticize Eleanor to her face was hardly to be thought of - she had never even wanted to carp at her, during all these years.

While she was still nervously seeking an opportunity to protest, the occasion came on her unawares. Eleanor went off into a tirade against a fellow research-student, and Hilary, who had just come in from the cheerful give-and-take of the Falkner household, grinned at her and, instead of clucking sympathetically, said, "Miaow!"

Eleanor stopped short, stared, and finally laughed; just as she had done when Hilary had cheeked her in her own garden, years ago. Hilary laughed too, with relief that she still really was the same Eleanor and not a metamorphosis brought about by years and change of occupation.

But this time she went stiff again in an instant. "What do you mean?"

"You're getting catty," Hilary said. "Catty and sour, and frightening me out of my wits."

Now that the unthinkable was actually in process, it did not embarrass her. Instead of sitting on the floor at Eleanor's feet, she had a feeling of standing on a step above her and looking down, good-humoured, sure of herself, and smiling. She did smile.

Eleanor did not. She looked away out of the window, her lips pressed together. Then she looked back, quite friendly, straight into Hilary's eyes. She said, "I know. I'm ashamed of myself. The fact is, I've been having what I suppose is rheumatism. Odd aches and pains - sometimes nothing much, sometimes quite bad, and always there. It makes me irritable. I'm not used to having to think about my health."

Hilary said, "Thank goodness!" and Eleanor threw back her head and laughed, and then clutched the back of her neck. "There - it gets me when I move suddenly . . . Why thank goodness for anything so annoying, anyway?"

"Well, rheumatism you can at any rate go to a doctor about. I was afraid you were hating being here, or that I'd done something to irritate you; that you were tired of living with me, or something."

"That's one way of looking at it," Eleanor allowed. "No, I like the work enormously. And if I wanted to throw you out, I shouldn't hesitate to say so." The affection in her eyes robbed the words of any possible sting, and only made Hilary say contentedly, "No, I suppose you wouldn't." Eleanor threw her once again that amused look of one who has inside knowledge, but Hilary, as usual, did not see it.

She was considering, busily, ways and means, conscious-stricken, a little, for stopping short at the fact of Eleanor's surliness and looking no further than her own nose for a reason. "You'd better see someone about it, hadn't you?"

Eleanor said, "I've made an appointment for to-morrow afternoon." Then, with a sudden descent from her heights of self-sufficiency, she caught Hilary's hand. "Come with me. I do so hate going to doctors. I'm terrified she'll say something frightful, like having my tonsils out. You can't think how I loathed that anaesthetic!"

"Of course I'll come! Fancy thinking for a second that I'd let you go alone!" Hilary was still penitent. Besides, it always gave her a warm feeling when Eleanor made one of her rare appeals. "What time, and where?"

"Half-past three, in Barnes Avenue, facing the Botanical Gardens. I don't know the woman, but Mrs. Fenner - the one I had to tea, you know - has her and says she's good. You don't know what a relief it is to have told you about it!"

There was no more snapping for the whole of the evening Eleanor was her old kindly, if rather acid, self, Hilary anxious for nothing but her friend's welfare. It was only when, the problem triumphantly behind her, she turned her thoughts languidly forward to the next day's programme, that she remembered that she had promised to meet Andrew for tea at a quarter to four. And that was on the opposite side of the town from the Botanical Gardens.

There was just time to send a post card to his home. One couldn't put off an appointment with a doctor for a tea-party. She would meet him after tea instead.

The rheumatism proved to be, most likely, due to a dead tooth, and nothing worse was set in train than X-ray and probable extraction, and some drops to be taken daily in milk. Hilary had tea with Eleanor and saw her into the train, and swung on to a bus for her meeting-place. The possibility of Andrew's not being there simply did not occur to her.

He was waiting for her, a shade of anxiety on his smooth face, for she was a few minutes late. He said, "I hope it's nothing serious. And that you've got a decent doctor."

Nice of him, Hilary thought, to mind about Eleanor, who was always so brusque with him. She said so.

"It's you I mind about really, of course. Anyway, she can't help being brusque. She's so stuffed with repressions that to get anything out at all needs a small explosion. I expect that's the cause of all the trouble, if the truth were known. Pity someone doesn't fall in love with *her* - it's the only cure. And no one ever will."

Hilary demanded fiercely, "Why not?"

"(*a*) She's not attractive, at any rate to men; and (*b*) she wouldn't let them."

"I hate you when you talk like that. As though different things attracted men and women - "

"They do, of course. Too obvious to require statement," Andrew said, unrepentant.

"Why can't they both be attracted by just a decent person? I am. A person who's humorous and trustable and charitable and brave - I don't care whether they're man or woman, I like them."

Andrew said, "Hoots!" and linked his arm in hers and marched her to the car. "Tell me what's the matter with her, anyway, and then I'll tell you whether your doctor's doing the right thing."

She chuckled at his ingenuous conceit, but he only persisted that there were good doctors and bad doctors and that there was nothing to laugh at all. When she said, "What's the matter is rheumatism," he stood still.

"And you put off my tea-party for a rheumatism? Hell cat! I thought it was something bad!"

"Rheumatism's bad enough if you've got it," she countered. "She was terrified to go alone; that's why I put you off."

He grumbled, "What on earth is there to be terrified of in *rheumatism?* If it had been something surgical I'd have sympathized - "

"Terrifying enough, to think you may be going to turn into one of those awful cripples - "

"Oh well - but it obviously wasn't that sort of thing, from what you've said. Muscular rheumatism doesn't cripple you."

She was irritated with him, "It's all very well for you - you *know* things like that. People who aren't doctors don't, so they get frightened. Nothing to snort at, in not having specialized knowledge. I don't snort at you because you can't tell me details of the War of American Independence! Besides, there was something surgical - or might have been; something about tonsils."

He grinned. "All right. I take it all back. I'd worked my

243

self into a state of sympathetic apprehension, that was all, and then it fell flat. It's queer, about patients, though. The most intelligent people, even, lose every particle of sense they've got when they turn into patients. A friend of mine, a physician, saw a woman the other day - a Headmistress - a highly educated woman, in charge of a couple of hundred kids and I don't know how many younger mistresses. She'd got T.B. and he told her so and told her the remedy. She wasn't very far advanced; she'd have got well all right, and she'd got the money, easily, for a year in Switzerland. But would she? Not on your life. She wrote to him, a day or two later, reproaching him for telling her what the trouble was - said she was too sensitive to bear even the mention of such a dreadful disease, and that she'd been to see someone else who said it was nothing but nerves and was sending her for a month to the sea. We still don't know whether the fellow was a knave or a fool . . . Too sensitive to bear looking the truth in the face when it's a matter of life or death! And she's not the only one . . . Why don't they bring kids up to think truth's the only thing in the world that matters?"

Andrew riding a hobby-horse was a delight. "Don't they? I suppose they don't. Her two hundred wouldn't get that idea, you may be sure . . . We did, I think, along with other things - "

He surveyed her contentedly. "You - yes, you're honest enough, I should say. For which thank goodness . . . Who's looking after your friend?"

"Dr. Bray. Helena Bray," she told him.

He seemed satisfied. "She's a good, sound, sensible lass.

Like her legs."

"Legs?"

"Like an elephant's. Very dependable."

She could not help laughing, both at him and at his attitude to women. He was so definite in his likes and dislikes of their physical attributes, so surprisingly willing to admire their mental ability just as he would have admired a man's. She wondered whether she would have liked him as much if he had been a woman.

He guffawed at the mere idea. And, indeed, it was ludicrous.

"No, you couldn't be you - and a woman."

"Any more than you could be you - and a man."

"Why not?" she defended herself indignantly. "I should hardly be different at all. Nothing but clothes - and a monocle, perhaps."

He hooted. "A nice sort of awful fright you'd look!"

They went for a drive by the light of a great full moon, had dinner at a wayside inn - Andrew knew very well where to find good food - and drove on, stopping on the open moor to talk and kiss. Hilary was growing used to this deliberate planning for embraces; had come, indeed, to wait eagerly for them, as chances to show Andrew how very much she loved him. She had been shocked, at first, that they should be anything but spontaneous, like the one on the rocky ledge. She wondered what would happen when the weather grew really cold. They could not sit in the car and talk on a foggy, frosty night. She wished suddenly, angrily, that her own household could be different. "If it had been Eleanor who'd wanted him, I'd have jolly well made it easy and nice for her!" Then was appalled at herself for the criticism of Eleanor's attitude.

As Andrew drove them slowly home, she gave herself up to the pleasure of listening to his talk. Dear Andrew, with his genuine, far-reaching knowledge of his own profession, his entranced dabblings in art, philosophy, history - all the things which made life interesting. He was quite the most stimulating person she had ever met: the only person whose vitality was equal to her own.

When she said something to that effect, he rejoined, "I could say the same to you. You've got a high standard, and it makes me love showing off to you. Sort of mental cold shower - keeps the brain on the alert. I like being kept up to the mark. I enjoy just being with you more than anything in the world."

There was a, deep note in his voice at the last sentence which made Hilary look at him sharply. It was as though he meant it so far down in himself that it did not easily come to the surface. She knew that feeling. She had it when she said, "Dear Andrew." She said it so often to herself that she felt self-conscious when it became articulate.

She said it now - "Dear Andrew. So do I, of course."

He cocked an eyebrow at her and they both chuckled, because things simply had to be moved to a lighter vein or who knew where they might have landed. These solemn moments, when both were unsure of themselves, were creeping more often into their conversations lately. Hilary was afraid of them and yet intrigued, curious, like a wild animal. They seemed to lead up to something and leave her gasping, relieved yet disappointed when the climax failed to come.

She was not late in getting home, but Eleanor had gone to bed.

"Only tired," she said, in answer to Hilary's inquiries. "I expect I got worked up about going to that doctor. Silly - but then, I'm not used to doing things like that."

8

The following week, Eleanor had several teeth out. The day after, her rheumatism flared up to such an extent that she had to go to bed and have the doctor to the house. She was in such pain and seemed so ill that Hilary was alarmed, in spite of the doctor's cheerful assurances that the flare-up was a good sign and meant that the trouble really was due to the teeth. She could not easily stay away from her own work, so she arranged for a nurse to help the little maid by day and rushed home as early as she could and managed for her during the night, which meant getting up a dozen times or so. For five days they had their hands full to keep their patient even moderately comfortable. Expeditions with Andrew were out of the question. Hilary wrote in a hurry and told him so. She had hardly time to miss him, and, after three nights more or less up, hardly the mental energy. He wrote by return, and at the end of a week came to the house.

In the little polished sitting-room, Hilary rushed into his

arms. "Oh, Andrew, it's been so beastly without you - and I'm so *tired!* I don't believe I've ever been really tired before!"

He gathered her in so that she leaned against him. There was not a chair which would have taken them both. "She's over the worst now, isn't she?"

"Dr. Bray says so. I suppose she knows. She had to have morphia for the pain!"

"She'll be all right in a bit, now the teeth where the germs live are gone."

Hilary was soothed by his calm. She said so.

"I wish I'd come before," he said. "Only I thought you'd wish me out of the way . . . Come out with me now and forget it for a bit."

"Andrew, I can't! The nurse is off, now, and Bella's as much use as a sick monkey!"

He argued with her. "There can't be anything to do except take up her food!"

"There might be. She still has to be helped to move - "

"Well, then, invite me to supper!"

"I'll do that, of course! Only I hope you're not too hungry - I haven't had time to bother much about food. I've lived on eggs, mostly."

"I'll sup off - " he glanced round the room - "nuts and bran biscuits if you want me to!"

"I don't!" she assured him indignantly. "Does it look like that? We're not, you know! Vegges or antivivisectionists or anything cranky!"

He grinned. "D'you like living here?"

She looked about the room, thinking of its memories; or

248

rather, of the memories of its furniture, for the room had few associations which had not been blurred by stronger things. She said sturdily, "Yes. It's the sort of life I'm used to. Simple, with the country close at hand. I'm not a luxurious person. And Eleanor and I make very few demands on each other, really . . . She can't help being ill."

He prowled round, looking at the pictures; Eleanor's pictures - Hilary had acquired none of her own; delicate, dainty things, all of them. Medici prints, Japanese woodcuts, an unframed water-colour or two which she had done herself. He paused at the small table on which papers lived, and turned them over - *Time and Tide*, *G.K.'s Weekly*, *The Nation*, *The Times Literary* and *Educational* Supplements, the *Journal* of the Royal Horticultural Society.

"It's a queer room," he said. "Not a woman's and certainly not a man's."

"An educated person's room, just?" Hilary suggested. He said, "The hive of a worker bee."

He lowered himself cautiously on to the wicker couch as though he felt, as he looked, too heavy for it. Hilary sat beside him, and before long they were happily talking the nonsense which Hilary had only so lately learnt. In the middle of it, a bell tinkled above in Eleanor's room. Hilary broke away and ran upstairs.

"She'd flumped down and couldn't get herself comfortable again," she said when she came down. "That's the sort of thing I can't leave to Bella."

He asked gloomily, "Do you have to lift her?" When she said serenely, "Of course," he grumbled, "You'll strain your self. It isn't good for you."

She laughed at him, "I'm as strong as a moor pony. You know that quite well; you're just being silly."

He said, "I know. I'm jealous," and Hilary hugged him. But he was not quite appeased.

The little room seemed somehow less stiff without Eleanor in it. They found that they could talk in it quite comfortably. They felt pleasantly domestic when Bella came in to set the supper and Hilary went into the kitchen to concoct an omelette. Eating a meal which one of them had cooked, together in a house, was so much more homely than being served in an inn. Andrew's second evening in her home was a success, and Hilary's hopes for the winter rose suddenly.

When the meal was eaten, Eleanor settled again, and they were sitting companionably by the fire, Andrew said, "You. know, not seeing you makes me definitely peevish. I could have quarrelled with you quite easily when I first came."

Hilary confessed, "I was resenting you a bit, too . . . I thought it was just being tired . . . I'm better now, aren't you?"

"Infinitely better," Andrew said, and looked at her so that she crossed the hearthrug swiftly and sat with her cheek against his knee.

"Only," he added, "we simply mustn't be apart too long again."

Hilary agreed, happily. It was going to be so much easier, now that the little house had stopped being antagonistic. Her love for Andrew underwent a change that day; turned into something calmer, less wild, something which looked forward to quiet evenings like this one, just the two of them together, instead of to the excitement of outings and battles of the mind.

After that day, Eleanor began definitely to mend. She was able to sit out of bed, and very soon to come downstairs. She remained, however, languid and disinclined to do things for herself. To keep the nurse would have been absurd, yet her departure made it increasingly difficult for Hilary to get away except when she had to for her work. She managed two afternoon walks with Andrew, and once he came back to tea. But the room had receded into its austere reserve and gave him no encouragement.

Margaret wanted her to go home with her one evening, but Hilary had excuses. "She's so sweet and grateful for what I do, I simply haven't the heart to stay out till late," she said. "I'm going to rush home right away."

"Then I shall rush with you," Margaret announced. "We can talk in the train. You don't mind, do you? I never get a word with you nowadays."

"I shall be delighted," Hilary said. "Only, I don't know what sort of a meal you'll get. I have to leave all that to Bella."

"Meal - as if I minded!" Margaret sniffed, and came.

She stayed all the evening, chatting, and cheered Eleanor enormously. The next day she delivered a crisp dictum to Hilary.

"It's cheek, offering you advice, I know. But I've lived with a lot of sisters and brothers, and I know how things happen. If you're in love you mustn't let anything – *anything* - interfere with it. If you're convinced that it's the

251

most important thing at the moment, you must *let* it be, and keep other loyalties from butting in."

"How do you know I'm in love?" Hilary demanded. She had come to know Margaret Falkner very well - but this evidence of observation amazed her. "And what do you mean?"

"I've seen you and Andrew together, haven't I? I like Andrew, he's a dear, and there's much more to him than most people see. Oh, you've seen it all right, I know. But he's always been - a bit of a spoilt child. Always gets what he wants. I wouldn't answer for him, quite, if he's neglected."

Hilary scolded, because she was alarmed. "But Andrew knows I wouldn't neglect him for the world - I *hate* neglecting him - if it wasn't a case of illness. He's a doctor; he knows what illness means."

"That's just why he put up with it while she was bad," Margaret persisted. "Now she's better - well, you know better than I do whether she's got more claim on you than he has. He's beginning to feel a bit injured."

"Has he been grousing?" Hilary asked. If he had, she would be furious.

"Of course he hasn't!" Margaret said. "Would he? No, I know Andrew. He's got the sulky, unbelieving look he used to have when he was a small boy and someone else had something he wanted."

Hilary could not stand that. Andrew, a small, hurt boy! And then, against him, she saw Eleanor, giving years of kindness, demanding nothing and then, in need, turning to the friend she trusted, and finding - no one. She looked at

Margaret helplessly.

Margaret was talking on with determination. "To-night, I'm going to look after Eleanor. We get on quite well, and I shall entertain her beautifully. And you'll go home - my home - and Andrew will be there and most of the others will be out."

It was too tempting to refuse. Andrew, when he saw her, came bolting across the room. He was there with just Mr. and Mrs. Falkner, and it was not long before Mrs. Falkner went off to see about supper, and her husband, mumbling something about brushes which needed cleaning, followed her out of the room. It was not long either, before Andrew was perched on the arm of Hilary's chair and Hilary leaning against him. She was too tired to talk, or even to listen very intelligently. But Andrew did not seem to want to talk, only to be there with her.

They had supper, rowdily, with such of the family as was there - young Don and Leila and their parents. After it, and some desultory conversation by the fire, Leila departed to her Girl Guides; Don to work, and Mrs. Falkner, with apologies, to a Women Citizens' meeting. Mr. Falkner showed an inclination to stay by the fire, but Leila, on her way out, reminded him firmly that he really must get some illustrations done to go off by the first post to-morrow if he wanted them accepted. He was proud of the success of his hobby, far prouder than of his business, and he took the hint.

Andrew and Hilary looked at each other and laughed. "A shame to drive them from their own fireside! But aren't they dears to go?" Hilary said.

If she was tired, Andrew was distrait. He had been in Fenchester very little during the past week. "What was the good, when I couldn't see you?" he said. "And I was having a busy spell anyway - things always come in rushes, in my job."

There was plenty to talk about, as always. But the conversation, this evening, kept trembling on the edge of expectancy and dying away, then pulling itself bravely together, to go on about Andrew's work, the car, the things they would do when the weather was warmer. Perhaps it was that Hilary could not quite keep her mind off Eleanor and so did not give Andrew her whole attention, and he felt this and was piqued by it; perhaps their relationship had come to a stage when it must go perceptibly forward or back. In any case the evening had something lacking.

He took her home and waited to pick up Margaret. To Margaret, Hilary said, "You're a perfect lamb, my dear, and I'm taking your advice to heart."

Margaret - sensible, matter-of-fact Margaret - squeezed her arm and said, "I think I want you to be happy more than anything in the world," and fled, leaving Hilary, moist at the eyes, looking after her.

Hilary thought involuntarily, "If Eleanor saw things that way, everything might be happily settled by now." But then, how could Eleanor see things any way at all, when she had not been told, really, anything about the business? Wasn't she justified in obstructing, when she was being unfriendlily kept in the dark? But Margaret had been kept in the dark, too, except for the light of her own observations, and she had seen. Then, horrified, how could

254

one possibly assume that Eleanor was obstructing? Poor Eleanor; she couldn't help being ill. People weren't ill, Andrew said, unless they were worried. If Eleanor had just wished, as Margaret did, for her friend's happiness, she wouldn't have been worried and she would not have been ill . . . This was all too far-fetched, too mixed up and muddled. Better stick to facts and stop theorizing.

The facts, however arrived at, seemed to be these: Eleanor had never been helpful about Andrew, and now she *was* obstructing, though a good deal of it wasn't on purpose. And she had been kept in the dark as to the extent of Hilary's preoccupation with Andrew, and that, considering the depth of their friendship, was unfair, and must at once be remedied.

She shut the front door behind her and went into the sitting-room. Eleanor looked up at her, determination in her face, and shot out, "Hilary, you must tell me - are you going to marry Andrew?"

Hilary's plans were all upset. She began, "No - " and before she could say any more Eleanor exclaimed, "Thank heaven!" and buried her head in her arms on the edge of the table.

Hilary sat down opposite her, intent on keeping calm. "Why 'thank heaven', Eleanor?"

Eleanor raised her head and snapped out, "He's not good enough for you, that's all. I've been so anxious . . . I thought you didn't see through him."

This was worse than anything Hilary could have foretold. "See through" Andrew . . . Not good enough for her . . . Eleanor had been thinking of her happiness after all.

Thinking of it so much as to risk losing her friendship by not humouring her. She must never deceive Eleanor again.

She said, "Eleanor, darling, I only said I wasn't going to marry Andrew because he hasn't asked me. If he does ask me, I shall say 'Yes'."

Eleanor dropped her head on her arms again. She said dully, "I was afraid so."

Presently she spoke again, carefully. "I must tell you what I think of him. If you hate me for it, I can't help it. I'm a pretty good judge of people. You're not. You're too un-suspicious, you take them at their own valuation. I should never forgive myself if you married him without any warning and then - were disappointed."

Hilary said involuntarily, "Then you have been worrying?"

"Worrying? Of course I've been worrying. Hilary, don't you see he's just a sham? He talks - he's clever, he can talk about anything you're interested in. He flatters you for your mind more than for your looks, because he knows you attach more importance to minds than to looks. But do you think it's your mind that attracts him? D'you think I haven't seen the way he looks at you? He's self-indulgent, sensuous, for all his cleverness. No one who wasn't could be so fat. I hate fat men. And he's stuffed with conceit. When he's got what he wants, he'll stop flattering you and expect you to flatter him. And if he doesn't get everything his own way he'll give you - hell."

In the silence, a tiny cinder dropping in the grate sounded like an avalanche. Eleanor's face was hidden again. Hilary was saying to herself, "It isn't true, it isn't true!"

In a minute, she heard herself speaking, steadily. "He may be - all those things. Like a naughty, self-indulgent little schoolboy. But there are other qualities in him too. And even if he is - all those things - I love him. We need each other, he and I."

Silence again. Then Eleanor, still dully, "Well, I've told you. I had to tell you. Oh, Hilary, take care of yourself!"

Hilary could not resent anything which had been done when Eleanor talked like that. She came and knelt beside Eleanor and said, "I ought to have told you before about it all. I've been enchanted - so happy I simply didn't think of anyone else's point of view. It wasn't that I wanted to deceive you. I suppose I knew, inside, that you disapproved, and that made me shy."

Eleanor stroked her hair with a thin, firm hand. When she had done that years ago, it had made Hilary purr with content. Now, because it was not Andrew's hand, she could barely control herself not to jerk her head away.

"I know," Eleanor was saying. "I got bitter about it. Bitter because you'd put me so completely out of your thoughts. Silly of me, I know. Love's like an illness, almost. You can't control it. But friendship's more important, in the long run. You'd have come back to me. Don't hate me, Hilary."

She rose, stiffly, for she still had pain about her. Hilary felt very strong and vital beside her. She thrust a hand under the thin elbow, to support her. "I couldn't hate you - how could I, after all these years? Andrew may be the froth, but you're the bread-and-butter that one depends on." She meant it, then - loving Andrew was a game, almost, beside the deep attachment to her friend.

Eleanor brushed a cheek across her lips and went upstairs, a sad, starved-looking figure, extraordinarily aged since the early days at Medling. Hilary was left looking into the fire, murmuring to herself, "It isn't true about Andrew - it isn't true."

Friendship was more important than love - but she had friendship and love together, with Andrew, and friendship had come first. What about all those arguments they had had - still had, in the intervals of making love? Old friends were the bread-and-butter - but one must have froth as well. "I must. I've never had any before. I can't live without it now."

The turn of the kaleidoscope had destroyed her carefully-thought-out pattern and left a dreadful muddle. Instead of the villain, was Eleanor to be the guardian angel? Andrew, instead of the hero, the treacherous friend? Was Eleanor's Andrew the real one, her own the product of enchantment? Did it matter? She loved him, whichever he might be.

9

After that, there was no real difficulty about going out with Andrew. Sometimes Margaret went to be with Eleanor, and even when she did not Eleanor made no complaint. She improved rapidly and was back at work in a few weeks, just as Andrew and Dr. Bray had predicted. When Hilary came home from her expeditions, Eleanor would look at her sharply and refrain from asking questions, and Hilary would give her an outline of where they had been and what they had seen, and nothing - or very little - of what they had said.

When she was with Andrew, she was as much as ever his. He charmed her with all his ways. He was a greedy little schoolboy, and she loved him for it. He was self-indulgent, but he denied himself for her. He was sensuous, perhaps - he loved her beauty and told her so, and she saw no harm in it. It was natural for two young, strong people who were good friends to have that feeling about each other. Eleanor's early years had sent her all wrong about that. Against his nature, perhaps, he treated her body, as he treated her mind, with respect. She loved him all the more for that.

Eleanor's queries had crystallized her ideas of the future. The natural outcome of this good fellowship was marriage, and to it she looked unquestioningly. It was foolish for a young man with his way to make to marry too soon; they had agreed about that, though not with regard, particularly, to themselves. When he had made his name, they would marry without a doubt. She was in no hurry. For him to have asked her if she was willing would have been foolish. He knew as well as she did that she was. That he did not ask her was just evidence of that queer chivalry which prevented a man from binding one until he could support a wife. The phrase made Hilary laugh. She did not think she would be expensive to support.

When she was not with Andrew, her mind went back, sometimes, to Eleanor's accusations. Perhaps it was reaction to these remarks which made her all the more spartan with herself. She wore her clothes plain, although she took care of them. She lived on the plainest food. She took cold baths and walked in the rain without an umbrella, and boasted a little of all these things to Andrew. He laughed at her.

Spring was coming; there was a softness in the air, a warmth in the sun and the buds were bursting. More than ever Hilary and Andrew could set each other's pulses racing, more than ever they tended to talk nonsense instead of theorizing with each other, to quarrel, a little, and passionately forgive each other, more than ever to be lovers rather than friends. Who could help it, with clear green sky above them, wild daffodils blowing in the woods and fairy blackthorn spraying all the hedges? It was after a magic afternoon when they had seen lambs gambolling, rooks making their absurd and clumsy love, and had felt the hot sun and the cold spring wind stinging their faces, that Andrew said, "Hilary, I'm going to be away from here for six weeks. Can we bear it? And is there the slightest hope of your coming up to town?"

Hilary considered. Six weeks - *six!* - without Andrew was unthinkable. But her work ended at one o'clock on Saturday and began at nine on Monday . . . And going to London would mean leaving Eleanor quite alone, and even now Eleanor was terribly easily tired.

Andrew was explaining: "Sir Nigel Priestley's going on holiday and he's leaving me his consultant work. There's a lot of it. It's a tremendous opportunity. I shall make a lot of money and, with any luck, quite a bit of a reputation. I never thought he'd do it - so soon."

Hilary said, "I'm terribly glad. He must think a lot of you, Andrew."

"More than I thought," Andrew agreed. And added, laughing and puffing himself out a little, "I knew I was pretty good. But I must say, this surprised me."

"I might come up for a Sunday," Hilary said. "Only once, because I couldn't afford any more . . . But I simply must do that."

"Better than nothing," Andrew agreed. "It'll be too foul, without you. I feel all horrible if I don't see you for two days . . . Let's hope I'll be so busy that I shan't notice it . . . You'll write to me, won't you? And - and not go off with someone else?"

She laughed with real amusement at the bare idea. "No, Andrew, I will not! When does it start?"

"To-morrow," he said. "I've been trying to tell you all the week, and couldn't, somehow - I don't know why."

He pulled her to him as though he were afraid of something's snatching her away; promised to dash to Fenchester if he could find half a chance; came bounding back to kiss her again, and was gone.

Although Hilary missed him, it was almost a relief to have him away. The conflict between his claims and Eleanor's was in abeyance. There was breathing-space to consider both of them. Eleanor had another tooth out and got over it with no trouble at all. Term came to an end. Spring was all about.

Eleanor was anxious that they should go away, and to Hilary, with the very slender chances of seeing Andrew in Fenchester, this seemed a good idea. She could go to

London for a few days, perhaps, on their way back.

They went to Redsands, dutifully. Hermione seemed hardly altered by the years. Rose Moore was mellower, far less apt to fly into rages, though as intent as ever on imposing her will. She was just a downright, rather difficult elderly lady now.

Eleanor's sisters had a house near the old vicarage where they had lived all their lives. Its orderly quiet was a contrast to Rose Moore's slap-dash methods of housekeeping - far more efficient - but Hilary felt less at home there. They seemed so peaceful that in a way she envied them, until some small piece of parish scandal cropped up and she watched them in amazement, sitting over it, mangling it, gloating over it and being shocked by it, returning to it in every minute of leisure, for days. How Andrew would have snorted. It was a little thing he would have taken in his stride, smiled at, perhaps, and forgotten in a minute.

"I'll give you your difference between men and women," Hilary wrote to him. "Men talk about themselves, or things. Women talk about each other, and the more uncharitable, in a thoroughly virtuous way, they can be, the more they enjoy it."

She wrote to him most days, because she simply could not help it: letters very much like their conversations, full of matters she had thought and read about; looking forward, every one, to seeing him again. If she had ever had any doubt in her mind - and during Eleanor's illness perhaps she had, though not articulately - as to which life, Eleanor's or his, she would choose to share, this spectacle of single women growing old together settled it. Security - and dullness and stagnation of body and mind, were its characteristics. Eleanor's sisters had been as well educated as she was herself. One, certainly, had never left home after her years at college, but the other had been a headmistress and recently retired. As mental entities they had no more existence than the hens at the bottom of their garden. Hilary could picture Eleanor and herself growing exactly like them in time.

Andrew's letters to Hilary were chaotic - sometimes two in one day, sometimes none for nearly a week. His life was chaotic, too, it seemed, with a popular London surgeon's work as well as his own to do. He wrote of crowded days and disturbed nights, sometimes of expeditions to operate in the suburbs; he commented jerkily on Hilary's letters, and longed above all things to see her.

She arranged to go to London for a week-end at the end of three weeks; three weeks which had passed more quickly than she could have thought possible. She had dreamed of Andrew more than ever, in his absence - she could see him; his smooth, pink face, solemn usually but ready to break into his pleasant, wide smile; the blue eyes which were lazy, piercing, tender, teasing by turns. She could hear his voice, too; not a Scots voice, quite, but deeper than most. She could feel him, the pressure of his lips which was gentle sometimes and sometimes hungry, and the firm, solid bulk of him. She acted scenes with him - some of which had really happened, some imaginary. She thought without fear of the home they would have together, of small, sturdy Andrews and Hilarys.

She could hardly believe that she was going to see him so soon again.

He met her at Paddington. The blue eyes gleamed for an instant straight into hers, then became lazy, quizzical, man-of-the-world. He had taken a room for her at a hotel near his hospital. He whisked her there, then rushed her round the hospital. He was proud of its great still wards, with their cold white walls and shining equipment. He loved it. Hilary, to her surprise, hated it, because of the looks on the faces which lay against the pillows above the red hospital blankets; and on the faces of the nurses who hurried about and eyed her curiously, coolly, as they passed.

He drove her about the streets of London and showed her this and that; and she hated the noise and the smell of petrol from the buses. He gave her his usual excellent dinner, and she simply could not eat it because she was so tired and wrought-up. She was furious with herself. She had never felt like this in her life.

They were going to a theatre, which excited her pleasantly, for she had never been to one in London. But while they were drinking their coffee, a messenger came from the hospital with a telephone call for Andrew. Could he go out, with as little delay as possible, to Sutton to operate on a man with a perforated gastric ulcer?

Andrew shrugged. "Just the sort of thing I was afraid of. It's no good setting one's heart on anything, in this job. Right, Smithers. Say I'll be there in an hour."

Hilary said, "An hour? Can't he possibly wait?"

Andrew, a taut, intent Andrew, shook his head. "'Fraid not. An hour makes all the difference between life and death in that sort of case. No, I'm afraid it busts our evening up . . . I made a covenant with a friend of mine to go to the show with you, in case anything like this did come along. I'll ring him up - "

"Can't I come with you?" Hilary said. "There'll be the drive - "

Andrew, without the slightest hesitation, said "No. It wouldn't be any good, as a drive, because I shall have to take my anaesthetist with me. And I may be goodness knows how long, and you'd have to sit and freeze in the car. And . . . I've got to keep my mind on the type of operation to do and all that, and I couldn't, with you there."

She felt dismissed, unwanted - foolishly, she knew. Andrew had talked so much of his work to her, she had felt as though she might become part of it. And now, when he was really in it, he didn't want her. She tried to tell herself that it was fun, to see Andrew as he really was when he was at work; still another Andrew, competent, absorbed, tremendously keen. She admired this glimpse of him, enormously; and, ridiculously, was jealous of it because it was not hers. All the time they were finishing their coffee she could feel that his thoughts were far away. She would have to grow used to that.

The friend came; an ordinary, pleasant young man with a toothbrush moustache, who looked her over amusedly, she felt. Her evening dress, the only one she had, was nothing remarkable - black lace, which showed up her lovely colouring and that was all. It had quite a lot of back and was not very low. It had done excellently for High School functions and would last, she hoped, for years. Andrew turned her over to him and vanished, swiftly, promising to call for her in the morning.

Well, that was that, and it wasn't any good being disappointed. If you loved a doctor, you must expect to play second fiddle to his work.

She did not enjoy the play much. It was meant to be funny - was funny, if you were in the mood for it. Her escort laughed uproariously. It was not at all subtle, but some of the jokes she failed to understand. In the interval, her escort was sought out by a party sitting a few rows behind - two young men and two girls. Hilary was introduced. She found their conversation almost unintelligible, and, seeing the girls, understood why Andrew's friend had given her that curious, unwinking stare. They had next to no eyebrows, their lips were scarlet bows, their cheeks an impossible but very effective pink. Their dresses consisted mostly of wide skirt and narrow shoulder-straps, their hair fitted closely to the heads like little crinkled caps. She felt frousty, dingy, immeasurably old beside them.

Back at the hotel, with no Eleanor to chat with, she felt more lonely than ever in her life.

Saturday was better. Andrew, spruce and smelling of soap, was there before she was up. He confused her by coming straight to her room, with the bed all in a heap, and watching the last stages of her dressing. "Bless you," he said to her apologies, "I spend half my life seeing people with a lot less on than that. And in their bedrooms."

She smiled, a lovely, dimpled smile, her eyes glinting grey-green under her lids, because she was so glad to see him. He kissed her with a possessive air which tickled her enormously.

He took her out to Richmond Park, and they wandered among the great old oaks, golden-green with catkins. He talked of what he had been doing; how he had made a brilliant diagnosis here and saved a life there by a timely operation when the doctor in charge of the case had been all for waiting. "I've got to go back and see that one in his nursing-home before lunch. And one or two others. The hospital ones, mercifully, are looked after by the house-surgeon unless they do something unexpected." No sooner had he mentioned these patients who must be visited than she sensed his eagerness to be with them. She suggested, "Let's go back now. I can sit in the car. I shan't be bored, with all the people to watch."

He agreed at once. "Don't you mind?"

"Of course not. You mustn't let me be in your way."

There was a sort of pride in his eyes as he looked at her. He said, "It's almost impossible to have visitors politely while one's working. It's ripping of you not to mind if I'm not polite."

She squeezed his arm happily, feeling as though, for once, she was giving to him instead of always taking. It was lovely, to give something to Andrew, even a thing as unimportant as one's pride. She thought of their long-drawn-out partings at Fenchester, and smiled at the promptness of his return to the car.

The nursing-home was in a square near Baker Street. People came and went from it continually; serious, clean-looking men like Andrew, who made one stride from car to

267

door and disappeared within; anxious-looking men, and women in fur coats, who lingered to talk outside, knocked on the door and waited in the hall. Andrew, returning, was waylaid by one such party, who treated him with deference, hanging on his words. She could see him choosing them, italicizing his encouragement by patting the elderly lady gently on the arm. She was crying, but she smiled through her tears at Andrew and looked after him, as he left them, as though he were a god. No wonder Andrew was conceited, a little, when people treated him like that. She wondered, in a panic, how it was that he had fallen in love with her, whose chief pleasure was not to pay him deference but to argue with him; who felt herself so unpolished and countrified beside all these sophisticated people of the town.

He leapt in beside her. "Those were my chap's relatives. Mother and father and fiancée - of the one, I mean, the G.P. didn't want to operate on. He's on the mend - "

Only once the day threatened to cloud. Driving round Trafalgar Square, Andrew slewed suddenly in to the kerb.

"I've got to meet a chap at Charing Cross Hospital," he said. "Just round here." Hilary's heart went down. Had she been dull? If she had entertained him properly, he wouldn't have thought of the "chap" all on the instant like that.

He went on, "I was going to leave you in the car again. But I might be half an hour, and I've just wondered if you'd like to look round the National Gallery. The Falkners always make a dash for it when they come up. I'll be happier leaving you if I know you're not bored."

She smiled at him, grateful at once for his thought for

her. He leaned over and opened the door, and she slid out into the crowd.

"Meet you here in half an hour," he called, and was gone.

Hilary, jostled and shoved on every side, tried to stand still. Of all these great buildings she hadn't an idea which the National Gallery was. She thought of asking someone, but the crowds ignored her, intent each one on his own hurried passage.

One bit of street seemed less packed than the rest, and she made for it, and walked along slowly, looking about. Not that there was much to see: a furniture shop, very grand and opulent; travel bureaux, narrow turnings lined with office buildings.

It was at one of these that she paused, realizing that she had lost her objective, looked along it for safety's sake, and saw flapping there a white flag with black lettering - "Exhibition of Sculpture and Painting - Henry Swain and Kathleen Verity."

Henry Swain. Sculpture. A red sandstone duck which had lived in her pocket until it was rubbed smooth. It was not there now, of course, though she felt for it, unthinking. She went swiftly up the little street and turned in under the flag.

It was not a big exhibition: two square rooms with pictures on the walls and the sculpture scattered on pedestals. Hilary went eagerly round them, not seeing the uniformed man who tried to sell her a catalogue and invite her to write her name in a book.

Most of them were heads. All were rugged, hurried-looking yet very strong, all of men; men with all manner of expressions - anxiety, pain, terror, interest, hope, calm courage, resignation, laughter; all different men, some young, some almost old. Hilary exclaimed to herself, "They're good. They're true." Then, slowly, memory welling up to join with the present impression, "Henry must have changed, to know all that. Grown up. Been - hurt, and got over it."

There were three ducks, certainly coming up from a pond at dusk on their way to bed, though there was no pond and no failing light, only something about the intent, solemn single file which told one; several animal groups, very lively; and one larger piece, different from the rest in that it was smoother, more finished, though still with that imprint of fine-drawn truth. In the prow of a boat, over a suggestion of waves, sat a girl, adolescent, a little awkward, her hair blown back from a broad brow, steady eyes looking into the distance, lips parted in an alert excitement.

Hilary stared at it for a long time. It had a familiar look which puzzled her.

Could it be Henry's daughter? And the familiar look a likeness to him? She found she could not remember, to order, exactly what he looked like. And anyway, he couldn't possibly have a daughter as old as that.

Perhaps he had a baby daughter and it was his dream of her grown up . . .

Suddenly a clock appeared in her line of vision. Half an hour Andrew had said, and she had been away forty minutes already. She swirled through the turnstile and ran as fast as she could down the little street.

The car was waiting, and Andrew's back looked stolid

and annoyed. Hilary shouldered her way through the people and slid in beside him before he realized that she was there.

"Andrew, I've found the loveliest thing - "

At her radiant face his exasperation vanished.

"I rather thought you'd like it - " in his showman's voice, just as he had spoken of their first sunset.

"You thought? Oh, but I didn't go to the National Gallery, I couldn't find it - " and she told him of the sculptured heads and the ducks and the girl in the prow of the boat, and of Henry.

"Who *is* Henry? You've never mentioned him before! Did you see him?"

"No, I didn't see him. I haven't seen him since the beginning of the war. He was just - a boy at the school where my father taught. I liked him, when we were both kids. I'd clean forgotten about him, till I saw that flag. I keep wondering if the girl in the boat is his daughter."

"Has he got a daughter?"

"I haven't the faintest idea!" She was laughing, a little, at the catechism. "He may have. He's married. I just couldn't explain why I thought I'd seen her before."

Andrew seemed to lose interest. "Well, I'm glad you weren't bored, anyway. Look, I really am free now. I've got someone to stand by for me. I thought we'd speed out into Surrey for lunch and have a stroll on Box Hill."

Hilary liked the little white-fronted hotel from the outside, but was doubtful about its dining-room full of chattering, smoking motorists. She would have liked a smaller place with Andrew to herself. She could not deny the beauty of the smooth slopes of Box Hill, but here again there were people, everywhere, walking or sitting under bushes, and she was not sorry when they went back to the car.

In the evening they went to a cinema, and she was idiotically pleased because Andrew seized her hand and held it in the dark. He seemed so far away from her in this different world, that she snatched at any evidence of nearness. But when they came out, he left her in the lounge while he telephoned, and then dumped her hastily at her hotel and shot off into the dark without even kissing her, the light of his own particular sort of battle in his eye.

He kissed her in the morning, though, before she left for Fenchester; hugged her to him joyously, protested that she had put new life into him by coming, and thanked her, almost shyly, for being so patient with his frenzied dashing from place to place.

Then, as though she had slept for these last weeks and dreamed some muddled dreams, Hilary was at home again. She told Eleanor, disjointedly, of the dreams and was not surprised that Eleanor did not find them interesting. She was surprised at herself for being so glad to be back and to meet her colleagues at the University and settle into its routine again. Was she leaving her enchanted life behind, or only growing used to it?

The horned-rimmed boy and girl were engaged now. The girl had left and someone not unlike her had come instead. Hilary wondered whether she would have to leave when she was engaged to Andrew.

Miss Cronshaw was snorting at the stupidity of throwing

up a good career for mere matrimony. Horn-rims had, it appeared, been an unusually brilliant girl. Helen Martin was talking to everyone at once, making everyone laugh. Even the men, so stand-offish at the beginning of the first term, strolled across the room to Hilary and asked about her Easter holiday. It was fun, to be back among them all again. She threw herself into her work with a zest equal to Andrew's own.

When Andrew wrote, saying that Sir Nigel was prolonging his holiday for another fortnight, she did not mind much. Having seen him at work, she understood the impossibility of his getting away. She was so very busy herself that she thought little of him. When she did, it was of the two of them working, as it were, on parallel lines, throwing each other, now and then, a friendly glance, both more intent on their work than on each other. She approved of the attitude as a healthy one.

It was at the end of the fortnight that, on her way out one afternoon, she found a letter from him in the college letter-rack. Funny of him to write to her there - he never did. But nice, for she would be able to read it in the train.

At the station, she ran into Blake, the museum man, going by train to see an archaeologist who lived even farther out than she did. He got into her carriage and talked archaeology, vividly, and she listened. Her mind was full of Crete and Mycenae, gold cups and bee-hive tombs, as she walked home from the station.

Voices startled her as she let herself in - Eleanor's and Margaret Falkner's. She wondered what Margaret was there for and, being there, why she had not travelled out with herself rather than with Eleanor. She was on the point of pushing open the sitting-room door and demanding answers to both the questions, when Margaret's rose shrilly, passionately, so unlike her usual tone of controlled banter as to be hardly recognizable. Evidently they had not heard her. She paused, and had heard Margaret's sentence before she had time to think.

"You *must* let her go! Don't you *see* that she isn't the sort of person to live your life? You kept her at home - a lovely, full-blooded girl she must have been then - all through the war. Did her out of any possible chance of marrying, then. Now she's got another chance - a real one - and you're doing her out of that. Clinging to her, because she's too kind to fling you off! You *must* let her go!"

Hilary turned and tiptoed upstairs to her room.

Margaret had got a bee in her bonnet.

Eleanor was not obstructing, now.

Should she go down and tell them they were being rather silly?

She had brushed her hair preparatory to doing so, a little puzzled by Margaret's vehemence, not quite sure how to deal with it, when she remembered Andrew's letter, and wondered suddenly whether it might be a request to meet him in Fenchester and that was why he had written to the University. Perhaps there would still be time to get back. She tore it open.

It was a long letter, for Andrew, written carefully in ink instead of his usual pencil scrawl. She sat down on the bed to read it. It began, as he always did - "Darling Hilary."

As to the rest, it was some time before she really took it in.

I hate writing this, because I believe, in my heart, that I'm letting you down and myself too. So I didn't write it until everything was settled and beyond getting out of. To-morrow you'll see it in *The Times*. I'm going to be married, to a girl my family's known - I've known - all her life. I love her, in a way. I always have. She's little and plump, dresses most beautifully and always smells of some subtle kind of scent. I'm telling you this so that you may understand and, if you want to, despise me. It's not the best part of me that loves her. I know that. The best part of me is yours and always will be. But I couldn't live up to your standard for long, Hilary. And if I didn't, you *would* despise me, and I couldn't bear that. I have to be admired, a little, or I go bad. *You* couldn't possibly admire me, if you knew me really well. You're too far above me. Lois looks up to me, always. You take me on the level, and very soon you'd be looking down. I'm honest, aren't I? And when I take liberties with her - liberties I should never dare even think of, with you - she's pleased. I don't admire her for being pleased, but I'm flattered by it. I must have my little luxuries, and with you I'm a bit ashamed of them. For everyday life, that wouldn't do. I must be pleased with myself, or I can't do my work. D'you see? I told you, once, that I was terribly fond of my food.

Please, Hilary, can we go on being friends? Your friendship is still as always the most precious thing I have.

I'm sending this to the U. as I'm not quite sure whether you and E.H. open each other's letters.

For some reason, the last sentence annoyed her more than the rest. She could understand it, anyway. She flung the letter across the bed. "As though we would! As though any self-respecting people who lived together would!" It showed her, suddenly, how little Andrew understood her. How could he understand anyone, when he was thinking all the time of himself? She said aloud, "So Eleanor's right!"

She thought, "I'd better go down and stop those two quarrelling . . . A nuisance, when one's friends quarrel. And there's no point in it, now."

Greedy Andrew, wanting to have his cake and eat it, both at once . . . Why, that was what she had tried to do herself - and now she had neither. Perhaps that was what he would do. But she knew that if he were free and wanted her again, at any time, he could have her. Too far above him! If only he could have known! "Go on being friends", he said. She did not think she could bear that. Besides, it wouldn't end there, she was sure. Perhaps that was what he hoped would happen. Then he would have his cake and eat it, just as she had thought she could do.

From the stairs, she could hear that Eleanor and Margaret were still talking. But by the time she opened the sitting-room door, they had heard her, and stopped. They both looked up at her and smiled, just as if it had been an ordinary meeting on an ordinary day. She hoped she looked ordinary, too. She began to explain how it was that she was later than usual, so that Margaret would not have to invent an excuse for being there; and went on to tell them of Blake's entertaining talk.

It was only when Margaret had risen to go that Hilary said, casually, as she had been rehearsing it to herself, "I've just heard from Andrew that he's going to be married. A girl called Lois, whom he'd known all his - no, all her - life. D'you know her?"

Margaret and Eleanor did not look at her, they gaped at each other; at first, both simply startled out of all pretence, then Eleanor, so mocking as to be almost malicious - Hilary had never seen her like that - shrugged her shoulders. Margaret threw Hilary one glance of horror and pity, and fled. They heard her rush down the garden path and slam the gate behind her.

Eleanor said, "My dear, I can't pretend I'm sorry. You know what I thought of him. But I know - I do know what you must be feeling, and I'm sorry for that."

Hilary glared at her. "You don't know! You can't possibly - you've never done it! How dare you think you know all about me?" she exploded, and groped blindly for the door.

10

She did not sleep - did not try to, just lay awake, stretched straight out on her back, and thought. She was not going to marry Andrew. She was not going to marry anyone. She was going to go on being a lecturer at the University all her life, to grow into someone rather like A.B.C., then someone like Eleanor's sisters. She was not going to have a home of her own, or children. The odd feelings which Andrew aroused in her, which she had rather encouraged than otherwise because she knew they were going to be satisfied some time, were to be wasted and would have to be squashed. Her whole life seemed to have conspired to prevent her being natural - the austere simplicity of the childhood with her father, and his habit of control, reaction against the passionate nature of her mother, both combining to make her bottle up all her own deep feelings; her mother's innuendoes - how well she remembered them now - smirching her relationship with Henry, and her own angry reply to that, deluding herself that boys and girls were all the same and friendship was a matter of the mind; her admiration for Eleanor, who shied at everything physical as at a bad smell; their life together, which accorded so well with her own principles but not, as she saw now, with her nature. Her nature longed for someone like Andrew, someone who belonged to the earth and extracted the uttermost from it. It was the real her, the natural, uncultivated Hilary, whom Andrew loved; the civilized veneer which had frightened him. If only she could show him that, everything would be all right . . .

She went over it all again and again, and presently her mood changed. No one could love as she loved Andrew and not be loved in return. If Andrew loved her - and he did - the hideous muddle would quite certainly be straightened out. She slept, after that - the dawn was already showing in the sky - till Eleanor called her in broad daylight.

The days that followed were a black dream. Hilary moved about, ate, even did her work and conversed with people. Margaret came to her frankly and said that she blamed herself for the whole thing and was never going to speak to Andrew again, and after that did not refer to it. Eleanor did not refer to it at all. She took trouble to see that Hilary should not be alone, quietly did small things for her in the house - saw that she had proper meals, put flowers in her bedroom, changed library books so that she should always have something to read in the train. How she herself behaved, Hilary had no idea. She was surprised one day by the grim set of her mouth, just as her mother's had been, as she saw it in the glass.

She saw Andrew once, and would have spoken to him. She was sure that in half an hour she could explain and change it all. But the beaming content of his expression appalled her and she slipped away before she should be seen. He had turned her life into a desert, and he could go about looking like that. She did not see him again, and did not write to him.

As the black dream began to lift, she became conscious of two things. One was that she had stopped feeling anything at all about Eleanor, hate, liking or love. It was not long-standing affection like theirs which turned to hate, but the quick, passionate sort. Here, there were so many little homely ties which could not be broken, doing oddments for each other because they had to be done and each knew those that the other hated doing; each being hurt, indignantly, when the other was hurt; like an old married couple, perhaps, who had pulled apart and come together again, drawn by just such bonds. They talked of nothing, now, but trivialities, but their life provided plenty of these.

The Staff were kind to her. It was Miss Cronshaw's quizzical glance which told her that they knew that something had happened to her. She was surprised that they should know. Her outings with Andrew had been, to her, surrounded by a golden haze which cut off all view of the outer world. She had not realized that those who lived outside it could see in quite well. It didn't matter, because nothing did matter, now.

A.B.C., after that first glance of amusement, invited her to dinner, swept aside her feeble protests that she could not come, saw her comfortably settled after the meal in a roomful of talkative people, and administered verbal prods whenever her attention showed signs of turning inwards. In the Common Room and at meals, she placed her solid bulk between Hilary and other people as though she had constituted herself her special protector, both against them and against self-pity.

Professor Hewer's contribution was to double her work, so that she hardly had a half-hour to herself in the whole week. Seeing her leaving her room late one day, he hovered in the corridor and met her, like a small, tidy, well-disposed bird.

"Am I overworking you?" he asked her abruptly. When she said No, he added, blinking and looking away from her, "Overwork's the best cure for any - er - disgruntlement which - er - leisure may have dealt one."

Hilary smiled at that. She was grateful for the old man's practical sympathy. She did work, as hard as she could, stayed late at college for extra coachings, and spent her evenings working at her M.A. thesis, at first doggedly, then with growing interest as it developed.

A sneaking conviction welled up sometimes, that all this intellectual effort was pointless, that to drum history into these young students was ridiculous, because what mattered was living, not amassing knowledge. She felt to blame, for leading them astray. Yet they, like her, would need some time an anchor which emotion could not shift. Perhaps she could give them that.

When she did begin to enjoy things again - music, books, poetry - she found that she sought instinctively the type of thing which did not play at all on the emotions but only on the mind. Bach, Chesterton and A. P. Herbert, Masefield - these she permitted herself.

In the work for her thesis, Blake the museum man was invaluable to her. He was willing to talk archaeology for hours, brought parcels of books for her to college and discussed them when she had read them. One day he suggested taking her to see a dolmen which had been excavated on the moor, and she went with him and enjoyed the expedition, soberly, with no magic in the enjoyment, but enjoyed it all the same. Blake, tall, bald, with rimless spectacles, strode beside her, spurting out exact information like a hosepipe all the way. When they parted, he thanked her extravagantly for coming. The next day when she passed the museum door he was peeping out, and pounced on her with a book they had been speaking of.

She began to wonder if his interest was entirely archaeological. It wasn't safe, to think friendship could be based on mutual interest. She considered what her own feelings might be, if not. Blake was a steady person, a bit fussy about his health, which he took pleasure in talking of, but a gold-mine of interest on his own subject. With revulsion, she saw how different he was from Andrew, who touched on twenty subjects, airily, in as many minutes. It was no good being revolted by everyone else's differences from Andrew. Blake was a good sort. One might live with him safely and contentedly. She thought about him quite a lot. At her mental image of Andrew, she put out her tongue, and felt the better for having done so. She could not hate Andrew. Sometimes she wanted him so desperately that she could have screamed. But that was no reason to let oneself be done out of one half of life altogether. One could not go about for ever with all these discontents churning about inside one. She looked curiously at the other single women of her acquaintance. What did they do about it? Had A.B.C. ever felt as she felt now? Or those two faded ladies, Miss Hawes and Miss Jago? Or Helen Martin? Or Eleanor? Not Eleanor, she was perfectly sure.

The next time she saw Blake was at a week-end. She and Eleanor were walking in a field which bordered on a country lane. A car passed them, slowly, and stopped, and a small boy tumbled out, followed by Blake. The child stayed doubtfully at the roadside, Blake came bounding towards them. "Why, Miss Moore! I've been wishing you could meet my wife - and here she is in the car if you'd come along. This is my small son Robin - "

Just a pleasant, plump, ordinary woman, Mrs. Blake, with a year-old baby on her knee. She greeted Hilary cheerfully, if without much interest, hoped, if she liked babies, she would come to tea.

Hilary laughed about it afterwards, not with Eleanor, just quietly to herself. Why shouldn't a married man teach a colleague archaeology?

She began to fear she was the kind of woman men did not

care for. There were certainly many such kinds, if Andrew were to be believed.

She said so to Eleanor, hoping for an indignant denial. But Eleanor's response was, dryly, "You shouldn't let that worry you. Most spinsters have a whole lot better time than most married women. Less worries, more life of their own, less misery, more fun. The best of men seem to me to be selfish wretches when you have to depend on them. And you've got every chance to live a successful life as a spinster - archaic word: 'single woman', shall we say?"

She tried Helen Martin, so trim and poised. Helen, sitting one afternoon in a deck-chair on the college lawn, wagged her head and said, "My poor friend! You'll get over it, really you will! Get on with your job!"

Hilary recited in a little mincing voice, "The *world* is so *full* of a *number* of *things*, I *think* we should *all* be as *ha*ppy as kings!"

Helen tossed it back - "True, if a bit trite! Are kings happy?"

"Anyway," Hilary persisted, "one's got to live as well as work! There'll come a day when one can't do a job but still has a life to live!"

"And if you haven't got a well-stocked mind when that time comes, heaven help you!" Helen rounded on her. "You won't be able to feed on your emotions then, my girl: it'll be the loony-bin for you!"

Hilary said deeply, "That seems to me as good as any place. If it's worth going on living at all!"

Helen glanced at her a shade anxiously. "See here, Hilary," she said, "I think this - affair Andrew - has thrown you right off your balance. Sent your values all wrong. You've lived an extraordinarily Spartan life, for these days. And just as the Spartan warrior went soft at his first contact with ordinary comfort, so you've gone - female, shall we say, at the first awakening in you of the life of the senses. Many of us - " she looked away from Hilary, up into the dark platforms of the cedar trees - "have known something of - love - from our very early years. Its effects on us have had time to dawn gradually. There are many women, even now, I think, whom it never troubles. They only know that they're never quite happy; the reason for it escapes them. But we who know what the matter is, recognize the symptoms and treat them according to the light - or darkness - that is in us."

Breathlessly, Hilary said, "I don't know what you mean!"

Helen brought her bright, straight glance down to her again. "I mean," her cool, clipped voice said, "that the whole thing's largely biological."

Hilary was so amazed that for some minutes she could not speak.

"D'you mean," she said at last, "that I don't really love Andrew at all? That I'm only trying to satisfy my own instincts?"

Helen shut her book briskly, as though she were bored. "I haven't the slightest doubt you were in love with Andrew all right, and he with you. So what have you? - only to get on top of it, for you. Any other solution . . . oh, no, not for you." And she clapped her deck-chair together and, carried it away.

Hilary thought cautiously about Andrew instead of

shutting him right out whenever he intruded into her mind.

Coaxed by Margaret and assured that Andrew never came to their house now, she still went to the Falkners on Sundays. They lived the greater part of their lives on the intellectual plane, with a wind of the spirit blowing and kind sunshine which kept them human. They held out inviting hands to Hilary to join them as she had so joyously done before. She could not take the step up. But she liked to watch them and listen.

She saw a lot of Mrs. Falkner, when the rest of them were out or working, and grew fond of her. She was very serene and sane, content with her life, yet not smugly so. She let her children keep her very much alive. Hilary, still searching for content herself, coaxed Margaret's mother to talk about her own past. Was this calm the inevitable outcome of happy family life, or had it followed after storm?

Mrs. Falkner enjoyed talking. She had married at twenty-one, and she still thought her husband the cleverest and kindest man in the world. She was naïvely surprised because her children were so successful and because they were still so fond of her, and pleased because their friends so often sought her out to unburden their troubles to her.

Hilary said, "You're awfully nice and sympathetic, and people like you because you're so happy. But you can't possibly understand us. No one who's married young can understand a single woman. We can understand you, all right. We all have the same instincts, married or single, and it's easy enough to imagine them satisfied. What you can never know is the stress of fighting them, single-handed, day in, day out, squashing something down that's stronger than hunger, just because we've got to wait for some wretched man to ask us to marry him. Yes, I know people talk a lot of bunk about sublimating. How can one, when one's young and strong?"

Mrs. Falkner, faded now and thin, blinked mildly over her spectacles. She was not shocked; it took wickedness to shock her. She said with spirit, "Why this rivalry? We have our problems, which you've never known. I'm not going to talk about them, there'd be no point in it. But, believe me, they exist. And you have yours, which we may have known, or may not. Many of us have had them, even if only for a little while. The best thing you can do is to get married to some nice quiet man and not expect too much of him. Very few of us get our fairy prince. I did - but I've known women who've got on very well with a cat's-meat-man."

Which, excellently meant as it was, had the effect of turning Hilary from her vow of hard work and hard exercise, to a watchful search for the nice quiet man of whom she must expect only the equivalent of cat's meat. She even considered an Indian student with marvellous melting eyes until Miss Cronshaw dryly gave her a lecture one day on child-marriage and she realized that the young man most likely had a wife already, of the age of ten or so, and moreover, that she was rather obviously making an ass of herself.

The next day, Saturday, she had no set work at all, so, instead of going to college to correct papers or read in the library as she often did, she made a parcel of food for lunch and caught a bus whose final destination was a moorland village.

She sat and hated its smelly stuffiness, and listened to the talk of the people round her, to keep her own thoughts from their tendency to whirl. A two-year-old, pale and solemn, stared at her. She screwed up her face at him and he broke into a smile. Presently he came unsteadily across to her, thrust a damp woolly toy into her lap, and remarked, "Wow!" She put the creature through some antics, and the child, leaning against her, squealed with delight. Its mother, opposite, grinned benignly, showing jagged occasional teeth. The wife of the cat's-meat-man, perhaps. She looked content enough. Hilary wondered how she herself would cope with a houseful of young children. She liked what little she knew of them and they seemed to like her.

Then the bus reached its terminus and she was out on the road, crunching uphill on gravel, with little streams at the roadside chuckling past her, grey rocks dripping above, coloured with liver-wort and lichen. She entered a beechwood, still, with shafts of sunlight dappling the grey trunks, and shuffled through drifts of last year's leaves. On the other side was brown moor, studded with whortle-berry clumps which keep the green of spring from April to October. Hilary bent down to one. It carried both waxy flowers and unripe fruit. She fingered it gently and let it go. Above a stream, farther on, the air quivered in the sun, rising in spirals of liquid gold. She climbed on until the sweat ran off her in drops, then flung herself down beside a big sleek rock. Was ever any bed as springy as heather?

She spent the day so, climbing and resting, not thinking coherently at all, just letting impressions chase each other over the surface of the mind.

She did not notice the great grey cloud which mounted behind her in the late afternoon until, turning reluctantly to go back to the bus, she felt its first drops sting her face. In a few minutes she was enveloped in a deluge.

Well, there was no shelter to be had out here, and no prospect, it appeared, of the rain's stopping. Hilary put her head down and charged through it, shaking it out of her eyes, and then, when shaking did no more good, just let it trickle down her neck and into her ears, and put out her tongue now and then to catch the drips from the end of her nose. Her skirt flapped heavily round her knees, her feet squelched in her shoes.

She had often been wet like this in childhood, on days when she had run out to escape the jangled atmosphere of home, but never, she realized with some surprise, during her years of teaching. Eleanor had always been there, then, or Andrew, and Eleanor and Andrew, in their different ways, had loved propriety and comfort and looked askance at vagabond wandering. She trudged on, hands in the pockets of her short coat, half enjoying her discomfort - and at last, for she had come a long way, neither enjoying nor resenting it, feeling nothing.

In the bus she dozed, and steamed, which did not matter, for there were few passengers. When she stumbled out at her destination, a biting wind met her. Well, she had not far to go.

She slipped in by the back door unheard, and changed her clothes and went to join Eleanor in their sitting-room. Eleanor, reading some solid tome, glanced up friendlily but asked no questions, and Hilary subsided into a chair. There was no fire - no need of one, really, except for a lunatic like herself - and the windows were open as usual. She wondered whether to tell Eleanor what she had been doing, which would result in a hot bath, a hot drink, fussing, bed - lovely, but so far from her habit that she was shy of them, and of the explanations that getting them would involve.

For the sake of some activity to warm her, she went into the kitchen and pottered over the supper, which was a cold one, and gave in to herself sufficiently to go to bed as soon as the dishes were washed.

She fell asleep at once, from sheer tiredness. But in the middle of the night she woke, aching all over, alternately hot and cold. She supposed she must be ill. Worry led to illness, Andrew had said - why must one always be harking back to what Andrew had said? A terrific dose of worry, she would need, to make her ill - he had said that too. Well, now she'd had her terrific dose, and she was ill. Or perhaps it wasn't illness, but the worry alone - for she never was ill - which kept her brain so painfully awake.

She threshed about her bed until her sheets were twisted into ropes. Coming to her unprepared by her early life, so entirely a matter of the intellect, after her unsought overwhelming by the affair Andrew, and the blind floundering in muddy waters which had followed it, Helen's frankness had been the last straw. She was more shocked by it than she could admit even to herself. It tarnished everything, love, friendship, even fastidious Helen.

Hilary was incapable of taking the sensible view of a human being as half animal, half spirit. She had never thought of her animal side, had never needed to, it had always been healthy and reasonably comfortable. Living with Eleanor, she had not come into intimate contact with the generation to whom the body's needs were a matter of course.

And so she translated her own state, not in terms of body and spirit but of her mother and her father; her mother, who ought to have married a rumbustious farmer and had a baby once a year; her father, who would have made a good monk. They were at war again in her as they had been around her in the mists of her childhood.

She knew without consideration that Helen's "any other solution" would not satisfy her; that she could never tolerate such a notion; that it was a home, children, quiet husbandly love which she needed more than passion. Her father worked against mere passion in her, substituting for it the things of the mind. She saw now how it was that her looks, her vitality, her mother in her, attracted men to her, while her father's asceticism, grafted on by her upbringing and fostered by Eleanor, had repelled them; why she had not kept Andrew; why, unless she could find another Gregory, she would never keep a man.

That flash of clear vision hurt her so much that she sprang up and prowled about the room, fighting to bury it, to pretend it had never been. Her mother had always been a fighter. Presently, she began to dress. Outdoors, even in the cold light of morning, was better than her small bare room.

It was so, pulling on her clothes in feverish haste, that Eleanor found her. Her face, till lately so smooth and youthful, was drawn and lined, her eyes were dark-ringed.

Eleanor's voice, sharp with anxiety, made her jump. "Hilary, what on earth's the matter? Are you ill?"

Hilary struggled to make her speech perfectly ordinary. "No. Just couldn't sleep," she said. "Sorry I made a noise."

Eleanor came in and sat on the bed, drawing the drab folds of her dressing-gown about her. The old attraction fought in Hilary with hatred for her thin spinsterishness.

"You haven't been sleeping for nights," she said. "Have you?"

"Not too badly, till to-night." Hilary did so hope that Eleanor was not going to ask questions. She did not want to talk about it all now. Certainly not to Eleanor, who would never understand.

But Eleanor was again the emotionless, impersonal individual who had ruled the girls at Medling. She asked no questions. She said, "I've been worried about you for weeks. Your nerves are all to bits, and if you're going to stop sleeping as well . . . Get into bed and I'll get you a hot drink and some aspirins."

In the morning, she was so stiff she could not move except with groans, and her temperature was 101°. Dr. Bray pronounced it nothing worse than a chill, though allowing that anyone less strong would have got pneumonia, and predicted recovery after three days. This duly took place, but left her so weak that she did not know whether to laugh or to cry at her wobbly progress down the stairs and the fantastic notion that she would be able to climb them only a few hours later.

Eleanor, having settled her in a chair, with a rug and, this time, a fire, announced, "I asked Professor Hewer yesterday if he would let you off for the rest of the term, to get right away."

The exaggerated firmness of her tone betrayed her expectation of opposition. But Hilary said indifferently, "Yes? What did he say?" She was so tired that she felt neither pleasure nor resentment at Eleanor's intrusion into her affairs. In any case she couldn't go back to work like this.

"Said he'd been thinking of suggesting it himself. So I've written to Janet to ask her to take you to that farm she likes so much in Devon."

A sudden longing assailed Hilary for the soft breezes of Dartmoor instead of the fierce gusts which swept the high country here; for rounded tors instead of jagged edges; for solitude instead of the bright conversation of the common room. She said, "That's terribly nice and sensible of you!"

"And you'll go? Next week, when you can walk a bit better?"

Hilary laughed. "Like an arrow from a bow. And teach myself to walk better all the sooner on purpose."

PART FOUR

The Professor

I

THE farm-house was on the very edge of the moor, accessible only by a path from a small village which was itself perched high above the road. There was a green garden shaded by a fringe of pines, and below it a miniature ravine, a tangle of ferns and rowan bushes, with a river chuckling in its rocky depths. All round were the sweet-smelling, heathery undulations of the moor itself.

For three days, Hilary did little but sleep; by night, beside an open window which showed her still tips of pine branches, like shaving-brushes, and the stars; by day, in the green garden, or, having walked and clambered for ten minutes, in the heather.

At first, her waking hours were dark, brooding, her ragged thoughts turned in upon herself; her only emotion, self-pity. Then she became conscious of the soothing rhythm which had been going on round her all the time; the river's music, the wind sighing in the pine-trees; the quacking of ducks, sheep calling, the clop-clop on the moist path of cows coming up from the marshes to be milked; and the fresh, sharp scents of the country.

Then she began to notice people; so different from the people she had come from that they took her back across them like a bridge, to childhood: the farmer's wife, rosy, sturdy, vocal only when she shouted to her husband and children; the children, bright-eyed, with darting glances trembling on the edge of cheeky speech; the farmer and the shepherd, indistinguishable at first, brown-faced, spindle-shanked, cheerful. Then, Janet, tall, straight, elegant even here, with wide, out-looking eyes.

Janet, who had come back from Geneva to take up Medicine, was the best possible companion for the days which followed. She had left Hilary alone - or had seemed to; really she had been quietly careful for her comfort all the time. When Hilary's energy began to come back, they walked and climbed the steep sides of rounded beacons and rocky tors, and sat in the sun with views which took in half Devon and most of Somerset. The rivers were their greatest delight, chattering over great rocks, shooting down waterfalls to make still brown pools which the sun turned to gold, flowing smoothly sometimes between deep banks, so clear that one could count the white stones at the bottom. Coming down to one of the pools on a hot day, they could not resist the impulse to strip and bathe, and, although there was only room for half a dozen strokes, the water was so delicious, like cool brown silk, that after that they always carried bathing-dresses. It was after a day when they had bathed, lain in the sun for a while and then tramped homewards in the clear, soft air which was somehow never too hot in spite of the sunshine, that Hilary began to sing. Janet, behind, watched her benevolently. People did not, in her experience, sing like that, spontaneously, unless they were at peace.

One day, passing through a village, they stopped at the forge and watched the blacksmith, a splendid man, with great rippling muscles under a brown skin.

Janet said, "He'd make a picture, against that dark interior, with the fire flickering on him, wouldn't he? Don't you wish you could paint?"

Hilary nodded. "'M . . . I wonder if he's married?"

Janet said conversationally, "He plays the bassoon in the village band, the small boy there told me. And he's courting the daughter of the man who keeps the pub . . . I'm sorry for her; fancy having a bassoon practised all over a small cottage. And he'll want enormous meals twice a day, by the size of him, and quantities of beer - too much sometimes - and have a bath once a week, in the kitchen, in spite of all that grime - and snore in his chair all the evenings."

Hilary laughed. It was fun, to have a friend you could not deceive, who knew your bad bits as well as your good ones and still believed in you. The blacksmith became, insensibly, a joke.

It was after that, that they began to talk, about things other than the scenery and the incidents of the day. Hilary began it, and Janet was glad. She said, "Could you tell me - about what happened to you during the War?"

Janet was careful; knowing that it would not take much to stir Hilary up and undo all the good the moor had done. She said, "There isn't much to tell. There was a man I nursed - he'd got a splintered thigh with a bad flesh-wound which I used to dress. He used to swear at me and then apologize. Most of the nurses were afraid of him. We got pretty friendly, and when he could get about on a splint, we went out together. When he was sent home, I got leave, and went to stay with his people. We ought to have got married then, I suppose, but we didn't, somehow. And when he went back, he was killed. That's all." She sat very still and composed on the heather.

The bald little story, somehow, pierced Hilary's egotism

297

for a moment. She put out a hand to Janet, and said, "Oh, my dear, how awful! And I didn't know . . . Why didn't you tell me? Write, or something?"

Janet, still serene, said, "I couldn't talk about it. I never can, about things that really matter. There were lots of girls out there in much the same case . . . We understood each other without talking, mercifully . . . And p'raps we felt that no one who wasn't out there, could."

Hilary had gone back to herself.

She asked, "How did you get over it? D'you mind my pumping you about it? What did you do?"

Janet's face came out of its repose into a smile. "No, I don't mind, now, and to you. I just worked like blazes. It was the only thing to do. It hurt, of course; but everyone was being hurt; one couldn't go about whining. And gradually - it faded. One feels a beast for letting it fade - but one must."

Into Hilary's mind a glimmer of light came; showing Janet's suffering as something real, something tangible, almost, from outside, which one was powerless to avert; her own, as something - was it? - manufactured to meet some need, hugged, nourished from within, something she had made herself. For an instant she understood those gay spinsters of seventy whose youthful *affaires*, oft-told, are little but invention. The glimmer faded. She let it fade - she had to.

She said, "But didn't you - want another taste of it? That happiness you had with him?"

Janet, sitting upright in the sunshine, shivered. She said quietly, "No. It was so lovely that I couldn't bear to have it spoilt. Nothing could ever be as lovely again."

She went on presently, in her pleasant, low voice. "That was why I didn't stay at Geneva. There was too much of - that atmosphere, all about. I knew it was a bit late to start medicine, for me, without even any grounding of science, but I decided it was the only thing I really wanted to do. There had to be no doubt that the job I was going to spend the whole of myself on was one that really needed doing. My people have been most awfully decent about it. They understood, I think, without my telling them. They knew - what had happened, of course."

"And now," Hilary said, "you like it?"

"I'm going to, when I really get going. I've only just started the hospital part - the part that matters. I'm busy, and tremendously interested."

Hilary wondered if she would be content, doing a job, like that, which took all one's energy and could be made to absorb all one's emotion. She said explosively, in a minute, "It's waste. Wicked waste, to have to use oneself up in that way!"

Janet grinned. "Well, what's the remedy? Polygamy? Of course it isn't waste, you old gump! I'm going to be just as much use in the world as a charlady with ten children, and most likely a good deal happier."

Hilary found herself actually interested in Janet, in an almost impersonal way. She encouraged herself in this. She had not been interested in anyone, except as they concerned herself, for a very long time. And Janet had grown up to an extent she herself had hardly visualized as a possibility.

On Sunday, strolling down to breakfast, she found that Janet had been to church: a walk of two miles or so down the rough path. She was curious about that, too. She asked, "D'you get any kick out of that - or why do you go?"

Janet was amused. "Kick? – no . . . That doesn't express it in the least. I've been going, again, pretty regularly, ever since I came back. I don't go for what I can get out of it, I think." She paused, then went on steadily, "I go in answer to a command, simply. 'Do this in remembrance of Me.' It's good to be - reminded - that someone immeasurably better than we are suffered, without grousing. And - well, who are we, anyway, to disregard a command like that?"

Hilary pondered that for many days and nights. She could see that it was an outcome of Janet's experience - but it was something more than that, too.

Another time, she burst out, "What's the *good* of trying to suppress a natural instinct? One doesn't suppress hunger; if one tries to, Nature comes back at one without the slightest compunction and makes one ill."

That was the only time Janet got cross with her. She said, "Now you're simply making your mind work crooked - talking yourself into believing something you know's false, just because you want to. You know hunger isn't comparable: it's a mechanism which is necessary to life. The other thing isn't, and that's that."

"It seems necessary, to me," Hilary objected. "But I suppose you know . . . As a matter of fact, I was going to tell you a conclusion I've come to about the Andrew business. (I never thought I should be able to talk of it flippantly like that, but I can!) I don't believe it was his not

300

loving me that bowled me over, or even the upset of all the plans I'd made for the future. It was the fact that I'd been so sure he did love me. Not being able to trust my own judgement, d'you see? It was like being whirled round and round. I couldn't trust myself or anyone else. I didn't know where I was. Even now, I don't know what to do - "

Janet said, "You'll come to it. You couldn't have dissected yourself like that a month ago, and it's a good sign that you can. It's a time we all have to go through, I think, making up our minds whether we're going to get married or not. It's ridiculously easy for some people - marriage presents itself and they take it; or, it never presents itself and they never think about it. For a terrible lot of us, the problem presents itself - just too late. And then, it's horribly hard, because one must either resign oneself, or fight. It's difficult for a woman to fight."

After a fortnight of Janet's common sense and the freedom of the moor, Hilary was outwardly, even to Janet, steady again. She had regained enough will-power to make herself say and do and even think - realizing that Janet could tell, somehow, the trend of her thoughts - those things which would fit in with the scheme of life of the world she would have to live in. But she herself knew that she was sitting on a volcano. She had not resigned herself, she was still fighting. She did not know yet whether her father or her mother was to have the upper hand.

The week-end before Janet had to go back to work they had planned to spend at Redsands. The sight of the Red Cottage, with white roses straggling over it, and the old lopsided tree in the garden; the sound of waves splashing in the bay, the smell of oil lamps and biscuits as they went in, seemed to liberate the energy which the quiet of the moor had piled up in Hilary. She called excitedly to Hermione, "Can we go and bathe? It's such a heavenly afternoon!"

Hermione, hovering in the sitting-room with the uncertainty of one who doesn't play hostess often, rubbed her hands together and twittered. "Yes, I should think so . . . Mother's resting . . . We didn't expect you quite so soon!"

Hilary bounded upstairs to collect towels, and came down to find her sister goggling at Janet's trim beauty and Janet trying to make her talk. "Aren't you coming, too?" she asked.

Hermione said, "I never bathe, now. It would be silly, Mother says, to risk another pneumonia."

They went out and left her. Hilary felt the old peace, as she had always done, at getting out of the little dark room into the green and golden garden. She said regretfully, "I suppose she'll never grow up, now. That pneumonia was twelve years ago - and it wasn't due to bathing, either."

It was a better bathe, even, than those in the moorland pools. Instead of caressing, the water buffeted and stung. The blue stones at the other side of the bay beckoned. Hilary met their challenge joyously. She had wanted only to bask, before. Now she was ready to make efforts. She and Janet raced each other across and Hilary won with the greatest ease.

Hermione would not come out with them on Sunday morning, either. It seemed that both she and their mother occupied themselves with church work, now, visiting the poor, sewing for them, presiding at Mothers' Meetings, even holding classes for Girl Guides; and so, they must set an example to their flock by going to matins. Hilary felt, uneasily, that she was missing something. Janet had gone off, as usual, before breakfast, the other two after it. And there was a change in the Red Cottage, which she had put down merely to the passing of the years. There was no friction, there was almost content. But then, Hermione had never resented her mother's authority, or Rose Moore her younger daughter's utter dependence on her.

When Hilary and Janet came back, in the afternoon, from tramping along the shore, they saw Hermione, in a sprigged frock and a big floppy hat, walking with the curate, a pale young man not unlike her in appearance. She left him at the church gate, and the curate held her hand a very long time, and Hermione looked down. That made Hilary restless. It seemed so bitter that her ineffectual sister should have what she, with her finer qualities, could not get and wanted so badly. Fine qualities, after all, did not seem to count. Her mother had married her father not for his intellect and his goodness, but for a certain childlike dependence on her strength. Any amiable half-wit would have done as well or better.

On Monday, Janet had to go back to town. On the way to the station she said, "I feel such a pig for leaving you. I wish I could stay."

Hilary, who was still feeling energetic and happy, said lightly, "Well, pray for me!" And Janet said at once, "I shall. I've been doing that all the time."

They stood back and looked at each other; Janet,

embarrassed, a little, Hilary simply surprised. It gave one a queer feeling, to be prayed for without one's knowledge. Hilary was not sure that she liked it.

2

In the days that followed, she made an effort to please her mother and Hermione. They let her do odd jobs for them, but always she had the feeling that she did not belong to their world now and that they knew it. She never had belonged to it, really. They were no more interested in her than she was, honestly, in them.

One day she ran straight into Hermione and her curate. It was impossible not to stop and be introduced. The man's glance for her was so full of admiration that she was sure that, if she tried, she could take him from her sister. How could it be otherwise, when Hermione was but a pale ghost of her, as she had always been? She turned away from them abruptly. It seemed such an easy way out of her tangle that she was tempted to take it.

The next day, the grey mist had given place to blazing August heat, with a hot wind flapping the drying trees and the sunblinds. Hilary walked through the village during the morning, on an errand for her mother. She spent some time in the dark recesses of the store, which sold everything from underclothes to bacon, and came out, blinking, into the sunshine. A black figure detached itself from the bridge, on which she had dimly seen it leaning, and came towards her.

"A wonderful morning, Miss Hilary. Let me carry your basket."

She protested, "You're going to work much harder than I am to-day, I'm sure!" But he took it from her, with a flourish, all the same. He looked, she thought, just like a curate out of an old *Punch* as he trotted beside her with it. "Your sister tells me you've been ill. I hope the sea air is doing its duty!"

She assured him that it was. He chatted, pleasantly, all the way. His voice was cultivated, and he had a whimsical sense of humour. She quite enjoyed the walk home. Then, as she thanked him at the gate, she saw Hermione's face at the window, incredulous, amazed. Hilary beckoned her hurriedly to come out, and Hermione smiled suddenly, and came. Hilary left them in the garden together.

She must get away from this, or she would be all in a muddle again.

3

She took some lunch with her, and made for her usual refuge, the road to the shore, the grassy path along the cliff. She walked quickly for an hour or so, till she reached the end of the headland. Here she stood, hot and wind-blown, looking back. The blue bay with its steep, straight sides; the little grey jetty in one corner; the houses, coloured cubes of yellow, white, and pink, rising higgledy-piggledy, one half behind another, eye-browed windows peering over, up the hill; each as she viewed it brought back ghosts of children - herself and Hermione, Kenneth and Henry, her father, whimsical, contemplative, pursued but not dismayed by sparks which emanated from her mother.

She turned towards the open sea, and saw there, very far away, a little boat with one sail, making leisurely landward. She sat down to watch it, as one does a boat, and to eat her lunch.

Whoever was sailing it knew how to sail. The sea was choppy, the gusty wind was in the wrong direction, but the boat, though it had to tack, was in no difficulty. After a long time, it came near enough for her to see that all the work was being done by one man. The other occupant was a child, or perhaps a big dog.

Moved by curiosity, Hilary strolled back along the cliff path, for she thought, and presently was certain, that the boat was making for Redsands Bay. She arrived above the harbour at the moment when the boat ran expertly alongside the jetty. An inevitable fisherman ran out and helped to tie her up, and to lift out a small girl who seemed annoyed at such an affront to her dignity, for she shook herself and smoothed her short skirts and did not appear to say "Thank you". A moment later a man followed her - a spare, long-legged man with a funny fair beard, and straggly fair hair, a tuft of which stood on end on the top of his head. He took hold absently of the hand the small girl held up to him, and, tilting his head back, looked about as though searching for something. When he saw Hilary on the cliff, he waved.

Hilary almost fell down the path from cliff to harbour. When she came to the bottom, the couple were waiting for her, the man's face eager, the small girl's doubtful.

"Hilary - what luck! I was sure it was you, when I saw you on the headland!"

"Henry, how lovely to see you! I'd no idea - I was just watching you come in and thinking that you could sail!"

They stood back, taking each other in, and then Hilary squatted down to talk to the child. "Is this your daughter? What's her name?"

A shy affection came into Henry's face. "Patsy, Patricia, really. Say 'Good afternoon', Pat."

The child had been staring. Now she said, "Taf' noon," in a deep voice, and smiled suddenly and thrust a hand into Hilary's and pulled it away again. Swinging her short, full skirt from side to side, she inquired, "Who's you?"

Hilary said, "A very old friend of your father's. He used to take me sailing, once."

Patsy looked interested. "Like sailing," she remarked. "Let's do it again." She tried to pull her father back to the boat.

Henry resisted. "It would be fun. But we can't go again now, little 'un. Don't you want any tea?"

That started a new train of thought, and the child began to pull in the other direction. But Henry lingered.

"We're just staying here," he told Hilary. "In the Manor, up by the school. You know, where the parents used to stay for week-ends. You're at your old home, I expect?"

Hilary nodded. "Yes. Mother and Hermione are still there. I've come for a bit of the holidays." She was glad term was over now; sick-leave somehow didn't suit her as Henry had known her.

He said, smiling, "Is Ma Greg as fierce as ever?" and then, without waiting for a reply, went on as though he had taken a sudden decision, "Come back to tea with us! I'd like you to meet my wife."

Hilary said light-heartedly, "I'd love to!" and they set off up the road. Patsy said, "Daddy - cally!" very soon, and Henry hoisted her pick-a-back to his shoulders, where she sat very contentedly looking down on them.

Following a glance of amusement from Hilary, Henry said, "Are you looking at my beard?" and when she grinned, explained, "I grew it in hospital when I was too ill to be shaved. That was where I met Kathleen - did you know? She was a V.A.D. Anyway, when it came off she didn't like me, so I very obligingly grew it again. And now it seems to suit the part, somehow - "

"The part?" Hilary queried.

He twinkled down at her. "I spend a lot of my time making War Memorials, and the Town Councils like me to look a bit peculiar."

Hilary said, "Not peculiar. Distinguished, rather. I somehow thought you'd go back to architecture after the war - "

He agreed. "So did I. And then I got going on this when I was convalescing, and people gave me commissions - one doesn't know how long it will last, but for the moment there's plenty of work. It's marvellous to have a job which is one's hobby too - "

Hilary was looking at Patsy, who was conversing quietly to herself as she jogged along; a chubby, snub-nosed little person with dark eyes and straight dark hair in two short, sticking-out pigtails. She said, "I happened in on your show at the Suffolk Galleries. I did - like them, Henry."

He turned to her with interest. "Did you recognize your-self?"

She stood stock still, and he stopped and smiled at her, for so long that Patsy, on his shoulders, bounced and shouted, "Gee up! Gee up!"

Hilary shook herself and said, "Good gracious!" and Henry threw back his head and laughed till the cliffs echoed, just as he used to do at some whimsy of Gregory Moore's or some flurry of Hilary's about her mother's tantrums.

Patsy said, "Daddy, you're nearly bumping me off!" "Are you insulted?" Henry was inquiring.

"Insulted! No, flattered. I couldn't think why I knew her by sight! I tried to make her into your daughter, and the familiar look into a likeness to you - "

Patsy was still lamenting, "You bumped me, Daddy!"

Henry disengaged a fat hand and nibbled it. "Sorry, lamb! No, she's not like me at all - she may be like her mother later on, if she's lucky. Anyway, you got your years a bit mixed, didn't you? She's four and a half. Did you like Kathleen's flower pieces?"

Hilary confessed, "I simply didn't see them. I was so taken up with yours - "

Henry began to speak, then changed his mind. "I think she liked doing them," he said.

They talked about his sculptured heads. "All of men I knew and sketched, some in the trenches, some in hospital," he told her. "You'll see several of them, bodies and all, on the memorials."

4

They came presently to the Manor, a solid country house, now turned into a hotel. Hilary knew that her father had dined there sometimes, with parents of the boys he had taught. She herself had never been inside. Henry led the way easily now, across the panelled hall, and Patsy ran ahead into a pleasant shabby lounge with french windows leading out to a terraced garden. A maid was laying a table in a corner, and several people sat in comfortable chairs. Patsy, after a glance round, sidled up to one of them and said, "Mummy, we're back!"

Hilary's first impression of Henry's wife was, "How pretty!" Then, "I wouldn't have expected her to be so fashionable!"

She was slim and dark, and she moved beautifully as though she had no bones, and she was perfectly dressed for a country hotel in rose pink linen with a white belt, white shoes and little white ear-rings. She fended Patsy off with affectionate horror.

"Go and wash, you grub! Henry, take her: you're sure to be all sticky and sandy, both of you - oh!"

She had become conscious of Hilary, standing beside her husband.

"This is Hilary Moore, Kathleen - you remember, the

310

original of the girl in the boat. And the daughter of the schoolmaster I was so fond of - "

Interest, sudden venomous hatred, studied charm, chased each other across the lovely chiselled face, so quickly that Hilary blinked. The charm remained - lips parted, eyes alert. Henry's wife said, "How very nice to meet you - I've heard of you and your father so often! Have you been sailing, too?"

Hilary explained. "No. We met quite by chance at the harbour. I'm staying with my people."

"Then you don't need to wash." Kathleen Swain patted the settee beside her, and Hilary sat down, watching a shade anxiously the disappearance of Henry and Patsy to make themselves tidy. Kathleen chatted, and Hilary realized with relief that she did not feel nearly as uneasy in this gathering as she would have done before her year of common room talk at Fenchester.

She heard that Kathleen Swain could not bear sailing and hated the country; that she could just put up with the hotel, which provided good food, a cultured atmosphere, and a number of artists with whom one could talk. But she did wish Henry would take his holidays at Biarritz or Le Touquet, where he would meet other famous people like himself. For he was famous now, did Miss Moore know? He could have afforded proper holidays which she - and he too, of course - would really enjoy, instead of always insisting on coming to this funny little place and doing nothing but mouch round and go out in his boat and treat Patsy as though she were a tough little boy instead of a girl.

Hilary was just tactfully inserting that she had thought

very highly of Henry's work when she had seen some of it in London, when Henry reappeared. His eyes met Hilary's with, it seemed to her, an appeal in them, and glanced away at once to his daughter who, spruced and polished, had followed him in.

Hilary added, "It's lovely for you to be able to exhibit together like that. Your dainty flowers and those rugged heads - such perfect foils for each other - "

Henry sat down rather heavily and took out his pipe. Hilary carefully did not look in his direction.

Kathleen Swain smoothed her already faultless dress. "Yes, it's marvellous for a husband and wife to share interests. Henry, don't make that child giggle so much - whatever will Miss Moore think of her?"

Patsy, who had been climbing on her father's knee, looked up at Hilary and was evidently tickled by her expression. She buried her head in a cushion and giggled the more, till Henry put down his head beside her and whispered something into her ear, when she, at once became perfectly decorous.

They lived in London, Hilary discovered as tea proceeded, in a flat in Kensington. Henry had jibbed at the suggestion of Chelsea. Patsy went to school already, being so bright, according to her mother, that she needed some employment for her brain.

Watching and listening to the conversation, Hilary saw Kathleen Swain as a charming spoiled child, lovely, and with a superficial cleverness; but intolerant of anything which clashed with her own comfort, whether her child, her husband, or a stranger provided it. She must be the centre of the picture, and as such centre she was good. But let her be shadowed for an instant and she would at once coax, thrust or scratch her way back again. The child seemed to accept both smiles and scratches philosophically. Henry waited on his wife, lit her cigarettes, let her have control of the talk and brought it back when now and then it eluded her. But often his eyes came round to Hilary, appraising her, sharing a point with her, approving.

"They keep each other very much alive," Hilary thought. "Flint and steel. Good for Henry, perhaps - "

She asked Henry what was going to happen to the "Girl in a Boat", and Kathleen Swain cut in, "Oh, that's just one of his useless ones - done to keep his hand in before he had many commissions - "

"Perhaps it helped to bring more commissions," Henry said. "Quite a lot of people saw it."

His wife said sharply, "Nonsense, Henry! How could a thing like that get you commissions for War Memorials? The heads did that, of course!"

Henry slewed round to Hilary to make sure that she was not hurt, and Hilary made a little gesture of agreement with Kathleen, who was still speaking. "The proper thing, of course, would be for the original to buy it. That's what happens to portraits!"

Hilary jumped. Ought she really to buy it? Then she was visited by a vision of it, occupying most of their little sitting-room, or presiding over the square of grass in their garden like an ornate tombstone. She snorted.

Mrs. Swain looked injured. "Was that a joke?"

"It was, rather," Hilary said. "I live in a very small house with a very small garden."

"Still with Eleanor?" Henry tried to turn from the subject, but this time Hilary would not follow him.

"Still with Eleanor. You must keep the boat girl, Henry, till I'm dead. Then it can go into the College chapel, as a memorial of me, not of the War - "

When at last she stood up to go home, Henry said, "Wasn't it luck, running into you like that? I've been here several times and always missed you, and I did so want you and Kathleen to meet."

Hilary said happily, "Marvellous luck!"

Kathleen Swain, walking into the hall with her hand on Henry's arm, said, "The more so as the time is so short. We're going back to town to-morrow."

Patsy wailed, "Oh *no*, Mummy!" and Hilary thought Henry looked surprised, though he said only, "A pity. But we'll be down again some time, to exercise the boat."

He disengaged himself to open the door for Hilary, and walked down the drive with her, and out at the gate, and along the road, though she paused, expecting him to go back. They talked, could not stop talking, as they had done so many years ago in the same place. He left her only at the cottage gate.

Hilary did not go in at once. When Henry had turned for a moment at the corner of the road, and waved, and disappeared, she went again along the cliff path towards the headland. This time she did not look back at the village. She sat on a rock, her hands clasped round her knees, gazing out to sea. The wind had dropped, the horizon was lost in the opalescent light of sunset. A gull flew over, another pursued it, crying. They tumbled out of sight and all was quiet.

The cool stillness, after a day of heat and blustering wind, accorded with the utter change in Hilary's mood.

With no word spoken, with no touch of hand, with no sign but the return of eye to eye throughout the afternoon and a long look, hardly broken, at their parting, she knew that Henry loved her, had always loved her, and would always love her, and that no word of it would ever pass between them to break up his life as it now ran. It was a love which stirred in her its natural answer, born long ago and sleeping until now, deep, comforting, friendly.

The affair Andrew clicked into place as an exciting, perhaps a necessary, experience.

5

Coming into Redsands, she saw Hermione, walking alone. Catching her up, she said mischievously, "What have you done with your curate?"

Hermione, without stopping to think, returned, "He's got his boys' Bible Class this evening." Then, suspiciously, "Why do you call him *my* curate?"

Hilary laughed. "I've seen you with him once or twice. You'd make a good parson's wife."

Hermione quickened her pace and spoke with agitation. "I must see less of him. If *you*'ve noticed, so soon, people must be talking. I couldn't possibly inflict myself on him, with health like mine. It wouldn't be fair."

A year ago, Hilary would have teased her. Now, instead, she said, "Your health's not too bad, is it, now? You seem to get through an enormous lot of work. And some men like a wife they can fuss over."

Hermione said, "I'm very anaemic . . . And there's Mother to think of: I couldn't leave her."

Well, it wasn't any good battling with Hermione, obstinate little mule. Hilary hoped the curate was persistent enough to get his own way in spite of her. It seemed a pity that they should both die unwed.

For herself, she saw now that she had missed her one real chance of happy marriage years ago, when she had let Henry go to France without a word of regret. She saw, too, that to do so had been inevitable. As always, Gregory's influence had been stronger in her than that of Rose.

She wrote to Eleanor that evening: "*I am now completely myself again, full of energy and hankering after work. I'd like to come home in a few days, and then couldn't we have a fortnight in Brittany or where you will?*"

6

Back at the University, the Vacation over, Helen Martin greeted Hilary as though nothing had happened, with a laugh and a gibe. Margaret Falkner gave her a searching look before relapsing, apparently satisfied, into her old attitude of affectionate respect.

A.B.C. plunged ponderously into an account of the Cathedrals of France, which she had been visiting. She wanted Hilary to fill in the gaps in her knowledge of their history.

Blake had been to Sicily, and buttonholed her to talk about it. Miss Hawes and Miss Jago discoursed on the beauties of the Perthshire Highlands. The younger members of staff welcomed her amiably among them. There were students to interview.

Professor Hewer suggested a new line of research, now that the M.A. thesis had been finished and approved. Hilary was astonished at the zest with which she was able to take up both this and her lecturing.

Even the cottage on the edge of the moor had an air of renewal about it. Eleanor had bought some big arm-chairs instead of the little wicker ones in which it had been impossible to do anything but sit upright. "We're getting old enough to need a bit of comfort," she said. They were upholstered in bright cretonne, and there were new curtains to match them.

Hilary, after saying how much she liked them, put forward an idea of her own.

"Mrs. Brown next door is going to Canada next month, to her son. I wondered if we could buy her cottage, and knock the two into one. It would be fun to have a bit more space. I've got a few savings."

Eleanor seemed anxious that Hilary should have everything she wanted. "It would be fun. We could have a spare room."

"And a bathroom - lovely to get rid of that tub in the

kitchen!" Hilary hitched herself forward in the arm-chair. "I've been thinking about it - I even got as far as drawing a plan - "

They pored over it together. "We should get a beautiful big room if we knocked the whole lower floor of next door into one - have the wall down between the two narrow little staircases and make one wide one. Then turn the back bedroom next door into a bathroom - it's over the scullery, so there ought to be some get-at-able pipes - "

Her enthusiasm infected Eleanor. "You're talking as though we'd got it already

"We'll get it!" Hilary vowed. She saw the remade cottages as a compact little house, its spacious living-room shabbily and comfortably furnished - perhaps they could get hold of a Morris wall-paper like that in the lounge of the Manor Hotel.

Indeed, no obstacle interfered with the plan. The owner of the cottage would sell at a reasonable price. The village builder and decorator took kindly to Hilary's ideas. They lived through three irritating but exciting months of dust and banging, and the little house was fashioned while they watched.

"There's a sale," Eleanor said one day, "at a big house over at Fenton. We could do with some more furniture, and old bits would suit it best."

Hilary could not always dissemble her surprise at this new, co-operative Eleanor who seemed to know and forestall her hopes while they were still being silently hugged. Queer, how their deep affection could still flower, after all these years.

Eleanor laughed. "I got the taste for sales when I bought those chairs."

The lounge, when it was done, fulfilled all their wishes. The Morris paper, a cream background with waving fronds of brown and green and here and there a pomegranate brightly set, went graciously on the uneven walls. A new window at the back of the house lightened the room, which would have been dark without it. The tiny fire-place had been enlarged and pleasantly modernized. There were rugs, richly coloured if a trifle old, from the sale, on the polished floor; Eleanor's arm-chairs and a couple of smaller ones, bookshelves, an oak chest, and the two small oak desks which had been in the old sitting-room, in opposite corners, each with a high-backed chair. The other room was now a dining-room.

"We must have a house-warming!" Eleanor suggested, and they did. Janet came to occupy the spare room. The Falkners came, and some selected students, and some friends whom Eleanor had made.

Mr. Falkner said, "You want a few pictures!"

Hilary told him, "You must choose them!" and longed, idiotically, for flower-pieces. She went on, "Did you go to my friend's exhibition of sculps at the Suffolk Galleries when you were in London just now?"

He nodded. "Yes. First class. He'll do some fine work if he sticks to it."

"What did you think of the pictures?" she persisted, and he shrugged and said, "Very little, if you really want to know. You do? Well, there was no drawing in them, no composition, and thin, muddy colouring. Nothing alive.

319

One wondered, if one saw them at all, how they got there."

Hilary explained. "She's his wife. Verity's her maiden name. She likes doing them."

"I shouldn't think he likes exhibiting them," he commented, "P'raps he can't help himself, poor fellow!"

"I think he likes to please her," Hilary said, and Mr. Falkner grinned wickedly and said, "It's like that, is it?" and left her wondering whatever false impression of Henry and his wife she had given him.

When the party had gone, and Eleanor, Hilary and Janet were gathered by the fire, Janet said, "Good show, wasn't it? Such a feeling of good will."

Hilary said, "Yes, weren't they kind? They do seem to like us - "

"And yet," Eleanor put in, "they're not *just* kind. They wouldn't think of being - they're all individualists with strong ideas. Even those young students are persons, in embryo."

Janet, laughing, said, "Well, after all, there's nothing formless about you two. Your integrity simply sticks out. That's why they, being the sort they are, like you."

"By no means everyone does so," Hilary said. "I have students who run at the sight of me - and there were girls, and staff too, who did the same to Eleanor at Medling."

"Individualists," Janet remarked, "are terrifying to people who like to melt into the herd. And most do."

Hilary, musing on this conversation, thought that her own integrity was only just now, and very late, detaching itself from the mists of adolescence. Eleanor had been a person long before Hilary had known her - but she herself?

She began to sketch in a mental picture of the successful teacher of history whom she had resolved to become.

She must know a very great deal, with absolute accuracy. Well, she had the brain, and would acquire the application, for that.

She must convey the knowledge and the passion for accuracy to her students. As long as she had those attributes herself and the students liked her, that would not be difficult.

The germ, she thought, of the perfect teacher was there. She did not realize how much she was building to her father's model. What she would *not* be, was an arid, grumpy steamroller of a woman like A.B.C.

She stirred, and Janet looked up and said, "You were very far away."

"On the contrary, very near. I was trying to see myself as others see me. Or as I hope they may."

"You've thought about yourself so little again, lately," Janet said, "haven't you?" And Hilary, startled as usual by accurate personal comment, agreed. "I suppose so."

Eleanor said, "Better so. That was one of your attractions, that looking out, not in."

Janet nodded assent. "No one ever gets a nervous breakdown except when he's completely concentrated on himself, and sorry for himself into the bargain. You were heading there, Hilary, and you missed it I think because self-centredness isn't natural to you. You could snap out of it. Lucky!"

"You snapped me out of it. You and a lot of other kind people," Hilary said. "And yet, one must look at oneself sometimes, mustn't one? Have an aim of some kind, and survey oneself critically from time to time to see how far one is fulfilling it?"

"Ah!" Janet said. "That's a different story altogether from being self-centred - "

Swinging down to the station in the morning, and conscious of the November sunshine and the elm trees, their brown depths scattered and crowned with gold, and the cheerful greetings of the villagers, Hilary agreed that she did not by nature long look inwards. She would guard against ever being driven by circumstances to do it again.

7

Towards the end of that same academic year, Hilary sat in her room in the college. It was not as bare as it had been. The beautifying of her home had made her discontented with it, and it now had rugs, pictures, and pots of flowers which the students kept replenished from their gardens.

The room was hardly ever empty of students. If no one was being coached, they would drift in to talk.

One of them had just left her now - a girl in her second year, not brilliant but a sound, hard worker with a steady future, if she could qualify for it. The trouble was that her father had just died, and her mother and two young brothers had to be kept. She had come to say that she must give up the remainder of her course and take a job.

Hilary had said, "Don't rush into that. You're too good to

be an uncertified teacher all your life, with limited oppor-
tunities and meagre pay." She had seen a light of hope flash
into the tense young face. "I'll see what can be done. Come
and talk to me again to-morrow."

As the girl went out, a young man's face came cautiously
round the door. Hilary glanced up, and saw that he was not
one of her students at all. She had, however, met him at the
Falkners. "Hullo, what's the faculty of Medicine doing in
the History Section?"

He came in, his sheepish impudence reminding her, with
a jump of the heart, of Andrew. "I don't want history as
much as help!"

She sat back, looking at him, and he went on hurriedly,
"It's about Phyl. Miss Gadsden. We're engaged, you know."

"I didn't," Hilary said a little grimly. Engagements
interfered so idiotically with people's work, and Phyllis
Gadsden was one of her more promising second-years.

"I'm practically qualified," the young man told her. "I've
only got Part Three to do, and that's next week, and I want
us to get married. I can go in as assistant to my father right
away; there's no difficulty about that. And now Phyl - " an
expression of hurt amazement told his point of view - "says
she won't till she's got her degree! Two - bloomin' - years!"
He slumped in his chair and blew his cheeks out in despair.

Hilary could not help laughing at him. "What do you
want me to do?"

"Talk to her!" he entreated. "She thinks no end of your
opinion! Tell her she's taking up room here that someone
else could make better use of! Tell her anything to change
her mind! What's the good of a degree to a married woman,

323

anyway?"

"A trained mind is a whole lot of good to a wife and mother, isn't it?" Hilary retorted, and he mumbled, "I don't know! It doesn't seem natural, for a girl to put that sort of thing before getting married. She knows what I want, too."

Hilary marshalled her arguments, and sent him away agreeing, albeit reluctantly, that some hospital jobs for two years before he went into private practice would make him a far more valuable person, and if he wasn't married he could do them, and that the girl's point of view must be given due weight as well as his own. "And if they did get married now," she said to herself, "he'd be jealous of his own children, just as he's jealous of her work. In two years he'll have grown up a bit - "

He bobbed back again to say anxiously, "Look here, you won't tell Phyl I've been here, will you? She'd be livid!" and she nodded her promise.

Then there was the young Catholic student who would twist every incident in history to glorify the Roman Church. She must be made to see that truth could not be so twisted - that the attempt to twist it did harm, not good, to a cause, muddled the past and gave no help to the conduct of the future . . . Hilary had a half-formed aim of writing a book which correlated the trends of one age with the trends of another.

She got through two half-hour coachings, one with an intelligent student who was a pleasure to teach, the second with a slick young man who wrote essays in flowing English about nothing at all and treated with superiority the suggestion that a background of solid fact would add to their value.

She then went to call on Professor Hewer to see what could be done about the student whose father had died.

She liked calling on the Professor. He was kind, not with the woolly kindness of the half-baked good, but with a definite, informed charity. His knowledge was profound, and he had that humility which the very learned sometimes have, which is ready, even expectant to learn from lesser people. His room had a graciousness which matched him well.

He greeted her with evident pleasure, and she plunged at once into the student's story. He nodded approval as she finished speaking.

"Yes. She could get a University Grant to cover her own living and tuition, if you think she's good enough. And we could tell her where to go to get some help from the County for the two boys. See her, and find out if that would meet the case. If it won't, we must think again. We don't want to lose her."

She thanked him, and he looked at her with a benign affection. "You had the same experience yourself, I believe," he said.

Hilary smiled. "I did. And there were no University Grants in those days."

"Yet you managed. A job - an honours degree - an M.A. You must have worked very hard."

"I did work hard," she acknowledged. "I don't regret it, but it did mean missing a lot of fun. I wouldn't like to condemn another young thing to it. And I don't think I could have done it myself if I hadn't been helped.

Encouraged. I've been very lucky in my friends."

"The power of attracting friends," the Professor said slowly, "and holding them, is no mean gift. We've become very fond of you, here, Miss Moore."

Hilary flushed at the unexpected tribute. It was seldom that the Professor ventured into personalities. "I'm happy here," she said, and was surprised that it was true.

"I'll see that your young friend is looked after," he promised, and she left him.

Queer, how one's past rose up at one - to hinder, sometimes, but often, if one used it rightly, to help.

After lunch, a restless mood came upon her, as it sometimes did in spite of her full and useful life. Quite simple things caused it - this time she supposed it was the student who had reminded her of Andrew; but the contemplation of other people's happiness could do it too, or a book or a film with a realistic love interest, or certain types of music. She deliberately avoided them as far as she could, and refused to be sorry for herself when they invaded her privacy without warning. She was thankful that she could now recognize both symptoms and cause.

The best remedy was a tramp on the moor, which tired her body and composed her mind, or recourse to preparation for this book of hers, in which her interest was becoming more and more centred. She was finding it easier, now, to jerk herself on to the plane of purely intellectual exhilaration to which her father had introduced her and of which her University studies had made her free. Twice she had lost her way there - at the High School, when there had been no need for it, and later here, when her emotional adventures had shut it out.

When she had attained that plane there seemed no happiness as intense as that which she found there.

8

And so the years passed.

The book was finished, typed, accepted, published. There was excitement in seeing it on the bookstalls in the University town, in reading reviews of it - reviews appreciative of both its learning and its general appeal; in hearing staff and students talk about it, whether they approved or carped.

One day her publisher called on her in her college room. It was his manner, a mixture of eagerness and deference, which made her realize that she had achieved a modest fame. Would she consider a series of books on ordinary people - a lawyer of the Middle Ages, an apothecary, a housewife? The mixture of sound knowledge and ability to put it over to the public was just what he wanted. Hilary was attracted by the idea, flattered a little, and let him talk of terms.

She discussed the series with the Professor, who was always ready to help. As time went on the books occupied her more and more, and each as it came out was eagerly read by the intelligent public and looked upon as a standard work by the students. They brought, too, a welcome addition to her funds.

A letter came from Medling, asking her to come and give away prizes at the Annual Prizegiving. She was startled to think that her notoriety should have travelled from the North of England to Kent. Eleanor persuaded her to go, and went with her, and the two of them chuckled at the Headmistress's description of her as "a most distinguished former member of our staff".

"D'you remember me? Just over twenty? On the mat for going on the river in a whiff in a gym-dress?"

"You were a darling," Eleanor told her. "Dewy and woolly, like a young bird!"

"And now most distinguished! Funny how absurd it sounds when it's oneself! And I should have got thrown out then, I think, but for you!"

"Do you do anything on the river now?" they asked the Head Girl, who was showing them round.

"Rather! We have a regatta every year, and every House has a boat. They still won't let us race, though," she lamented. "I suppose you couldn't make them? Look, here's a photo of last year's boats - "

Strapping girls in shorts, with sweaters round their necks, stood holding their oars. She listened politely while Hilary told of earlier days. "We wear shorts for all games now," she said, and added, grinning, "and so does the Gym mistress!"

The living-room at the cottage was seldom without visitors now. A regular Thursday evening "At Home" had been instituted, with the idea of bringing to a provincial University, where most of the students lived with their families, something of the atmosphere of Oxford and

Cambridge, where the Dons reckoned hospitality as one of their privileges. Hilary had said, "They'll never bother to come! It's different when you're living in college and probably the Don is too!" But now "Miss Moore's Thursday evenings" were a feature of University life. Invitations were prized as evidence that a student was in some way interesting, and were eagerly sought after. Yet there were no games, seldom any entertainment at all at these gatherings, nothing but talk, though that was flowing and of the best. Professor Hewer was nearly always there, and other members of staff, and students of every "shop", and, once invited, they came again and again.

The spare-room, too, was seldom untenanted. Old students came, and Eleanor's sisters, and very often Janet. Hilary's own people had never been persuaded to make the long journey north. Hermione had married her curate. He had a country living now, with a big rectory. Rose Moore had two rooms of her own in it, and helped greatly with Hermione's two small boys, who had arrived in the most normal way possible.

Hilary had never again been back to Redsands. Her spells of restlessness now took her to the Continent; usually to some University city, where she could gather more historical knowledge, to be bent to her own uses - correlated, interpreted, and passed on. She had come to have a passionate belief that the common man must know and understand the past in order to control the present and to mould the future, and she contributed in every possible way to that end.

Sometimes Eleanor came with her on these expeditions;

often she stayed at home. For although she and Hilary were now nearer, perhaps, than ever in spirit, they had many interests apart.

One day, as Hilary was leaving one of the big shops in Fenchester, a car drew up at the kerb and Andrew Fraser tumbled out of it. She wondered for an instant whether he had stopped there on purpose, but the surprise in his face told her that he had not. She made no effort to avoid him, and at her smile he stared, then thrust out a hand and strode after it.

"Why, Hilary! What ages since I've seen you!"

He was successful, contented, self-possessed; Hilary no less so.

They shook hands. Hilary was thinking, "I could never have been happy with him - never, never! He was perfectly right. It would have called for changes neither of us could possibly have kept up."

In the car was Andrew's wife; small, plump, vivacious, pink-and-white. She wore expensive clothes in excellent taste. To Hilary she was friendly in a shrill, bright-eyed way. Hilary was sure that, like Andrew, she was terribly fond of her food.

9

Hilary had been lecturer in History at Fenchester for twelve years when Professor Hewer called her into his room one spring morning. She had, as time passed, become more and more fond of the old man, more and more ready to lean on his kindly wisdom in the solving of problems both of work and of human relationships.

He seated her comfortably and gave her a cigarette. Then, going back to his own leather chair, he looked at her over the rims of his flat-topped glasses and said, "My dear, I'm resigning at the end of next term. I wanted you to be the first to know."

Hilary, leaning forward and gripping the arms of her chair, exclaimed, "Oh, must you? Must you really? It wouldn't be the same place without you!"

A smile glinted over the frail old face as he fixed his straight glance on her. "A better place, perhaps. I've no use for people who hang on to their jobs till everyone says, 'Oh, *that* old nuisance!' "

She protested, "No one ever would, of you!"

He went on, "Anyway, I'm very old and tired. I would like some leisure before I die. And the reason I wanted to tell you in good time is this - I do so hope you'll apply for the position."

Hilary opened her mouth and shut it again. "Me? Professor of History for the Northern Universities? I couldn't, possibly!"

He smiled again, very kindly. "I can think of no one - no one at all, and I have a wide acquaintance - who would do it better. It will have to be advertised, and there will be other applicants. We've never had a woman in a University Chair, and there will be some opposition. But I think, with your attainments and my backing, that you would have a fair chance of being elected."

Hilary was sitting upright, flushed, gazing into space; thinking, "I must have made myself - a bit - the sort of person I wanted to be, or he'd never have thought of me, knowing me as he does"; wishing her father were alive, to be proud of her - only that, even now, hurt too much to think of for long; wondering what Eleanor would say, Eleanor, whose progress lately had been so pedestrian that she was still a research student and would never, now, be anything else; thinking, "Janet'll be glad."

She said rather wistfully, "Do you think I could really do it?"

The Professor asked, "Why not? You've served a very proper apprenticeship!"

"I don't seem - intellectual enough. The real highbrow intellectuals - except you, and you're a real person, not a highbrow - don't think much of me."

He said: "A real person. That's it, I think. You certainly have a humanity which the arid type of intellectual lacks. And a gentleness with people. The gentleness of strength, perhaps. But those are positive gains, of which the pure highbrow is a little afraid. *I* want you to follow me – selfishly - because you would carry on the tradition which I've built up on the foundations which were laid for me."

"I would do that," she said quickly. "I learned something of that tradition from my father before I ever met you."

"One's past, again," the old man commented. "One can't escape it. Have you ever noticed how the characteristics of the very old are invariably the crystallized tendencies of their own youth? They're the same people - simpler, harder - but the same."

Hilary, stretching out her hands to him, said, "You must have been - a very sweet person, when you were young!"

He twinkled at her as he took her hands. "That's nice of you. And I would be glad to know you when you're old! No, one can't dodge it. But one can use it. If you know the sort of person you are by nature, if you are honestly aware of your tendencies, you can turn them into the right channels. The aggressive man need not fight for himself, nor need he force himself to become an unhappy doormat. He can use his fists for a cause. It's *not* knowing what you are, what you can do, letting yourself be poked into a wrong-shaped hole because your own shape is hidden from you, that makes for frustration, hatred, violence."

Hilary said, "That's what I've been trying to show, in the books - of nations, too - "

"I know," he said gently. "And you'll apply for this post? Get busy on all the bother of testimonials?"

"I'll be proud to," Hilary told him.

10

Time and again during the next few weeks she said to Eleanor, "I can't do it. It terrifies me: to be the last authority, to have no one to appeal to; to be on a lot of committees and councils and have to *talk* at them, not just sit and listen and be dumb - I'm not that sort of person at all!"

Eleanor said, " 'He rules best who rules unwillingly' -

true, I think. The unwilling ruler doesn't abuse his power."

"But am I doing just the thing Professor Hewer said one must not do - letting myself be pushed into the wrong hole? Anyway, I may not get it - "

Eleanor laughed. "That would settle it. And you'd be horribly disappointed. I must say the hole seems to me to be very suitable. You come of a line of teachers. You've picked up somewhere the knack of making people like you - "

Hilary nearly said wistfully, "But not love me - or not love me enough - " then decided that this, after all, was an argument on Eleanor's side, and remarked absently, "That's only a matter of being interested in them."

The deafening applause which re-echoed in the college hall when the appointment was announced did much to reassure her. Afterwards, people thronged round her with congratulations which seemed so sincere that she was amazed and touched. And by the end of her first term as Professor, she was sure that her hole was the right one for her. She grew used to the deference which was paid to her. She enjoyed making people unbend by refusing to occupy, even for an instant, a pedestal. Yet, when she felt strongly, as she often did, about some proposal, she could be so firm that her decisions always carried weight. She was, as Janet would have said, definitely a person, and liked it.

It was some two years later, on a December evening, that a small car nosed its way along a dark lane, through driving rain. Its occupants, three women and three men, all students, clung together and groaned as they were bumped up and down. Once, as the hill grew steeper, it stopped altogether. The driver swore under his breath, "What a road! No, she *will* start again, and you *won't* have to get out and walk! There she goes - "

The girl next to him laughed at his tone of patient resignation. "It's worth it, cherub," she said. "Courage! *Avanti!*"

"I hope it is. I've never been to one of Miss Moore's shows before. Can we smoke?"

"Smoke? You can do anything you like, within reason! I don't know *why* her evenings are such fun, but they are. If they weren't, you wouldn't get people flooding out here to them, would you?"

"You would not. Lord, that was a near thing!" as the car lurched up the edge of a bank and down again.

The girl was still talking. "'Tisn't as if we *do* much, either. Good food. *Very* good talk. Music, sometimes, if people want it. It's the atmosphere more than anything, I think. Something peaceful about it, like rest after a storm. And yet - fun. Oh, great fun! I do think Miss Moore's an awfully wise sort of person, don't you?"

From behind, another man commented, "I must say I've never heard any lectures that were a patch on hers. She's got a damned fine mind, and she knows how to put the stuff across. The place has got quite a reputation for scholarship in history, a chap told my Pater last Vac, since she was made Professor."

A girl said, "I'm dying to read her book on Queen Elizabeth. It's due out next week. I've read all her earlier ones. There was a bit about it in the *Litt. Supp.* yesterday. The man called it 'monumental' or something. 'The first real light on a difficult reign, unbiased by religion or anything else.' Real honest diggings into history."

"What strikes me as odd," the driver put in, "being new and knowing nothing about the lady, is, how a woman professor, properly learned and all that, makes people like her. Not only women, not only students, but everyone. Women professors are such *sticks*, generally

The girl beside him mused, "And yet, I suppose they've all had private lives to live - outside their shop, I mean . . . I bet Miss Moore has . . . D'you remember, Joan, the end of last year - " she slewed round and spoke into the darkness behind her - "when I was off my nut about Billy and came down in my first-year exam? Well, she didn't send me down, as she very well might have done. She made me tell her all about it - goodness knows how, for I'm not one to bleat about my affairs - and then just said, 'I thought it was something like that. Well, I expect you think you'll never get over it, but you will, and be all the better person for having been through it. The things that last are the dull, rather matter-of-fact affections, not these thrills . . . and I'll set you a test at the end of the term.' You don't expect understanding like that from a person who writes learned books and fairly flays you if you're not plumb accurate in your essays . . ."

The car jerked to a standstill. Someone said, "I'll open the gates, John, if you wait a jiff - oh, they're open already. O.K., you can drive in - "

Light was streaming from the cottage door. The party straggled in, and stood looking into the sitting-room.

Before the fire Eleanor Hunt sat, thin, weather-beaten, clever-looking, chatting with Blake. Helen Martin, well-dressed as ever, if a little sharper in face and manner, perched on the arm of Mrs. Blake's chair. A man from the Medical School and another from the Art Department stood looking down at them.

Hilary Moore came forward to greet the influx of new guests. The bright hair had streaks of grey in it, the stern mouth was balanced by the kindness of her eyes. The friendly warmth of the room embraced the party, made them at their best, eager, at ease. She hustled the students out to take off hats and coats.

Blake's wife, glancing about, remarked on two new photographs. "Those weren't here last time. The children - they're charming! Who are they?"

Eleanor answered her: "This little imp is Hilary's niece. Her sister, you know, married a parson down in Devon, and this is her third child. The boy and girl, twins, are Margaret Falkner's - you remember her? They're coming to stay with us next week. They'll keep us pretty active, I expect - "

Hilary, returning, called out, "What about supper? We've put all the food on the sideboard, and will you all please help yourselves, as there's such a crowd? There are still one or two more to come - "

They moved past her into the other room, a pleasant, contented group. Hilary, smiling, turned out the light and followed them.

11

At breakfast one winter morning, Hilary handed a letter across the table to Eleanor.

"Look at this!"

Eleanor read it out - "The Hellenic Society's Cruises. Spring Cruise 1937." There followed an invitation to Professor Hilary Moore to take part in the cruise as a guest of the Society and to lecture from time to time to the company on board ship.

"What lovely things happen when one is rather eminent," Hilary said. "Seems like magic, to me!"

Eleanor said, "You must certainly go."

"And you must come, too. We can afford it. If I'm to be a guest I shall insist on taking you!"

"I should like it. I've never been to Greece," Eleanor acceded.

"Where do we go? Start from Venice - Sparta - the Dardanelles - Istanbul - Rhodes - Athens - Corinth - Ragusa (doesn't it sound lovely?) - and expeditions to places I've never heard of. Three weeks - oh, heavenly!"

"As long as these rumours of war don't come to anything"

"D'you think they will?" Hilary asked.

"You should know. History in the making. You ought to read the papers more."

"I read the weeklies," Hilary protested. "They give one a far better idea! The dailies blow hot one day and cold the next and I can't stand them. Anyway, I don't think there's going to be a war this year."

Eleanor looked suddenly into the back of her head as

though to reassure herself about some memory which was there, and said nothing.

"You will come, won't you?" Hilary asked her, and she said, "I really think I will!"

Their brief meetings during term were filled with preparations, and talk was mainly of the expedition. One day a long envelope arrived for each of them, and Eleanor opened hers while Hilary looked at some official communication about examinations. She glanced up from these for a moment to ask, "What is it?"

"Plan of ship. I'm just finding out where they've put us. Oh, here we are - lovely big cabin with a port-hole. And there's a passenger list."

"I shan't know anybody," Hilary grumbled. "You may. Parsons and people. There are always parsons on these trips, aren't there? Following round after St. Paul?" She tossed her envelope into her desk unopened.

"We shall get to know them soon enough," Eleanor said absently as she scanned the list. Then she, too, put her envelope into her desk.

A few days later she came to Hilary with another letter, her face troubled. "From my sisters. The old one - Beatrice - is apparently very ill. Emily wants me to go and help."

"You can't, possibly," Hilary said. "If you do, it'll mess up the cruise."

"I *needn't* go on the cruise," Eleanor said slowly, watching her. "You'd get on perfectly well without me." And although Hilary begged and entreated, argued and grew angry, she was unexpectedly obstinate.

"I can't let them down. They don't often ask for help!"

"Send them some money to pay for a nurse!"

"I can't do that, they'd think I was dreadfully hard-hearted, and be insulted as well!"

And Hilary, hurt and bewildered by the sudden change of plan, had to stand by and watch Eleanor's passage cancelled, the big double cabin exchanged for a single one, to see Eleanor off hurriedly for her sisters' home and return, lonely and rather forlorn, to make the final preparations for her own hitherto eagerly-anticipated trip.

She had two letters from Eleanor; one written on the day she arrived, saying that Beatrice really was quite ill and the younger sister very tired, and both so pleased at her arrival that she felt a pig for ever having cavilled at going to them.

"You didn't, visibly!" Hilary grumbled; but she was mollified, a little, by the hint that Eleanor had, after all, suffered some internal struggle about her desertion. Funny, she thought, how, at a crisis one's family always came before one's friends. Even a family one had grown right away from before a friend who was almost part of oneself. She supposed that if Hermione had called for help, she herself would have given up even this marvellous expedition to go to her.

The second letter, which came just before she was due to leave, sent all such kindly understanding out of her head. The old sister was much better, but would hardly let Eleanor out of her sight. Eleanor was planning to bring them both back to the little house, because it was so much easier to run than their own old-fashioned one, and so infinitely warmer, and they would need a change anyway. *"They are so fond of our house!"* Hilary read. *"I think they*

would like to spend the rest of their lives with me there.
Beatrice said so quite frankly the other day. She loses all
her inhibitions, like a child - or, I suppose, like the very old
woman she now is - when she's ill. But we must talk that
plan over when you come back."

Hilary gasped. "We'll do no such thing! Or, if we do, my
contribution will be brief and to the point! The idea of
those two old hens filling up our spare room - permanently!
I really think Eleanor's gone mad!"

She brooded crossly over that letter throughout her
packing, and during the duller parts of the journey across
France. She had arranged to meet the main party at Venice,
where they were to board ship, because they were to spend
a night in Milan and she preferred one in Venice, which
she had never visited. The main, object of that had been to
explore Venice with Eleanor.

However, the gem-like perfection of the place on a fine
spring evening could not but enchant her, even by herself.
She was carried by gondola from the station, along canals
which wound between shadowy buildings, piercing the
clear sky with pointed roofs and turrets, and mirrored,
lighted windows and ghostly walls, in reflections which
were splintered by her passage. By the time she had come
to her hotel, she had recaptured the familiar excitement of
contact with unfamiliar places and almost forgotten that
Eleanor should have been with her. She slept like the dead
and awoke entirely refreshed.

After a leisurely breakfast, she made her way to St.
Mark's, and found it ornate but very lovely. She was
overawed by the prison, so packed with history, much of

341

which she knew, and so, for her, packed too with ghosts, its bars glowering over the sad grace of the Bridge of Sighs. She sat in the sun in the pink stone square by the Doges' Palace and gazed up the slender pillar with the Lion of Venice at the top of it. She wandered into the church of San Paolo and was amused by a little bored marble angel whom she found there. That, somehow, reminded her of Henry, and sent her to find Leonardo's Collione statue. She was admiring the vitality of the thing, the springy step of the great, thick-necked bronze horse, the tense strength of the armoured knight, when she became conscious of a man who stood beside her and regarded, not the statue, but herself. A little indignant, she looked up at him, and he smiled down at her, sheepishly, as though he had been stalking her, secretly, and expected to be sent packing.

"Hullo, Hilary!"

"*Henry!* What on *earth* are you doing here? And where's that beard? I like you better without it!"

He passed his hand over his clean-shaven chin; a good chin, pointed and definite, which strengthened his thin, sensitive mouth.

He said, "I thought you would."

"How," she asked suspiciously, "could you think anything at all about me? How did you know I was here? I didn't see you on that train! And where are Kathleen and Patsy? Patsy must be grown up by this time!"

"Yes, she is grown up," he said absently. "She's staying with a school friend. Kathleen - " he looked away, and his face had a queer, strained look - "Kathleen's dead."

Shocked beyond speech, for she had no memory of

342

Kathleen Swain except as the lovely, vital, jealous woman of so many years ago at Redsands, Hilary gripped his arm.

"Henry! I'm so terribly sorry! I didn't know - "

"I thought - you might have seen it in the papers. Eighteen months ago, now. She had cancer of the breast. Operation, and all sorts of treatment, but it wasn't any good. They say it's more deadly if it catches you young than old. She hated it so - "

Hilary, knowing so little of illness, could imagine Henry's pain better than his wife's. She could only say again, "I *am* sorry, Henry!" and voice her earlier thought, "She was such a vital person, it seems impossible."

"It did seem so," he said.

They had wandered away from the statue and were sitting now on a low marble seat. In the silence, Hilary's thoughts oscillated between sadness at the breaking up of Henry's life and the question which came bubbling up and had to be denied emergence. How is it that you're here, with me?

He turned to her, as though continuing a conversation which had already begun. "We used to fight a bit, Kathleen and I. She was an exacting sort of person, you know. Must have attention, and must have the very best of everything. Even one's work had to go by the board if she said so, and that's difficult; specially, I think, for an artist. But she was - such good company. Kept one up to scratch. I have all sorts of regrets that I didn't give in to her more - "

He stopped, and after waiting a minute, Hilary put in, "I believe people always feel like that when someone's - died. I thought you were most sweet with her - that once I saw

343

you together."

He gave her a grateful look and went on. "I was so lonely - so mortally lonely - I couldn't fasten it on Patsy. She's a lively, pretty thing who can't help enjoying life, and she saw very little of her mother as she grew up." He was quiet again for minutes, during which Hilary could have wept for him. Then he turned to her again. "I kept thinking - and thinking - of the comfort of talking to you."

Hilary could say nothing. She was so dreadfully sorry for him, so infinitely glad he had found her, so humbly doubtful of her ability to help him. She led the talk crisply to a more practical plane.

"I'm glad you thought that. But Henry - I can't think how this meeting happened. You seem to have come up out of a trap door like something in a pantomime."

He smiled. "Not a demon. I assure you, not a demon. That was easy, anyway. I'm on the executive of the Hellenic Society, and I help to choose its guests. See - but you must have seen it already." He pulled out the little blue passenger list, with his name among others on the cover, and Hilary's with the other lecturers just inside.

Hilary, confused, said, "I just didn't look at it. D'you believe that? You would, if you knew me better. I was reading something else when it came, and I just didn't look at it. Eleanor did - "

Their eyes met, like those of conspirators; like those of the boy and girl at Redsands. The thirty-odd years between then and now had fallen away, and with them had gone some far more recent recollection, vaguely connected with Eleanor, which Hilary had for an instant tried to recapture.

Henry was saying, "We'd better get some lunch. And then go on board, and find our way about the ship before the main-gang comes. You can't think how glad I was when I found you were stopping here instead of at Milan with the rest of them. I did so want to get you to myself . . . I knew I should run into you somewhere."

They had lunch at Hilary's hotel, talking all the time as though they could never stop, then strolled across the piazza opposite the Customs House to look at the ship which lay at anchor there.

She was a squat ship with two funnels, dazzling white in the sunlight, with gleams of brass upon her. About her, gondolas plied busily with luggage and stores, and farther over, little fishing boats, like Goya's, darted with coloured sails, red, yellow, and brown, some brightly new, some patched with grotesque shapes.

Henry passed his arm through Hilary's, in comfortable, friendly fashion. She looked up at him, startled, and he hugged the arm to him and smiled down at her, his sudden, whimsical smile. His voice when he spoke was strangely deep.

"I'm not going to let you go - again!" he said. "I don't know how I've done without you all these years. I haven't, very well."

He looked out again at the ship.

Hilary's thoughts raced suddenly away from him, away from Venice and the sea and the sunlight, back to England and Eleanor.

Eleanor hadn't gone mad. She had read the daily papers, and seen of Kathleen Swain's death, and kept quiet about it

345

lest her friend's ordered life should be disturbed. She had seen the passenger list. She had known about Henry, known what was going to happen, and had given up the cruise to leave the coast clear for Hilary to make up her own mind. For, after all, old Beatrice was often ill, and Eleanor had never gone to nurse her before. And that last letter was to say that she would not be left lonely, that she would not, now, resent Hilary's going if she wanted to go. Dear Eleanor!

Her eyes followed Henry's. The ship had become a magic ship, voyaging to unexpected happiness, to that second chance so often hoped for and so seldom given.

She reminded herself sternly that she was forty-five and a Professor of History whose business was to lecture to the company on board. But she returned the pressure of Henry's arm. "Oh, Henry," she said, "we'll have such fun!"